To Bashabi Barua

Your presence is woven throughout this book; you were there when *Shokhi Rongomala* was in inception—beside Rongomala's lake and the ruins of the zamindar palace—and you were there to read the first draft of *Beloved Rongomala* with your insights and passion.

One day we shall meet again, beloved friend, to talk about books over a steaming cup of tea, and we will bask in the radiance of your gentle, smart and kind spirit.

We miss you. May all the world's light carry you home.

Shaheen Akhtar, Shabnam Nadiya

Beloved Rongomala

Shaheen Akhtar is an award-winning novelist from Bangladesh. She is the author of six novels and six short story collections, several of which have also been published in West Bengal. She also edited the three-volume *Soti O Sotontora*, a curated compilation of representations of women in Bengali literature from the twelfth century to present day. In 2004, her novel *Talaash* (translated into English as *The Search by Ella Dutta*) won the Prothom Alo Book of the Year award; in 2020, the Korean translation of the novel (translated by Seung Hee Jeon) was awarded the 3rd Asian Literary Award in South Korea. Akhtar was presented with the Shera Bangali 2014 award by India's leading Bengali news channel ABP Ananda, and in Bangladesh, the Bangla Academy Literature Award in 2015. In 2015, she also received the Akhteruzzaman Elias Katha Shahitya Prize and the IFIC Bank Award for her novel *Moyur Shinghason* (*The Peacock Throne*), and in 2019, her novel, *Oshukhi Din* (*Unhappy Days*), about the 1947 Partition, won the Gemcon Literary Award. Her most recent novel, *Eksho Ek Rater Golpo* (*The Story of a Hundred and One Nights*) is forthcoming from Prothoma Prokashon, Dhaka.

Shabnam Nadiya is a Bangladeshi writer and translator, settled in California. A graduate of the Iowa Writers' Workshop, she is the recipient of the Steinbeck Fellowship (2019) for her novel-in-progress, *Unwanted*; a PEN/Heim Translation Grant (2020) for her translation of Mashiul Alam's short fiction entitled *The Meat Market and Other Stories*; and the 2019 Himal South Asian Short Story Prize for her translation of Mashiul Alam's short story 'Milk'. Nadiya's translations include Leesa Gazi's debut novel *Hellfire* (Eka/Westland, 2020), and Moinul Ahsan Saber's novel *The Mercenary* (Seagull Books, 2018). Her original work as well as her translations have been published in SAAG Anthology, *The Offing*, *Joyland*, Amazon's Day One, *Gulf Coast*, *Copper Nickel*, *Wasafiri*, *Words Without Borders*, *Asymptote*, *Al Jazeera Online* and *Flash Fiction International* (WW Norton).

Shaheen Akhtar

Beloved Rongomala

Translated from the Bengali
by Shabnam Nadiya

eka

eka

First published in Bengali as *Shokhi Rongomala* in 2010 by Prothoma Prokashon

First published in English as *Beloved Rongomala* in 2022 by Eka, an imprint of Westland Books, a division of Nasadiya Technologies Private Limited

No. 269/2B, First Floor, 'Irai Arul', Vimalraj Street, Nethaji Nagar, Allappakkam Main Road, Maduravoyal, Chennai 600095

Westland and the Westland logo are the trademarks of Nasadiya Technologies Private Limited, or its affiliates.

ISBN 9789395073356

10 9 8 7 6 5 4 3 2 1

This is a work of fiction. Names, characters, organisations, places, events and incidents are either products of the author's imagination or used fictitiously.

Typeset by Jojy Philip, New Delhi 110 015

Printed at Manipal Technologies Limited, Manipal

Cast of Characters

Adam Ali: Ayna's husband who works as a merchant seaman

Amena: Karim Sheikh's youngest daughter who is mute

Atma Ram Nor: Rongomala's father; follower of the Vaishnava tradition within the Hindu faith

Ayi-Ma: Ethin's grandmother, who also has magical powers

Ayna: Karim Sheikh's daughter; wife of Adam Ali; mother of Najar Ali

Bhelu Chowdhury: Younger brother of King Inga Chowdhury

Bishwambhar Sur: Founder and forefather of the Chowdhury dynasty

Black Moon: A mynah; Phuleswari's favourite from her aviary

Chanda Bir: Rajendra Narayan Chowdhury's chief henchman; Chanda is known by his title, 'Bir', meaning brave and/or warrior

Chandrakala: Daughter of a high-caste Brahmin family; she singlehandedly repels Raj Chandra when he attacks her

Chullu Singh: The guard Raj Chandra arranges for Rongomala

Durga: Rongomala's chief maidservant and surrogate mother

Ethin: Burmese woman, who allegedly bewitched Adam Ali into forgetting his wife and child

Golap Raiya: Rongomala's drunkard brother

Gulbadan: King Inga Chowdhury's second and favoured wife; a bi-racial woman from the western lands

Harendra Ghosh: Nayeb-e-reasat, or chief tax collector of Babupur

Heera: Heera is a dashi, a maid or a slave, bought at an auction by Phuleswari's father, and acted as surrogate mother after Phuleswari's own mother died

Inga Chowdhury: Muslim zamindar of the neighbouring kingdom of Dewanganj; Raj Chandra's ally

Jaggeswari: Heera's maternal grandmother; abducted and impregnated by a Portuguese pirate; ended her life as mistress to a merchant

Jamiruddin the midget: A villager who tries to ingratiate himself with Raj Chandra by drawing his attention to Shoiop Mala, the weaver's wife

Jugindor: King Raj Chandra Chowdhury's personal servant

Kala Jugi: A weaver; Raj Chandra Chowdhury attacks his wife Shoirop Mala when she's alone in the house

Kali Charan Guha: Salt trader from Lamchor; father of Phuleswari Rai; owner of Heera

Kalitara: Mother Shumitra's elderly maidservant

Karim Sheikh: Chief boatman of the royal family

Khhanto Moni: Chief maidservant of Second Thakurani

Mangal Singh: One of Chanda Bir's men

Manohar Gazi: Ruler of Meherkul; elder brother of King Inga's first wife Mehrab

Mehrab: First wife of Inga Chowdhury; sister of Manohar Gazi; rumour has it that she cast a spell on Inga's second and favoured wife to drive her mad

Mother Shumitra: Mother of King Raj Chandra Chowdhury

Najar Ali: Ayna's son, born while his father was still at sea

Nasir Mohammed: Son and heir of Inga Chowdhury

Panna the whore: Heera's mother who auctions her off to Kali Charan Guha

Phuleswari: Also known as Phuleswari Rai; barely out of childhood, she is the daughter of a salt merchant and the young queen of Babupur

Prafulla Kumar: Grandson of the Regent Rajendra Narayan Chowdhury; his mother Shunonda is the Regent's daughter

Raj Chandra Chowdhury: Hindu zamindar, or king; heir to the throne of Babupur; Phuleswari's husband and Rongomala's lover

Rajendra Narayan Chowdhury: Acting Regent of Babupur and the uncle of rightful heir Raj Chandra Chowdhury

Ram Bharari: King Raj Chandra Chowdhury's constant companion and chief lackey

Ram Goitya Guja: The humpbacked villager who weds an unwilling Rongomala

Ramya Mog: Chief of the Mogs, a clan that originated in the Arakan mountains of present day Burma

Roma: A female barber, who is traditionally responsible for makeup, hairdos and other accoutrements; Rongomala's confidante

Rongomala: Mistress of King Raj Chandra Chowdhury, Rongomala was born in a Nor family, a low-caste people known for singing, dancing and theatre

Second Thakurani: Wife of the Regent Rajendra Narayan Chowdhury

Shamsher Gazi: Legendary Muslim ruler of Tripura, who was born in a peasant family, Gazi was known for his benevolent rule, during which he granted tax exemptions to farmers and increased access to education for the general populace

Shoirop Mala: Wife of Kala Jugi, the weaver; unwitting object of Raj Chandra Chowdhury's lust

Shunonda: Daughter of Rajendra Narayan Chowdhury

Shyam Shundar: Shyampriya's lover who betrays her

Shyama Shundori: Rongomala's mother; follower of the Shakta tradition within the Hindu faith

Shyampriya or Shyampriya Vaishnavi: Former mistress of the Regent, and go-between for Raj Chandra and Rongomala; a child-widow, Shyampriya converted to the Vaishnava tradition as a young woman when she eloped with a young man (in the Hindu traditions, widows could not remarry)

Somiron Bibi: Karim Sheikh's wife; mother of Ayna and Amena

The Sahib: Unnamed, the Sahib is an officer of the East India Company, whose friendship with Raj Chandra is based on their lechery

One

Even before dawn broke, the news that Chanda Bir was approaching the palace with Rongomala's severed head arrived like a storm. Earlier, flocks of black crows had swarmed the skies, flying in from who knew where. Their caws echoed across the courthouse, and through the palace corridors and balconies and the orchard and the banks of the pond. The palace was in uproar. From the commotion, it didn't seem as if it was a low-caste woman's head that was arriving but a wildfire blazing across the Roopsingh Plains, a fire that threatened to wipe out the entire Chowdhury dynasty. Raj Chandra Chowdhury lay unconscious in the outer house, still stoned from drinking bhang the evening before. Everyone—men, women and children—was terrified. When he woke up and, with Rongomala's decapitated head in hand, commenced upon a dance of destruction like Lord Shiva, who would stop him?

Heera dashi, the slave, darted though the palace searching for Phuleswari Rai in each wing. She stormed through the rooms, entering through one door and exiting through another. Her only misadventure was stumbling and falling over Mejo Thakurani's hookah pipe, pulling down the whole contraption. The stale tobacco water ruined her favourite fancy rug; however, the Thakurani barely had time to glance at it today. She was desperately seeking a hiding spot for Prafulla Kumar, her daughter Shunonda's son and beloved of the household. There was no telling from which direction disaster would strike. Doomsday had come upon them—if they had been Muslims, they would have been chanting *Ya nafsi, ya nafsi* in Arabic. Where was Phuleswari Rai at this calamitous moment?

Phuleswari was sitting on her swing in the orchard, rocking herself while counting crows on her fingers. Crows cawed and shrieked as they soared overhead in the hundreds. The birds flailed their wings and squawked in the aviary, raising a grand furore. Phuleswari couldn't keep count. As soon as she made it to twenty, she lost track and had to begin all over again. '*Didimoni, Didimoni*!' Heera's sudden shouts broke through her preoccupation, ending her counting game.

'Sister dear, sister dear!' Heera stopped to breathe and said, 'I've been searching every corner of the earth for you, and you're sitting here?' Just as Phuleswari poised herself to leap and grab her by the hair, Heera released the dreadful news like an arrow.

Rongomala's severed head in the courthouse!

'Come, you. The warrior Chanda Bir cut off her head and carried it here. Maharaja Rajendra Narayan's decree has been fulfilled.'

Just then, they heard heavy footsteps trampling through the garden shrubbery. Who was fleeing through the backway? Wasn't that Rajendra, Regent and uncle to the rightful king, followed by Chanda Bir? The flock of crows took to the air, following them while shrieking in chorus. In the blink of an eye, the palace emptied of crows.

Heera raced through the palace wings again and returned to tell Phuleswari that although Raj Chandra, the king, still lay snoring in the outer house, everyone else had latched their doors from the inside. Forget the hum of juicy gossip; there wasn't the slightest sign of any of the slaves or servants. The cookhouse had been abandoned. The Brahmin cooks had run for shelter to the woods behind the pond. The Brahmin priest thought his head was on fire. His head, adorned with the holy tuft of hair at the back, was bobbing like a coconut shell in the pond facing the courthouse. The queen mother, Shumitra, sat in her prayer room, chanting God's name with her hands folded and her eyes shut. Hers was the only door that stood open.

Raj Chandra might excuse his mother, but would he show any consideration to his wife? Phuleswari was surely the prime culprit. Though Rongomala had not been granted the formal status of co-wife, she had been more than that. When Raj Chandra would fail to find anyone else at hand, he would most certainly lash out at Phuleswari, the wife who wept day and night, the one driven insane after being spurned. Did this witless woman understand that? The last year seemed to have washed away Phuleswari's intelligence and reason. In her present state, she was worse than a lunatic. The signs didn't bode well to Heera, the slave. She dragged Phuleswari's leaf-thin body to her room. For a moment, she considered latching the door from the inside and feigning sleep. But what if Raj Chandra kicked it open? Before Phuleswari could get a grip on what was happening, she found herself a prisoner in her own bedchamber. Heera had padlocked the chain from the outside and fled with the keys.

'You lowborn whore!' Phuleswari cursed Heera as she hammered the locked door with her fists. 'I just want one glimpse of Rongomala. Open up!' As she wailed, tears scored her cheeks. Of the two people who were supposed to respond to Phuleswari Rai's plaintive cries, one, her mother-in-law, Ma Shumitra, was praying, 'Thakur, Thakur!' with her eyes shut tight; the other, her chief maid Heera, had vanished into the woods by the pond where she was currently besieged by venomous ants.

Exhausted from crying, Phuleswari finally calmed down. Was Rongomala really dead? Was she dreaming, or was this really true? That unfortunate girl had perished because of her fancy to have a lake cut in her name—an honour a lowborn woman couldn't claim. What a horrible way to die! At Rajendra

Narayan's command, his ruthless bodyguard Chanda Bir had cut off her head.

What use was it to Phuleswari now that Rongi was dead? Phuleswari Rai was adrift like a clump of weeds in the waters of this world. The time to sink her roots had passed.

Phuleswari wanted to weep again. She hadn't been able to get a good look at the woman who had destroyed her life while she had been alive. Rongomala, that woman who had turned her into a grass widow. And now she wouldn't even get to see her dead face. If seeing in dreams counted, though, and if her reflection in the water was indeed her true self—then Phuleswari had actually seen Rongomala about a year ago. Even now Rongomala's laughter, one that could shatter dams, floated like the sound of weeping on the distant night winds.

Two

Just a year ago, before Phuleswari Rai had been dubbed a madwoman, she was known widely as the daughter of the eminent salt merchant. Despite her husband's obvious lack of regard, she had wanted for neither affection nor care in the royal household.

One night, Phuleswari had a dream: the five-flamed prayer lamp flickered as it circled in the air by itself in coils of smoke, round and round. There was no sign of a priest or a puja pavilion anywhere nearby. Neither were there the sounds of drums or bells. Like fog, the dream wove itself into Phuleswari's eyelashes after she awoke.

In her dream, she saw a sudden shaft of light pierce the smoke and pause, resting on the gold crown of the goddess, Ma Durga. The light flickered and disappeared. Again, the five flames returned, like light travelling from afar. They didn't move too close, nor did they disappear completely, as if they hinted at some secret, while keeping their distance. Phuleswari grew desperate and tried to follow. This time she didn't have to wait. The greedy flame tongued the gold crown, flowed past the tight curls that clung to the goddess' temples like clusters of black grapes, and touched the glittering earrings. Before the inchoate beauty of Durga's idol vanished into smoke, Phuleswari scrambled herself awake in her bed.

In the dim light of dawn, her eyes moved to her sandalwood chest. The padlock hung lopsided from the iron ring, undone. The bunch of keys was still tied to her sari-end, jangling when she walked. With the strength of a demon, she lifted the lid of the chest with one hand, while with the other, she fastened the wooden latch that propped it open. The smell of camphor flooded the room. From the secret chamber, she pulled out the large red velvet pouch that contained her jewellery. It was half-empty. She ignored the fact that it had been emptied so much that it weighed less than before and clasped the pouch to her chest as if it was the fabled treasure of seven kings. She carried it to her bed, untied the noose of the gold drawstring and poured everything out.

The large diamond earrings were gone. Phuleswari paid no attention to what else had disappeared. She sifted through the pieces, searching for the earrings she had seen gleaming in the light of the five-flamed lamp moments ago.

How strange for such a disaster to strike while she slept! She hardly ever opened her sandalwood chest. It wasn't customary for the wives and daughters of the royal household to dress up unless there was a festival. Their everyday pieces of jewellery sufficed. Who knew how long ago the diamond earrings had been stolen? Phuleswari's little heart ached. Raj Chandra had known that those earrings belonged to her dead mother, and yet he had taken them anyway. Her old grandmother used to say, 'If doubt you must, then better first to doubt your own eyes.' People depart, but their words remain. She dropped her jewellery pouch and stood up. She struck a flint and lit a candle. One by one, all the tapers in the candelabra blazed. The dazzling light was bright enough to find a needle in a haystack. Whether she found her earrings or not, at least she could resolve this confusion between her eyes and her heart.

Phuleswari tucked her sari-end into her waistband and began her search. She shifted each item in the chest. She combed through every piece of clothing. All she could do now was to call on Ma Shumitra and complain about her son. But what could Phuleswari tell her? That the diamond earrings had vanished from her chest? That they were now in the possession of Goddess Durga? While

Phuleswari wasn't brave enough to dismiss her dawn dream with a snap of her fingers, she didn't entirely believe in it either. Even before her mother-in-law had warned her to keep a close eye on her keys, she had figured out who was stealing her jewellery, and how. She had been too afraid of Raj Chandra to open her mouth before. But now he had assailed the memories of her dead mother. That stonehearted man had struck a blow to her heart. Whether goddess or witch, Phuleswari now *had* to see the one whose ears were graced by her diamond earrings.

'Heera, do you know the way to the Nor house?' Phuleswari's calm voice made Heera dashi, the servant, shiver. What hell was this even before the day had begun? She had been standing by the mynah's perch with a bell-metal bowl in hand, feeding chickpeas to the bird. At Phuleswari's question, the bowl slipped from her hands and fell to the ground. Chaos descended. The crows converged on the chickpeas, cawing raucously. Black Moon, the mynah, was furious at being robbed of his feed. He was cursing Heera, calling her a slave. '*Baandi*! *Baandi*!' Today Phuleswari couldn't stand the word she herself had taught the mynah. She plucked Black Moon from his perch and went to sit on the plinth built around the medlar tree.

Heera squabbled with the crows to get at the chickpeas strewn on the ground. Phuleswari glared at her. 'Stop that, you slut,' she exploded. 'Do you know the way to the Nor house? Why don't you speak?'

Although she remained silent, Heera slowly moved forward and plopped herself down at Phuleswari's feet. She raised her face like a thirsting bird. Phuleswari's neck, the line as graceful as a swan's, was taut as she gazed into the distance—beyond the aviary, beyond the lotus-bedecked pond, to the other side where a dozen storks stood one-legged and meditating. The child-bride had grown older in the past few days, as if she had doubled in age. Black shadows ringed her eyes, and the blue shade of privation was etched in the lines of her face. Oh, Lord, by whose curse did the flower wither before it had even had a chance to bloom?

Heera was but a bought slave, bound to serve. Still, she had fallen to her knees pleading with Phuleswari's father, Kali Charan Guha. 'Don't give her in marriage there, just don't. Have you plugged your ears with cotton wool? You wish to hear neither good nor evil! Let me just say this—better to chop the girl into pieces and throw her in the sea.'

Big talk from the mouth of a menial! Kali Charan had pinched her cheek and strode off to the outer house, the end of his dhoti swinging to his gait. It was the Lord's endless bounty that he had advanced from a small clerk in the salt trade to a merchant so rapidly. He had already bought a zamindari, the landholding that would smooth his entry into the landed gentry. What he needed was a way to gain acceptance into the ranks of the aristocrats. That path had opened up with the arrival of the proposal: for his daughter to be given in matrimony to the house of the Chowdhurys of Shindurkait. Kali Charan pledged everything he had to ensure that this opportunity didn't slip through his fingers. He began spending money like water. What he ignored was the need to investigate the groom himself, his history. Even those who made it their business to meddle in weddings had to depart with their tittle-tattle unheard. It was the groom's side that profited. No matter how aristocratic their lineage, the groom himself was wayward and wild. The Shindurkait Chowdhurys needed a bride, no matter what kind, to put a leash around his neck. Now with that bride arrived chests full of gold and a convoy of bullock carts weighed down with goods. Heera herself had witnessed the people of Babupur sniggering at the grandiose antics of the Lamchor salt merchant through a chink in the blinds.

Heera sat in the palanquin with Phuleswari. The girl was so laden with jewels she could barely sit straight. She kept toppling onto Heera. A kingdom's worth of terror showed in her face.

Although she had jumped into the palanquin when she had heard that Heera was going with her as well as her birds, as soon as she lost sight of her father's house, she began to cry. There was no way to stop their palanquin. The palanquin bearers and the guards were all unknown, as was their route. Even Heera, who had walked all kinds of roads in this world, had never set foot hereabouts. She had grown up with the winds of the riverine islands playing against her skin. Heera's heart wept as they left Lamchor behind.

Beauteous Radha sits by Jamuna's shores and weeps,
Why can I not hear the melody of his flute?
I ache for Shyam Chand, my Dark One,
I ache from the harsh words of people,
Oh, my heart's love, my friend, I want to beat my head against stone.

Phuleswari had dozed off. As their convoy entered Babupur district, they were mobbed by onlookers who seemed more entertained by the long procession of bullock carts than the glimpse of the new bride behind the palanquin's veil. The sentries and guards wielded sticks and spears, swords and guns, but they could barely control the throng. Phuleswari clutched Heera in terror. The sun was setting behind a horizon lined with ripe rice paddies. The reddish gold light of the vanishing sun illuminated the endless line of people snaking along the earthen ridges bordering the fields. Like ants, they were scurrying towards the royal palace.

At the first glimpse of Phuleswari's mother-in-law, Ma Shumitra, a weight had lifted from Heera's heart. No matter how the husband turned out, it was as if this motherless child had finally found refuge in a mother's arms. *Don't place her on the ground where bites the snake/Nor in the water where waits the crocodile*—the queen mother had chanted the required invocations.

She cared for the girl. Phuleswari kept herself busy feeding her birds, marrying them to each other in play, just as she had in her father's household. If today the magpies were to be wed, tomorrow it was the hawks' turn or the parrots'. Bright-hued flowers and leaves adorned the cages; the birds were made to exchange wedding garlands, everyone was served sweets—the weddings in the aviary went on and on. Any disruptions, and the girl sulked at her mother-in-law, or climbed a tree in a huff. Ma Shumitra would stand beneath the tree, a plate of milk and rice in hand, pleading. Phuleswari climbed up and above, as high as the highest branch. She hid in the branches, imitating birdcalls. Days passed, months passed, years went by.

The trouble began once the young girl reached puberty. The mother-in-law couldn't make her see sense. At night, if she pushed the girl into her son's room through one door, Phuleswari promptly escaped through the other. They had to set a guard at the door to keep her in there. When she heard Raj Chandra's footsteps approaching, Phuleswari squeezed herself against the cold wall behind her. When she could shift no more, she would press her lips to the wall and whisper, 'Oh, wall, please turn into a tree. I'll climb right to the top.' How long could this go on! The young girl's entreaties were swept away in the surge of her husband's desire. One morning, a dishevelled Phuleswari emerged from her bedchamber. With Heera's help she moved the dovecote far away from the hawk enclosure.

How strange! All these years, all those talismans and blessed oils—nothing had worked. But now that she had heard her husband was spending his nights at the Nor house, suddenly she was pining for him. If this had happened earlier, there might have been time to do something about it. But Raj Chandra had been wetting his beak at that particular pond for about two years now. All and sundry for miles had already chewed and digested this bit of gossip by the time the poor thing had finally sat up to take notice. Who was going to deal with this now?

The storks by the pond had gorged themselves on fish and flown off. Phuleswari didn't let up. She stayed where she was and prodded Heera. 'I want to visit the Nor house tonight. Arrange it.'

Leaves crunched behind them. Heera spun around. It would spell trouble if it was Khhanto Moni, chief maid to Rajendra Narayan's wife, the Mejo Thakurani. Not only was that whore a shrew, she was also a scandalmonger. The gossip would race before the wind. Phuleswari was the goose that laid golden eggs; it would be Heera, her chief maid, the one who had no one to speak on her behalf, who would be sent to the chopping block. Heera tried to throw whoever was hiding in the bushes off the scent. She began the bedtime story she used to tell Phuleswari, 'Oh, Didimoni, you know that time when my grandmother was taken by the Portuguese pirates …'

'Forget about your Portuguese *harmads*. I don't care.' Phuleswari set the mynah aside and pounded her fist on the plinth. Who was the girl angry at? If hitting and punching were giving her satisfaction, why didn't she strike at her misfortune?

'Tonight!' Phuleswari pounded the plinth again and let loose the final arrow from her sheath. 'I *must* go to the house of the Nor tonight. That woman has disguised herself as Ma Durga!'

Heera had no way of knowing who had disguised themselves as the Goddess Durga. But she sighed in relief when she saw that Phuleswari's noisiness had flushed out a tiny rabbit instead of Khhanta Moni from the ixora bush. The rabbit blinked in surprise. Perhaps this was the first time it had come upon humans. It loped off through the rear gate.

Minutes later, Ma Shumitra entered through the gate, her wet sari wrapped around her. She had just finished her bath at the back pond. No longer did she push her daughter-in-law to bathe every day. The queen mother had lost face. Her son's tomcatting was eating away her fierceness; it dwindled like the waning moon. Her health was headed the same way. Day after day of fasting was taking its toll. As if, like a fallen leaf, she could float in the wind and disappear among the trees.

Now she would change her clothes and enter her prayer room, not to emerge until her belly cried out in hunger. A Hindu widow, Ma Shumitra ate only what she cooked herself. She allowed no other hand to touch her food, performing all the chopping and grinding too. It would be late afternoon before she was done. Who would deal with Phuleswari until then? Would she just sit here without eating, without bathing? And was Heera just supposed to watch? Or did it make more sense to call the healer when someone was bewitched?

Heera said, 'Dear Didimoni, Budha the Mad One has returned to the village after travelling many lands. Shall I get some blessed sindoor from him?' Budha the Healer prayed over and dispensed sindoor; it was an infallible remedy to rein in one's wandering husband:

If this blessed sindoor betides a defeat
May Mahadev's locks fall at Goddess Uma's feet.

Heera's well-meaning words invited abuse. 'You husbandless woman, why don't you slather your forehead with sindoor, go on. Here,' Phuleswari wrenched off the silver amulet from her upper arm and hurled it at Heera, 'wash this amulet and go drink that holy water.'

What irreverence for a sacred token! Heera busied herself looking for the amulet. Forget Budha's sindoor, the amulet had to be returned to its ordained place, or misfortune lay ahead.

By then Phuleswari had locked herself inside the osprey pen. A fierce bird of prey, yet there it perched, dozing this early in the morning like an old opium eater. Life in a cage had turned it feeble. Phuleswari poked the osprey till it roused itself. It didn't pay much attention to her and just shifted sideways. What nuisance this morning! And that from one who should know better!

How long should Heera wait outside holding the amulet? Phuleswari thought she was being so sly locking herself in. Begging and pleading had no effect, and Heera finally rid herself of the amulet by promising to take Phuleswari to the Nor house. Phuleswari exited the osprey's cage in a cloud of feathers.

Phuleswari had unburdened herself by passing all responsibility to her chief maid—she sat in the swing and trilled like a bird. As if, instead of Raj Chandra, she was the one who had been invited to the house of Atma Ram Nor tonight. And along with her, all her pet birds had been invited, even the owls and the bone-swallowers. They couldn't take flight inside the cages, so they showed their joy by capering about. As a species, birds were as selfish as the women of zamindar families! Heera sighed. She barely had an appetite at lunchtime. As soon as the sun moved towards the western sky, she began preparing for the night's journey.

First, Ma Shumitra's chamber. She granted Heera permission to visit the boatman Karim Sheikh's house right away. All it took was for her to hear that Heera needed a burqah so she could secretly visit the shrine of the Muslim saint Miran Shah to procure blessed oil for Phuleswari.

Even Karim Sheikh's daughter Ayna believed it when Heera told her. But she ignored Heera's haste. She lowered her baby to the ground and, instead of going to grab the burqah, went off to get betel leaf. The baby crawled in the yard, cramming whatever it found into its mouth. The boy Najar Ali had never seen his father Adam Ali, who had taken a job as a boatswain and sailed off on a merchant ship when Ayna had still been pregnant. That was when Ayna's fortunes had burned. Although all the other men had returned, of Adam Ali there was no sign. He had fallen prey to the wily arts of some witch in a foreign port.

But that was nothing new for the handsome menfolk of Sudharam village. Ayna's father Karim Sheikh had mounted a search for Adam Ali but had given up soon enough. Since then,

Ayna had found shelter at her father's house. Was her son supposed to eat from a silver bowl and sip milk from a golden spoon instead of gnawing clumps of dirt? Despite Heera telling her not to, Ayna settled herself comfortably with the paan box by her side, leaving her son to graze in the yard.

There was a certain glee in getting all the gossip about Raj Chandra and Rongomala straight from a royal servant. Even a babe in arms would forget to suckle at its mother's breast, and here Ayna was a young woman in her prime, a grass widow at that. But today her demands felt toxic to Heera. Each time she pulled at Heera's sari to sit her down, Heera straightened like an unsheathed arrow. But what use would it be to return home without the burqah!

'The nerve of that Nor girl!' Ayna shook her head as she smeared slaked lime on a betel leaf to make paan. 'Since childhood I've been seeing Raj Chandra roam about on his horse. He patrols the land day and night, gun in hand. I swear by Allah, I've never raised my eyes to him, not once.' Another day Heera would have mocked her about this claim; she would have pinched Ayna's pockmarked cheeks and asked, 'Why didn't you raise your eyes? You're no less of a beauty than Rongomala, are you?'

But today Heera was in a different mood. She pretended that she couldn't see Ayna's mother Somiron Bibi gesturing to summon her to the cookhouse again and again, sticking her neck out like a stork. The woman was desperate. With one hand she was stuffing straw into the stove's maw; in the other she clasped an iron spatula. As soon as the thinly sliced onions were browned in oil and spices, she would throw in the boiled duck eggs. In the meantime, she held taut a strand of her hair and used it to slice each boiled egg into two. Heera sneered and averted her eyes.

The only exception in this household was Karim Sheikh's mute daughter Amena. Her wide eyes seemed vague, but she took no respite from her chores. She had penned the ducks and the chickens, and now she hunkered down on the ground with a bamboo funnel, filling lamps with the oil of swamp barb fish. It was almost time to light the evening lamps; when would Heera manage to extricate herself from Karim Sheikh's family? Somiron Bibi twitched like a headless chicken by the stove. She couldn't miss this chance to hear Rongomala being badmouthed. When she saw Heera leave with the burqah, she stood in the doorway of the cookhouse and shouted, 'Heera, stop by on your way back from the shrine! I shall bless the holy oil as well.' The woman must be mad, trying to lord it over God Himself!

Heera heaved a sigh of relief when she reached the road. Ayna was like a vine, twining around her. If her baby hadn't stuffed a worm in his mouth, Heera would never have managed to get out of that house so easily. The call for the Maghreb prayers had sounded—she was lucky that Karim Sheikh wasn't back yet. That man had a knack for worming out secrets; he was an ace at digging one's guts out of one's belly. He wouldn't have let her off just because she was Phuleswari Rai's chief maid. He would keep talking and throwing questions at her until he got at what she knew. The Chowdhurys would have done better to make the man their qazi or judge instead of their boatman.

Late at night, Heera exited the palace through a back entrance, with Phuleswari in tow. They had barely reached the adjacent pond when a thorn pierced Phuleswari's foot. It was a tiny thorn from the tiger claw tree, but still, a bad omen at the outset of their journey. Heera returned to the palace to tuck a pair of slippers under her clothing and start anew.

Shod in Chinese slippers, Phuleswari's feet made slapping noises with every step. The black burqah she wore reached below her knees. A pair of eyeholes in the veil allowed her to see where she was going. Heera had clad herself in Muslim garb as well. Glass bangles covered her arms, an enormous stud sat on her nose, and her sari-end was shaped into a pointy *ghomta*—a head-covering—shadowing half her forehead. They barely recognised each other. The rest was in God's hands.

Phuleswari hid herself in the bamboo grove beside the Nor-house pond. A cottage stood on stilts in the middle of the water. Chandeliers illuminated scenes of carousing. The king lolled on pillows, pulling on his hookah. In front of him, paan wrapped in edible gold and silver *tobok* were arranged on an ornamental platter. The servant Durga was running from one end of the stilted cottage to the other, carrying pitchers of wine and spittoons. With such attendants everywhere, why should the king bother to return to his own house?

Suddenly Phuleswari's breath caught. Rongomala had entered the scene like the shimmer of moonlight on gentle waves. Was this a woman or some divine creature? She was draped in a white muslin sari embroidered all over in gold, with a matching white bodice. She was covered in jewels that sparkled every time she moved. Just like in her dream, Phuleswari strained to see her. She couldn't tell what kind of earrings lent their glow to Rongomala's face. She wore no crown, but a fan-shaped gold ornament was attached to the side of her head, fencing in her black curls that were half covered with her sari-end. She couldn't see her clearly, and the little she could see of Rongomala through the whorls of smoke emitted by Raj Chandra vexed her even more. For a moment, it seemed to Phuleswari that she was actually seeing Rongomala's reflection in the water, not Rongomala in the flesh, an experience as far from the real as her dream. Could Phuleswari recognise Raj Chandra himself? Such a jovial mood and tender gaze could not be his; they couldn't belong to that thuggish husband of hers. This had been a fool's errand—to have followed this stranger.

Phuleswari couldn't bear to wait a moment more. As she rushed out of the bamboo grove, the hem of her burqah caught on a branch. Before she could untangle it, her eyes caught sight of a scene that made her freeze. Raj Chandra had picked up

Rongomala and was carrying her into another room. Their laughter was like undammed water; they were laughing so hard it seemed Rongi might fall from his arms. Phuleswari shut her eyes. When she looked again, the door had been shuttered, the candles dimmed. The candelabra stood outside like a guard, its many eyes flickering. Phuleswari felt truly forsaken. She could hear nothing except the beating of her own heart. When she couldn't breathe, she grasped Heera's hand and moved away from the pond.

The field ahead of them was awash in moonlight. Their hearts felt flooded, yet not a single word crossed their lips. The world had fallen apart in a moment. Phuleswari's hand was cold and hard in Heera's. This girl, flighty as a bird, always laughing—what solace could she be given in this moment? Heera's eyes had been scorched by Rongomala's beauty, her mind numbed.

It wasn't as if the gods had not granted Heera some beauty. If Rongomala owned a gold coin, then Heera could at least boast of a few pennies. When her mother had auctioned her off at the Lamchor market, even if there hadn't been much flesh on her bones, her ocean-blue eyes and long legs had raised her price from fifty silver coins to a hundred in a flash. That is what Kali Charan Guha had paid for her. Phuleswari was yet to be born back then.

Although Kali Charan Guha had three wives, Heera was summoned to his quarters whenever the whim took him. The salt trader wouldn't brook a moment's delay. Her lord and master would strut into the servant quarters, his clogs clacking on the floor. As she licked the salt off her master's skin, Heera dreamed of becoming the mistress of his household. Then Kali Charan Guha's second wife died during childbirth, and Heera's fortunes plummeted. She was granted permission to live in the main house, but not as the mistress. She was to tend to Phuleswari, the motherless babe. The master passed the responsibility of his dead wife's baby and her birds to Heera and turned his gaze elsewhere. The rest of her days she carried the bitter taste of salt on her tongue; let alone a husband, she hadn't even been granted the chance to serve as a kept woman. Still, beauty had two sides to it and it wasn't a thing to be spurned. If she had been ugly, Kali Charan Guha would simply have sent her off to the salt flats instead of taking her to his bed.

Phuleswari vaguely knew all of this. Although she had deduced some of it when she had grown up, Heera had never told her the whole story; Kali Charan Guha had warned her not to. Even the story of Heera's grandmother, Jaggeswari, she had only been told just enough to serve as a morality tale at bedtime. Today there was no need to hide anything anymore. The girl was no longer a child. Today she had watched her husband take a whore to his bed. To say anything about that would just feed the flames. Heera fumbled for words. The southern wind that blew over the pond brought with it many tales of joy and loss. The stories buzzed at her ears. Although they spoke of the magic batons of silver and gold that could grant life, these stories had no 'the king and queen lived happily ever after' at the end. They were more like a flowing river that flooded both its banks.

The bells jingle under the mango tree, beneath the banana tree to be wed

Waits the groom of the beautiful maiden, and a crown sits on his head.

The women of the inner quarters ululated; the conches sounded. Drumbeats travelled far in the night breeze. In the darkness, *kosha* and fishing boats sliced through the heart of the river against the current. Oars churned the water. No other noise broke the silence.

When the *kosha* fleets of the Mog and Portuguese pirates hit the riverbank, Jaggeswari had been standing under the wedding canopy. The daughter of a high-caste family, she had turned eighteen by the time they found a proper match for her. Her beauty merged with the holy fire. The bride and groom had already exchanged garlands and *shubhodrishti,* the ritual exchange of glances. The bride was about to be given away; her sari-end had just been tied to the groom's clothing when the cries heralding a pirate attack pierced the village. The ululation, the conches of the wedding festivities—all other sounds were tamped down. The groom jumped off the wedding stool and bolted like a racehorse. His ceremonial *uttori*-scarf was still tied to Jaggeswari's sari-end in accordance with wedding custom, and so, slipping and falling, she was forced to run behind him, slowing him down. They had barely reached the end of the yard, when the groom flung off his uttori and raced away, leaving the bride to be captured by the harmad. At the entrance to the inner house lay Jaggeswari's father, moaning. He had been shot but was still alive. A tall man with equine features, sporting a pointy hat—whose blood flowed in Heera's veins today—dragged Jaggeswari towards the riverbank through the congealing blood of those who had been decimated. Canoes were berthed at the bank in serried ranks. He aimed at one and launched Jaggeswari towards it like a bird into air. Jaggeswari landed in the dark chasm of the boat's belly. A wooden cover rumbled shut above her head.

The pirate boats sped like hawks as the wind hit the sails. The Mogs and the Portuguese harmads stood guard, guns in hand. The sound of weeping arose from within the boats. The captives could not see each other. Each had had a long, thin, sharpened piece of cane pierced through their palm like a shackle, so they couldn't escape. The night passed as did the day. They lay in heaps without food or water. Some of the prisoners scrabbled around the bottom to eat the handfuls of dry rice that the pirates threw down. Pain and fear caused the grains to stick in their parched throats. They sailed one night and one day, and the next night they docked beside a seagoing ship anchored in safe waters. That night, a harmad jumped down into the boat where Jaggeswari was confined. He released her from the cane shackle and made her climb a rope ladder onto the ship. A home set up in the heart of the sea. Jaggeswari was surprised beyond belief. The harmad held out food towards her, a thing like a longish cake, and chattered to her in the tongue from the land of her forefathers. 'Bread! Eat, girl! And then come and sit by me. I love you so much.' Hunger possessed her like a demon. Jaggeswari grabbed the bread to her mouth and shoved it down her throat. Her left palm was bleeding again.

She did not return to the kosha. The Portuguese pirate was besotted with her. He held her thick hair close to his face so he could smell it, caressed her flame-hued skin and gazed, enraptured, into her jet-black eyes. Jaggeswari's urn-shaped buttocks, her large breasts—the harmad loved every bit of her. He claimed he would marry her when he had enough money. This abandoned village by the forest of *goran* mangroves was their secret hideout. Apart from the earthen houses, there was no sign of people. This was where the local merchants and procurers came to buy slaves from the pirates.

From above, Jaggeswari witnessed the kosha boats emptying out day by day. It wouldn't be long before he had enough money. The harmad would take her to church, convert her and wed her. She had to escape before that happened. Luckily, she soon had her chance. The pirates ended the last day of their trade with a magnificent celebration. They had hunted spotted deer and jungle fowl. From sunset began endless feasting fuelled by meat and liquor. In the first hour of the night, the ship rolled this way and that as the pirates went wild and danced. Jaggeswari poured some rum down her throat from a wineskin. Coaxed by the pirate, she had become used to drinking; it made her feel quite sprightly. She placed her hand on her lover's back and danced on unsteady feet. She was wearing a ghagra and blouse, her neck adorned with a spray of pearls, her arms covered in *belwari* bangles. Although the largesse of the pirate chief made sure that she wanted for nothing—clothes, jewellery or food—she had grown as thin as a lath. But that made her even more mesmerising. The pirate's eyes closed in rapture. His arm slackened around her waist. Jaggeswari pretended to feel unwell and retired to her cabin. Once there, she changed her clothes. When she emerged again, the night was in the small hours. The great roistering had ended. The drunken pirates lay heaped on the deck, like dead soldiers, and snored. There was no longer any need for armed guards as there were no more prisoners in the boats.

Jaggeswari walked to the ship's rail. The star-studded sky hung low above the calm sea. Diamond coronets glimmered at the tips of the small dancing waves. An old Mog was keeping watch in the crow's nest, thirty or forty arms' length above. He made no signal as she descended the rope ladder. Perhaps he was asleep. Silently, a wooden plank tucked in her armpit, Jaggeswari lowered herself into the water.

Behind her, the harmad pirates; ahead, the green shoreline. She held onto the plank and swam for her life. The night was brightening into dawn, and still there was no sign of the shore. The green line she had seen from the ship seemed to have vanished. Around her all was water, glittering in the sun. She must have kicked off in the wrong direction in the darkness. Thirst turned her throat into parched wood. Her arms grew numb. There was no hope. She lay her head on the plank and drifted into deep sea as the ebb tide pulled her along.

At day's end, a boatload of fishermen spotted the barely-alive Jaggeswari floating like a tree trunk. Her belly was swollen from all the saltwater she had swallowed. The fishermen pulled her onto their boat and then lay her face down, a water urn keeping her torso raised. When the seawater drained out through her mouth and nose, they let her rest flat on a mat. They fed her coconut water with a seashell spoon until finally she found her voice. The fishermen were from her father's land, Bhola and Mehendiganj. Having hauled in their catch from the sea, they were on their way home. The next day, she ate *loitta* fish and rice that the Muslim fishermen cooked. The worst had already happened to her. Losing caste by eating food prepared by Muslims wouldn't make much difference now.

After three days, Jaggeswari finally reached the dock near her home. Her mother was just coming back from washing the rice in the river. She didn't recognise her mother, dressed as she was as a widow in a white sari, without her conch-shell bangles and the sindoor in her parting. Her mother was startled. As if she had seen a ghost, she dropped her rice basket, and in the darkness of the milkweed tree, mother and daughter embraced and wept quietly. Their sorrows had hardened in their hearts and turned to stone. Even the house looked blighted. A month had gone by, but the fences and the walls remained in ruins, just as the Mogs and Portuguese pirates had left them. As if the house was unable to recover from the loss of that one person. And to add insult to injury, the daughter had returned, but tainted by the foreigners. Would the villagers understand that having her daughter back was like having the moon handed to her!

At daybreak, her mother pushed Jaggeswari into the loft and shuttered it. Jaggeswari lay there throughout the day, with her torso twisted to fit the confines of the space. She even breathed slowly, so she was no louder than a fly's buzz. At night, after the evening lamp was doused, she descended in the dark to sit beside her mother and eat. A single meal had to last throughout the day. Not a word crossed their lips. Even their tears had dried up. They could see no way out. The rituals required to purify Jaggeswari were expensive. Where would they get that kind of money? The Mog and harmad pirates had killed them in more ways than one. Besides, thinking of the ritual acts for purification made their blood run cold. Being made to drink boiling-hot ghee and hold clay platters full of glowing coals in her hands and on the top of the head—it was worse than death. All these anxieties receded, however, when, coiled in the loft, Jaggeswari felt the movement of a baby inside her.

Four months after her escape from the pirate ship came another dark night. Jaggeswari removed her sleeping mother's arm from around herself and walked out the door. When she had leapt into the sea from the pirate ship, Jaggeswari had known that she was returning home. Now she was walking the same, familiar path, but out towards an unknown world. With each step, she left behind all the joy and sorrow of her eighteen years. As dawn broke, she climbed aboard a passenger barge. Her destination: Laxmipur, the port town on the eastern shores of the Meghna. Jaggeswari, the daughter of a high-caste family, was born anew in the storm that raged over the river.

Thus began the life of the whore Moti, who survived this world by selling her body. Already pregnant, she became the mistress of a merchant at the port. There she gave birth to a strong, healthy baby. The merchant looked on the baby as his own. His generosity allowed Jaggeswari to earn enough to build a grand house by the river. A hijol tree standing on its edge drooped into the river on one bank, while the other bank was lined with coconut and areca nut trees. Although her flesh was her ware, in her tree-lined mansion, Jaggeswari was a woman to be reckoned with. No one cared about a whore's caste.

As a child, Heera had seen her celebrate Kali puja with pomp and ceremony. By then, Jaggeswari had turned into an old lady garbed in white. In her lifetime, she had attained all the rights that she could, except the right to wear shoes.[1] Panna, the daughter

---

[1] Many marginalised identities were prohibited from wearing shoes. For example, peasants beholden to zamindars were known to be punished if they didn't take their shoes off and carry them in their hands while in the presence of the zamindar/zamindar's family, or even while crossing the zamindar's house/

born of her womb and from the loins of the Portuguese pirate, had inherited neither her courage, nor her beauty, nor her wits. Alongside his equine features, Panna the whore's father had bequeathed her a taste for opium, which eventually led to her downfall. When her mother's comforting presence was gone, poverty became Panna's constant companion. By then she was past her prime. She auctioned off her blossoming daughter for a thick wad of money. She needed cash, lots of it …

Phuleswari bickered over the claim that the blossoming young girl of Jaggeswari's tale was actually Heera. So be it; it was quite enough that the desolate clouds had passed tonight. Who knew what the future held? Jaggeswari's story had shepherded them back; they were at the far end of Rupsingh's Plains now. One by one, many breeds of birds were alighting on the water and on the shore, their calls melding together. The moonlight had died away, leaving the eastern sky awash in a bloody red. The crown of the royal temple of Kali pierced the red like an arrow.

---

mansion. This is similar indication that while Jaggeswari was able to carve out a decent life, she was still a sex worker and as such, no matter the money she made, she would never be accorded quite the same level of acceptance or respect that 'normal' people/women would get.

Three

It was still dark when Shyampriya, the vaishnavi, her body burning with fever, stood on the lakeshore near the palace. She had wrapped herself in a torn quilt and was carrying a pot. She was destitute and weary, ravaged by illnesses. And there was Raj Chandra, practically living at the Nor house. The roosters were crowing already, and still no sign of that philanderer.

Once people got what they wanted, they didn't bother to remember their benefactors. For two years now, Shyampriya had been dogging Raj Chandra's steps in the hopes of getting her reward of one hundred silver coins. As soon as he spied his creditor, Raj Chandra would take off, leaving Ram Bharari, his lackey, to charge at Shyampriya with raised fists. But Shyampriya was not one to let things go. Today, if Raj Chandra didn't pay what he owed her, he would have to climb over the vaishnavi's hungry body. She would leave him no choice.

A little later, Phuleswari Rai and Heera came down the path. Shyampriya had settled herself against a tree, wrapping herself well in her quilt. Her head hung low and her chin rested on her chest. She was sleepy and her eyelids kept drooping shut. She thrust her head out like a turtle when she heard the footsteps of the daughter-in-law and the maidservant from the royal household. Not a sound crossed her lips. Her eyes flashed like steel from within the shadow of the ragged quilt.

No matter what people said about her, Shyampriya was a person, and an old-fashioned one at that. This was Koli Jug, the

Age of Vice. How was she to know that the royal daughter-in-law had decided to spy on the Nor house in the dark of night to see the woman for whom her husband left home night after night? Even if that woman was a whore? This was what the world had come to; this was what Shyampriya had to witness as she leaned against the old areca nut tree by the side of the road. And that too *after* the visit, not before.

In the blink of an eye, she could rouse a furore in the palace that slumbered peacefully behind her. But to whose advantage would that be? Neglected by her husband, this young queen was like the walking dead anyway. If news of her nighttime jaunt spread, she would be scorned by all, and besides, it would make Shyampriya's sworn enemy, the Mejo Thakurani, wife of the deceased king's brother, Rajendra Narayan Chowdhury, rejoice.

Shyampriya had been the thorn in Mejo Thakurani's side when she was a young woman, because the Thakurani's husband, Rajendra Narayan, had been her frequent visitor. That was when the door to the palace's inner quarters had been slammed shut in her face. That was when she had lost the chance to earn a few coins from performing songs of love and faith before the women of the palace. Apart from that, it had been Shyampriya's routine job to supply the bark of red lotuses and oleander to rid the maidservants' wombs of trouble. These earnings were a bonus. Poor people always got kicked in the belly. Mejo Thakurani didn't have the nerve to persecute the dancers at whose feet Rajendra Narayan wasted his money and his nights.

Evenings used to descend on the zamindar's lakeside pleasure house to the beats of the bayan-tabla and the tinkling of ankle bells. Resplendent in kohl, attar, bangles and long scarves, like celestial nymphs flying down from the heavens, the tawaifs would glide onto the soft carpet and wait, bent at the waist, in welcoming obeisance. The subtle smoke of perfumed tobacco floated in the air. Belwari glass chandeliers danced overhead, twinkling in a thousand points of light. The heart of the gathering, Rajendra Narayan, would show up early in the evening, doused in attar and swinging his dhoti pleats, only to return home drunk as a lord when the night was done. In the morning, Mejo Thakurani would arrange all the accoutrements for her husband's bath and then settle herself with her legs splayed out, ready for a good bout of weeping. Her heartrending wails could crack a stone, but left no impression on her husband. One by one, she released each arrow in her quiver. Twice she left for her father's house by boat. No response from her husband. Eventually, she had to come back the way she had left—by herself. To avenge her loss of face, Mejo Thakurani took to liquor, setting the kingdom abuzz with scandal. Yet, from her husband she could provoke no reaction.

Once darkness fell, it was impossible to keep him home. As if his palate, jaded by the richness of palace food, relished the dried-fish tang of the vaishnavi. Clad in only a knee-length dhoti, his feet muddy, like a crow he cawed a single note: Priya, Priya. Shyampriya was dressed in the ochre garb of the vaishnavi, her everyday *rasakali* and *tilaka* painted on her forehead and down the bridge of her nose. Her hair was twisted into a topknot. That was enough to slay Rajendra Narayan; the grand style of kohl, scarves and bejewelled skirts favoured by the tawaifs vanished from his mind. Their nights passed in the twinkling of an eye. In the mornings, when Rajendra Narayan galloped out of her yard, his horse caparisoned in red broadcloth, Shyampriya's heart trembled like the brass and silver bells slung around the horse's neck.

That was ages ago. Now Rajendra Narayan was a toothless, clawless old tiger with sagging skin. He might still be out and about lugging his pudgy body and throwing his weight around, but in truth he was nothing more than a windup toy. It was Chanda Bir, that demon king, who was winding his key behind the scenes. The lakeshore pleasure house was like a haunted den these days—phantoms danced in the dark of night, and every hour owls hooted in the echoing emptiness.

Although the palace had scaled down its excesses, Rajendra Narayan's nephew Raj Chandra Chowdhury was hard at work maintaining the standards set by his forefathers. He was Shyampriya's walking cane in her dotage, keeping her on her feet. But he wasn't really. She had gone to all that trouble to pair him up with Rongomala, but now whenever Shyampriya showed up to ask for her hundred-coin reward, he set his dog Ram Bharari on her.

Shyampriya had never seen a hundred silver coins in her life, not even in her youth. While she jingled her hundred coins in her dreams, Raj Chandra's white steed galloped away right under her nose. After him came Ram Bharari. Shyampriya couldn't tell whether it was man or horse that kicked her when she stood in the way, but suddenly she was tumbling down the steep lakeshore with her quilt and her water pot. It took a while for her to reemerge from the lake. By then Raj Chandra had dismounted and was walking towards the palace. Ram Bharari was haltering his horse to the mango tree by the lake. He raised a warning hand to threaten her as the vaishnavi stood in water up to her chest. He pointed to his own curls and shouted: if she ever tried to ask for a reward again, he would rip out the few strands of hair left on her head. Shyampriya barely blinked. Ram Bharari grew angrier. He girded his dhoti into a loincloth, implying that if she didn't come out of the water right away, he would go there and hold her down.

Ram had reviled Shyampriya and hit her many times in the past. She never took it to heart. Not only was she losing that one hundred silver coins promised to her, but also her value, now that her youth was ebbing. Even beggars tried to kick her when they saw the chance. She couldn't take this humiliation anymore. Even an old snake had some venom left in its fangs. By the time Shyampriya climbed out of the northwestern corner of the lake after dunking herself in the water a hundred and one times, Ram Bharari had disappeared with his black horse. The white horse was still grazing, tethered to the tree.

Shyampriya was awash in the tears streaming from her bloodshot eyes. She needed a white pullet this very moment, no matter what condition it was in. A white pullet was essential, according to the shamans, to cast a spell. Although her guru had warned her not to misuse her arcane skills to bring harm to people, sometimes she had no choice.

But where could she find a pullet she wouldn't have to pay for? These days she wasn't even able to solicit supplies for herself from the marketplace. When she did try to beg, they threatened to kick her out. Maybe she could get hold of a free chicken from Karim Sheikh's house. They were the only Muslim household nearby that kept fowl.

Shyampriya's wet clothing dried on her body. Scared of mongoose attacks, the chicks stuck close to the house as they pecked around. That mute daughter of Karim Sheikh's was a pain. As if she had somehow smelled the impending danger, she brandished a cane as she patrolled the yard. Shyampriya waited in the incline behind the house, hidden by the tall flax. She would pounce like a hawk as soon as the girl relaxed her guard. She was ready. But all was lost as the day progressed. The vaishnavi's fever-wracked body wilted in the reeds from hunger and thirst. The rays of the sun gradually moved away from her as it prepared to set.

In front of Shyampriya's fevered eyes floated a white pullet and the young queen Phuleswari Rai. Phuleswari was as foolish as the chicks were smart. Instead of soldiers, she was taking a flock of chicks with her to the Nor house to catch her husband in the act. Rongomala crouched, sharpening the curved blade of a boti. They were celebrating something at the house of Atmaram Nor. They had set out a seat for Shyampriya as well. Sweets, *kopta*, *kaliya* galore—a royal feast indeed. What to eat and what to leave! She had no qualms about eating fish, so she would have some. Just as she was grabbing a tail piece, a chicken flapped its way onto her plate.

Shyampriya shook herself awake. Was it a dream or some vision? The sun had already set; the whole day had gone to waste. Was she to return empty-handed? Roosters and hens of varying colours stormed towards her as if it was dawn and they had just been released from their coop. Shyampriya crouched and jumped, skinning her elbows. She came away clasping a handful of fluff. If only she had managed to grab one! All the chickens seemed to vanish into thin air. Where were they? A flock of quacking ducks fled this way and that. A moaning arose from Karim Sheikh's house. The vaishnavi remained immobile, still hunkered on the ground as if she were crawling. She was bereft even of the strength to be surprised. The hubbub seemed to be growing. It wasn't safe to stay here anymore. Shyampriya bent low and ran out of the clump of flax, keeping herself hidden behind the screw-pine shrubs. She crept into her own home like a thief.

Home was a shack with a flax thatch, walled with bamboo slats. It stood behind the little algae-covered pond belonging to the Chowdhurys. This was where she did everything—ate, cooked, slept. Aside from her cat Chandramukhi, there wasn't another living soul near her. None. She had no one. Shyampriya had never let herself be bothered by this. Since she had left home, she had nursed a rage against everyone—all of society and people. She had reached her sari-wearing age already clad in the widow's garb of white; her fate had already been written. She had taken a broom to her destiny at thirteen, or maybe fourteen. The dark-skinned flautist Shyamshundar had eloped with her. It was he who had named her, his lover, Shyampriya—beloved of Shyam or Krishna. The lovebirds donned the attire and accoutrements of the vaishnavas and returned to the village with their heads held high. That summer, the heat raged high as people argued over their return. But those who had found shelter within the vaishnava vessel of faith had no compulsion to abide by the laws of the sanatana faith; they were under no obligation to conform to caste norms. Shyamshundar and Shyampriya spent that rainy season playing the *khanjani*, begging for alms, eating occasionally, and mostly going hungry. Their melodious voices failed to quench the fires of their hunger. But once winter settled in, the rats in her own house gnawed a hole in her walls, seeking a way out. Shyamshundar undertook ritual purification by ingesting cow dung and was returned to his caste; but the villagers would not allow Shyampriya back. All she had when she took to the streets were her voice and her youth. Still dressed in her vaishnavi clothes, she drifted her way to the royal palace. The waters of life hid undercurrents at every turn. Although Shyampriya bobbed and gasped as they pulled at her, she had never drowned. Somehow, she had managed to earn enough to survive. Now Rajendra Narayan's days were giving way to the new regime of Raj Chandra. Nothing seemed to be within her reach anymore. More so than old age, illness and abuse were exacting a price from her.

Shyampriya pulled down another torn quilt from the loft and shivered her way to bed. The fever had come back in full force. She kept waking up. Chandramukhi, her cat, meowed a few times wanting attention, and then, failing, she crept under the quilts too.

At dawn, Shyampriya's fever drenched her in sweat and left. What didn't leave her was her desire for a white pullet. But the pace and shape of her thoughts changed altogether. She had planned to place the pullet in a newly fired clay pot and plant it in the path of Raj Chandra and Ram Bharari. Well, she had failed to get the pullet because she had no money. There was also the cost of the new pot and the shaman to consider. If she could just get the royal daughter-in-law eating out of her hand, she would be able to take care of all these expenses. Women happily gave away not only their jewels to punish and capture a philandering husband, they flayed their own skins without batting an eye. That's how mad they were. It would be easier if she could gain access to the palace's inner quarters. However, that wouldn't happen as long as Mejo Thakurani lived. With the kind of flesh she had on her, sending her to the cremation ground would require the deployment of a diamond charm, which would require another white pullet, another newly fired clay pot, more money for the shaman. When the mistress of the palace died, the chief maid became more than a mistress. Until she got rid of Khhantamoni, Shyampriya was pretty certain she wouldn't have access to the inner quarters.

Thus, before the night was over, half the people in the palace fell prey to conjurations of the diamond charm in Shyampriya's mind. The vaishnavi only let Phuleswari off because she needed money from her. She had many dreams about her, though. Even if Shyampriya couldn't enter the palace, Phuleswari herself would come out, drawn as she was by Rongomala. Goddess Radha swaying in the lap of her lover, the god Shyam—witnessing it filled one with delight. It evoked a different kind of pleasure. That young queen with her burning body, what could she do other than quench her thirst for milk with whey? There was only one path she could take while returning from the Nor house—she would have to cross the lakeshore where Shyampriya had waited swaddled in her quilt, her water pot in hand.

Yesterday, on her way back from the Nor house, Phuleswari had thought Shyampriya was a bundled-up quilt left by the roadside. Although Heera was knock-kneed from fear, Phuleswari Rai had marched ahead. Beyond the clearing lay the tiny pond for the palace's inner quarters, and beyond that was the back entrance. She didn't have much time. It was already growing light. She had to do it now.

She ignored Heera's entreaties and entered her bedchamber to hang a dirty broom from the door's lintel and place her muddy sandals on the bed. The birds had begun to chirp in their enclosures. It was almost time for her husband Raj Chandra to return home. Phuleswari trilled to herself softly, like a tailorbird. The birds echoed her in chorus. Black Moon swung on his perch. She wasn't interested in her birds this morning. Phuleswari prodded Heera until she hid her tall form behind the hawk pen, and then she left to get some sleep in Heera's bed. Before leaving, she scanned her bedchamber once more. Her arrangements to welcome back her lord and master after his night of dalliance with his beautiful damsel were quite suitable. After being jabbed by the broom hanging from the lintel, he would forthwith make the acquaintance of Phuleswari Rai's muddy shoes in bed. She had ordered Heera to hide in the aviary to witness the Shiva-like dance of destruction that he would surely commence upon afterwards. Then Heera was to run immediately to Phuleswari in the slave quarters and relate the whole episode in detail. Until then she needed to sleep.

Although it felt like she lay on a bed of thorns, the exhaustion of her restless night brought sleep to Phuleswari's eyes. Sleep that came and went. Her satisfaction at arranging the perfect punishment for her philandering husband was absent in her dreams. The current pulled her towards an endless sea. At least Jaggeswari had had a plank to hold on to; Phuleswari didn't even have a straw to grasp. As she floated, she suddenly recalled—wait, she had a pair of wings! She was human in name only; in truth she was a bird! Why was she floating so helplessly? Supine on the water, she flapped and spread her wings. Water, like pearls, trickled off her and vanished. Her wings pulled her weightless body out of the seawater. But before she could fly too far, she crashed.

The very roof of the palace shuddered at Raj Chandra's roars and howls. The next moment, there was a woman screaming.

Phuleswari was confused: those screams that seemed to be ripped out of someone's throat, they weren't hers, were they? Ma Shumitra thought the same. Phuleswari heard fabric slapping as her mother-in-law ran out in her wet sari, and then she heard her shout, 'He's murdering her, this son who is no son of mine, he's killing my daughter-in-law, murdering her!' Oh, for such a mother to have borne such a son! Was a daughter-in-law anything more than someone else's daughter? As she heard her mother-in-law wailing, Phuleswari began to sob. At that moment, Heera pushed open the door and entered. Her blue eyes, bugging out from excitement, were shining with joy. Because the one being beaten up good and proper by Raj Chandra was none other than Khhantamoni. The slut had rushed over unbidden to bear witness to their escapade last night. Who knew what she had actually seen with her sleep-muddled eyes? She had assumed that with her husband away, the royal daughter-in-law had gone out to carouse for the night, only to return at dawn. How dare she! To be a daughter-in-law of the royal family and think she could behave like the men! Also, she thought that Heera needed to be brought down a few notches. Two birds with one stone! Khhantamoni had lain in wait—as soon as Raj Chandra returned, she was ready with her bit of tittle-tattle. And she ran straight into the mouth of a cannon. 'Oh my, Didimoni,' Heera panted, 'it was like when a palmyra fruit falls from a tree in the month of Bhadra! He thumped her hard with that same *goom-goom* noise! Raj Chandra Chowdhury gave her a drubbing hard enough to break her bones! She'll be bedridden the rest of her life.' Phuleswari was about to rise when Heera winked at her. 'No, no, don't go, don't. Chowdhury has realised his mistake. He's looking for you now.'

Phuleswari lay down again but couldn't go back to sleep. There was a bitter taste in her mouth. Who was being punished for whose crime? Was the malefactor punishing the innocent? His royal highness was like an arum leaf; no dirt clung to him. By now he had probably cleaned himself up and was lighting up the courthouse. And here was Phuleswari, being bitten by bedbugs. Not to mention that a tremendous quarrel had broken out in the slave quarters as soon as the day had begun. The language! And everyone screeching like hawks. Even with her ears covered, the words burrowed their way in. Phuleswari peeked through the bamboo slats. The two servants had now stopped cursing each other and were busy tucking their saris tightly in their waistbands as they got ready to charge at each other. The amply-fleshed servant Tepi stood in the middle with her arms akimbo. She kicked the two quarreling women, as if playing with two balls at the same time—and they flew off in different directions. Nearby, a baby bawled. A few moments later, one of the fighting women sat down to nurse the baby. The other woman went off towards the pond, humming a tune, carrying a huge load of dirty pots and dishes. Well, that was that. Phuleswari moved away from the hole in the wall. That wasn't the end of it, though. On the other side, the horseplay had begun again, as had the dancing and the jumping. Four maidservants sat down this time to separate chaff from the rice while they jabbered and gossiped in a manner beyond her imagination. Phuleswari was astonished—to think that these were the people responsible for making sure that the constantly turning wheels of the royal palace never stopped!

Morning had passed into afternoon. Everyone was still scared stiff of Raj Chandra. Ma Shumitra had located Phuleswari and sent Heera down with her lunch spread out on a brass salver. The meals for the servants and slaves were prepared separately in the servants' wing: a curry of rotten swamp barb fish, dried fish with red chillies, old *kalai* lentils. As if to spite her mother-in-law, Phuleswari ate the servants' food for her meal. She rinsed her mouth out at the back entrance, at the base of the papaya tree that bore fruit all year round. She dried her fingers and her mouth on her sari. The mother was quaking in fear of her son;

she didn't have the guts to welcome her daughter-in-law back to her own rooms. She must have sent the food prepared for the royal meals down here in secret. If it was acceptable for Phuleswari to stay here, then she might as well eat what the servants ate. His royal highness was surely eating food prepared by the hands of that Nor woman, wasn't he? When Phuleswari ignored Heera's admonitions and opened the gate, the palace was casting its long shadow on the front yard that had been daubed with cow dung. The serving women sat in a long line in the shade, styling each other's hair and picking lice, as if a wedding was being celebrated in the household. Nearby, a group of naked toddlers played horses. One child would go down on all fours as the horse. The naked rider would whip him and chant:

Mango leaves grow in pairs
I whip and gallop as I dare
Hey there, woman, step aside
Here comes my crazy ride.

Phuleswari Rai snapped her fingers and joined the game. The mad horse bucked his rider off his back. The naked rider rolled around in the dust, still hanging on to his whip. The maidservants were unsure about how to react: the long line of asses were now stuck to the stools. The nimble fingers teasing out hairdos were stilled. As Phuleswari whistled, mimicking the call of the shyama bird, the fear-struck children began giggling. And then she hooted like an owl. The children rushed into the courtyard. In a minute, the fun hit a peak. Phuleswari cock-a-doodle-doo'ed like a rooster. And now an easier lesson: the cooing of pigeons. The children shouted, copying her, as if they were repeating their times tables: *coom—coom—coom.*

As Phuleswari mimicked each of her birds, she failed to notice the courtyard growing crowded like a village fair. Young Prafulla Kumar, the other bird-mimic, was the first to hop over to her like a playful bird. Behind him arrived all the women of the inner wing. It was only when she felt the damp hand of her mother-in-law on her back that Phuleswari finally understood that it wasn't admiration that she was hearing—the courtyard was throbbing with derision and mockery. As if the shame belonged only to the mother-in-law, Ma Shumitra grasped her daughter-in-law's elbow to remove her from the scene. Mejo Thakurani stood in front of her, arms akimbo. Her eyes were spewing fire.

As the cosseted daughter-in-law disappeared indoors, clasping her mother-in-law's hand, Heera stood like a stone in a corner of the courtyard. No one bothered to rein in their tongues. They were speaking lies, untruths. Mejo Thakurani's howls sounded like she was ready to call forth some exorcist or shaman. Khhantamoni's thrashing at the hands of Raj Chandra would be avenged by punishing his wife—the wife he couldn't be bothered about. According to the one-eyed Mejo Thakurani, this was justice. But then Phuleswari Rai's audacity was astonishing. Off she had gone to the Nor house last night. Then she had strung up a broom in her doorway. And now she had played an animal-mimic in the servants' quarters. She had brought this ignominy upon herself. The things she had done one after another—it was difficult to keep that girl on a leash. But what could an exorcist do? The only medicine that would work was Raj Chandra himself. If Phuleswari had been a mother, it would have been different. But what kind of man spurned a blossoming young wife like this? Heera scurried towards Ma Shumitra's chambers to speak in Phuleswari's defence.

There, another drama was unfolding. When Ma Shumitra heard what her daughter-in-law had to say, she felt the sky was falling on her head. The royal daughter-in-law had gone to the Nor house! At night! What if something had happened on the way—would there have been any way to accept this girl back in the household? As if that risk was nothing, the girl continued relating her adventure to her mother-in-law as if she had just come back from a *naiyor* visit to her father's house. Whether the girl was naïve or mad, all the blame lay with that wretched Heera. That deceitful whore! Trying to fool the consort of Pratap Narayan with all her song and dance about procuring blessed oil!

Though a vulture might fly in the sky
Its eyes never leave the pigsty.

It made no difference that Heera had grown up in the household of a reputable merchant—she had been born in a brothel. The flood of wealth that the salt trader had poured into the royal palace had also granted entry to a lot of muddy, salty water. Ma Shumitra spat into the spittoon as if some bitter taste sat on her tongue. Then she locked Phuleswari in her chamber and made her proclamation—Heera the slave was not to move even a hair's breadth beyond the inner wing. From this day forward, the elderly slave Kalitara would tend to Phuleswari Rai's birds.

That night, Phuleswari lay in her mother-in-law's bed as her thoughts strayed across heaven and earth. The light from the sconces wavered on the enormous, covered chandelier that dangled overhead. Ma Shumitra slept beside her, facing the other way. Her expression had been thunderous all evening. The royal daughter-in-law had gone, on foot, to the Nor house; for such things to happen while she still lived!—this was the mantra she had recited every few minutes. As if, had she only known, she would have sent Phuleswari off with an entourage of guards and such in order to witness Rongomala and Raj Chandra's dalliance. Phuleswari realised the truth all of a sudden. Even if the inside was hollow, what counted was the shine and sheen outside. It was all show—her mother-in-law's adoption of white yardage as her only clothing, or her covering up the chandelier, after her husband's death. She was very strict in her observance of the rule-bound life the scriptures allotted for widows. She ate once a day, early, and all she ate was unsalted cooked vegetables and sun-dried rice on a stone platter. She painted a sandalwood *ulki* on her forehead and wore *rudrakkha* beads around her neck. Her thick black hair barely made it beyond her scalp. A maid shaved her head regularly. The people sang the widow's praises with a hundred tongues. She was so proud about this that her feet barely touched the ground. She was Phuleswari's respected elder. Perhaps she even loved Phuleswari, her daughter-in-law. But she loved the money of Phuleswari Rai's father more; the money that made sure even Mejo Thakurani sought permission before stepping foot into Ma Shumitra's quarters. That was how well-guarded she was.

What good did any of this do to Phuleswari? Her mother-in-law was smart; she was using the greens to hide the tiny serving of fish. Afraid that her son's shenanigans would become public knowledge, she was secluding Phuleswari from everyone. It played into her plans that Phuleswari kept herself occupied with her birds. Now when someone should be put in chains, she let her son off the hook without even the pretense of fairness, while her daughter-in-law was shackled. The same son who had no qualms about stealing the earrings of his dead mother-in-law!

But had he actually stolen them? No matter how hard she had tried at the bamboo grove by the Nor house, Phuleswari had failed to spot the earrings on Rongi's ears. Perhaps she hadn't worn them last night, perhaps she was wearing them tonight. Perhaps tonight she had dressed herself as another apsara, a celestial nymph. His royal highness was leaning against the bolster and pulling on his hookah. Smoke wisped in the air. His eyes were half-closed in lust. When the jangling of jewellery near his feet grew silent, he pulled Rongomala onto his lap in a swift motion. He couldn't restrain himself. Kissing and such right out in the open—Durga the servant fled to save her eyes from such a sight. The joined silhouette of the couple rocked atop the waves. The king straightened his dhoti pleats and carried Rongi into the bedchamber of the stilted cottage. The flowing sound of their laughter rippled across Rupsingh's Plains, entered through the palace entrance and slammed against Ma Shumitra's door.

The door was chained shut. Ma Shumitra had locked her daughter-in-law inside and was now snoring away. She wasn't keeping track of where her son was or what he was up to. In her rage, Phuleswari wanted to strangle her mother-in-law.

If you disliked someone, then anything and everything they did were like thorns in your side. Before menarche, Phuleswari had slept in this same bed for two years, sucking on her thumb, her leg thrown over her mother-in-law. She still sucked her thumb. But the water-rot odour of Ma Shumitra, from washing and handling water hour upon the hour, felt new. The hours passed. Birds began to warble and chirp. Phuleswari shoved a pillow against her face but she still couldn't get rid of the smell.

While Phuleswari was tossing and turning in the locked bedroom, Shyampriya, the vaishnavi, was by the lake, still wrapped in her torn quilt, still carrying her water pot. The kura bird was calling, and yet there was no sign of the royal daughter-in-law. The security at the palace was so tight, who knows if the young wife had been caught red-handed trying to leave! That would end her hopes of making money.

A while later, two riders emerged in a cloud of dust. Shyampriya's ears were pricked for the jingle-jangle of jewellery. Which was why she didn't hear the clopping of hooves. But she managed to jump off the roadway into the water before Ram Bharari's kick landed on her. It was only after they had disappeared that she realised that the two riders were the ones in her debt, and she was the creditor, and yet it was she who now stood in neck-deep water like a criminal.

When the same thing happened two days in a row, Shyampriya grew anxious about herself. Her beauty had disappeared long ago, and now it looked like her wits were leaving her as well. She should leave this damned land and head towards the haven of Naba Dwip while she still had some sanity left. The Maha Prabhu was no longer there, but the streets were strewn with the dust of his feet. Not to mention the ashrams and vaishnava-akhras! It was a site for pilgrims—the last bastion of hope for the forsaken, such as Shyampriya.

At day's end, Shyampriya sat in front of her hut swathed in her quilt, humming to herself. The branches of the silk-cotton tree in front of her were covered in red flowers. The cuckoos flew in and out all day long. Bashanta, high spring, the king of seasons, was on his way out; where was the ferment of youth? Although her body's hunger was over and done with, a hankering still lingered in her belly. Chandramukhi was pregnant again. She would birth her kittens at the end of the month; she wanted to eat well. Shyampriya stroked the cat. She shrugged the quilt off her shoulders and entered her hovel. A fistful of bug-infested chaff sat at the bottom of the pot. She cooked it with some water and hurried Chandramukhi. 'Chandra, there's no oil in the lamp. Come, eat early.' Their plates overflowed with the watery gruel. The cat sat beside her, waving her tail. The fever had stolen Shyampriya's appetite, but even Chandramukhi meowed in complaint as she moved away from her plate—the gruel was that tasteless. Tomorrow Shyampriya would have to go out with a begging bowl, if only for Chandramukhi. Her trudging feet would keep the cat fed.

The next day she bathed early. She dressed herself in her clean sari, drew the tilaka on her forehead and the rashakali on the bridge of her nose. She reddened her lips by chewing paan and dried tobacco leaf, stuffed her khanjani in her bag and left home. Under the cover of her *madhukari*, the ritual act of begging door to door as if she was a bee seeking honey, she had always been more engaged in bringing lovers together. She was the merchant of love. Age as well as betrayal and oppression had slowed down her body, but nothing had succeeded in keeping her down. As soon as she hit the road, the songs came to her lips and her khanjani slid into her hands almost of its own volition:

I see him, I see him, I see him but once
Is it the heart-stealer under the kadamba tree?

True connoisseurs, whether of songs or of love, were a vanishing breed. Left and right, up and down, Shyampriya had peeked into the inner quarters of many households throughout the day, and had spotted none to rival Rongomala. Had God just created that one creature and gone off to take a nap?

As she walked home, Shyampriya stopped at the threshold of the Nor house. She hadn't stepped foot in there for nearly a year. It stunned her now to witness how a home could be transformed overnight, without much effort. The only remnant of the original Nor house was the bamboo grove balancing precariously on the sloping bank of the pond. The old shacks thatched with flax had been pulled down to make space for a two-storeyed structure. In the middle of the pond stood a gorgeous cottage on stilts. A bamboo walkway sloped up towards it. The guard sitting under a canopy of flowers, preening the moustache spanning his face, could very easily trample a dozen Shyampriyas beneath his feet.

Shyampriya smiled at him condescendingly. She lived right next to the palace of the Shindurkait Chowdhurys. This moustachioed warrior, this Chanda Bir lookalike, was merely a servant of this new Nor house which was trying to imitate the royal palace. Raj Chandra had posted him at the entrance to keep an eye on Rongomala. A lover's heart is forever uncertain. He wins over his love, but his fear remains. Shyampriya thought of spending some time chatting up this giant to get on his good side.

His massive body stood rigid. His lips were locked. He responded with silence to everything she said, whether good or bad. Shyampriya's greetings seemed to bounce off against a stone wall. But the vaishnavi didn't give up. Finally, from the man's speech, which sounded like gibberish, she figured out that not only was this Chullu Singh a foreigner, he was also quite harmless. That enormous pair of moustachios had seemingly been glued to his face to give his clay body at least some life. His half-closed eyes announced that he had no objection to a quick whiff of ganja often and whenever. Seizing the chance, Shyampriya opened up her pouch and swiftly assembled a hit. If she pulled on it once, Chullu Singh took ten puffs, making the bong rumble. He inhaled so strongly the bong almost exploded. Their surroundings darkened with the smoke. When the guard's eyes had all but disappeared, Shyampriya found nothing else hindering her entry into the inner quarters. But she couldn't muster the courage to go in; the reason for her fear lay elsewhere.

Just a year ago, there had been a fence of areca nut fronds where the entry room stood now. There had been no sentry then. Durga herself had tucked her sari-end into her waistband and grabbed Shyampriya's hair to throw her out. Behind her drifted the high-pitched laughter of Rongomala. The games people played once they had their hearts' desire in the palm of their hands! Shyampriya hid her sadness and pulled out her khanjani to sing.

Rongomala sat on a mat in the veranda of the inner house with her legs stretched out. Roma, the hairdresser, was painting her feet crimson with alta. Durga stood behind her holding a wooden comb in one hand and a bowl of perfumed oil in the other. Shyampriya's song floated towards them from the entrance. Rongomala listened intently. Why was there such sorrow in the vaishnavi's voice? She hadn't brought some bad news about Raj Chandra, had she? That man had enemies in his very own house. Her heart was imagining misfortune just because she had not seen him one day. Despite Raj Chandra cautioning her against Shyampriya, Rongomala called her into the inner quarters.

'All praise Radha.' The vaishnavi put her palms together and waited below in the yard, her bag on the ground. She stood there, bent at the waist. Paan juice stained her lips a luscious red as if they belonged to a sixteen-year-old. The old slut had the mannerisms of a *jatrapala* dancer. Rongomala couldn't decide whether to laugh or cry. She thought of ridding herself of this annoyance by giving Shyampriya some rice or money as alms. Yet her heart yearned for some snippet of news about Raj Chandra.

Shyampriya stood motionless in the yard, her big toe digging into the earth. Her manner betrayed that her heart still harboured the hurt from Durga's assault. She wasn't going to open her mouth unless she was made to feel welcome. Rongomala wiped the surface of a sandalwood stool with her sari-end and pushed it towards her. 'Oh, sister, come seat yourself. How are things? You haven't come this way in such a long time!' Done with the alta, Roma had left with her bottle and brush. Although Rongomala had gestured to Durga to disappear, Durga glowered at Shyampriya before she left. It was enough to make Shyampriya's heart drop to her stomach.

Much of Rongomala's jabbering, as she opened her heart, went to waste. Shyampriya listened but registered nothing as her gaze roamed the four chambers of the house like a spinning top; she was busy ogling the pomp and show of the Nor household. 'Have you brought any news from Raj Chandra Chowdhury, sister? Why don't you speak?' When Rongomala finally asked, the vaishnavi's gaze had come to stop at the cockscomb flower bush in the corner. Her eyes were sucking the red from the flowers, grain by grain. Although she heard Rongomala's pleading question, she didn't respond. Suddenly her bloodshot eyes brightened. It was clear as day that the Nor girl had not yet heard the saga of Raj Chandra and Shoirop Mala. With such a guard at the entrance, even a mosquito would find it hard to get in, let alone people who came bearing tales. Although she lived right next to the palace, had Shyampriya herself known about the incident? Today, because she had been out on the streets, she had been able to snare this day-old scrap of gossip from the winds. But was this new for Raj Chandra? For him, this was as humdrum as the everyday rice and lentils. Shyampriya had digested the gossip while she was still on the road. When Rongomala displayed her infatuation so openly, the scandal surfaced from the bottom of her belly like a sour belch. Who wouldn't take advantage of such a chance for revenge? There wouldn't even be any bloodshed, as there would have been if she had cast a hex. She could stay behind the scenes and still twist Raj Chandra Chowdhury's ears. The only worry was that neither hexes nor scandalmongering remained hidden for too long.

'Sister, why do you look so pale? Haven't you eaten today?' Rongi's words barely dropped from her lips when Durga leapt onto the veranda. In one hand, she carried a bell-metal platter holding a couple of *khoier mowa*, popped rice and jaggery balls and a *shabri* banana, while in the other, there was a pot of drinking water. Shyampriya settled herself. But she was too afraid to make eye contact with Durga. The whore wasn't satisfied with assaulting her physically; now she was looking daggers at her. Well, at least she wasn't kicking her in the belly. Placing the water pot on the ground, Shyampriya bit into the mowa and watched Durga stomp in the yard jangling her silver jewellery. Roma was also hanging around there. She could tell that both the women had their ears pricked her way. They would come onto the veranda at the slightest excuse. Who knew whether they would beat her up again!

Rongomala allowed Shyampriya to calm her belly, but not her thoughts. 'I am in such a state! Raj Chandra said he would come last night, but he didn't! Is there any bad news, sister?' Shyampriya shook her head slowly and examined Rongi. Where had the Nor girl's sharp tongue disappeared? Her eyes no longer possessed the glint of a honed blade. Her gaze was like that of a milch cow. Her happiness dribbled down her plump body like oil. Her body, which once had lines sharp as swords, and had sliced Raj Chandra

Chowdhury in two—on the one hand his desire, on the other his caste—had been spoiled by the fat that had accumulated in places wanted and unwanted. The woman who allowed herself to give in to the ocean of joy without fear of consequence had no recourse in the end but to wash up, like the abandoned trunk of a banana plant, on the shore of a whorehouse. Did the Nor girl not know this?

'What lesson can I preach to you with my lowly tongue?' Shyampriya asked her humbly, as befitted a vaishnavi. 'It's getting dark. Give me leave to go home.' But as soon as she tried to rise, Rongomala grabbed her bag and forced her to sit down again. She had shifted from the mat and was now sitting on the bare ground with a crazed look in her eyes. 'I don't understand what you're saying, sister. I beg you in God's name, just tell me clearly what you're trying to say.'

Before Shyampriya opened her mouth, she looked Rongomala over. She was covered in jewels. Shyampriya glanced at the ostentation of the Nor house; she examined the flash of white silver on Durga's black skin. Then she remembered the one hundred silver coins which were hers by right, but which she had never received, and she put her palms together and raised them to her forehead. The Lord knew, she who brought lovers together would never rip them asunder. But what else was she to do at this moment? As she held a blazing flame close to the beehive of Raj Chandra and Rongomala's love, she pled forgiveness from Him, the Omniscient.

Four

Rongomala suffered the bee stings unleashed when Shyampriya flamed the hive all by herself. And the vaishnavi, who lit the flames, had to go into exile. No one could get away with trying to gain the upper hand with Raj Chandra. He had been wild since boyhood. Like a demon, he sped wherever his heart pointed. The first male child of the royal line, he was spoiled rotten at home and elsewhere. In his childhood, his father and uncle had left no stone unturned to make sure he received a proper education. First came a Hindu pundit. Later they hired a Muslim munshi to tutor him in Persian. The pundit began teaching him the alphabet by chalking letters on the ground. But as soon as they graduated to numbers written out on palm leaves, the pundit's *tiki* was stolen—sliced off neatly with the sharpened stem of a palm frond while he slept. This incident ruined Raj Chandra's chance to use a reed pen on paper to scratch out his Bangla letters, to make them perfect like pearls. After the pundit's departure, for a while Raj Chandra dressed himself in a gold-embroidered *qaba*, sported a turban on his head and plagued the munshi's lodgings. His elders thought at least the boy was becoming proficient in Persian, a language essential for ruling a zamindari. Also, tomes such as the *Pandnama*, the *Gulistan* and the *Bostaan* would give him enough moral and ethical lessons. He would grow adept in his manners, his appearance, his conduct. But then came the day a live turtle crawled out from under the boy's qaba. The munshi quit on the spot; he packed his things and left. That was the end of any attempt at schooling. Raj Chandra's father Pratap Narayan went to an early grave, bearing the sorrow that his son lacked a proper education. Rajendra Narayan became the orphaned Raj Chandra's guardian. He disciplined Raj Chandra one day and indulged him for three. The teenaged Raj Chandra spent his days roaming around, his double-barrelled gun for bird hunting perched on his shoulder. No one in the Bhulua region could rival his horsemanship. The neighbouring lands clamoured: *Be warned! Be warned!* Rajendra Narayan's chest swelled with pride. If anyone was worthy of carrying on the proud name of their first ancestor, Bishwambhar Sur of Mithila, it was his talented nephew. The boy's horsemanship proved that it was pure blue blood coursing through the veins of the Chowdhury clan.

Raj Chandra's voice was cracking and deepening, fronds of moustache and beard shadowed his face, and already he was losing interest in hunting birds. He was losing his appetite as well. Until Chandrakala, a daughter of the Thakur caste from Maizdi, lodged a complaint, Rajendra Narayan was completely in the dark about the fact that his nephew had recently become interested in women travelling in palanquins as well as the women belonging to the households of their *raiot*, their serfs.

That day, as soon as the royal court convened in the outer house, news arrived of a flock of birds ravaging the ripened rice harvest at the Karimpur lake. Rajendra Narayan, the incumbent zamindar, was thunderstruck. The year before, people had died of starvation; cows had become mere fodder for leeches. This year, tax collection would be well-nigh impossible if the birds ate the harvest. The East India Company was auctioning off estates right and left for the fault of tax dereliction. Although the Chowdhurys had lost much of their old glory, Bishwambhar Sur's blood still flowed in their veins—they couldn't allow themselves to rule under the thumb of roving bands of dacoits like those zamindars of Shimulia. Although, to be honest, since being granted the *Diwani* as vassal states under the thumb of the British, it was more useful these days to maintain a band of dacoits instead of a zamindari.

Raj Chandra had been out all day. Even a summons to the inner quarters failed to bring him to the court. Find him! Even though he was yet a youngster, the boy was a master marksman. He could easily rid them of this bird infestation in a single afternoon. Where did the bastard disappear as soon as he woke up? Rajendra Narayan paced indoors and outdoors in his *nagra* shoes.

At that very moment, Raj Chandra was just a couple of miles away. He was sitting by the Damdama lake, playing his flute and sending lightning-swift glances at the household of a raiot on the other side of the lake. Not even a mosquito buzzed in response. Only a milch cow swished its tail as it stood feeding at the trough. Raj Chandra's breath turned ragged as he blew on his flute, his throat as arid and cracked as a pond in the month of Chaitra. Beside him sat Ram Bharari, fixer of all problems. Ram had carried water from the lake in a banana leaf. Raj Chandra held the leaf like a bowl and drank deeply. His flute lay on the ground beside him. He threw a few clods of earth into the calm water of the lake. Ram Bharari supplied him with the clods, carrying them in the fold of his dhoti from the ploughed field nearby. He was finding it very difficult to keep up with the future king. Walk through the ploughed field, down to the water, then again to the ploughed field—all this trekking up and down was doing him in. Raj Chandra threw away the clods of earth and picked up his flute. But instead of holding it to his lips, he shut one eye and held it to the other like a telescope. His manner was borrowed from a British sahib at the *kuthi*, the textile bungalow. That sahib was a lustful lover indeed: a conical straw hat resting on his head, clad in pantaloons and gumboots, he spied upon the washerwomen by the riverbanks with his telescope every single day. There was magic in that hollow tube. It was unnecessary to take a single step out of the house; just peeking through the blinds was sure to land a prize. In the blink of an eye, the far-off damsels were standing practically nose-to-nose with him. They laughed and talked, displaying the sides of their breasts and the curves of their waists as they laundered clothes. If only he possessed such a device, the ladies on the other side of the lake would never escape Raj Chandra's keen gaze. They would weep and buzz like little flies caught in a spider web.

The white stallion tethered to the tree stamped his hooves. Like his master, he had an impatient nature. Raj Chandra jumped astride his horse and made for home. Ram Bharari ran after him. Back then he still used to walk everywhere. It would be years before he would become the rider of the black steed.

When Rajendra Khura asked him to go and hunt the birds, Raj Chandra agreed at once. But he demanded a telescope before setting out on the mission. Rajendra Narayan had never seen a telescope in his life. He had no idea whether it was a thing one ate or wore. He blinked at his nephew for a few uncomprehending moments before flaring up for no good reason. 'My son, can you just go! First, uphold the honour of your father and forefathers. Afterwards, this telescope or whatever it is, I'll see to it.'

'No, that's not happening. First you give me your word, and *then* I'll go.'

Now was not the time to bicker over the price of a telescope. If the birds weren't finished off fast it would spell the end for everyone. Grumbling in anger, Rajendra Narayan gave in to his nephew's terms.

By noon, the birds of Karimpur were finished. Two servants headed for the palace, carrying large wicker baskets stuffed with black birds. But Raj Chandra made no move to return home. He roamed the forests and the pathways nearby, his gun slung across his shoulder. Ram Bharari stuck to him like a shadow.

Chandrakala, daughter of the Maizdi Thakurs, was riding in a palanquin on her *naiyor* visit, when a married daughter returns to her father's house. The winter's afternoon disappeared as fast as it arrived. The darkness of night often called forth marauding bands of robbers and dacoits. The palanquin bearers took the narrow path that angled its way between the forest and the rice paddies.

Chandrakala lifted the veil draping her palanquin and gazed at the splendour of the golden harvest. Every single thing her eyes alighted upon in the land of her forefathers seemed drenched in beauty. Everything felt comfortingly familiar. This rice field shimmering in the wild breeze, the gold of sunlight at day's end, the birdcalls trilling from the forest on the other side, in the distance the gauzy awning of fog—as if all this was to celebrate Chandrakala's return home. Her mother, driven mad by the absence of her beloved daughter, had been waiting the whole day for her arrival.

Suddenly, something sprang out of the forest: not tigers or bears, but two men. The palanquin made a sudden, juddering stop. The four bearers threw down their turbans and ran before the gun barrel descended on their backs. Chandrakala kept her wits about her. She had glimpsed the attackers before dropping the veil of her palanquin, and she recognised him: the gun-wielding man trying to prove his manhood was no other than that idiot Raj Chandra of the Shindurkait royal house. He might have grown taller and broader, but he was still the boy from one of the houses her father's clan visited to perform priestly rites. Chandrakala descended from her palanquin and unveiled her face. But she was barely on her feet a second before Raj Chandra seized her from behind and threw her on the ground. Their struggle flattened the golden-hued rice paddy.

Twirling his stick, Ram Bharari returned to the scene of crime after chasing the palanquin bearers beyond the forest. Chandrakala stood in the middle of the rice paddy, her demeanour as fearsome as the Goddess of War's. Curses were pouring from her lips. Raj Chandra crouched on a raised border by the field, his palm cupping the corner of his mouth. Even when the palanquin turned towards Shindurkait instead of continuing in the direction of Maizdi, he didn't come to his senses. He was still licking the salt of his own blood from his split lip—blood that had mixed with the paan juice in Chandrakala's spittle.

However, Raj Chandra didn't need anyone to tell him that Chandrakala had stirred up a veritable hornet's nest. As soon as he set foot in his home, he faced an explosion. Rajendra Narayan came after him, brandishing a shoe, and Ma Shumitra slapped her own forehead so hard it seemed she was trying to split open her skull. 'Oh, Divine Mother, I've borne a lowlife in my womb, and now these people come to our palace to humiliate us! Oh, God of Death, take me! I no longer want to live!'

That wasn't the end of it. The Thakur's daughter created such a ruckus when she reached her father's house that, the next day at dawn, over two hundred Thakurs marched to war, wielding their sticks high. They swore an oath that they wouldn't touch a drop of water until they had imprisoned Raj Chandra and enslaved every single resident of the palace, man or woman. Chandrakala's father, Sri Dhar Thakur, led the clan. Their dhoti pleats swung with their martial gait, as did their rattail tikis. The farmers ploughing their fields twisted the tails of their oxen and chanted,

Off to war march two hundred rats
If they all fight, then who nabs the cats?

The mockery did not change the Thakurs' resolve a whit. When they had trooped a little farther, an elderly Brahmin pundit stood in their way. In his opinion, it did not behoove Brahmins to fight. And anyway, they would certainly lose against the warrior Chanda Bir. Could sticks ever win against guns and cannons? Instead, they should sit calmly under the tree and think it through. They needed to avenge the insult and loss of honour their daughter had suffered. Accordingly, two hundred warriors laid down their weapons and sat under an ancient banyan tree. Every single ritual—prayers to the gods, birth–marriage–death—which, if any of these, were possible without the Brahmin as intercessor? That very day, straight from the banyan tree, messengers went out to all Brahmins far and wide. Thus was laid the brickwork for the social ostracism of the Chowdhurys.

Because of the Karimpur hullaballoo, a document fixing the auspicious astrological hour for Raj Chandra's wedding was put together with due haste. The groom's entourage was ready, but a priest to officiate was nowhere to be found. All the Thakurs had gone into hiding. Drumming for them did not work; neither did threats of setting their houses ablaze. The auspicious hour for the wedding was almost past. The bride's father, Kali Charan Guha of Lamchor, was rushing around like a monkey whose tail was on fire. He was most invested in entering into a relationship with the Chowdhurys. Now was not the moment to weigh the good or bad deeds of the groom-to-be. He began sending his people to every single Brahmin household with gunnysacks full of coin. Thus, the hard-sworn oath of the Thakurs was bought off by gold. The perpetrator wasn't brought to justice. Despite her courage, Chandrakala was defeated.

Raj Chandra was not one to learn a lesson from anything or anyone. The master of all he surveyed, he galloped wherever his desires drove him. He had obtained a wife, and coins to jingle in the bargain. Once the wedding festivities were over, his desire for a telescope surged anew. Although his first chance to procure a telescope had been scotched by Chandrakala's intemperate aggravation, now he had a new, wealthy father-in-law. His desire did not remain unfulfilled for long. His child-bride was busy with the feeding, bathing and play-weddings of her pet birds. Outside, the whole world was Raj Chandra's Brindaban, like the playground of the divine lover Lord Krishna. Raj Chandra discarded his flute and left early in the morning with his telescope in hand. It was late at night when he returned. With him went his old friend Ram Bharari. He would occasionally try to spend time at the courthouse, but he couldn't bear it there. As soon as he was faced with the obligation to examine documents or deeds, he began to yawn. Days passed in the pursuit of his manifold whims. By the time he grew tired of the telescope's magic, rumours of Rongomala's great beauty had spread on the wind and reached his ears. Shyampriya vaishnavi agreed to bring the two together in exchange for a hefty reward. It was as if, finally, Raj Chandra Chowdhury had found his place.

There were many reasons for Rajendra Narayan to lose his tenderness towards Raj Chandra. It wasn't as simple as his nephew reaching majority and thus his guardianship coming to an end. No. Rajendra Narayan's only daughter Shunonda had returned to her father's house a widow. With her had come her four-year-old son, Prafulla Kumar.

The time of their forefathers had passed. Rajendra Narayan's grandfather, Mahesh Narayan, had obtained the rule of this administrative pargana from the nawab of Murshidabad. The land had prospered in the able hands of Uday Narayan, Rajendra Narayan's father. At the time, Nawab Alibardi was having a lot of trouble even retaining his own throne. The old nawab was besieged by attacks from the Portuguese pirates, the foreign merchants' bids to increase their power, and palace conspiracies one after another. Who had time to pay any attention to the tiny pargana of Babupur, way out there by the sea, where the rivers swallowed up the land? Uday Narayan filled in that little gap with his determination. The beneficent gaze of the gods rewarded him. He closed his fist on a handful of ashes, and they turned into gold, right in his palm. Yet fate determined that Rajendra Narayan would fail at holding on to the gem that was Babupur. Even before his rule began, the Battle of Plassey had taken place. The twists and turns since then! Now just paying for the five-year lease on the zamindari was draining his resources. The rapacious fist of the East India Company was relentless. They were reneging on their promises and raising taxes every single year. That Rajendra Narayan had foregone his own comfort and indulgences and was walking on a bridge as thin as a strand of hair—who was all this for? If the zamindari was divvied up among the various heirs, what would remain? And given Raj Chandra's nature, he would destroy himself running wild after women. This wasn't necessarily a bad thing. Rajendra Narayan began plotting on settling his own grandson on the throne before he died.

The expenses for Raj Chandra's attempts to turn the Nor house into a palatial mansion were being paid from the royal treasury, but not from Raj Chandra's monthly allowance; it was all on loan. The documents showed the expenditures swelling and swelling. The young man who had even recently flailed blindly while counting his money had his eyes open now. He was demanding a full accounting of his father's inheritance. Rajendra Narayan was balking him with his repeated refrain of the property falling into the wrong hands. Even the cats and dogs of Babupur knew quite well that the zamindari would be sold off in lots once Raj Chandra managed to get his hands on it. Everyone understood this except Shumitra Devi. She was blind to her son's faults. She was also plotting to regain her position as the mistress of the royal palace—the position she had lost after her husband's death. She was trying to regain her power through her son. Rajendra Narayan had even played the loyal, obedient brother-in-law, like Lakshman from the Ramayana, to try and keep her ambitions in check. All for naught.

When Raj Chandra attempted his raid on the Jugi family and was repulsed ignominiously, mother and son had stopped talking to each other. The conflict between them had temporarily resolved the conflict between Shumitra and Rajendra Narayan. It was that same event that Shyampriya had tattled to Rongomala, striking at Raj Chandra like a snake without venom. It was as if a three-pronged attack, from sky, earth and sea, had been launched against him. Raj Chandra still couldn't fathom what had happened, and how.

The other day, Raj Chandra had paid a visit to the Dewanganj residence of Inga Chowdhury, the Muslim zamindar, to complain about his uncle. On his way back, he ran into Jamiruddin, the midget, at Madhab Patni's marina. The man was a leech. Every time Raj Chandra tried to move away, Jamiruddin clutched his feet. 'Hujoor, you're more than our fathers or mothers.' Raj Chandra thought distractedly, Jamiruddin probably didn't have enough to pay the ferryman, and so was asking for a few coins. In his mind, Inga Chowdhury's words were rising and falling like the river in high tide. With no guarantee that he could wrest Raj Chandra's estate from his uncle, Inga Chowdhury had demanded a deed promising him one-fourth of the entire estate. That damned Muslim! Although he was well known as a brave warrior, his reputation was on the wane. What if he broke his word? Ram Bharari was usually a reliable solver of almost any problem—except when it involved paper and pen. He was illiterate. He had been sulking on the return journey because Raj Chandra had bawled him out. Now he was shouting at the midget instead of dealing with him by shelling out a couple of coins. As if it was Jamiruddin's fault that Ram was illiterate! Raj Chandra couldn't be bothered to carry money on his person. He roamed around with a light heart and empty pockets. But now, it looked like Jamiruddin was probably not angling just for a few coins; he was after bigger fish. The tiny man was also a Muslim—another one for scheming! Raj Chandra was about to mount his horse and use his crop, when Jamiruddin stepped right in front of him. This time he didn't grab his feet; he brought his mouth close to Raj Chandra's ears. Before Ram Bharari had the chance to charge at Jamiruddin, Raj Chandra's demeanour had changed. He had the same reckless expression as when patrolling his lands with his telescope. And Ram Bharari would have to dance to his crazed tune. It was true that the telescope had brought the doings of Shoirop Mala, the wife of Kala Jugi, to Raj Chandra's attention.

He had ridden his horse fast that day, but not fast enough; by the time he had reached, she had vanished like a mirage. Now he had Jamiruddin with him—Jamiruddin would make sure that every possible exit the woman could take would be sealed shut.

Jamiruddin's proposal pushed the concern over Inga's demand for a quarter share right out of Raj Chandra's head. Raj Chandra further shed the burdens he carried by rewarding Jamiruddin with the fine mulmul scarf wrapped around his neck—the scarf that Inga had gifted to him two hours ago.

A cloudburst before he had even prayed for water! In his glee, Jamiruddin mouthed many prayers before breathing on Raj Chandra to transfer the blessings. Ram Bharari stood apart and smirked. Let them get to the entrance to the Jugi house first. He would make sure that scarf was returned to his master's neck in a heartbeat.

Jamiruddin sat behind Ram on the horse, holding onto his waist, weaving side to side as the horse trotted. Raj Chandra's horse was ahead of them. This area had no proper roads or pathways. It was all fallow land, covered in undergrowth. The horses stepped slowly. Jamiruddin took the chance to let go of Ram Bharari and raise the kingly fabric to his nose, rubbing it and sniffing at it. The king's lackey may walk on branches, but Jamiruddin was crafty enough to make his way on the leaves. Although the scarf was lacking in width, it was pleasingly long. If he ripped it down the middle, he could have double the show. The best of both worlds: kill the snake without breaking his stick. People didn't care whether they had food in their bellies or not. But when they would see Jamiruddin and his son Nuruddin strolling down the streets with their fancy scarves dancing in the wind, the whole neighbourhood would take note. It would teach Ram Bharari a good lesson too. As soon as he thought of it, it was as good as done. Jamiruddin jumped off the horse near Kala Jugi's house and ripped the scarf in two. Raj Chandra was astonished and couldn't understand the deeper meaning of the midget's actions. At any rate, he was more interested in the inner quarters of the Jugi house. Ram Bharari scoffed in utter rage. A dog's belly cannot abide butter! The midget smiled with all his teeth. He raised his hand in an extended salaam and vanished, abandoning them at the entrance of the Jugi house.

Kala Jugi's wife, Shoirop Mala, sat on her stoop, spinning yarn. She heard hoofbeats. There wasn't a single soul anywhere near. The end of the yarn was still in her hand. She hadn't even had the chance to thread it through her wheel when two men rushed into her yard. Shoirop Mala ran into the main room. Her heart thumped in fear. She could barely think: where to run, where to hide? She clambered up the beam to the platform near the ceiling. Raj Chandra dismounted and ran after her. The Jugi woman didn't know he could climb trees like a squirrel—reaching her atop the platform was nothing for him.

There was a scuffle up there. Ram Bharari stood alert in the yard, his eyes surveying the surroundings. Yet Shoirop Mala somehow managed to run past him, and inside, Raj Chandra's voice rose in a scream, 'My knee! My knee!' As you sow, so you reap—the king had tripped on the hole dug for the spinning jenny, and was now, hands clutching his knee, thrashing about like a chicken with a slit throat. Ram Bharari checked and realised that the injury was serious. There was no chance that Raj Chandra could stand up by himself. He needed some sort of remedy.

Ram Bharari sat in the yard and concocted a nostrum, mixing juice from the stem of a taro leaf plucked from behind the house, slaked lime and sooty cobwebs recovered from the thatch of the cooking house. He kept track of Shoirop Mala's movements out of the corner of his eye. Although she had first concealed herself in the banana grove, the hiding place did not seem to please the poor woman. Ram noticed a flurry in the murtaq reeds that grew in the slope behind the house.

While Ram Bharari was busy applying his nostrum to Raj Chandra's knee, she exited the clump of reeds and slipped under the fence in a corner of the yard, which escaped Ram's eyes. She was so scared she had taken leave of her senses. When she saw Raj Chandra limping in her yard, she lost her wits altogether. She ran to the pond and jumped in. The water came up to her neck. Ram Bharari dragged her out by her hair.

At that very moment, Jamiruddin the midget was walking past the Jugi house with his son Nuruddin. Nuruddin carried a grocery basket on his head. In it sat two chickens from their coop; they would trade these for oil, salt and other supplies, and return home while it was still daylight. Otherwise let alone the cooking fire, even their lamp would stay unlit. The three of them would have to flail in the dark with stones tied to their hungry bellies. Despite the taunts from his wife, Jamiruddin and his son left their house like twins, their royal scarves streaming in the wind. By then Raj Chandra had bound Shoirop Mala to a pole in the yard and was whipping her to punish her for her impertinence. The man whose meddling had brought poor Jugi's wife to such a pass could no longer hold his tongue. But Jamiruddin did not have the courage to stand up to the lord of the realm. He ran to the Rajganj marketplace with his son, where Kala Jugi stood with half of a mosquito net draped on his body to attract customers, while the four mosquito nets that his wife had woven that week lay neatly folded in front of him on the ground.

When they spotted the father and son, the whores taunted, 'Oh, look at the twin nawabs go by!' They were assembled at a shack adjacent to the marketplace. Their pimps repeated their jibe. On this busy market day, the brothels were hard at it even before evening had descended. The chickens cackled from the basket. Yet Jamiruddin could find no proper comeback to such a highhanded welcome from the whores. He hung his head low in shame. Not only was his young son with him to witness all this, if he couldn't deliver the news in time, Kala Jugi's wife would be murdered—a murder in which he would be complicit. This was the midget's nature: he would tell the thief, 'Go, steal!', and then tell the homeowner, 'Go, catch him!'. He hid their scarves under the chickens, instructed his son to tarry by the wayside and slipped into the marketplace.

The Rajganj textile bazaar was busy with trade in the late afternoon. The marketplace had been established by the Chowdhury clan. The zamindar's representatives were present to collect tariffs on all trading. The market was abuzz with foot soldiers. A few armed soldiers from the East India Company were also present, like jackals in a pack of dogs. They were remarkably insolent. In all this hustle and bustle, Kala Jugi was like a mosquito, hard to locate. Perhaps, spotting the soldiers carrying guns, he had hidden behind the mosquito nets woven by his wife. The man wet himself even chancing upon his own shadow; how was he going to stand up to Raj Chandra Chowdhury's lust-crazed gaze? He would turn to ashes. There was no point in taking him along to try and salvage the situation. Jamiruddin slipped towards the area where the weavers were assembled, and, alighting like a crow, he exploded the news.

Only Allah knew how much the mob actually understood as the news travelled mouth to ear. In a second, the marketplace was in uproar. The weavers and the traders banded together like rice and lentils mixed in a hodgepodge. Bundles of fabric were strewn everywhere. The traders pulled down their shutters as hastily as they could. The market dispersed. Even the soldiers firing blanks into the air failed to restore order. The buyers who were originally heading towards the whorehouses now joined the gaggle of weavers.

Jamiruddin's son Nuruddin had been standing by the roadside with his basket on the ground. The scarves were covered in chicken shit. He couldn't figure out whether he should throw them away or wrap one around his neck again. They hadn't bought any supplies for home yet. Scared of his mother's fists, he started to wail and sob. The people from the marketplace surged ahead, pushing right past him. Ahead of them all strode Jamiruddin the midget. Kala Jugi walked beside him, clasping his hand. They had gone partway when Jamiruddin was numbstruck upon realising that Kala Jugi was night-blind. At this rate, by the time they reached his house, the night would be over. Already it had taken him all of the early evening Maghreb hour to get this mob together. Raj Chandra had probably vanished by now, his flunkey in tow. The Chowdhury courthouse was actually on their way. Rajendra Narayan sat totting up the account ledgers in the light of castor oil lamps. The Dewan sat beside him, explaining away this and that. The palace guards and sentries had not yet been dismissed for the night. They were scattered here and there, smoking ganja, concealed by the shrubs and bushes. Although the shouts and clamour of the swarm from the marketplace had stopped Rajendra Narayan's heart in its tracks, his men in the bushes didn't stop passing the bong around for a second. Jamiruddin and his horde took the chance to rush into the courtyard of the Chowdhury palace.

All these people were there without any prior notice. Rajendra Narayan was unable to move his finger on the ledger; it was stuck like an ant in molasses. He stood thunderstruck—as if life had drained out from his body. His brow was creased. The Dewan had disappeared; only the pleated end of his dhoti could be seen from under the tall stool meant to store documents, waving slowly like a gecko's tail.

Although they had sent no word ahead, Jamiruddin the midget and his followers had no intention of scaring anyone. They were there to seek justice. The complainant was Kala Jugi; his wife was being tortured. He was pushed to the front, to stand in front of the zamindar. Kala Jugi put his palms together and began trembling. His jaw had locked. Now, Hindu or Muslim, who among the weavers could speak on his behalf? None of them really knew what was going on. In the end, Jamiruddin the midget, eyewitness to Raj Chandra's criminal doings, stepped up. Upon hearing his report, Rajendra Narayan's knit brows slowly smoothed over. The Dewan exited from under the stool, dusting off his clothing. What a relief, this tumult had nothing to do with tax collection! If this had been a dacoit attack, by the likes of Devi Singh of Rangpur, there would be no exit from under that stool tonight—his time on this earth would have ended right there.

With his composure restored, Rajendra Narayan began storming about. If he called for Chanda the warrior one moment, he called for Mangal Singh the next. Chanda had, at this odd hour, gone off to the *akhra* to practise his cudgel-wielding skills. Rajendra Narayan would have to make do with the ganja-head Mangal Singh. There was no way he was going to let this opportunity to humiliate Raj Chandra slip through his fingers. Let the denizens of Babupur witness the actions of the son of his brother Pratap Narayan; Raj Chandra might be the lawful heir, but he was a blot on the family name. Let them also witness Prafulla Kumar, a child divine. A child who had yet to grow all his milk teeth was one whose bite held no fear.

Raj Chandra could hardly believe it—the guards and sentries who were employed by his own zamindari were coming to capture him? But he was on his way home! Because of his injured knee, his progress was slow. The five guards Mangal Singh had brought with him were all doped to their gills—they could barely keep their eyes open, and were following Mangal Singh's orders blindly. Before he could get the hang of things, Raj Chandra's double-barrelled gun was confiscated. The big lugs accompanying Mangal Singh tied him up with his hands behind his back. He was about to kick one of them with his good leg when a slap landed on his cheek, making his head ring. Ram Bharari had spotted their flaming torches from afar and fled. If he hadn't, he would have been in for it too. It was beyond him to hold his own against these five lumps.

Helplessly, Raj Chandra surrendered himself to Mangal Singh. They pulled him off his horse and tied a rope around his waist to drag him to the courthouse. The crowd from the marketplace surrounded him to witness the spectacle, as if he was a captured dacoit leader. Some hid in the shadows and shouted out sneers and barbs. Clods of earth, gobs of spittle landed on him from different directions. He felt as if Kala Jugi and Jamiruddin were apparitions, although they were right there in front of his eyes. Raj Chandra Chowdhury could only think of the episode as a nightmare, nothing more.

When he finally came to, Raj Chandra realised he was in the outer chamber of his quarters. His personal servant Jugindor was solicitous. 'Hujoor, you haven't opened your eyes for a full day and a full night. Open your mouth—let me feed you some lemonade.'

'Get lost, you bastard! I might have my eyes shut, but I'm not blind.' Forget about lemonade, Raj Chandra wouldn't deign to touch the water in this household. But where was he to go? When Rajendra Narayan showed up to place a hand on his forehead, he kept his eyes closed and feigned sleep. The man was a two-faced snake. He had sent Mangal Singh to shackle him and drag him back, and then he had undone those shackles with his own hands. It was all a ploy. He was trying to present himself to the peasants as their saviour. The grandson of the saviour was also an avatar of the gods—he had descended to this earth directly from his divine abode. The throne here was being prepared for him.

On whom should Raj Chandra's anger descend? Who but Jugindor was around? Even the babes suckling at their mothers' breasts could work out that Mangal Singh and his sidekicks had been granted sudden leave to save them from Raj Chandra's ire. No one was saying a single word to him. As soon as his knee felt better, Raj Chandra would again cross Madhab Patni's marina. He was fine with Inga Chowdhury's demand of a quarter of the estate.

In a niche in the wall sat a bottle of turpentine. Jugindor also procured castor oil and sea salt from the marketplace. A massage with a castor oil and sea salt mixture, and applying hot turpentine compresses, would alleviate the master's pain. But Raj Chandra's heart hurt more than his flesh. Another night had passed, another day almost gone. No one had summoned him from the inner quarters, no one had come to even peek at him. Despite her widowhood, Ma Shumitra wasn't proscribed from coming to the outer chambers. She did come out when needed. So where was she now? Had she also taken the side of that black viper? Forget about picking apart his uncle's treachery with her, Raj Chandra couldn't remember when he had last sat down and talked things over with her. Phuleswari was keeping her distance from him ever since the day she had hung up the broom in the doorway. All he knew was that she had taken refuge in his mother's chamber.

The rough winds of the afternoon's Nor'wester banged doors shut all over the palace, while thunder rent the sky asunder. It made him yearn harder for those who were dear to him. Raj Chandra could no longer stay in bed. As soon as the wind died down and the rain let up a little, he limped his way to the inner quarters. The inner courtyard was strewn with dead leaves and storm-ripped branches. Limping with the aid of a cane amid all that debris was like trying to row a boat in waters clogged with weed. The maidservants massed to sweep the courtyard watched him, hiding their laughter in their sari-ends. Raj Chandra barely made it to his mother's chamber. As soon as he set foot on her veranda, she said, 'I do not wish to see that disgraceful face of yours,' and lowered her blinds. As he was returning to his chamber a failure, Ram Bharari prostrated himself at his feet at the entrance. Raj Chandra felt a fire course through his veins. He held his head, brought low in shame, high as before. Ram Bharari didn't even have to provide his excuse as to why he had vanished upon sighting the flaming torches of the guards. Raj Chandra ordered him to saddle his steed, and began to get dressed.

The day was all but done when the storm was finally over. Although the sun was blazing in full force, the roads were still wet. Raj Chandra's horse kept sinking in the muck and the puddles. His knee ached in the damp, chilly breeze. The night had descended with such deep darkness, he could barely see an arm's length ahead. They left the fields and rode on to the roads. Although he had left the palace intending to visit Inga Chowdhury, Raj Chandra soon changed course. Ram was an understanding fellow; he understood that even more than his zamindari, what his master needed right now was a soft bed, and a softer pair of hands. Even if the world had turned upside down, these still waited at the Nor house.

From the spinney of palmyra and areca nut trees nearby, the hooting of owls, in pairs, sounded in the darkness.

Five

That day when Shyampriya took her leave, Rongomala's perfumed hair oil congealed in its bowl, her meal spoiled in the pot and the bright red alta patterns on her feet turned blue with jealous anger. Not a word passed her lips. When her servant Durga came to light the evening lamp in her room, Rongi was lying in bed, neither awake nor asleep.

Rongomala could not stand the odour of castor oil. Wax candles burned in the wall nooks, exuding blue smoke. A burnt smell wafted in the air. Durga sat outside on the veranda, waiting to rush in with taper, flint stone and jute stick as soon as the room grew dark. She was an old hand at Atmaram Nor's household; although the financial circumstance of the family had changed in the past year, she still kept her fist tightly shut. She lit the evening lamps in each room as was the custom, but then she made a second round to blow them right out. The rooms were empty. Who were the lights for? The house itself had grown, but the people within had disappeared alongside the shrubbery that had been lopped off. Nearby there were a few households where Atmaram's relatives lived. They had used thorny branches to fence off the paths used by their daughters and wives. Rongomala's own parents hadn't been able to stomach her indecent doings; they had gone off, into self-imposed exile. Who could blame her extended family? Her brother, Golap Raiya, was better off gone. He spent his days and nights tied to the sari-end of his whore mistress and visited every few days asking for a handout. He oozed the noxious stench of palm wine while cursing, fit to turn the air blue. As soon as he had some money in his hand, he would clasp Rongi around the neck—it was hard to tell at such times whether he was laughing or crying. The brother was funding his prurient lifestyle with his sister's broken fortunes. All their misfortune had initially been occasioned by Golap Raiya when he had tried to marry his sister, the beauteous Rongomala, to Ram Goitya Guja, called Guja for his humpback. Shyama Shundori, their mother, was the one who had fanned the flames of that particular destruction.

All this Durga had witnessed with her own eyes. When Durga had arrived at the Nor house, Golap Raiya was still a toddler as naked as the day he was born, and Rongi had just begun to crawl across the yard. Atmaram was eternally busy with his *jatra*-plays. Atmaram's wife, Shyama Shundori, took care of all household affairs. They were dirt poor, without two pennies to rub together. The gaps in their walls were big enough that foxes crawled through—and yet man, woman, child, they were, all of them, joyful. Durga was astounded. Depending on their commitments for performances, month-long rehearsals went on—sometimes it was *Nimai Sanyas*, sometimes *Man Bhanjan*, sometimes *Ram Leela*. Men of all sorts entered the house in those days. They sat and smoked and chewed paan. The burning lamps, the songs and the music turned night into shining day. Then one day, Atmaram would receive an advance, and leave with his troupe for far-off lands. It was as if the whole household would settle down to draw breath. Silence surrounded them like water. Even a crow cawing on the rooftop startled them into glancing at each other. With Durga's help, Shyama Shundori mended the broken fence with jute stalks, neatened the yard with cow dung water, helped the gourd vine climb up the bamboo trellis, hummed while embroidering quilts and counted the days, hoping for Atmaram's return before the rice in the fat-bellied jar emptied. Otherwise, those two children would drive her crazy, crying for rice. When their father was home, neither hunger nor thirst ever seemed to touch them. Both of them were as mad about music as their father. The jatra rehearsals continued in the outer room, and Rongomala danced in the yard, tinkling her ankle bells. The Nor girl learned to dance before she learned to walk. One year, Golap Raiya played the part of Lord Krishna, the divine butter thief, in the Janmashtami play, the day celebrating the Lord's birth. The zamindar of Amirabad rewarded him with a gold bud for the performance. Shyama Shundori sold it off the next rainy season, during their days of penury. The commotion that created! Atmaram broke every single pot in the kitchen and went after his wife. The children were just like their father. None of them understood Shyama's travails. Both of them were vagabonds. When Atmaram was gone, they spent the first few days at a slow tempo, drifting here and there. Then, as soon as they got out of bed, they would go out to steal fruits and vegetables from others' gardens. Brother and sister spent whole afternoons fighting over a single unripe cucumber. If possible, they would have snatched the food right out of Durga's mouth. Atmaram came home as soon as his jatra played out; he bribed his daughter with a doll and his son with a toy flute, and they both quieted down. Even his wife, Shyama, would be beside herself with delight when she received a bamboo basket or a palm-frond fan instead of money. But even that Atmaram couldn't bear too long. As time and again he played the parts of the drunken louts Jagai and Madhai who were converted to the spiritual path, somehow he himself transformed into an ascetic like Lord Nimai. The rehearsals at home gradually stopped. He started visiting the akhra of the kirtan singer Loknath. There he danced with one hand raised toward the heavens, ankle bells on one leg, or he sang devotional kirtans while playing his khanjani.

Hare Krishna, Hare Krishna
Krishna Krishna Hare Hare

—the *naam-kirtan,* consisting only of the names of God. He would return home, wrapped in a yellow scarf adorned with the God's names, singing the many names of Lord Hari as they did at funeral pyres. Whenever domestic needs were brought to his attention, he responded, 'I can't be bothered. Go talk to Golap.'

Golap was a growing boy. His mother's tears fuelled his determination. Day and night, he cast about for ways to make some money. Once he signed up as a mercenary for the zamindar but returned with his head split open. Even before hair grew back on the wounded patch, he was sitting hunched under the tree where the villagers would gather. The opium eaters there advised him, 'Someone with such a pretty sister shouldn't have to worry about money! Are you mad? Arrange a match for that sister of yours; the groom's people will measure out at least five seers of gold for you. We'll take care of the groom search for you, don't worry.' They decided on a groom in that single meeting. Ram Goitya Guja, son of the pinchpenny Nosi Ram. Guja showed up the very next day with a wad of cash, which he had obtained by knifing open his father's strongbox. Any delays in this propitious event, and surely Nosi Ram would claw at his son's hump until he got back all his money.

Golap left Ram Goitya waiting under the kadam tree by the pond before entering the house. Atmaram seemed uninterested, although the marriage of his one and only daughter was impending. He said, 'I don't want to see the groom. Tell Golap's mother to peek through the fence and take a look at him.' Shyama Shundori passed that responsibility on to Durga. What Durga glimpsed through the fence, waiting under the kadam tree, was a dry-season owl, clad in dhoti and shawl. He was peering this way and that, as if he was out at night, hunting for rats. As soon as she reported this to Shyama Shundori, she came at Durga with a broom: 'You miserable woman, what does a man's looks count, what will you do with it—wash and drink that holy water?' Once she was done cursing Durga, Shyama sent Golap out to promise Rongi to the man.

The neighbourhood women arrived in droves as news of the imminent nuptials spread. They needed no prompting to launch into songs. Although their songs began with laughter and play, the women wept as they sang, their cheeks drenched in tears. A wedding was a moment not only of joy, but of loss. Durga's eyes were like an arid desert. The women pulled her into the gathering, but no song emerged from her throat, as if she had swallowed ground glass. Her heart had been distraught ever since she had seen the groom.

The wedding was completed in haste. Rongomala's beauty that day was beyond description. Born of a poor family, all she had to wear throughout the year were two saris: they were woven from thread they spun themselves, no longer than a mere ten arm lengths. When the women draped a gold-bordered *meghdombur* sari around her, bedecked her in *hashuli* earrings and a crescent *makri* necklace, adorned her face with vermilion and sandalwood paste, it was as if the very moon had lost its way and risen inside their hovel. Her fiery beauty dazed all eyes. But it took no time for that fire to be snuffed out. At her first look at the groom, Rongomala ripped the eight pieces of jewellery off her body. She pulled her topknot loose like a madwoman. The houseful of relatives and neighbours tried to stop the bride's wailing: some grabbed her mouth, some stroked her hair, some bit their tongues in shame and stopped up their own ears. Nothing worked. In the meantime, the night was almost over; crows had begun to caw. They forced the young girl into the bridal chamber and left.

A man of weak physique, Ram Goitya's arms and legs were like reeds; he had no neck at all, and a massive hump sat between his shoulders. Despite being a man, he lacked resolve. Rongomala tossed him from the bridal bed into the yard with a single kick. He took the door with him, and scampered off at a run. One day passed, then another. Ram Goitya didn't return. However, Nosi Ram was not as easy to dissuade as his son. He now called upon the village elders to hold a mediation underneath the big tree. The purpose was to dissolve the marriage. This was a marriage where the holy fire itself was a witness; it wasn't like those *jabans*, those Muslims, that one could just do a talaaq and everything would be business as usual. Whether she ate of her husband's earnings or not, until the day she ascended the funeral pyre, a woman must wear the conch-shell bangles and the vermilion in her hair parting—the signs of a married woman. All that remained to resolve was the matter of the money stolen from Nosi Ram's coffers. That day, Golap Raiya had to count out every penny, and return it before he could make his way back home.

It was as if a storm had ravaged the hitherto peaceful household. Atmaram spent several days with his door latched, too ashamed to go out in public. Although Golap had been thoroughly humiliated, there was no way for him to hide indoors. He had to go out to seek work. This was Shyama Shundori's fate: to have to keep a married daughter. She wiped her tears with her sari and continued to try and sustain her household with a patch here, a mend there. Although she was an extra mouth to feed, Durga had nowhere else to go. The place she came from was being eaten away by the river. She had lost all she had and had finally found refuge as a maidservant in this household belonging to her distant aunt. Where could she go? And Rongi could not survive a moment without Durga nearby. Although she was not living with her husband, it was as if the waters of marriage had washed her body with pure beauty. Flames that had been choked by ashes blazed bright one day or another. Rongomala was downcast, but only for a few days; soon her lively spirit made life hard for everyone else. As if her whole life was meaningless unless she could display her wares of beauty and youth. But where were the connoisseurs who could truly appreciate what she had? The cessation of the jatra rehearsals in their house meant that the coming and going of the many men had ceased as well. So, although there was a perfectly good pond for bathing right beside the house, one day Rongi just had to visit Shayor Lake to bathe, and the next day she needed to go to Damdama Lake.

Rongomala strolled ahead with Durga as a chaperon. The rowdy wind carried word of her beauty everywhere. The demon Ravana had abducted Goddess Sita when she had stepped foot outside of the Lakshman Rekha, the boundary drawn by her brother-in-law, Lakshman. Rongomala invited the storm of destruction to her home when she summoned Shyampriya the vaishnavi to their inner quarters. Durga was ordered to call her, but she did not like the idea a whit.

No matter who came begging, whether they were blind mendicants or men and women of the vaishnava faith, the custom was to give them alms and bid them farewell from the front door. Rongi's young heart grew restless when she heard Shyampriya singing outside. She sent Durga out with instructions for the vaishnavi to sing a few more songs on Radha and Krishna's love-play. But the vaishnavi was stubborn. It would leave her unsatisfied, she said, if she didn't see the face of the person requesting these songs. When Durga and Shyampriya's argument over this hit a peak, Rongi tiptoed her way to the outer house. Shyampriya dropped her khanjani when she saw Rongi. Was Shyampriya a woman, or a man in disguise, to be so affected by Rongi's beauty?

Whether man or woman, anyone who truly appreciated Rongomala's beauty was welcomed with open arms by the wife and daughter of Atmaram Nor. They forgot about the songs, and busied themselves with where to seat the vaishnavi, what to feed her—Durga received one order after another. Shyama Shundori stood in the doorway and smiled indulgently at her daughter. What could Durga do by herself? Neither Atmaram nor Golap were home to break Shyampriya's fangs and rid the house of the black viper.

Shyampriya settled herself comfortably, smoking, and chewing on paan. She chatted about many things, carefully finagling all she could from Rongi. The evening lamps had been lit. She kept repeating she had to be on her way, but made no move to leave. She closed her eyes and tinkled her *mandira* cymbals. 'You glanced at me and my heart did steal,' she sang. The vaishnavi's melodies had roused Shyama Shundori as well. Disregarding how her voice sounded, Shyama Shundori set out coins in a bell-metal platter, emptied out her pots and pans to find half a fistful of rice and descended from the stoop, singing:

Oh, Shyampriya, take your alms, leave my platter free
Leave your blessing for these two, my Golap and Rongi.

Wonderful! As if mother and daughter were competing in tomfoolery. The vaishnavi took her leave that evening after bestowing numerous blessings. But she turned up again the very next day. This time she came prepared. Although Golap Raiya was home this time, the whore couldn't be stopped from walking straight into the inner quarters. Apparently Shyampriya's sister had drowned as a child, and she had looked exactly like Rongi—such a tale would call forth tears from anyone. And this tale opened the gates of the Nor house wide for the vaishnavi.

Durga spied on them from behind the door. She could hear Shyampriya whispering in Rongi's room, giggling now and then, then singing a few lines, tinkling the khanjani. 'What, is there a man in there? What are you spying for? I'm in such a hole with you, you wretched woman.' Shyama Shundori's taunts forced Durga to move away, but her heart remained by Rongi's door. Where did this slut just fly in from to nest in this house? If she wasn't aiming to oust Durga, what was her purpose here? It wasn't long before it became known.

'Oh, Ma, my heart is aflame—what am I to do?' Damdama Lake was nearby. Rongi had been taken there to bathe at Shyampriya's suggestion. Ever since her return, the girl was chanting a single mantra day and night: Chowdhury, Chowdhury.

'Who is this Chowdhury?' Atmaram asked his son. Golap just looked at him blankly. Although Durga had witnessed the moment when the two pairs of eyes sought each other and met by Damdama Lake, she had kept her mouth shut. The only Chowdhury that the father and son knew of was at the royal palace of Shindurkait, the zamindar of the Babupur district. One might get a glimpse of the stars in the night sky—but a zamindar? Never. Well, no matter what people said, Rongi was merely suffering from a fit of mania. Just wrap a poultice soaked in chilled oil around her head and make sure she stayed in the shade on the terrace.

One evening, before Rongomala's madness had had a chance to dissipate, just as father and son had settled down on the moonlit stoop outside to share an after-dinner smoke, the clop-clop of horses sounded outside. Shyama Shundori and Durga poured water in their unfinished plates and rose swiftly; they didn't even have a chance to wash their fingers clean. The earth beneath Golap Raiya's feet trembled. He stumbled a few times but managed to stand a few feet away from the pair of horses, with his palms pressed together in obeisance. Here, at his doorstep, stood the man who could not be glimpsed even if one lay down a thousand coins. Before Golap had managed to verify what his eyes were seeing, Raj Chandra Chowdhury proposed that Rongomala prepare a platter of paan for him. Standing beside him was Ram Bharari, who held out a sheaf of money. Golap Raiya had performed in many jatras; in fact, he had been dubbed *Raiya* because of his portrayal of the role of Lord Krishna's lover Radha, but at this moment, the only gesture he could manage was to keep his palms pressed together, and the only words to emerge from his lips were, 'I beg you.'

'You lousy bastard!' Raj Chandra descended from his horse and took hold of Golap Raiya's tender chin with his index finger and thumb. For a split second, it seemed as if he would lean in and kiss those eyes that were so similar to the doe eyes of the sister. Instead, he roared, 'Take the money and get your sister ready. I am coming into the inner quarter.' Durga heard Raj Chandra's raised voice and rushed outside. When she ran into Golap, he told her to spread out a mat in the outer room, and strode to Rongomala's bedroom.

Rongomala had just finished lining her eyes with kohl, and was holding a mirror up to her face to perfectly position the crystal bindi on her forehead. A slight smile played on her paan-reddened lips. The house was in uproar, and here was his sister whoring herself up! Golap Raiya threw the bundle of money on the floor and left. Atmaram had discarded his hookah and retreated to his room a while ago. He could no longer deal with all the hustle and hassle of this earthly existence. Today the very core of his being had been shaken. It was one thing to accept the asceticism of a holy man—like Lord Sri Chaitanya. But this, this was violation—this was rape! How could he, a father, watch this happen and not want to leave this life? He said to his son, 'Take Rongi and leave this land. I'll hang on to our homestead even if I have to bite down on the ground.' Foolish old man, he had almost reached the end of his life and was still clueless about how far the claws of kings and zamindars could reach. Even if they hid Rongi inside the very earth, there would be no escaping Raj Chandra Chowdhury. His great rage would decimate the whole family.

And for whom would they fight? The remedy lay in the disease itself. Shyama Shundori beat her forehead in despair as she exited her daughter's room. She needed her husband at this moment, even if he had turned away from worldly things. Perhaps he would understand her sorrowing heart! Golap Raiya stood at the doorway to his father's room. When he saw his mother, he began to wail. 'What kind of a daughter did you birth, oh Ma? If I had known, I would have chopped her up and thrown her into the river.' Atmaram sat unmoving like a statue, while his wife and son grieved. He pursed his bloodless and pale lips tightly, while in his mind he repeated a shloka from the Gita:

Asato mā sad gamaya,
tamaso mā jyotir gamaya,
mṛityor māmṛtaṃ gamaya.

Lead us from untruth to truth; from darkness to light; from death to the eternal. Teardrops hung from the tulsi necklace hugging the old man's neck.

When Golap Raiya left through the thicket behind the house while wiping his tears, a different game was unfolding inside. Raj Chandra had not deigned to visit the Nor house to sit on a rush mat in their outer house and smoke or chew paan. He knew quite well what was in the girl's heart. When the wailing inside stopped, he sprang up. Ram Bharari was patrolling outside. Raj Chandra strode to the middle of the yard. Durga stood there, leaning against a pole, her mind scouring heaven and earth. Before she could spread her arms out like wings to deter the zamindar, silver coins glinted in front of her eyes. Raj Chandra Chowdhury himself was holding out the coins. Durga had never had a dime to her name. She folded back her arms, brought her palms together with the two coins pressed between them and touched her hands to her forehead, her eyes closed in ecstasy.

All Durga was responsible for was pointing the way to Rongi's bedroom. She didn't want to be deprived of the chance to provide some care for Chowdhury. She stuffed a paan loaded with catechu and slaked lime in her mouth and walked towards Rongi's room with the paan box. She had barely reached Rongi's room when a hairy arm pulled the door shut from inside and slid the latch. Durga stood immobile by the stoop, with the paan box still in her hand. The two silver coins, knotted in her sari-end, swung against her back.

That night, if she had untied the silver coins and left them at the door, it would have made no difference to anyone's virtues or vices. The world would have continued to turn. But Durga was trapped by the silver. Rongomala's father ripped asunder the bonds of love. He abandoned his daughter to follow a righteous path, and her mother followed. Durga was merely a distant cousin, working as a maidservant for them at that. What responsibility did she have? She herself had remained a virtuous virgin, keeping herself safe from the quicksand of life. Her sun was now at its peak. She still tossed and turned alone in her bed, her body calling out. That night, she went to bed holding the silver coins in her hand. They sang her a lullaby: tinkle, tinkle, tinkle, tinkle. This lullaby was all she had gathered for this life and the next—whatever else remained was all lies.

Six

When Rongomala's room darkened, Durga ran in with a lamp in hand. Her shadow shifted behind her. Rongi was still in bed, moaning. Durga lit the lamp and left. Rongi sat up, rubbing her eyes, looking this way and that. Evening had just descended—the whole night lay ahead of her. What provocation had Shyampriya left her with? She couldn't get rid of the spectre of Shoirop Mala. Rongi couldn't deal with this demon by herself.

Chullu Singh, the guard from the western lands, was at the entrance. His frequent slapping of mosquitoes sounded like cannonballs exploding. He was a nuisance. Raj Chandra had posted a big lout as the guard to make sure not even a fly could get in or out. Even Rongi couldn't leave. She was a prisoner now in her father's house.

Durga placed the candle in the wall niche and disappeared; it was hard to tell whether she was in the house or not. She was a solitary person by nature. Perhaps it was because she rarely opened her mouth that Raj Chandra trusted her so much. She also did her best to tend to his needs. But even if that fool Raj Chandra couldn't tell, Rongi knew in her bones that all of Durga's service was due to the silver.

The whore's tongue seemed to itch whenever she spotted Shyampriya. Durga mocked her with ditties that made fun of the vaishnava people. Without warning, Durga would sometimes tuck her sari-end in her waistband, preparing to fight with Shyampriya. As if they had been co-wives in another life. There was no difference between telling Durga of her sorrows and trying to talk to a tree. The only other choice was Roma, the hairdresser. She lived a few miles away. Roma's virtues were too many to count. As she smeared a paste of turmeric and *gila* on Rongi's skin, she learned every single detail about Raj Chandra.

It was Roma that Rongi needed.

Chullu Singh had barely taken his first step to patrol the house while holding aloft a blazing straw torch, when Rongi peeked at the mirror hung on the wall. Her swollen face floated there like a dead fish. Her eyes were swollen; they were stretched as tight as drums. She slapped herself a few times and looked in the mirror again. When Sri Krishna had returned after spending the night at Chandrabali's grove, what had the wounded Radha looked like? Like a dead fish! That shameless hussy Chandrabali—how had *she* looked?

When Chullu Singh entered the house with Roma in tow, Rongomala was singing by the window with her hair loosened. The plaintive tunes of songs about Krishna trying to coax Radha out of her anger drifted in the air.

Roma guessed that she had not been summoned to Rongomala's chamber at this odd hour to help her get dressed. This beauteous maid had decided to punish the louche Raj Chandra. She was finding it hard to remain strong in her resolve though. And so, she was sitting here, singing these songs of yearning. But at this moment, she needed more rage than sorrow.

Roma left her bundle of alta-dye and manicure tools outside on the stoop and tiptoed in. She was addicted to betel leaf and tobacco. And anyway, what sort of merrymaking took place without intoxicants! She had barely got the words out before Raj Chandra's silver hookah was brought over from the stilted cottage. Roma trembled in fear. On the one hand, there was Rongomala insisting, and on the other, the room was awash in the aroma of the *amburi* tobacco—it was enough to let her desire triumph over her fear. There were four or five different nozzles resting in a wall niche. No one paid any attention to them. Raj Chandra's hose was passed from one hand to another. When Rongomala's bout of coughing was over, Roma began her chatter. 'Didimoni, let me give you one bit of advice. Don't let the flying line of the kite slip from your hand. Let the kite soar in the sky. Pay out the line, but hold it taut. Raj Chandra Chowdhury won't be able to move. He will wait at your doorstep, a beggar for your love, for the rest of his life.'

Rongomala had drunk some of the bhang, laced with opiates, on an empty belly. Everything the hairdresser said was making her giggle. Her man tripping over the throstle-hole and desperately yelling, 'My knee! My knee!' Who could hold back laughter at that! Roma was adept at pulling together the threads of all the gossip from the villages around them.

On the one hand the bhang, on the other the slew of talk from Roma—the news of Raj Chandra's broken knee floated away like a piece of straw in water. Rongomala listened wide-eyed as if she were hearing stories about someone else.

That day, while Shyampriya was still sitting on Rongomala's stoop, Roma had left her alta bottle and made her way to Kala Jugi's house. Villagers milled around the house as if there was a wedding taking place; they wanted to get an eyeful of the whiplashes on Shoirop Mala's back. The ploughed field next door had been flattened by so many people coming and going. A long line snaked from the yard to the door. Shoirop Mala sat lotus-style in the middle of the room. Beside her stood Kala Jugi, holding an oil lamp high, like a flaming torch. In great detail, he was describing the story of Raj Chandra's shameful behaviour. Roma had barely touched Shoirop Mala's bare back when she hissed like a cat displaying her blackened teeth. The oil lamp didn't hide the fact that the Jugi woman was also cross-eyed. What eyes that Chowdhury had! Well, such is desire.

Durga had seen Shoirop Mala with her own eyes. She knew Kala Jugi's petite, dove-like wife wasn't as ugly as Roma was claiming, but she kept quiet. Right now, the aim was to staunch Rongomala's ache and hurt. Everyone was colouring the event as they saw fit. Durga herself was unlettered. Still, she proclaimed quite ostentatiously that Raj Chandra's calligraphy was more like chicken scratches than letters. Rongomala picked up the refrain from her maid and described how Raj Chandra had overturned an inkpot while trying to compose a missive and had placed the blame squarely on the Chinese paper. Roma was also eyewitness to Raj Chandra rolling on the ground as his uncle Rajendra slapped him around; that had happened not too long ago, just after Raj Chandra had wed. Roma had been returning from the Rajganj bazaar with a portion of swamp barb fish wrapped in a banana leaf. She had heard the hullabaloo as she neared the royal courthouse and had stopped to watch the drama unfold. It had been summertime. When her fish had begun to exude a rotten odour, Rajendra Chowdhury had forgotten about his nephew on the ground and rushed at Roma in a rage.

Rongomala started to weep. It was unclear why. She wiped her tears with her sari-end, and fell asleep in the middle of explaining that once the lights were out, there was no difference between a humpbacked Ram Goitya and the son of a zamindar. Their party was over. When Roma started homewards, there were only a couple of hours till sunrise. The birds had not left their nests yet; they were merely chirping at each other.

It was the following afternoon when Rongomala finally woke, and that too because of the roiling Kal Baishakhi storm. Before the storm, she had heard Atmaram's voice. As if her father was returning home with his troupe. He was having an argument with Shyama Shundori in the cooking house: no food, no bathing, and you're already setting up in the outer room with your drums and all! She could barely hear the hum of her mother's voice. Her father paid no heed. They had begun singing the songs from the *Nimai Sanyas* musical play, accompanied by small cymbals:

> *Nimai, do not become an ascetic, do not renounce this life*
> *Stay home and call this wretched one 'mother'.*

Now and then, the songs soared over the storm's howl.

Rongomala broke out of her daze. The wilder the storm raged, the louder the conches and the ululations of Durga, the cook and the seven maidservants sounded. They had thrown several pots and pans into the yard for the storm to come and sit still upon. Chullu Singh was probably smoking his weed in the guardroom at the entrance. Not a single sound came from there. The blinds near Rongi's head weren't lowered. Where was the outer room of the Nor house? The little cottage on stilts that stood in the middle of the pond was swaying from side to side as if it would topple into the water.

Golap Raiya paced like a caged tiger in the stilted cottage. He had entered this room that he thought of as hell out of a sheer need to sing to the accompaniment of the *khol-kartaal*. The storm arose while he was singing, and now he was trapped in here. How similar the voices of father and son sounded! Were the mother and daughter's voices similar too? Rongi would never again have the chance to sit all four of them together and compare in this lifetime. A storm raged inside her heart, complete with gusty winds, lightning and rain. An orchestral chamber for the *nowbat* had been erected in the Nor house, spiritual joy had been replaced with the hookah, and Atmaram, the man mad about music, had left through the backdoor with his wife. Such was fate.

It felt as if it was Queen Shochi's sorrow at losing her son Nitai rather than the storm that was roiling this household so. Rongomala wanted to run through the storm to her brother's side and clasp his neck. 'Where did our parents disappear, Dada? Tell me!'

Golap Raiya was like stone. Although the rain had let up, the gusts of wind were breaking tree branches everywhere, and he had to leave right in the middle of all this. Where was he going? Who made you swear an oath that you had to leave right now, Dada? Rongomala couldn't bring herself to demand an answer. How could the two of them coexist? They had tethered their boats to different shores; there was no way for them to meet. They could only change the shores they were tied to. The day that Rongomala's boat would finally dock at the Rajganj brothel was the day he would drift back home on the ebbing tide. In between, their relationship was made only of money. Golap collected a tax from her. He might not bring guards and soldiers with him, but if he didn't get enough money from her, he smashed things and ruined her house.

Today Golap Raiya didn't need to go on a rampage. He bit his tongue in shame when Rongi held out the money towards him. The singing had made him feel generous. He still had about half a bottle of liquor left. Although his sister wasn't Raj Chandra Chowdhury's lawfully wedded wife, still she was a queen of sorts. She deserved some token of respect from those who sought her presence. He placed the bottle at Rongi's feet with a gesture of respect and left the house jangling the coins.

As soon as the storm quieted, everyone came out to gather the mangoes now strewn on the ground. Durga and the cook stood gleefully to the side, counting basket after basket brimming with the mangoes brought down by the storm, as if they were consolation enough for the scare the storm had given them. Rongomala stood nearby, holding on to the door. The bhang she had taken a day and a half ago was still potent; she felt as if she would fly off if she loosened her grip. Durga's joy at all the mangoes made her prattle like a young girl. Flame-hued sunlight caressed the green mangoes streaked with vermilion. The rays of sunshine at day's end sliced through the clouds. Durga's teeth glinted when she reported that the mango tree planted by Shyama Shundari herself had been split in two by the storm.

Forget the tree. No one even remembered Shyama Shundari anymore. In the last two to three years, everything had been wiped clean. And the one because of whom all this had occurred, where was he? Two days and two nights had passed, and now the third day was moving into night. Where was he?

While Rongomala sat pondering, Raj Chandra sat with his sprained knee in the outer chamber of his palace, getting ready to go out. Although the sun had painted the earth carmine before slipping away for the night, lightning glinted in the darkness. The lightning startled Rongi. Had her lover gone off to visit Shoirop Mala with his banged-up knee? *The vermilion dot on the forehead, the line of kohl.* The melody didn't seem to flow from her voice tonight. The cross-eyed gaze and blackened teeth of the Jugi woman were floating in her head, ruining her song. Perhaps she should send Chullu Singh to get Roma again.

Durga came running when she called. Chullu Singh was right behind her. But by then Rongi had changed her mind. She wanted Raj Chandra tonight, for sure.

By the time Raj Chandra started off for the Nor house, despite the ill-omened owls hooting at him from the copse of palymra and areca nut trees, Rongomala had gulped down the remainder of the bottle her brother had left her. As if it were manna, not poison. She started singing in a high-pitched voice. She tied bells around her ankles and danced. Durga clapped in time. A few brass and bell-metal pots and pans thrown out during the storm still lay in the yard; Chullu Singh banged his stick on them, keeping time, as if he were a music connoisseur present at a soiree featuring professional dancers. With every other beat, he shouted, *waah*!

> *Radha Monyung Porihoro—Radha, cast aside your petulance, I have come.*

Raj Chandra limped his way to the inner quarters of the Nor house. The neighbouring children who had flocked to listen to the music quickly dispersed. Durga stopped her clapping and fled. The stilted cottage in the middle of the pond was dark. She would have to change the water in the hookah. Rongi had neither dressed nor painted her face. Her hair was loose, her sari practically falling off. Almost like a madwoman. Although Rongomala's song and dance stopped as soon as she saw Raj Chandra, who could stop Chullu Singh's enthusiastic clanging! His eyes were closed, and he was swaying to the music like a dancing snake. What school of music did this idiot belong to? He was about to burst everyone's eardrums. Leaving Ram Bharari to deal with Chullu Singh, Raj Chandra entered Rongi's chamber.

There he was with his sprained knee, limping with a cane. So the rumours were true. Rongomala sat on her bed, hissing like a snake in anger. Her ankle bells jangled now and then as her leg banged against the bed. Raj Chandra was too afraid to move from the doorway. Yet to stand there like this was also cowardly. He had to admonish Rongi about what he had just seen. She had even beguiled that big lout. No wonder Muslim princes and kings only employed eunuchs at their harems. In their hands, pearls and precious stones and fine shawls and women were all safe. One needn't worry about the safekeeping of one's possessions. He should immediately start searching for a *Kafri*[2] eunuch to take care of Rongi. In the yard, he could hear Ram Bharari giving Chullu Singh a thrashing. Let him. There was no way he would allow Rongi to eat and breathe on his dime and step a foot astray. Raj Chandra turned up the lamp with the end of his cane. A pair of bloodshot eyes flashed at him. 'Raj Chandra Chowdhury, you here? You didn't go to work the looms at the Jugi house?'

---

[2] The term used in Bangla to indicate people of African origin

What did she just say to him? Raj Chandra did not respond to jibes. He had never bothered making excuses or explanations to anyone. When the need arose, he knew how to unsheathe his sword or fire a bullet. But this was a woman, and his loved one at that. This woman from a low-caste family, she had never had the chance to learn any genteel behaviour—what could be done!

Rongi was possessed by poetry. With a slanted smile, she slurred,

There are those who are bees, for honey they love
They drink and then flee, that's what they're made of.

Raj Chandra could neither recite poems nor sing. He lacked the learning to engage in this call and response with Rongi. It was humiliating to have to swear in God's name that he was no bumblebee suckling honey from flower to flower. He was about to say something, when Rongi gestured towards him and said, 'If I'd known before, I would have kicked such love right in its head.' As if the kick had indeed landed right on his head, Raj Chandra banged his cane on the ground and roared, 'Silence, you Nor woman! Another word and I will slit open your throat. I am Raj Chandra, son of Pratap Narayan. I swear on my forefathers; I will crush your arrogance.'

Raj Chandra's white steed galloped under his whip. Ram Bharari rode ahead of him on his black pony, holding a flaming torch. He was forced to whip his pony to gallop ever faster. He was astonished at the Nor woman. That whore had no shame. What had happened to Raj Chandra? He had limped his way out of the haveli as if kicked out by the pretty damsel. Not a word crossed his lips. Well, the true master showed his hand at the last moment. Even if his lord and master Raj Chandra let this incident go, these Nor people would get no mercy from Ram Bharari.

Raj Chandra dismounted from his horse and stood by the lake near the palace. The chambers in the royal mansion were brightly lit; one could even hear voices. He would be a laughing stock if he returned to the inner quarters now like this, all dressed up for his night's tryst. Neither did he want to stay in the outer chamber with Jugindor to look after him. But how long could he just wait here in the dark like a thief? The decaying moon played peekaboo through black clouds lined with the gold from its shine. The light played on Raj Chandra's face. When Ram Bharari stabled the horses and started for home, Raj Chandra was still waiting in the light and shade by the lake. In a slow rhythm, his cane rammed the earth.

Seven

After almost a week, Ma Shumitra sent Phuleswari back to her bedchamber. Although she had pulled down the blinds right in her son's face, her heart had started to melt right there and then. Her poor child, leaning on his walking stick, had limped all the way to her through the muck in the courtyard. He seemed so defeated by the pain in his knee. And to top it off, the humiliation from that stone-hearted Rajendra. She felt confused at times—was all this being done for the good of Raj Chandra or not? There was no one to whom she could open her heart. Human children were like those of birds—as soon as they learned to fly, they took wing away from their mothers. But Raj Chandra had a wife. No matter what kind of man the husband was, it was a wife's responsibility to take care of him.

Although she had no idea regarding what dangers her husband faced, Phuleswari touched her mother-in-law's feet like a good girl, as if she had taken her advice to heart. Then she tucked her side pillows under her arms and crossed the courtyard, her anklets tinkling. Such a short walk, yet there were so many eyes trained on Phuleswari Rai. As if she was a newlywed bride, about to enter the bridal chamber.

Phuleswari's bedchamber was lined on either side by different kinds of trees. The rain-washed vines and leaves let the moonlight slip through and melt onto the veranda and the door, creating a lattice of light and shadow. Phuleswari paused. Two more steps, and there awaited her bedchamber and the bedstead intended for husband and wife. An evening lamp guttered in her empty room as the fragrance of incense wafted in the air. The other day, she had tied a broom to the door lintel and left her mud-spattered slippers on the bed. There was no end to the furore that had been created. Had his royal highness' anger abated? If not, so what? She had returned to her quarters after so many days! Her aviary, her heart's delight, was so nearby now. Phuleswari Rai's heart swelled in joy.

She tossed her pillows onto the bed and pulled up the blinds in the window that overlooked the garden. Sudden gusts of wind brought the scent of fresh jasmine, champak and gardenias. She hadn't needed to use a loofah to scrub off the fishy, dead-water smell of her mother-in-law from her skin; it had somehow disappeared by itself. After all, this was her own domain. Here sat the bedstead measuring ten arms' lengths—the people here had had to saw the door wider to get it in when she had arrived. The jewel-encrusted canopy over the bed had also come with her from Lamchor. Under the bed sat a domed lamp made of moonstone. Before lighting it, Rai pulled it out and cleaned it herself. It glowed like a perfect pearl. The old maidservant Kalitara stood shamefaced in the doorway to tell her that Raj Chandra was not to be found anywhere. He had limped off somewhere early in the evening; Jugindor could not say where. That servant walked around wearing blinders. Was the man playing hide-and-seek with his mother? Ma Shumitra had sent her daughter-in-law back; it would be scandalous now if the son did not appear.

Phuleswari was taken aback at first; then she started laughing. As if the king paid attention to anyone! It wasn't Jugindor who was blinkered, it was Kalitara. Her eyes must be blinded with cataracts. She would be unable to tell if an elephant walked right by her! God only knew how Phuleswari's birds were faring in the hands of such a sightless one. Phuleswari rewarded the maid and dismissed her as if the news that Raj Chandra was not to be found, that he had limped off somewhere, was good news. At least for this night she would be left to her own devices for a few hours.

But Phuleswari wouldn't get even an hour to herself. A week had passed since she had ventured to see Rongomala. Now that she had been finally permitted to reenter her own rooms, the king himself was on his way back after being kicked out by the beauteous courtesan—a fact Phuleswari had no way of knowing. She lifted the door latch and sat on the bed, her casket of jewels in her hands. No matter what devices and ploys her mother-in-law resorted to, Phuleswari's heart could never be fettered. The tighter the bind, the looser the knot. As Phuleswari, the highborn virtuous wife, gazed into her mirror, her reflection was replaced with the face of the harlot Rongomala. The same face that had glimmered that night in the pond by the Nor house. Phuleswari Rai adorned herself with her jewels just like Rongomala. She lined her eyes with kohl and wore vermilion in the parting of her hair. Her pair of *ratanchur*, the bracelet to which five rings were attached with chains, had lain unworn at the bottom of the chest. Ma Shumitra had never allowed her to wear them, even on festivals, for these were ornaments more suited to a dancing girl than a king's bride. Phuleswari pushed apart all the stuff crowding her chest to get to the ratanchur at the very bottom. From her clothing chest she pulled out a white muslin sari embroidered in gold. Even her tiny bodice matched the white of Rongomala's. There was no difference between Rongomala's appearance and hers. As soon as Phuleswari entered the skin of that celestial nymph who had floated on the rhythm of the waves, a low knock sounded at her door.

Although soft, surely those knocks were Raj Chandra's. So this was how the king announced his arrival at Rongomala's door. One could barely hear it unless one was listening for it. It would have been better if he had called out *Rongi, Rongi* instead of *Rai, Rai*. Phuleswari Rai would have opened the door, and like Rongi, she would have glanced at him from the corners of her eyes and smiled as she welcomed him. The king would have picked her up and carried her to bed. Their undammed laughter would have fused together before the lamp was doused.

But as Raj Chandra entered the room, Phuleswari backed into the corner. She had no idea where to hide her body, as if it belonged to someone else. But here came the king, limping with his cane; it was impossible not to take his hand to help him rest on the bed. Everything was spoiled in the blink of an eye. None of her plans—welcoming the king as if she were Rongomala, him picking her up, their laughter joining—came to be. He pulled Phuleswari out of her corner and began intercourse. Divested of her sari and bodice, Phuleswari felt as if this was indeed Rongi's body, to be spread out and offered up like a lotus. Mesmerised, she watched everything that happened to her. The nipples that called out to the king's spittle-wet lips and the bellybutton where his fingers danced: all of it was Rongomala's. Phuleswari listened to her own moans as if eavesdropping on some other woman. The king pressed his lips against Rongi's trembling mouth. A storm raged across the bed. Even with her eyes closed, Phuleswari could see Rongi's nubile body twisting in deep pleasure and gradually growing still.

'Oh, my knee! My knee!' Shouting, Raj Chandra crashed onto the bed like a felled tree. Phuleswari's foot had banged against his sprained knee. What a disaster! Phuleswari crouched on the ground in contrition and touched her husband's feet one moment and thumped her head against the bed in the next. How would she repent such a terrible sin? Everything was her fault. Her mother-in-law's quarters were more a fortress than anything else. She had been locked up there all this time. She had heard that her husband was limping. But no one had told her that he had broken his leg. How had this happened?

'I fell off my horse,' Raj Chandra told her in a low voice with his face averted once the pain subsided. While she tidied the clothes on the bed and put away her jewel casket, Phuleswari prattled on about things she had heard on why horse-riding was not a particularly safe pursuit. Raj Chandra smirked to himself—it was a lucky man whose wife kept birds. She had no sense of east or west, truth or lie. And there he was, nosing about in the mud when he had such a gem right here at home.

As the night deepened, the pain in his knee took hold of him. As if there had been poison in Rongi's laughter and the lines she had recited, a poison which now tormented him. Phuleswari slept peacefully beside him, sucking on her thumb. She was growing older, but that wasn't at all reflected in her comportment or her actions. Tonight she had dressed up like a slut on who knew whose bad advice. What was fun for some was disaster for others. What was a bed of roses for Phuleswari Rai was a bed of thorns for him. Raj Chandra jumped out of bed despite his sprained knee. That Nor woman—she had mistaken a tiger for a cat. He had indulged that lowborn whore so much that she had grown uppity. She would understand who her master was as soon as this night was over. She would pay for her insolence.

The next day, Ram Bharari showed him the way. They just needed two men to snatch Golap Raiya from the Rajganj brothel. The fellow was worse than a woman. The moment he saw soldiers coming after him with pikes, he fainted. Ram Bharari took a different route to show up at the Nor house. Rongomala should be the first one to learn that Golap Raiya had been imprisoned for defaulting on taxes. Then they would see who would fall weeping at the king's feet.

While Raj Chandra plotted, Phuleswari sat on a swing on which trees and light and shadow played into a pattern. The cuckoo perched on top of the medlar tree was annoyed. If he cuckooed once, the human sitting below him cuckooed back three times.

The caged birds were also annoyed. Phuleswari Rai had returned to the garden after a long time, but she wasn't paying any attention to them at all. Such a storm had raged yesterday; and yet the cages had remained uncovered. So many eggs had fallen out of the nests and been smashed, so many little chicks were still soaking wet, and here she was, playing with that vagrant cuckoo instead of cooing at and petting the chicks. Who knew where Heera had disappeared? Kalitara was half-blind. The only reason the falcon hadn't pecked out Kalitara's eyeballs when she offered him the chickpeas was its loyalty and love for Phuleswari. They might be birds, but they were guests at the house of Phuleswari Rai's in-laws. They too were responsible for keeping Phuleswari Rai's good name and reputation unsullied. Black Moon, the mynah, could barely chirp out a word, so pent up with emotions he was. He side-eyed Phuleswari and fluttered his wings again and again. Phuleswari barely looked at him. The hour had grown late. There was much she had to do.

Phuleswari's intervention secured Heera's release from her prison in the servants' quarters. As the day wore on, an air of festive preparation took hold of the palace. Phuleswari herself was folding paans, wrapping them in gold and silver foil and laying them out on a silver platter. Heera brought the silver hookah and the attar holder. She fetched the scented amburi tobacco. The gardener Haradhan delivered wicker baskets full of freshly cut flowers. Phuleswari put aside the silver platter and sat down to arrange the flowers in vases. Heera wove together a pair of enormous matching garlands composed of hibiscus, gardenias and nageshwar. Phuleswari smeared her skin with turmeric and cream, and bathed in rosewater. She emerged like a lamp in twilight, her light subdued, but everywhere. Heera settled down to dry Phuleswari's hair in incense-scented smoke. She recalled watching her grandmother Jaggeswari, who knew how long ago, make incense with agarwood, sandalwood and camphor.

This delightful item was not used much in the palace. The other slaves and servants crowded the chamber, drawn by the fragrance. Heera fended them off and sat down with a comb in hand to do Phuleswari Rai's hair. She had to redo it three times before it took the exact shape of the tight coil that Rongomala had worn. Around it she looped a wreath of fragrant white flowers. It took almost the whole afternoon to crimp two locks of hair to frame Phuleswari's forehead. Beauty flowed from the girl's body down into the earth; Heera could not look away. Ma Shumitra had sent the night's dinner for husband and wife arrayed on a silver tray. With it came a separate drink for Phuleswari—a glass of hot milk laced with ground almonds and pistachios. Phuleswari took small sips until the glass was empty. Then she dismissed Heera and latched her door. This hour, she needed to be by herself.

Perhaps the king would not like the same sari every day. Still, white muslin had brought her luck. The perfect creases of her bodice had been ruined last night. Phuleswari smoothed out the fabric with her palms and placed it beneath a stack of pillows. She brought out her jewellery casket and sat cross-legged on her bed. Rongomala's face was reflected in the mirror in front of her. Even when she had completed her transformation into the other woman, no knock sounded on her door. She peeked through the blinds. It would have been lovely if the courtyard was a lake and her bedchamber the cottage in the middle. Surely Rongomala took her paan with some camphor. Mejo Thakurani, Raj Chandra's aunt, smoked her tobacco in a hookah. Apparently, she used to drink liquor in the past. Phuleswari tucked a paan in her cheek and was about to reach for the nozzle of the hookah when the king appeared in the inner courtyard. He staggered this way and that, and tried to nuzzle her door open like a cat, his stole half-dragging on the ground. Let alone the three-legged hookah, even Phuleswari herself escaped his attention. He crashed onto the bed, his shoes still on. When Phuleswari pressed him to sit up and eat dinner, he exclaimed in annoyance and turned to his side, hugging his cane. Soon his snores, like a groaning beast, filled the room.

It was probably late. The birds in her aviary were silent. She could hear the guards at the palace gates, banging their staves. An old bat slowly flew by her window, flapping its wings. Phuleswari was woken by Raj Chandra's fingers moving inside her bodice. She began backing away towards the wall as she had in the past, but stopped. She had fallen asleep at some point while counting the beams in the ceiling. She hadn't even pulled down the blinds. The light of the lamp in the wall niche fell on the bed through the filigreed frame of the bedstead. Raj Chandra hovered over her face. His gaze seemed familiar to her—eager and tender. Phuleswari had seen this gaze only once before, when she hid in a bamboo grove; it had been directed at Rongomala. Her eyes closed in rapture.

She held her breath and endured Raj Chandra's hot exhalations saturated with the smell of liquor. She tried to conjure the faint visage of Rongomala in her mind. By then, her bodice was loose, and her sari was no longer wrapped tight around her waist. Raj Chandra abandoned her paan-reddened lips and moved downwards. As if Rongi's naked body was the endless water of the lake, swelling and foaming as the king churned it. The melody of the crashing waves played in the curves of her body. Lightning sizzled through her. Her raised knees trembled with desire before they fell. When their bodies became one, Phuleswari saw a shadow slip away from beside her window. Whether that shadow was Heera or someone else, it was certainly an agent of Ma Shumitra's.

Although the platter of food was returned untouched the next morning, Ma Shumitra rued nothing. No one died from missing a few meals. Her son had returned home, head and heart: this was enough to bring her joy. If the daughter-in-law became pregnant during this sojourn, her cup would overflow. True, Phuleswari's nightly attire pricked her eyes—whoring it up with that gauzy see-through sari. But if her husband was so taken with whores, what could the young wife do? It was best to pluck one thorn with another.

Phuleswari was immersed in bliss. The pleasures of the flesh were new to her. The pleasure she experienced from her birds was nothing compared to this. But it was the beauteous Rongomala—the one who was more than a co-wife, the one who was Raj Chandra's true mate—who brought both joy and tears to Phuleswari. Rongomala was not a thorn between husband and wife; she blossomed like a flower between them each night they spent together. If the king did not return to Phuleswari's bedchamber—all would turn to dust.

It didn't take long. On the fifth day, when afternoon shadows lengthened and Phuleswari began her daily ritual to prepare for the king's nightly visit, Roma stepped out of the Nor house to deliver a missive from Rongomala.

Eight

Dewdrops cannot dampen earth, not until it rains,
The heart is not sated with news until the eyes behold the beloved.

Raj Chandra's eyes were stuck to the sheet of cotton-pulp paper. He was quite taken with this couplet from Rongi's letter. He read it again and again, and smiled to himself. He hadn't even noticed when Roma, her sari clamped to her lips to staunch her laughter, had vanished. His white steed was haltered nearby, stamping his hooves. The horse couldn't wait to go to the Nor house. Although he didn't understand the letter, he could read his master's mind. Annoyed, Raj Chandra raised his eyes. The sun changed course behind the ruined walls of the abandoned pleasure house, which was once used by Rajendra Narayan. Summer days never seemed to end. The heat was intense. It was just him and his horse in the overgrown courtyard of the former pleasure house. Since Roma had disappeared, there was no point in sweating over writing a response. He might as well just show up for his pretty one.

Golap Raiya was still in a pillory in the palace dungeon. Today was the fourth day that he was paying penance for his sister's insolence. Although every line of Rongomala's letter was filled with yearning at her lover's absence, although there was not the slightest hint of Golap Raiya's imprisonment, Raj Chandra knew quite well that she would make his life hell, nagging and arguing about it as soon as he set foot in the Nor house. There were very few who were not afraid of Rongomala's tongue. Yet this missive, so permeated with sweetness, was not to be discarded so lightly. Raj Chandra was now stuck between the sweet and the bitter. Now only if Ram Bharari could exercise his brain and solve this dilemma.

It was past midnight when he finally got Golap Raiya released from the dungeon. Rajendra Narayan would do anything for money—once the son of Atmaram Nor had been caught, he couldn't possibly be let out without paying some, even if a little, of his defaulted taxes. Raj Chandra went to a lot of trouble to secretly procure money from the treasury with one hand, and then offer it to his uncle with the other. Chanda Bir was standing right beside them. As the old man counted the money, Chanda sneered, 'Master, why bother to count the money from the big chest so many times? Just close your eyes and put it back where it belongs.'

The audacity of that uppity fellow! Raj Chandra burned inside. But this wasn't the time to embroil himself in fights. Otherwise he would have taken on Chanda Bir. He kept his mouth shut and exited the courthouse. His white horse stood ready at the gate. There was no sign of Golap Raiya anywhere. He had taken off for the Rajganj marketplace as soon as he was released. It was more the lack of booze than the crush of the pillory that had bothered him during his incarceration.

Rongomala awaited Raj Chandra like a queen, dazzling her surroundings with the light of her beauty, as if she wasn't at all interested in her brother's fate. The arrangements to feed Raj Chandra Chowdhury were as regal and pleasing as Rongomala's appearance. Durga touched his feet in obeisance as soon as she saw him enter, and left Rongi's chamber. Rongomala spread the *dastarkhan* tautly over the lush carpet to lay out the food. At a single stroke, both mistress and maid had turned beautifully obedient. Niceness never yielded results. Raj Chandra washed up in scented water. He rinsed out his mouth in the metal washbasin. In front of him waited mounds of food. Nearby sat a freshly dressed silver hookah on a tripod. Paans were arrayed on an enamelled plate. The colourful paintings depicting different stages of Radha and Krishna's love had been concealing their faces; now they had come out of hiding to assuage Raj Chandra's anger. Raj Chandra settled himself comfortably and began to eat. His stomach burned with hunger. Ever since he had received Rongomala's letter, he had been so busy trying to finagle the money to get Golap released, buttering up the treasurer and the rent collector, he hadn't even had the chance to have his afternoon tea.

Rongomala fanned him with a palm-leaf fan and watched him eat. For four days straight, her brother had lain in the dungeon without food or water. Rongi herself had been unable to eat anything. She had made a bundle of flattened rice and puffed rice and sent it to the dungeon with Durga. Durga had returned weeping: far from being able to give Golap the food, she had had to flee when the guards at the entrance had poked her in the ass with their staffs. Rongomala had seen the true face of her father and brother when they had married her off to Ram Goitya. The past years had shown her the face of the rest of the world. She had seen it all. The poor were corrupted because of their poverty. And the zamindars were simply made of stone. They were ready to murder for the slightest wound to their pride. Love and affection weren't worth a dime. Raj Chandra Chowdhury might have no qualms in accepting the rice she cooked and served with her own hands, but still, she would forever remain a low-caste woman, in every cell of her being.

The Nors were dancers. Her father had told her that once the Nors had been considered high-caste. They had been praised to the heavens, for their singing and dancing pleased the gods. Once, a master Nor visited Lord Indra's court. He was dancing and singing while beating his drum. Indra, the king of gods, trembled in rapture. His courtiers were mesmerised. The Nor stopped for a drink of water and sipped with his drum still strapped to his body.

The drumhead was made of cow hide. That did it for them all—that one transgression brought all the Nors down. Indra wrinkled his nose: oh, this Nor, he was fallen! Even Rongomala's beauty could not conceal that original sin. Like the blemishes of the moon, that caste-sin reared its head again and again. Who could avert what the gods had ordained!

She who made her bed in the ocean, what fear had she of the morning dew? Rongomala picked up little tidbits and served Raj Chandra herself. Like a baby bird, she opened her lips and accepted chewed bits of food from Raj Chandra's tongue. In a little while, the two of them would sit on her bed, and while they chewed paan and smoked tobacco, they would engage in lovemaking. There was no way to move through this life without forgiveness.

I sought and found I had none
You, my moon, the only one.

Whether Raj Chandra Chowdhury had understood these lines from Rongomala's letter or not, they were true. If he, the one through whose power she was holding onto her father's house, abandoned her, her body would become fodder for all the vultures out there. Yet Raj Chandra's love seemed now to be an ebbing tide. His heart roamed the sewers and the jungles. What use was a beautiful topknot if it was coiled with false hair!

When Raj Chandra turned to face her at daybreak, Rongomala asked him for a favour: she wanted to go on a pilgrimage. It was clear that she was speaking from her heart. She had spent her sleepless night thinking about this, and now she had decided. Her face looked puffy, her eyes pleading. She hadn't thought, however, that she would get him to agree so easily. As an advance reward, she pulled Raj Chandra close. Although her lover was in a hurry to get home, he was quick to respond. The room was filled with the pallid light of early dawn. They could hear people alongside chirping birds. They didn't have much time. Rongi quickly pulled down the blinds, disrobed and returned to bed. Her gestures and movements changed every moment. Every other minute, her body spoke a new language. There was no way to separate her desire for a pilgrimage from her desire for love. Such was the Nor girl's skill in the art of dalliance.

Although Raj Chandra did not exactly promise her the pilgrimage, he nodded on the spur of the moment. Rongi needed to be reined in. She was doped to her gills with opium day and night. Raj Chandra was no longer willing to watch her do the *khemta*-dance like any other drunk nautch girl. Once she turned towards faith, all her bad habits would fall away like dirt. Other than Raj Chandra, no other man, not even that upcountry *khotta*[3] Chullu, would be able to go near her. Chullu Singh was walking around with a long face ever since he had been beaten up by Ram Bharari. Last night he had barely saluted when Raj Chandra arrived, and had stood at the entrance like a plank of wood. The tiny guardroom at the outer gate was as far as he was allowed in—if he wanted to keep his job. What else could Raj Chandra have done! It wasn't so easy to find an African eunuch, especially in these days of penury. And since the subject of money had come up, how was Raj Chandra supposed to fund this pilgrimage? Was he to go out with a begging bowl? Atmaram had been a Krishna-follower, so his daughter was probably hoping to visit Mathura-Brindaban. He might just leave it all to the augur. That might be easier. With the barrel of a gun pointed at his chest, the priest's finger would quite easily point eastwards instead of west. There was only one pilgrimage site in the east—Mount Chandranath at Shitakundo.

The first obstacle came from Ram Bharari. When Ram heard of the pilgrimage idea, he couldn't decide whether to laugh or cry. The devil quoting scripture—here was a whore yearning for a

---

[3] A derogatory word for people from certain regions, like Bihar

pilgrimage. Who had ever heard of such a thing! But all he said aloud was, 'Hujoor, why would you want to spend all that money for nothing? First, reclaim your zamindari; then when you're old, you can start thinking of pilgrimages and such.'

This was the problem with illiterate folks. He didn't understand that to Raj Chandra money was like dirt. It had to be thrown here and there to keep his own hands clean. However, in order to keep his hands clean, he needed to get them on some money in the first place. His monthly allowance from the treasury barely lasted a week. He was fed up with having to scrimp and cajole to make it through. If he asked for a fair share of his inheritance, it would lead to war. But war required preparation. His other choice was to steal from the treasury. But thieving for a holy act did not seem to be a nice thing to do.

Of course, just like he had a wife in his house, he had caskets full of her jewellery. So, although he had had to beg before his uncle Rajendra when he repaired the Nor house, he had not had to ask anyone for the tokens of his esteem that he regularly presented to Rongi. The Nor house was no longer what it used to be. And the old fool guarding the treasury no longer had the chance to hand him fifty silver coins and record five hundred. He was sitting there sucking his thumb. It was his illiterate crony, Ram Bharari, who had given him the idea. He had also advised Raj Chandra that instead of giving all of Phuleswari's jewellery to Rongi at one go, he should take it from the casket one at a time and hand it over one at a time. This way, he could keep both his wife and his mistress under his thumb. Because Raj Chandra's real conflict was waiting ahead—with his uncle Rajendra. Why muddy the water needlessly before that showdown?

Still, it made no sense to pay attention to Ram Bharari's advice and wait until he was nearing death before going on a pilgrimage. All expenses for the trip would be taken care of somehow; his expenses always were. But slowly. Let his knee heal first.

Baishakh was almost gone, and the month of Jaistha was almost here. The mango and jackfruit season would be over in a flash. Before the hard heat of summer dissipated, the rains would arrive, turning everything into mud and sludge. During those days, it was hard to even walk down a regular road; trying to climb up eight thousand wobbly steps to visit the mountaintop temple was out of the question. That was not something this wretch was willing to do. There was a saying that the life of the faithful was like that of the climbing perch fish—hard to get rid of. If he had been one of the faithful, that would have been one thing. Only because of Rongi he was being forced to undertake this pilgrimage before it was his time. It would be fine if he just looked for an auspicious day for the journey, and then announced it at some point. All of that would take at least six months. Even if his pretty girl was patient, could Raj Chandra Chowdhury himself accept the delay? He disliked having to wait for anything.

Nine

Raj Chandra's knee healed. Shyampriya the vaishnavi had been evicted from Shimul Tol. She had caused no apparent trouble. But she had already known that her gossip-mongering would have consequences. She had grabbed her cat and fled one evening before Ram Bharari had shown up with five goons. Her cat Chandramukhi wailed and wept in her stead until they reached the dock. The vaishnavi headed for Naba Dwip on a dinghy meant for pilgrims. At her age, it would be a miracle if she reached. The hardship during the journey might kill her off. Raj Chandra was also done with being cautious with Rongi. He had abandoned his brazen nature and was walking the straight and narrow as far as Rongi was concerned. The few nights in between, when he had shared Phuleswari Rai's bed were throwaway memories—they didn't even feature in his thoughts. Raj Chandra always needed something to keep him busy; he always had to have something he could chew on to pass the time. His biggest annoyance right now was that the day of departure for their pilgrimage wasn't arriving fast enough.

The months of Baishakh and Jaistha had passed by. Since then the rains had not let up at all. This year was bad. Several regions were already waterlogged. Even to visit Rongi he had to organise boats and boatmen before he could reach the dock adjacent to her house. As if he was a young bride returning to her husband after visiting her father's house—the whole neighbourhood was alerted to his visits. The entire situation annoyed him. If he couldn't whip his horse and gallop to his love amid the shadows of night, what was the point in having a mistress? He'd much rather sit at home like a woman and play cowries or chew on *chaal-bhaja*.

On one such day, Ma Shumitra showed up at the outer chamber without prior notice. She sat beside her son, chattering about this and that. If one did not know how to swim, one could drown even in the pond belonging to one's father. No matter how cunning Rajendra was, if Raj Chandra did not give up, if he just continued to show up at court, someday it would yield results—there would be no need to beg or cajole for them to survive. Did people remain the same throughout a lifetime? People changed, grew different at different ages. When the number of mouths to be fed in a household grew, the household itself grew hungrier. She had to think of the future. The royal lineage of Shindurkait had long been of good repute. The year of her marriage, Shumitra Devi had heard from her own mother-in-law about Bishwambhar Sur, the king of Mithila, the first king of Bhulua, the founding father of the line of the Chowdhurys.

People from one land ended up in another. War had been raging everywhere when the jaban-Muslims began their reign. If the faith could not be protected, what was the point of anything? Even a throne of gold seemed to be made of thorns. Bishwambhar Sur had gathered his men and gone on a pilgrimage by boat. His destination was Mount Chandranath at Shitakundo. It was during the return journey that trouble began. In that vast river blanketed in dense fog, the boat's crew couldn't tell where there were hidden peaks or where there lay deep water. Day after day they searched and drifted directionless until finally they berthed at a deserted island. That night Bishwambhar Sur had a dream: Goddess Barahi appeared in front of him and said, *I have been submerged in the deep waters beneath your boat for many years now. Raise me up. Invoke my presence and make offerings. There is no need for you to return to that Muslim kingdom. You will be king of this deserted land. This river will be silted over. A harvest, like gold, will grow.*

The next day, Bishwambhar Sur's crew carried out all the instructions the goddess had given him. But in the fog, they made one mistake. Instead of sacrificing the goat with the goddess facing eastwards, they had her facing westwards. When the fog lifted, the men cried out, '*Bhul hua! Bhul hua!*'—A mistake! A mistake! And since then, Bishwambhar Sur's kingdom came to be known as Bhulua.

Raj Chandra knew this story. He had visited Goddess Barahi's temple at Amishapara many times with his mother, swaying inside her palanquin. His ears had been ready to fall off from hearing this story so many times during their return trip. Here was that same story, again, after so many years! There had to be some reason. Soon the reason became clear. Today, as in his childhood, his mother was telling him the same story because she was anxious—Raj Chandra was the fruit of the same line that had once settled this land; his kin were all looking to him. If he brought shame to his lineage, where would his widowed mother hide her face?

Aha! Behind his mother's storytelling lay the desire to shackle the son! Raj Chandra's skin crawled in anger. But he couldn't just get up and leave. He sat there, squirming like an eel and cracking his knuckles. Suddenly, when he heard of Phuleswari's pregnancy, his hands went numb. He felt dizzy. Although other men of Raj Chandra's age had already fathered many a child, probably none of these sons or daughters were direct results of the amulets their wives wore on their arms or the blessed water they had consumed. Actual intercourse was required for this to happen.

Raj Chandra began sweating. He had no memory of intercourse with Phuleswari. And there sat Ma Shumitra, babbling in joy. Kalitara had made all that dried mango, her back burning under the summer sun—well, she had not even been able to retrieve the dried fruit. Phuleswari had gobbled it all, straight from the banana leaves on which they were spread out in the sun. Every summer the tamarind was cut into jars meant to last the whole year. Heera had reported that all those jars now stood empty. Ma Shumitra's daughter-in-law was also eating pickled elephant-apples and *koromcha* by the bowl. To top it all, Phuleswari had stolen the jar of chunky amchoor that Mother Shumitra kept in her room. Not once had the girl considered that this was the only thing the widowed, old mother-in-law ate with her meagre diet of lentils and rice. All women become pregnant in their lifetimes, but this behaviour was too much!

Raj Chandra stared at his mother goggle-eyed. It was hard to tell whether she was praising or castigating. Her tone changed as she stood up to leave. Her face darkened, and her voice was tinged with a forced sadness. Ma Shumitra's daughter-in-law was newly pregnant; she couldn't hold any food in. Even the tamarind that she gobbled up was vomited out whole, complete with seeds. But her son was so cold-hearted that the poor girl did not even get to see her husband at day's end. While Ma Shumitra stood in the doorway, bellyaching, her son's brain was aflame. Another few moments and he would explode like a cannonball.

There were still a couple of hours before evening descended. The sky was overcast. As soon as his mother left, Raj Chandra ordered Jugindor to bring him a glass as he settled down with his liquor. It had long been his habit to take his drink solitary. He dragged on his hookah between sips. His eyes would change colour even before he began his second glass; he was suffused by the impulse to shoot off into the skies like a firework. Yet today it was as if this confusion over the when and whether of intercourse with his wife had him stuck to the ground—even four glasses of alcohol could not make him fly. Perhaps marijuana would help. Jugindor was watching the drama from behind the door. He dressed the hookah with ganja at Raj Chandra's order. Raj

Chandra pulled deeply on the hookah with his eyes closed. At times it felt as if he was ascending to heaven in his earthly body as he inhaled. He might truly have ascended, except a spark from the hookah spattered onto his lap and he jumped up, his trance broken. He could no longer keep still on the rug. Outside, it was drizzling, accompanied by sudden gusts of wind. Before Jugindor could open an umbrella over his head, Raj Chandra lurched his way into the darkness.

❖

Heera was sitting on the bed doing Phuleswari's hair. Phuleswari had been spending her days in bed, and her hair was tangled into knots. The teeth of the comb were pulling her hair out in clumps. Heera dipped her fingers in a bowl of oil before running them through Phuleswari's hair, trying to tease the strands apart. But every time she tried the comb, Phuleswari moaned in pain. Black Moon screeched, '*Bandi! Bandi!*' at Heera from his perch by the bed.

Phuleswari had transferred Black Moon to her bedside ever since she had begun feeling sick. She felt more fondness for her birds than she did for her servants and slaves. Heera slathered oil on her palm and rubbed it roughly on Phuleswari's scalp. The friction between hair and oil heated her head. Once Phuleswari fell asleep, Heera would take the mynah and settle his perch outside. Then she would lay out her pallet on the floor by Phuleswari's bed. This was the routine these days.

Phuleswari Rai's hair was not done when the mynah began screeching *'Rat-chandra, Rrrat-chandra'*. Phuleswari flinched. Heera glanced at the door. The latch was lowered. No one would fault her for thinking it was a cat or a dog fumbling at the door, trying to push it open. Heera dropped the comb and rushed to the door when she spotted the red border of the dhoti. Raj Chandra was so far gone, he was incapable of even opening a door. Sopping wet, teeth chattering, he kneeled at the threshold. He tried to stand up but weaved sideways and fell again. Heera held the door wide open. A few moments passed before their lord and master entered, lurching, barely managing to take each step. He reached the bed before toppling over.

When he awoke in the morning, Raj Chandra recalled that he had not resolved the issue which had brought him to Phuleswari's chamber. He had snored like a water buffalo all night, and that too beside a woman who, without copulation with her husband, now carried a child in her womb. Weak and unwell, Phuleswari was still asleep. When she was rudely awakened by her husband shoving her, she felt sudden nausea, as if her very innards were pushing their way out. She tried to climb down from the high bedstead and fell onto the cement floor. Instead of helping her up, Raj Chandra let loose a string of curses and oaths, as if once the husband suspected perfidy, the wife lost her right to live. On the left panel of the doorway, the mynah screeched and jumped, flapping its wings, 'No more! No more!'

What was going on! Ma Shumitra rushed into the room with Heera. Behind her streamed an unbroken line of water. Her son was taking such good care of his pregnant wife that she hadn't even had time to wring out her sari after bathing. All her advice yesterday was having the opposite effect. Who knew what kind of man Bishwambhar Sur had been! Ma Shumitra couldn't fathom it. God had gifted her son neither wits nor judgement, but spirit and brawn in good measure. Full of flaws, but none of the virtues. How could he evade the curse of his blood?

While Heera helped Phuleswari from the floor and tried to clean her up, Ma Shumitra set aside all sense of propriety and shame and sat down to face her son's allegations. She had many witnesses at hand to affirm that Raj Chandra had indeed had intercourse with his wife for four successive nights following the evening of the Kal Baishakhi storm. Phuleswari had stopped menstruating in the month of Baishakh. There were two days left before Jaistha would roll into Ashaar; Phuleswari had been with child a full ten weeks.

The ruckus resolved Raj Chandra's doubts about intercourse. But it was Phuleswari who paid dearly for his suspicions. At three months, she lost the child; the blood flowed out of her without pause. Heera could barely keep pace changing the bedclothes and washing her clothing. Phuleswari had grown so pale her skin looked like chalk. Heera fed her hornbill fat from tiny clay bowls, and fresh pigeon blood. Amulets and talismans covered her body. The physician from Lamchor sent by Kali Charan Guha had returned. It was a battle between Yama and human strength. Old wives' remedies and brews were their only hope now. Ma Shumitra came to sit at Phuleswari's bedside after she was done with her daily ablutions, and her prayers and offerings to the gods, careful not to touch Phuleswari in this state of impurity.

Although it looked as if the blood flowed again under the skin of the young queen, any hopes of an heir were gone. Her fall from that high bedstead had ruptured a vein. The poor thing could no longer sink her roots into this household. No matter what wealth her father commanded, as a barren wife, Phuleswari would have to take second place once her husband brought home another queen. She would be subjected to taunts and harsh words at every turn. Still, how could Ma Shumitra not arrange another bride for her son! If she didn't, it would be Rajendra's line that would grow heftier, leaning upon that child Prafulla Kumar. Pratap Narayan's lineage would be destroyed before it was barely a seedling. Nothing in this world was achieved without effort. If the father wasted his days in the gutter, once the son attained majority, he would get to work, reclaiming the zamindari. But everything would come to pass only if Ma Shumitra managed to coax Raj Chandra to sit once again on the wedding *piri*. Why should they worry? There were examples, even among the very forefathers of the Chowdhury dynasty, of enjoying a kept woman outside the house while marrying many times. However, the thick purse of the Lamchor in-laws and an unworldly girl like Phuleswari had been a match made in heaven. Such a perfect fit was not easily found. Right now, Mother Shumitra had unfettered access to all the money and goods of Lamchor. But once a co-wife to his daughter arrived in the household, what father would be eager to send money and gifts anymore?

This dilemma rent her asunder. The daughter-in-law was marked a loss the minute she miscarried. But what of Mother Shumitra herself? Who could evade destiny? ... The queen mother exited Phuleswari's room with a sigh.

The mother-in-law had washed her hands of Phuleswari Rai. It was only Heera, the servant, who continued to tend to her. She rushed around ceaselessly, trying to gather anything and everything anyone suggested, even if the suggestion involved sourcing tiger's milk. One day she even dared to smuggle in a bearded mullah to the inner quarters, disguising him as a woman. He was to bestow blessed water on Phuleswari Rai. He chanted his Muslim mantras ferociously as he blessed the water, making Heera's inner soul tremble. She shuttered all the doors and windows with haste. Phuleswari's eyes were still closed. For two days, she had lain with her jaws clenched shut, unconscious. Until her lips parted enough to dribble some water in, the Mullah sat at the head of the Hindu girl, chanting:

The Prophet visits this girl's house
The girl suffers childbed fever
Rise, girl, cleanse yourself
Say your fazr prayers
La Ilaha Illallah, illness be gone.

The human hand carried out God's will. It is difficult to say how the illness was cured. Whether it was the blessed water or the constantly chanted mantra, Phuleswari Rai blinked her eyes open on the second day. She even smiled when Black Moon mimicked the mullah from his perch and sang out *La Ilaha*. Alongside the blessed water, Heera continued with all other remedies and interventions. She brought a mortar and pestle from the three-legged stand beside the bed. She crushed the medicine with honey, and dipping the tip of her finger in it, fed it to her patient smear by smear. She dripped milk from a seashell through Phuleswari's barely parted lips. Black Moon sat overhead, chattering day and night. A barn owl flapped at the blinds at night by rote. As if it was another drug for the sufferer, Phuleswari slumbered deeply as long as the owl sat at the window, gazing at her with glowing eyes.

Triumphing against all ill will, the glow of health returned to Phuleswari day by day. Her skin-and-bone limbs began to accrue flesh. But with this improvement, a new symptom manifested—heartrending tears for some reason or none. There was no answer to the question of why she was weeping or what it was she wanted. It was as if she hadn't been able to weep earlier because she had no strength; now that she could, she would. Only once did she ask—when was her *shaddh*, the day when she, as a mother-to-be, would be indulged by all in food and gifts and blessings? Heera could find no words. She covered her eyes with her sari-end and left. She had made so many plans: during the shaddh, she would adorn Phuleswari in eight kinds of jewels and drape her in a gold-embroidered red *cheli* sari. She would place Phuleswari's dainty feet, painted crimson with alta, upon a stool, and everyone would prostrate themselves at those feet. Slaves and servants would compete to get to her first. Khhantamoni's flat face would finally be flattened forever. If they had been impressed by the wedding, the Babupur folks would be slack-jawed at the pomp of Lamchor's gifts and offerings for their pregnant daughter.

But God had not destined such joy for her.

In the beginning, Heera would run to Ma Shumitra when Phuleswari wept. And Ma Shumitra would come as soon as she was called. Now the queen mother grew annoyed if Heera tried to bring her to Phuleswari. She had enough troubles of her own. She could barely keep her mind on her devotions to God. She spent all day in the pond, immersed to her neck. The only thing she hadn't done was clasp Raj Chandra's feet and beg. Other than that, she had done everything she could. Raj Chandra had not agreed to a second marriage. Instead, he was going off on a pilgrimage with his whore in tow. Even if the common people accepted such behaviour, would the gods accept it? Ma Shumitra's skin crawled in fear of their divine wrath.

Ten

The news of Raj Chandra and Rongomala's pilgrimage spread far and wide. Heera was stunned when she heard the news from Karim Sheikh's daughter Ayna—Heera was a resident of the palace's inner wing and yet she knew none of this! She was throwing away her life watching over Phuleswari's madness. Did she have the time anymore to keep her eyes and ears alert?

Ayna felt like a fool as Heera flailed about. She wanted to kick herself. This was not what she had come here to talk about.

Two nights ago, Ayna's husband, Adam Ali, had entered the house by cutting through the thatched wall. Fumbling in the dark, he had lit a lamp and held it above the sleeping Amena's face. The moaning and wailing of the mute young girl had disrupted the sleep of the whole neighbourhood. Ayna had slapped the lamp out and pulled her still-asleep son Najar Ali to her heart. Her man should have fled through the opening he had made in the wall, but he didn't. He stood right at her head like a block of stone, with a meagre loincloth wrapped around his waist and stinking like a buffalo. You reap what you sow. He might have died from the beating the gathered mob gave him in the dark, but Ayna and Amena's screams made Somiron Bibi bring out a lamp. Adam Ali had already been administered a round of beating by then and was being shoved towards the yard. Somiron Bibi began to lament, '*Yah Allah*, who are they beating? This naked thief is Najar Ali's father!' Karim Sheikh dropped the stick he had been wielding. The other men stood back as well. Adam Ali scrambled to his mother-in-law's feet. 'You've been a mother to me. Save me!' His nose was broken and bleeding. The man who had returned was not the man who had left—and he returned as if he was a thief! Their family had been humiliated in front of the neighbourhood. When the neighbours returned to their own homes, Karim Sheikh helped his son-in-law up from the ground and then hit him with his shoe. Even that did not lessen his rage. Najar Ali was crying, his mother was crying, Somiron Bibi was crying—as if the entire house was a Karbala in itself. Amid all this, Karim Sheikh shoved Adam Ali and beat him as if he were a dog, before finally dumping him outside the village.

'Your father's done the right thing getting rid of that nuisance. Why do you weep?' Heera tried to shrug off Ayna. Ayna was sticking to her like a leech. Heera's belly was bursting with the news of Raj Chandra's pilgrimage. She had to tell Ma Shumitra as soon as she could.

'Sister! My heart tells me I should drink poison and die. Najar Ali's father is waiting for me by the murtaq reeds on the lakeshore.' At Ayna's words, Heera turned and looked at her. What a fuss! If this loin-clothed man decided to climb out of the clump of murtaq on the bank, there would be such a commotion in the palace. They had enough of their own troubles to deal with. Heera forgot about her bath and, grabbing her sari and other things from the lakeshore, ran homewards. Ayna ran behind her. They latched the back entrance to the palace grounds, and sat under a tree, resting their cheeks in their hands. This was a safe spot.

Ayna wept and laughed at once as she spoke. Since that night, she had given up all hope for Najar Ali's father. The last two days she had eaten and drunk nothing in sheer sorrow. This morning she had visited the pond for some water. As she climbed up the side of the pond, balancing her full water pot against her waist, she had felt someone tug at her belly-chain. It was Najar Ali's father. He clapped her mouth shut and pulled her down to the scrub of murtaq. The man was stone-hearted; he enjoyed his wife right there in the mud and the sludge. Then he talked and talked the rest of the afternoon, now and then touching her hands and feet. If Somiron Bibi hadn't started shouting Ayna's name, husband and wife would probably still be lying together in the middle of the reeds.

It was fate. Otherwise, here was a man bound to his wife's sari, a man who had, before he set sail, named his son Najar Ali while he was still in the womb—how did such a man fall prey to the devices of a foreign witch?

The witch slept all day, and in the evening, after plastering her face with sandalwood paste, she went out to make her rounds. She wrapped a *khami*-skirt of two and a half arms' length around her and wore a floral bodice that didn't leave much to the imagination. Her hair was cut into short bangs, and she tucked a kadam flower behind her ear. When she wept, her tears fell like pearls. Instead of fresh fish from the sea, she ate *ngappi*, fermented fish. Every single thing she did was topsy-turvy.

Adam Ali and his crew had finished their work. They had unloaded tons and tons of paddy and areca nuts from the merchant ship on to the dock. It was time to make haste for the journey back home. The crew was out purchasing all the fancy things their wives and children had desired. It was hard to walk the streets. Hundreds of women, like shoals of fingerlings, were crammed into the alleys and byways of the marketplace. All the men were indoors, engaged in cooking and cleaning. Adam Ali stood to the side, watching the spectacle of the marketplace. When the witch saw him by himself, she disguised herself as a beauteous maiden and plucked him with a magical gesture of her hand. They took a forest path to a huge wooden house that stood by some hillocks. The only other person there was an old crone, the witch's nanny.

When she heard the girl call, the crone descended to the wooden porch, carrying a candle as thick as a tree trunk. In between the porch and the witch, there was a sliver of a garden. On this side of the garden, behind the golden-dodder fence, Adam Ali stood with his toes digging into the earth. He was still wondering whether he should enter the house or flee to his ship. The young woman turned around when she was midway across the garden and made the same magical gesture with her hand. In the blink of an eye, Adam Ali flew to Ayi-Ma, the crone, and his arm was around her waist. The monstrous laughter of the snaggletoothed crone reverberated around the hills. The doves took wing from their nests in the crossbeams of the house. Adam Ali had lost control of his senses. Like a wooden puppet he stood inside the wooden house. Three days later, in accordance with local custom, by virtue of eating from the same platter for three consecutive days and sharing the same bed for three consecutive nights, Adam Ali and the crone's granddaughter Ethin became man and wife.

The next few days, he felt like he was in heaven; he had completely forgotten this world. Such joy and such delight! He had never dreamed of anything even close. At dawn, the two of them walked amid flowers, clasping each other's hands, and chased butterflies. In the afternoon, they bathed in the sea, and when one of them dived, the other broke through the water like a dolphin. In the evenings, he pressed his lips to the lips of this sylph and drank her honey. As if Adam Ali was the prince of his homeland Sudharam and the witch girl, a southern princess.

Adam Ali, the prince, was clad in clothing from the old crone's chest. The princess didn't bother with dressing up. She danced with wildflowers in her hair. In his princely attire, Adam Ali sat atop a hillock by the waterfall and watched her. Then, gradually, those days of happiness came to an end. He was awoken one morning by the crone hollering. Ethin was not in his bed. He himself was buck naked. The princely clothes he had laid by his head before falling asleep were gone. The crone turned everything in the house upside down. Her wails echoed through the neighbourhood as she struck her forehead again and again like a madwoman. She tried to trick him into believing her various explanations—her best friend was on her deathbed and Ethin had to go in a palanquin to take some medicine to her, and she left at daybreak, and she couldn't see well in the darkness so she took his clothes instead of her own, and she'd be back in a moment.

Adam Ali paid no attention. Whoever had removed his princely clothes had also removed the effects of her witchcraft. Suddenly he regained his clear sight. *Yah Allah*! Didn't he have a wife back home? Hadn't his bonny child started crawling by now? Not a moment more would he tarry in this witch's abode! He walked beyond the golden-dodder fence and onto the road. The vines and leaves of the hills trembled at the old nanny's weeping. The waterfall had stopped flowing. The birds mourned.

Heera exhaled slowly. Who knew what happened after that to Ethin, the girl from the southern lands. Such was the way of the world.

Bring the shovel, dig a hole
what price tears, what price yowl.

If there was shadow at one end, the sun rose in the other. The most important thing was that Ayna's lost husband had returned home. If Heera had been married off at the right time, she would have had a child about Ayna's age. Phuleswari's mother and Heera, both had conceived at the same time, give or take a week. The fruit of Heera's womb had been ripped out through the administration of red oleander. And in due time, Phuleswari had arrived, lighting up the whole house. Kali Charan Guha's ventures with his women had yielded different fruits.

Why was Karim Sheikh such a stone of a man? He had made Ayna take an oath by placing the Quran on her head and making her face the *qibla*, the direction in which they prayed to Allah. She had had to swear she would never see her husband's face as long as she lived. Then she had bedded her husband in the reeds by the lake. Ayna was willing to die with the burden of sin on her soul, but she wasn't willing to renounce her husband. The husband who was rending asunder heaven and earth like the woman Behula of legend, searching for his loved one …

Adam Ali was in quite a predicament when escaping from the witch's nanny; he had not a stitch on his body. The old crone was pursuing him. Ethin might return anytime in her palanquin. With a single gesture of her hand she could again transform Adam Ali into a sheep. For two days, he hid in the deep of the woods, eating fruits and roots and drinking from the waterfall. With tree bark wrapped around his waist like a loincloth, he finally reached the seashore. There were many kinds of boats anchored in the bay: sampans, dinghies, jaliyas, sloops, koshas. They sailed chanting the name of Badar, the Muslim saint to whom sailors of all faiths prayed for safe passage. No one wanted to take on this bearded lunatic clad in bark; they shooed him off. Adam Ali haunted the docks like a madman. He yelled at random people on the street. He picked garbage off the streets to eat. The thought of going home writhed in his brain like tiny cobras—biting every other moment. Their venom dreadlocked his matted hair and beard. Nobody took pity on mad old Adam Ali; nobody offered to take him aboard their boat to sail the bay for free. The new shirt he had begged off a foreign merchant had ripped, and the shreds stuck to his skin. Then he discovered ten traders who had gone bankrupt and were planning to cut down wild bamboo from the forests to build a raft. Adam Ali managed to get taken on the raft. As if theirs was the legendary raft of Behula, there was no end to their travails during the journey. They set sail with their raft, basking in the mild southbound breezes of the month of Phalgun, and they finally reached home six months later in the palm fruit-ripening heat of Bhadra.

Of the eleven travellers, only five survived the trip. They had seen strange creatures and stranger doings. On the right side of their raft stretched the shoreline, on the left was untamed sea. Occasionally they spotted uninhabited islands. Coconuts clustered ripe on the trees with no hands to pluck them. Hundreds of overripe coconuts floated on the sea. Adam Ali and his fellow travellers salvaged them with bamboo poles and broke them open. That was their food and drink. The real travails began when they had travelled farther: thirst and hunger. The islands were sandy wastes with no trees or grass. Crocodiles incubated their eggs there and hatched their babies. Gigantic tigers swam from one island to the next. During the dark nights, they swam onto their raft, drawn by the smell of human flesh. Two of the traders were eaten by tigers; one was dragged into the water by crocodiles. Three others convulsed to death from thirst. None of them received burial shrouds, or prayers for the dead. These men, once so familiar to the rest on the raft, travelled to an unknown eternity with the rolling waves. The rest of them were not meant to live either. Yet the ways of God were unfathomable.

Adam Ali had recounted all these sorrowful tales to his wife while in the reeds, and swayed her to his side. There was no way to make Ayna change her mind again. She was seeing her husband covered in lice, his body all skin and bone, hard like wood. But he didn't lack in passion. And this had completely seduced Ayna. She grabbed Heera's feet and pleaded with her to make it possible for the two of them to be together. But who could persuade Karim Sheikh? The vaishnavi Shyampriya, the one who acted as clandestine go-between for illicit lovers, had disappeared since the day of the Shashthi Puja. People said she had boarded a dinghy heading for the pilgrimage at Naba Dwip, but had died of cholera on the way. The only one left who could do anything was Ma Shumitra; Karim Sheikh could never disregard her words.

Eleven

Ma Shumitra hissed like a water snake as soon as she spotted Heera. This whore was always coming by to fan the flames lit by her son. A friend in need indeed! Ma Shumitra didn't even want to talk to her, let alone get into an argument. She would have dismissed Heera right away, but since the topic of conversation was not Phuleswari, she settled down to listen. She didn't stop her cursing though. Ayna wanted to live with her husband—fine, let her. Weren't the women of the royal palace keeping house with husbands who were insane, lecherous or even barbarians? Who did Karim Sheikh think he was, to be so arrogant? To want better for his daughter? A mere servant, he was trying to live better than the zamindar!

When a jubilant Heera left, Ma Shumitra sat down to lay out her plans. Raj Chandra's pilgrimage could not be prevented. Karim Sheikh had been the chief boatman of the royal pleasure boat since her husband's reign. He was trustworthy to a fault. To reach Shitakundo, the pleasure boat would have to cross both the Feni Major and Feni Minor rivers. The mouth of Feni Major was foggy and turbid; the boatman could pull off almost anything there. He could pretend to show that Nor girl gulls and push her into the hair-ripping waves—although it would be easier to simply poison her food.

Karim Sheikh sat with his gaze lowered. Such ill-considered ideas could only occur to women, especially the kind that spent their days in the lap of luxury with one foot resting on the other.

They paid his wages, however, so he couldn't say it to their faces. There was more disgust than respect in his eyes. Ma Shumitra sat in her chair, swinging her bare feet; he watched as they appeared and disappeared from his view. Although her body was as slender as a bamboo sapling, her ankles were as thick as cudgels. Her skin was as crinkled and pale as cowries. If she stopped moving, he could easily mistake her feet as belonging to a drowned corpse. Every time Ma Shumitra summoned him, Karim Sheikh arrived to find her sitting in the same way on this chair, swinging her bare feet back and forth. The only difference this time was that Karim Sheikh was not standing in the doorway, gripping the door panel. She had called him into her chamber under the pretext of seeking advice, and made him sit on this embroidered seat. He had been served a platter of *pera*, *sandesh* and puffed rice. That is how he had come to examine her feet so closely. Now his head was buzzing with conjectures about how she walked, her mannerisms; oddly, Karim Sheikh had never actually seen Ma Shumitra walk.

The woman who stomps, and rolls her eyes—when she is the wife,
The husband will die years before he's used up the span of his life.

Pratap Narayan had died with many years of his life unused. Early thirties were nowhere near a full lifetime for a zamindar. Now the respect that the young widow had gained because of the early grey in her hair would be squandered because of her rash behaviour. Murder was murder—even that of a whore's. Ma Shumitra's whispers were like the dirt on Karim Sheikh's skin. He would dust them off as soon as he left. But what hazard had his miserable daughter created for him? She had come to the palace to snivel against her own father! Even if Adam Ali wasn't a fraud, he was mad. He had been driven mad when he supped on the hawk meat prepared by those Burmese witches. If Ayna wanted to play house with him, let her. She would no longer be allowed anywhere near her father's house. Karim Sheikh was a man of his word.

Ma Shumitra knew this as well. Although Karim Sheikh had not actually agreed to her idea of throwing Rongomala into the river, she accepted his silence as consent. When the boatman asked her permission to leave, she, Pratap Narayan's widow, felt as if she were holding the moon in her palm. All the slaves and servants were summoned to her chamber. They were assigned their tasks depending on what was appropriate for their castes. She didn't have that much time. She ordered all the things Raj Chandra loved to eat, as well as things he didn't like that much. Her son was embarking upon a pilgrimage. His heart was turning towards faith. At such a time, a mother could not remain aloof. Ma Shumitra's forced laughter grated on Heera's ears like the late-night call of the kora bird: sad, but harsh enough to burn the heart. She stopped in the middle of stirring grated coconut into sugar syrup with a spatula. She could make no sense of Ma Shumitra's moods. What had Karim Sheikh advised her that was making her so joyful at the prospect of her son's pilgrimage? That Muslim man's insides were as twisted as a jalebi. Heera herself had unwittingly dug the canal that let in the crocodile. She should not have been so distressed over Ayna's situation. The coconut *narus* fell apart in her hands—the sugar syrup had not thickened enough. And there was Kalitara, usually clueless about everything, producing one perfect *chandrapuli* after another shaped like the full moon. Even the *poa pitha* that Bhabani and Korali were deep-frying were swelling into perfect chubbiness, just like their cheeks. The washerman's wife sat in front of a clay pot containing hot sand, in which rice popped into *khoi* like clusters of jasmine. That whore of a sweetmaker was churning out thick sandesh, her basket overflowing. Their feet barely touched the ground in their pride. Heera made the excuse of checking in on Phuleswari and left the cookhouse.

Such a hubbub throughout the household and Phuleswari Rai lay fast asleep. All those birds that used to be her heart's love—she barely even asked anymore whether they had been fed. Starvation had turned Phuleswari into a wrinkled raisin. Her skin was no longer smooth and silky like an arum leaf. Heera brought out a couple of sandesh from beneath her sari-end. Phuleswari stuffed both into her mouth at the same time and spat them out, the sweets spraying across the room like dabs of wet cotton. More work for Heera the slave, more annoyance. This damned girl with addled wits was just making her situation worse. While Phuleswari hid her face in her hands and slept day and night, Raj Chandra was emptying out the gold and jewels from her casket. This thievery was probably how he was funding his pilgrimage. Ma Shumitra was fanning the dishonest flames of her son's actions. She was telling all and sundry that a barren daughter-in-law wasn't worth a penny. Messenger after messenger was travelling to Lamchor carrying her missives. She wanted to bleed Phuleswari Rai's father dry and then dump the girl back in her father's house as soon as she could. A strange world, this, where a good person could turn evil in a matter of moments. If only she knew how to write, Heera would have sent her own message to Kali Charan Guha. Arthritis had him bedridden these days. Cinnabar fumes and other nostrums were being applied day and night. Neither of Phuleswari's stepbrothers had turned out well. The minute the salt merchant breathed his last, Phuleswari would lose her right to her husband's household as well as her father's.

When she thought of what lay in store for Phuleswari, Heera couldn't help but think of her own fate. Like an ox and its yoke, the two of them were headed down the same path. How could Heera the slave unyoke herself and flee? It had been years since Panna the whore had left this world in a final opium daze. Jaggeswari's house had been overrun by rats and bats. The river had eaten away a part of the house. Heera had been heartbroken when she was robbed of the chance to see that old mangrove tree one last time. Jaggeswari used to clasp the low-hanging mangrove branches and gaze unblinking at the other shore, her white hair streaming in the gusty river breeze. Mangrove blossoms fell at her feet.

So much water had flown through the Meghna river since her youth; yet somewhere across the river, who knew where, lay Jaggeswari's home. As if the stone-hued mansion behind her, paid for by her blood and her sighs, where her own daughter and eight other young girls brought in undesirable men, where day and night there was cursing and brawling—as if all that was merely a dream. That is what Heera felt when she heard her grandmother talk to herself, her bare feet blanketed in mangrove flowers. Like her grandmother, Heera too had decided that home was an unknown village somewhere beyond the enormous waves, where her great-grandmother waited cheek in hand for her to show up. Great-grandmother wore a white sari. Behind her stood a broken gate, unrepaired since the pirate attack due to lack of money.

The whore Panna was quite aware of what transpired in her daughter's heart. After Jaggeswari's death, she conspired with her pimp. The mansion already felt like a haunted house. The young girls had all disappeared in pursuit of their own fortunes. Panna stayed on in that haunted mansion with her daughter and her pimp. Even the cracks in the stonework whispered to them, humming into the very air. One day, Panna tricked Heera into dressing up and climbing into a boat headed for 'home'. The tiny dinghy hugged the riverbank as it sailed, the oars slapping into the water. Heera sat at the prow. To her right lay a hair-thin line of earth, beyond the great waves, where she believed her great-grandmother awaited her return. Heera tried imagining her face. Suddenly the boat veered left. It entered a side canal, and, twirling once like a top, sped like an arrow with the rising tide. Heera lost her balance and fell into the bilge. In a second, the hairline riverbank disappeared, leaving Heera stunned. She had no reason to trust her mother. Had Jaggeswari grown daft in her old age? Ignoring her own home and forever pointing to the other side! Heera plucked a water lily with a preoccupied air. She broke open the seedpod, picking out and chewing the tiny black seeds. Once the moment of crisis had passed, Panna the whore acted calmer. She stared vacantly at her daughter. Heera had gathered herself and was sitting at the prow again, a blood-red water lily in her hand. A little gift for her great-grandmother.

The boat docked at Lamchor. It was market day. Heera, still holding on to her water lily, followed her mother as they made their way through the crush of people, sheep, ducks, chickens and other goods for sale. The sun blazed overhead. Her mother made her stand in the shade of a peepal tree and walked to a storage shed with a long veranda. She entered and exited many doors that were standing wide open. Eight men came out and they stood together talking.

Heera couldn't tell that the wholesalers and her mother were counting on their fingers and negotiating. She thought her mother was asking for directions to her great-grandmother's house. The men actually pointed eastwards while talking to her. Panna the whore bought a whole stick of sugarcane and handed half of it to Heera. She began peeling the remaining half with her teeth as they walked eastwards. There was no humble earthen cottage with a broken door at their journey's end. Instead, they stopped at an enormous tower adjacent to an enormous mansion. Stubbornly, Heera clung to a pillar at the gate—nothing would induce her to go in. Her mother beat her with the sugarcane until it broke on her back. The shreds of water lily petals lay scattered at the cement entrance like drops of blood. Heera fell on the ground, flailing her limbs. Panna, already out of breath, couldn't control her.

Suddenly two men rushed out, bellowing at the top of their voices, *rey rey rey*. Turbaned heads, earrings, red tabards and moustachios—the two men were guards. Heera grabbed an earring, ripping an earlobe, and got slapped in return. That did it for her. While she was still dazed, she was sold for a hundred silver coins. When she came to her senses, she was already locked up in a cage meant for mad dogs. Her long legs wouldn't fit in there no matter how she tried. Day and night her blue eyes brimmed with an ocean of tears. Finally, even that stopped. In the end, all that emerged from her were puppy squeaks.

Heera might very well have turned into a dog if Kali Charan Guha had not returned from his travels and released her from her cage. Her body was covered in yellow pustules like segments of a ripe jackfruit. Flies swarmed over her. In accordance with the salt merchant's instructions, an old maidservant bathed her every day in water boiled with neem leaves. She smeared sandalwood paste in a thick layer on her pustules. Three times a day, she made Heera drink glasses of milk. She spread out a soft pallet on top of a straw mattress for Heera in the slave quarters. When the year made its round, it was the same maidservant who prepared her with hair oil and kohl and sent her to Kali Charan's bed. Before that, once, her pustules still unhealed, Heera had escaped her soft pallet. By the time she reached the Lamchor dock, mad bells were ringing out behind her, slicing through the night's silence. The boats anchored at the jetty listed in the water. Heera clenched her eyes shut and clamped her hands to her ears.

When she opened her eyes, a massive fire blazed in the terrace, heating up a falchion. Ten servants, male and female, stood in a row nearby. Their sleep-swollen eyes were clouded with terror. The old maidservant sobbed with her sari clasped to her mouth. Kali Charan Guha was supervising everything. His sideburns seemed aflame. His rings glinted in the firelight when he flicked his fingers. At his gesture, a muscular slave bared Heera's back and held the red-hot iron of the falchion against her skin.

The lesson of a lifetime. Since then, Heera had travelled by boat from the Lamchor docks up to the Meghna river many times. The breaking waves echoed in her voice through many songs of joy and sorrow. The past had vanished; like the burnt skin on her back, it had sloughed off, taking with it flesh and blood. Today you couldn't see the scar unless her back was bared. Heera couldn't even tell when the salt merchant had tamed her through tenderness and fire. When she woke from her daze, she, the whore whose womb had been scoured clean, was already cradling the babe of another woman in her lap. As if the gift of a garland took away the pain of the shoe slapped on the cheek.

When Heera emerged from Phuleswari's room, the air in the whole palace was sticky with the smells of *pithas* and sweets. The cookhouse stood empty. All the cooks had bathed at this late hour and congregated in the long veranda behind Ma Shumitra's bedchamber. This was where all the eatables for the pilgrimage would be bundled and packed. Heera turned toward the Mejo Thakurani's wing. Rajendra Narayan's daughter Shunonda sat like a queen bee on a rug near the threshold, surrounded by her companions. They were playing cards. She was as deft at sleight of hand as her father. Heera had come uninvited. Khhantamoni swept past her. Shunonda's son Prafulla Kumar stood in the yard with his finger on his lips to keep the grownups quiet, and chirped, *Chhie jhit jhit jhit*! Exactly like a wagtail bird perching on a tree with its tail feathers swaying. Here was another one for the birds! These ones had sorrow written across their brows—Heera knew this well from watching Phuleswari. Even though his mother or grandmother never came anywhere near them, the little boy liked to visit the aviary. He stood beneath the window near Phuleswari's bed, mimicking birdcalls. A few days ago, he had suffered a fall when he tried to climb the window grille while holding a tailor bird's egg. Phuleswari Rai had not appreciated his token of esteem. She had howled so loudly hearing the mother bird cry *ti-ti-ti* at losing her egg that Prafulla Kumar had dropped, egg and all, straight onto the ground. His dislodged kneecap, a result of that fall, still hadn't healed properly. Now he hobbled behind Heera, drawn by the possibility of birds.

Here was one in the royal household who made no distinction between this wing and that. Yet it was this child's existence that made Rajendra Narayan ready to throw down the dice in this game of *pasha*. Heera had been burned before. She could easily spot the signs of the coming storm. Ma Shumitra arranging all these pithas and sweets, Shunonda playing cards, dressed to the nines—all this was a dream. The next morning, when the pair of palanquins bearing Raj Chandra and Rongomala ran past the palace, Heera put her palms together and held them to her forehead in prayer—oh God, oh *Bhogman*!

Twelve

Rongomala opened her silver case and stuffed a paan in her mouth. The swaying of the palanquin was making her queasy. She held the tiny compartment open, yet her trembling fingers couldn't get the slaked lime to stick to the stem of the betel leaf. Why were the palanquin bearers rushing like this? Without the slaked lime, the juice from the betel stem stung the insides of her mouth. Rongi lifted the drapes to peek outside. Their pilgrimage caravan was speeding past the royal palace. And not in front of the palace either; they were taking the back way, crossing over back creeks, as if they were fleeing thieves. Phuleswari Rai, that woman to whom Rongi was more than a co-wife, must have been smirking when she saw them go by. Raj Chandra Chowdhury never seemed to lack for ideas to humiliate Rongi. She sat in angry silence with the burn on her tongue.

This was the first time she was leaving her own land to visit a foreign place. That, too, in a brocade-covered palanquin. Uniformed servants ran alongside. And then there were the mace bearers, the pike bearers, the personal servants, the cooks, the boxes, the chests, and so much more. Who would have thought that the daughter of a Nor, who lived a hand-to-mouth existence, would one day seek pilgrimage in such style! Even her brother, Golap Raiya, had grown goggle-eyed when he heard. 'Talk about luck! When you reach, sacrifice a pair of goats in my name. Pray that Yama comes soon to snatch my life away.' Golap had always been one to twist things. These days, he couldn't bear anything good happening to his sister. Who could tolerate anything good happening to Rongi?

They had left the palace behind quite a while ago. But all her joy from that moment when she had climbed into the palanquin had turned to ashes as if the trident on the dome of the Kali temple had skewered her heart. She couldn't even seek comfort through conversation. If Roma had been her travel companion instead of Durga, the atmosphere in here would have been quite different. Raj Chandra Chowdhury had grown quite enamoured of Durga, the woman with the lust for silver, and had refused to bring anyone other than her with them. Also, he couldn't stand Rongi's friendship with Roma. These days, he wouldn't even tolerate any mention of her. Rongomala slammed her paan box shut and opened her little box of opium.

Rongomala had performed the Shiva Brata for two whole years, praying for a husband like Lord Shiva. Each Chaitra Sankranti, the last day of the year, when the crows awoke at daybreak, her mother spattered cold water on her face to get her out of bed. The still sleepy Rongi would weave and sway her way to the pond. After bathing, she would sit right there, and with her tiny fingers, fashion a Shiva out of clay and place him beneath a palm-leaf parasol. She made the god offerings of bael leaves, akanda blossoms and sun-dried rice. After all that work, she had received humpbacked Ram Goitya as a husband. She had not spoken of her sorrows to anyone. Now she was on a pilgrimage to Mount Chandranath, the very abode of Shiva. This would have made her mother so happy. The hardships of their poverty-stricken household had not compromised or diminished Shyama Shundori's faith. Every Tuesday, a priest visited their home. Incense—clay lamp—flowers—sandalwood—sun-dried rice—areca nuts. Carefully, she used her fingernail to parse out eight kernels of rice. With cotton threads, she bundled the rice with eight strands of durba grass to craft her offering to the gods. This is how her mother carried out the Mangalchandi Brata, praying for the welfare of her household.

In the outer room, Atmaram sat with his copy of *Sri Chaitanya Bhagbat* open. He had an ongoing battle with his wife over her faith in Goddess Chandi, the slayer of disaster and misfortune. He wanted to get the children on his side.

Krishnanam bhaktishunya shakal shangshar
Pratham kalite hoilo bhabishya achar.

The words that Atmaram chanted were as dry as the torn, black-inked yellowing pages he read. Golap Raiya sat yawning, but Rongi escaped as soon as she could. So what if she wouldn't be getting a share of the delicious offerings Shyama Shundori had cooked for the gods? Her tiny heart would be in turmoil as she watched her mother bowed like young grass, praying to get their fence mended, or to be able to serve good food to her children. The melody Shyama Shundori chanted tugged at Rongi's heart, as did the dance-like gestures she made with her hands and the movement and sound of her conch shell and coral bangles.

When Raj Chandra raised the palanquin's drape, Rongomala was fast asleep. Durga lay in a heap in a corner, dozing. Even in the narrow confines of the palanquin, Rongi's body spread out in luscious curves. Her cheek rested on her palm. The many-hued gems set in the ratanchur that covered the back of her hand added a glow to her face. A rainbow played across Raj Chandra's vision. He had purloined the ratanchur only last night from Phuleswari Rai's jewellery box. All this time, Kali Charan Guha had thrown his pearls before a swine. If he could have seen Rongomala today, his eyes would have been blessed. So what if she was someone else's offspring, the daughter of Atmaram Nor!

Durga emerged from the palanquin. Her dark skin was almost invisible in the blue darkness of the disappearing sun, as if she was the glint of countless stars on a moonless night. Her silver jewellery tinkled as she walked. The royal pleasure boat was anchored at the dock. Karim Sheikh stood at the stern, combing his beard with his fingers, his eyes narrowed to slits. He mistook Durga for Rongomala, and, after honouring her with an elaborate salaam, he stepped aside. He realised his mistake almost immediately as Raj Chandra climbed into the boat, clasping the Nor girl's hand. That fool Raj Chandra had covered Durga in silver. Durga wasn't a mere servant; she was as deceptive as a green-skinned ripe mango. Rongomala's beauty and the glitter of her jewels merged together. Outshone by her, even the lamps on the boat hid their faces in shame.

Karim Sheikh's hands were covered in calluses from pulling at oars since early childhood. All he had to show for it was a tax-exempt house and a sliver of arable land that yielded a rice crop. Somiron Bibi had never owned a single piece of gold jewellery other than the tiny stud on her nose. He shouldn't even bother thinking about his daughters. What sin had made Allah turn His face from His faithful follower? His younger daughter couldn't speak, had never managed to even call out 'father' or 'mother', let alone demand anything of him. She adorned herself in mute smiles and garlands strung from the flowers of velvet apples. He couldn't bear to see her like that. And the older one had ripped his heart to shreds and run off to set up house with a madman. Forget about jewels, who knew whether she even had rice in her belly. Now his wife had begun to have fancies. She was growing old but turning into a young girl. Karim Sheikh was tired of hearing 'You cheapskate!' Day and night, Ma Shumitra was beguiling him with dreams of land and property.

When the wives or daughters of zamindars loosened their fists, they rained gems and jewels for the rest. He could fulfil Ayna's mother's fancies. But who would fulfil the fancy of Pratap Narayan's widow? She was knocking on the wrong door. These days, Karim Sheikh was more used to killing flies, not people. Chanda Bir was the chief guard now; he was the one who tramped ahead of Rajendra Narayan, flourishing a stick or a pike. It was child's play for that butcher to hack the head off a person. Although the two of them had begun training together at the same place, today they were oil and water: they didn't mix. Karim Sheikh completed his prayer ablutions in the river, and through the cloudy water, he looked at his calluses. They looked like charcoal cakes, black on his white palms, round and hard like whole areca nuts. The boatmen were waiting on the afterdeck for him, Karim Sheikh, the chief boatman of the pleasure boat, to lead them in their prayers.

A carpet was spread out on the afterdeck after the men performed their namaaz and left. Moonlight, bright and white like popped rice, illuminated the night. Bathed in the moonlight lay bolsters and pillows, hookahs, attar and roses. The breeze carried the clinks of carafes and glasses, and sudden gusts of laughter. Karim Sheikh preferred to keep his distance. He had done so even during the reign of Pratap Narayan, when he had been a young man. Raj Chandra's father had never left the boat for land. A few days of smacking the tabla, the tinkle of anklets, waves of amusement—that was it. Like a duck, the man would shake off the water that clung to his feathers and return home. But this fool was playing with fire in his lap. When it caught him, he wouldn't be able to smother it with a quilt. Karim Sheikh was right here on board the boat, a man his father's age, yet Raj Chandra saw no need to show any respect for his presence. Doomsday was nigh. Ma Shumitra was a harebrained female with zamindari blood in her veins. Which was why she thought murder would resolve the matter. Karim Sheikh rubbed his rough palm against his beard. Ram Bharari, currently waiting at the base of the steps, was a perfect example that one could not hold on to the wages of sin. Like a sly cat, the man was forever seeking mouse holes. His hair had greyed from all his years of toadying; and yet his house still had a leaky thatch. He didn't have permission to ascend the steps to the afterdeck at this hour, so he was stuck down here, whispering in Durga's ear. They couldn't have enough of this vileness in their own homes, so these vulgar people had to have their fun in the guise of a pilgrimage. It was a sin to even witness their doings.

Karim Sheikh cleared his throat and shouted at his men. It was time to perform the *Esha* prayers. The crew was sitting around smoking, killing time. The aroma of food being fried and five spices wafted up from the kitchen right beneath them on the gusts of wind. Separate meals were prepared for the Muslim crewmen. For them it was unmilled aush rice, duck eggs and a thin soup of pigeon-peas. They got the same food for lunch and supper. In between, they had been served some of the sweets and cakes sent by Ma Shumitra. The slippery wood of the deck was quickly covered by rush mats. Once their evening prayers were said, the crew would slurp up their plates laden with rice and go to bed. Before daybreak, they would cross the river. On the other side, they would sail through Jorarganj and then Mirsarai. Shitakundo was a full day's journey via palanquin from Mirsarai. There awaited Mount Chandranath.

Thirteen

Thick fog surrounded them, billowing skywards like smoke. It was hard to see someone standing just a few yards away. The wobbly stone steps gave rise to fear of slipping and falling. Below, nol vines and water spinach embraced each other by the creeks and runnels, while purple and white flowers raised their dewy heads. Nearby grew a jasmine tree. As they climbed upwards, the vegetation began decreasing and eventually disappeared. The feet of hundreds of pilgrims had denuded the mountaintop of grass and turned the ground white, like a bald head. Rongomala crouched low and plucked flowers from the vines. She touched her bare feet to the sensitive touch-me-not plants as she walked, making the fronds close in on themselves. She was dressed very simply today. She looked like any other married woman on her way to view Chandranath. Durga walked ahead of her, carrying the basket of offerings. After two visits, they knew their way well. They could gauge the route they were supposed to take to the mountaintop, but not completely without fear.

At night, tigers roamed the area. The first night, exhausted from the journey, everyone slept like corpses. The next night, the heart-stopping roars began even before it was dark. The very beams of the mansion built during Uday Narayan's reign shook. Raj Chandra was ready to head out with his gun in hand. Ram Bharari could barely keep him indoors even by invoking Ma Shumitra. Finally, he laid down his gun and came to bed like a good little boy when Rongomala applied her skills. He had just entered her when, in the middle of their lovemaking, a tiger roared. A wet spot on the bed was all that happened that night. To assuage that blot on his manliness, Raj Chandra left with his retinue at cockcrow. He returned with neither a tiger, nor a bear, but a pair of porcupines. The same thing had happened several nights in a row. Today, when Raj Chandra went off to hunt, Rongomala left her bed. Lord Shiva was calling out to her fiercely …

When Raj Chandra was nearby, Rongomala felt untouched by fear or anxiety. She wasn't the bride to whom he had sworn an oath beside the divine fire; but still she wasn't a throwaway nothing. When Raj Chandra had placed a pearl necklace around her neck, she had reciprocated with a double-stranded garland of champa blossoms. From their very first night together, they had both wept at each other's sorrows. If she had not found a place in the palace, she had found her place in the temple of love, which stood on a strong foundation. Let their destiny be written by the gods on a palm leaf: the life and death of lovers are joined together, no matter where; on water, on land, in the heavens. They had spent their nights together on the boat wrapped around each other, like twins in a womb.

At dawn, when the boat set sail, Rongi had given in to caprice. Instead of annoying Raj Chandra by raising the window drapes, she stepped out of their cabin and climbed to the roof. The pleasure boat was suspended in space like a bird. A miasma drenched both banks of the river. She could see neither the oarsmen nor the sailors. But the slapping noise of oars told her it was indeed their efforts that was making the boat move through the river. A gull flew overhead, loudly flapping its wings. It settled on the main mast, sharing space with another gull. Both posed aggressively, as if saying—Look at me, look at me! There was no one else around. Suddenly she felt a hairy arm whoosh past her. Before the vision disappeared, out of the corner of her eye, she glimpsed a pair of glowing eyes and a grizzled beard. She glimpsed a sliver of a greyish shawl. Was it her eyes or a gust of wind tricking her? It wasn't as if she had spotted a fly—she had seen a person. Surely she would have run into him on her way up or down from the roof. Although she was no longer paying attention to the gulls, Rongomala stayed up there until the sun rose.

When she was about to descend from the boat, she felt her heart stop. The chief boatman was supervising the unloading of their boxes and luggage. Bright eyes, grizzled beard, grey shawl tied around his head. Through the rest of the journey, Rongomala couldn't close her eyes for a moment. What if someone raised the drapes of her palanquin and slid a knife across her throat? All this time, she had thought Raj Chandra Chowdhury was the one with enemies. Now it seemed assassins were shadowing her as well!

As long as there was life, there was hope. Rongomala reached the top of the mountain and stood panting. Her continuous climb up the steep mountainside was making her body steam. She couldn't stay on her feet. She leaned against a skinny koroi tree. Sunlight played hide-and-seek on her skin. Nearby, a stray dog, fattened on the generosity of the temple, shook itself, spraying dust everywhere. Durga picked up the offerings basket and sat on her haunches at a distance, like a milk vendor with her wares. No one paid attention to their two husked coconuts, the spray of kabori bananas, the pair of bael and the four red hibiscus flowers. The priest and the votaries—everyone was busy purifying the courtyard by sprinkling it with a mixture of cow dung and water. Yet, a couple of days ago, their group had been the centre of attraction. Raj Chandra had drawn everyone to them with his donations, his prayers, his pomp and his stature.

Golap Raiya was constantly on Rongi's mind. She still hadn't broached the subject of the sacrificial goats with Raj Chandra. But the next day, Rongomala sprinkled water on the holy fire of Barob Kundo and prayed for her brother's longevity. Durga wasn't returning empty-handed either. No matter what the price, she had to have a black stone Shivalingam for herself. She would install it in her wall niche and worship it morning and evening.

Rongomala looked at herself as if she was gazing at someone else, as if the clothing, the body wrapped in the red-bordered white sari, the arms with the conch shell and coral bangles, all belonged to someone else. Her feet were muddy and covered in bits of straw and leaves. The heat had drained from her body, leaving her chilly. Feeling shy, she draped the shawl with embroidered peacock tail feathers around herself. Nearby, the pathway spiralled down to the falls. The water, as clear as a crow's eye, chattered as it flowed over small pebbles. Ice cold. Rongomala washed her face and hands and splashed some water on the spray of wildflowers she had laid out on the rocks. This was her offering at Shiva's feet.

The prayers and rituals were over. Rongomala felt hollow. Look to the east—all those high mountains wearing little cone hats of mist. To the southwest spread the silver sea, shining in the sunlight. In Barob Kundo the miraculous fire blazed on top of the water. It never went out. The soft murmuring of the leaves overhead was as old as the hills. People came and went; but these wondrous divine creations had no demise. Rongomala had grown to love this place in just a few days. The thought of leaving made her want to weep.

She would return empty-handed. But what could she ask for? What could she desire for herself? What happiness was there in lying in a bed of gold or silver coins? So many widows and orphans had funded ponds and lakes by weaving and selling yarn. The water of the yarn-spinner's lake in Amarabad still ran clear; it was a lifesaver for the villagers and the travellers during the harsh, hot days of Chaitra. People passed away, but their deeds lived on. Rongomala wiped her tears with her sari-end, and with trembling hands, she tied a strip of fabric to the seven-leaved bitter-bark tree. Her strip seemed to laugh as it flapped in the wind, surrounded by many other colours—red, blue, yellow, green.

If her wish was granted, like everyone else, she would return to untie her strip from the tree. If such was her fate. No matter how long it took to dig this lake, six months or a year, it would carry her name: Lake Rongomala.

Fourteen

> Everyone sings love, love, love,
> Not knowing it's a garland of thorns.
> The flowers of the forest remain
> Beautiful to the eye.

They were anchored again at Madhab Patni's dock. The smitten Raj Chandra was on his way to Dewanganj. Forsaking his comfort and undertaking this journey while it was still dark was the price he was paying for his love. Rongomala lay deep in slumber, wrapped in a quilt. Now and then, she laughed or wept, still asleep. The water burbling in her dreams was Lake Rongomala. It was so large the other side was invisible. Its waves were washing away all the people and the cattle in the kingdom. Heartrending wails broke through the air.

Raj Chandra had averted his eyes. If he sat here watching the shows she put on, the night would be over. Even after being with her the past few years, Raj Chandra still couldn't tell east from west when he suddenly woke up at the Nor house. It felt as if he had been out on a hunt and gone to sleep in a tent, ready to head home the next day. But Rongomala's moon-like beauty and sad gaze jumbled up everything. Each day began with new edicts from this beautiful girl, and Raj Chandra girded his loins to do her bidding right away. It was unbecoming for Uday Narayan's grandson to shy away from any challenge. So far, he had passed every test she had set for him. But now, his night's rest had been disturbed by anxiety—would he fail this grand test of having a lake dug in her name?

Ram Bharari was still snoring in the outer chamber. Raj Chandra ordered him to saddle his horse and stood at the southern slope by the Nor house. It was a quiet night. Five palmyra trees raised their heads above the undergrowth in the darkness. Beyond them lay fields of grain. Altogether, about two *drons* of land had been earmarked for Rongomala, and she had already planted four banana trees in the four corners in accordance with custom. The digging had to commence soon, so that the work could be completed before the rains arrived. Rajendra Narayan was unwilling to fork over a single penny for the lake. Raj Chandra couldn't get him to agree by any means. The old man was also refusing to loosen his death-grip on the zamindari. Since he wouldn't hand over Raj Chandra's inheritance while he still had breath, Raj Chandra's only recourse was to seek help from Dewanganj's ruler, Inga Chowdhury.

By the time Raj Chandra reached Madhab Patni's dock, Venus was twinkling in the eastern sky. Slowly, night turned to day. The other side of the river was still shrouded in fog. This winter, with its harsh bite, had attacked suddenly like harmad pirates. Raj Chandra was bundled up in a thick woolen shawl; on his head, a turban. Ram Bharari shivered beside him in the cold wind blowing across the river. His thin shawl over his cotton vest and dhoti was inadequate and unable to keep him warm. The whip kept slipping from his numb fingers. But once they reached the court of Inga Chowdhury of Dewanganj, he would have no worries. The greatest virtue of these jabans, these Muslims, was that they had large hearts and open hands. He might find good food, fire to warm himself, and even be gifted shawls and wraps. Raj Chandra was, after all, the moon who had come to rest on Inga's palm. A gold mine. A pearled oyster.

Gamecocks crowed, welcoming them, as they approached the entrance to Inga Chowdhury's court. The squawking roosters were loud enough to rattle them, but the feathered splendour of the birds soothed their hearts.

Inga and his brother Bhelu Chowdhury held court, rivalling the gamecocks in their magnificence. Inga was garbed in churidar, with a floral-embroidered Kashmiri shawl draped over a long robe. A gem-studded turban graced his head. The nagra shoes discarded beside him must have cost at least a thousand coins. His fingers sported rings set with precious stones such as topazes and moonstones. Inga leaned lazily against a pillow as if he was a nawab. In one hand, he held a silver cane; in the other, a gold box. Inga put his cane down now and again and opened the gold box to extract paans, which he slid into his mouth. His hennaed chin-strip of a beard swayed rhythmically as he chewed. Five toadies took turns at holding his spittoon. All this pomp and pageant hid the truth that Inga was a zamindar worth no more than a penny. Most of his zamindari was being auctioned off due to unpaid taxes. Rumour had it that he had lost his entire landholding under the East India Company's Quinquennial Settlement for land revenue; he had lacked the cash flow to be able to pay the required revenue. The man was now subsisting on a monthly allowance from the East India Company. This was all hearsay, though. Or maybe the product of Ram Bharari's imagination.

Raj Chandra paid no heed to such gossip. If a man like Inga were placed in a hot frying pan, he would still yield gallons of fat. Inga's brother-in-law was Manohar Gazi, the awe-inspiring zamindar of Meherkul. He was heir to the line of Shamser Gazi, who had conquered Udaypur Palace after defeating Tripura's king Krishna Manikya, whose name still evoked terror in the hearts of the Bhulua kings. If war became inevitable, Inga would surely call on his brother-in-law for help.

Raj Chandra had sworn an oath to himself before entering Inga's residence today—whatever his fate, he would not return home without making some solid arrangements. But he seemed to be starting off on the wrong foot. His ears were burning with humiliation. Uday Narayan's heirs did not need any lapse in etiquette to be pointed out to them; they were born with a fine-tuned sensibility. Raj Chandra was made to wait at the entrance for longer than a second. Then Inga Chowdhury remained seated when Raj Chandra entered his presence, and merely gestured at him with his cane to seat himself. One by one, as was the custom, rosewater, sweet drinks, fancily dressed paan and dried tobacco leaf, a separate hookah with different kinds of hoses—all of it arrived. But every gesture lacked the tender warmth of sunlight on a winter's afternoon. Inga Chowdhury was irked at Raj Chandra for simply disappearing after his last visit. These faithless, feckless sons of zamindars were poison in his eyes. They broke their word at every turn. They took no account of anything in this world other than their own interests and comfort. They cooed to themselves when times were good; the minute times turned hard, they folded their wings and came straight for help.

Bhelu Chowdhury's young face turned the hue of a dead leaf as soon as he spotted Raj Chandra. Although they looked similar, the two brothers, Inga and Bhelu, were vastly different in nature: if one was a tiger, the other was a kitten. Bhelu lived in terror of Chanda Bir. He had gone to Babupur during the previous season to collect additional revenues. Chanda Bir had stolen his achqan and let him loose in the fields. Buck naked. Bhelu Chowdhury still carried that humiliation with him. He was lobbying for his older brother to remain uninvolved in Raj Chandra's business. But how long could the tiger sit still with a grudge when the prey was right in front of him?

Inga was frugal with his words. He barely parted his lips. He guessed Raj Chandra's intent and gestured at someone to bring pen and paper. Raj Chandra signed a deed promising one-fourth of his zamindari to Inga Chowdhury. Bhelu Chowdhury fidgeted the whole time, as if someone had rubbed stinging nettle under his achqan. When Inga dipped the gold nib of his pen in ink and began writing a missive on Chinese paper to Rajendra Narayan, the younger brother could no longer remain silent. Black fire burned in his surma-lined eyes. 'Esteemed brother, forgive my impertinence. I beg, my palms together, your forbearance. You do not know Chanda Bir's strength. He will destroy, turn to dust, every last one of us.' He had just begun to mumble out the events related to the additional revenues from last year, when Inga's flunkey Aman Khan rubbed his hands together and stood up. 'Hujoor, this is no lie. This I have seen with my own eyes.'

'Silence!' Inga Chowdhury roared liked a tiger. The complaints of his younger brother or the championing of his favoured acolyte left him unmoved. These young fools, what did they know of the world, what did they understand? But some of his anger oozed towards Rajendra Narayan. 'With no further delay, you will, with urgency and immediacy, consign his inheritance to Babu Raj Chandra, son of Pratap Narayan, and in the event you pay no heed to this warning and do not desist in such unwarranted hounding, then know that Babupur will be no more.' With this indirect challenge of war, his missive ended. Inga Chowdhury spat into the spittoon, his saliva red from paan, and thumped his silver cane on the ground. Raj Chandra's heart quivered. When the courier left with the message, he almost fainted. He barely managed to hold himself together. Once an arrow was loosed, there was no bringing it back. And did he himself not want to wield the stick over Rajendra Khura?

Inga Chowdhury had returned to his earlier mood. He was cutting jokes, laughing uproariously every other minute. When the master laughed, how could the others not? And the one making everyone laugh was Aman Khan, Inga's favoured courtier and cousin to his new wife. The courtiers were abuzz. Raj Chandra was seeking an excuse to go—but he wasn't granted leave. Was he supposed to just wait on someone else's pleasure? He had not been born to listen to the smarmy chattering of someone else's toadies. He stood up. Inga Chowdhury jumped up from his seat and came at him with a shout. Rajendra's nephew was surely planning to tarnish his good name in the afterworld. Khuda ta'Allah was the master and provider of sustenance, and no one should be able to claim that a guest had returned from Inga's home with his belly unfilled. Why should Raj Chandra protest? It was late in the day—the sun was high in the sky. And there was no fear of losing his caste. Why, Inga's chief clerk himself was a Brahmin. He had arranged for a little something to be prepared for Raj Chandra in his own kitchen. The food would be served by Hindu servants. Inga Chowdhury placed a hand on Raj Chandra's back as if they were the dearest of friends and guided him to a long room adjacent to the inner wing. The room was divided into two by satin curtains, at head height, running the length of the chamber. On the carpeted floor, a dastarkhan was spread out, on which his meal would be served. If this was 'just a little bite', then what would a grand meal look like?

Although Raj Chandra's belly was hungry, his mouth had no appetite. At Inga's insistence, he broke off a piece of luchi fried in ghee and placed it in his mouth. He could barely swallow. His hand was mistakenly reaching for the carafe again and again, hoping for liquor. One who had never eaten at Inga's haveli would never know how many kinds of beverages existed in this world. The man was becoming penniless simply by feeding himself and others. The call for prayers sounded from the royal mosque in the western wing. Inga Chowdhury left, with a promise to meet again after the Friday prayers. Raj Chandra felt confused. There was a *chilamchi* pot in front of him to wash his hands in, but there was no water in it. How was he supposed to clean his fingers? Perhaps the custom here was to lick one's fingers clean of the ghee-yoghurt-sandesh and wipe them on one's shawl. Suddenly, from behind him, came the tinkling of belwari glass bangles and bubbling laughter. Raj Chandra quickly removed his fingers from his mouth and turned around. A pair of emerald-green eyes, lined with surma, gazed at him from behind the satin drapes. What divine beauty! The drapes rustled and the eyes disappeared. Otherwise, Raj Chandra would have thought he was dreaming. Could a human being have such gorgeous eyes?

When Ram Bharari heard about it, he chuckled. His belly stuffed with all kinds of good food, he was in a generous mood. He had managed to spend the morning and the afternoon in the sun in the southern field beside the outer house, on the pretext of tending to their horses, doing nothing much. There was no lack of paan or tobacco. As a bonus, he had found several companions to pass the time with. He had even managed to find some opium. He had smoked up and mouthed out at an even pace.

The one that Raj Chandra had mistaken for a nymph was actually Inga's second bibi, his younger wife: Gulbadan, the mixed-breed woman from Iran. His first wife was Mehrab, the formidable lady from Meherkul. Mehrab, although she had failed to stop her husband from marrying a second time, had cast a spell on the new bride on the very first night of the marriage. That night she had fed Gulbadan leeches, thus addling her wits. Since then, Inga could barely keep her in his bed. He would wake up at night to find her sitting on the doorstep, or smoking, or dancing with her hair down, stark naked. Bibi Gulbadan had quite possibly been a dancer in the past. Mad people had no sense—she became unsettled whenever she spotted even the shadow of an outside man near the inner quarters. There was no end to her coquetry. Bibi Mehrab's hard work had all been for naught. Even if he couldn't keep Gulbadan under control, she was still the grey-haired Inga's favourite, his heart's true treasure. He felt transformed when she was near, and lifeless when she was out of sight. He would leave his court in session ten times a day and show up at the inner quarters on ridiculous pretexts. It was this precious doll, this madwoman, who Raj Chandra was now setting his sights on! Raj Chandra would be whipped to death! Inga Chowdhury always kept his guns loaded. Raj Chandra would do well to keep that in mind.

Raj Chandra pulled on his reins. He turned for a last look at Inga Chowdhury's mansion. Tight security at the main entrance. The other three sides were guarded by a moat the width of sixty arms' lengths. Even in the heart of winter the moat was brimming. There was no way to cross without a boat. Did half-breed women from the west know how to swim? When he had left the narrow, long room, the curtain behind him had rustled once more. The tinkling of bangles on restless arms had continued without pause. Raj Chandra had not been able to get a good look because the chief clerk had been with him. Before he exited, from the corner of his eye, he had glimpsed an enormous nose ring flanking a perfect nose. Raj Chandra didn't deal in glimpses and glances. He wanted the whole thing, all at once. If Inga Chowdhury had pressed just a little more, he would have stayed the night. So what if Inga's guns were loaded? Love was stronger than bullets or gunpowder.

What had he come for, and what was he leaving with! Many thoughts seethed in his head. No one seemed to be bothered by the thought that Inga's letter must have reached Rajendra Narayan's court by now. They were taking their time, dawdling. They walked their ponies through the harvested rice paddies, crushing the remaining rice stalks, and entered the fields of kalai. The fragile seedlings were just raising their heads. As they crushed them underfoot and made a turn by the forest, they came upon fields of mustard spreading out over a dron and a half. The blood-hued gold sunlight of the waning day unfurled gently over the fields. The northerly breeze carried the pungent yet sweet smell of mustard flowers. As if it was a royal invitation, clouds of bees and butterflies teemed in the fields. All of this—the fields, the swarms—had been here in the morning when they were on their way to Inga's. The newly bedewed flowers had been glittering in yellow and gold. Yet none of them had drawn Raj Chandra's attention. The need for money turned people blind. Although his money troubles still weren't over, and Inga Chowdhury was now out fishing in muddied waters—Raj Chandra's vision was suddenly besieged by the beauty of the mustard flowers. He saw again those surma-rimmed emerald eyes against the backdrop of the yellow flowers; they wouldn't let him go, they pulled him back.

The winter's afternoon went fast. At Ram Bharari's cajoling, Raj Chandra moved homewards before the yellow disappeared from the mustard blossoms. His cracking whip pushed his horse to the limits of endurance.

Raj Chandra was angry at Inga really; the small spark of his anger raged into full flames with the unsteady motion of horseback riding. But he wasn't exactly sure whether he was angry because Inga had taken it upon himself to send a missive to his uncle's court, or whether it was because he was keeping Gulbadan from the west imprisoned. It was probably the latter. If there was war, he would kill off Inga first. His hands shook in anticipation.

They rode beyond the crop fields and came to a stop beside a massive lake. Darkness was descending amid the water hyacinths covering the lake. Fish speckled the black water. Cormorants splashed in and floated with only their necks above the water, their bodies the same colour. Like Raj Chandra they too were footloose, with no motivation to head homewards. They were splashing around at this odd hour. Raj Chandra, astride his horse, pointed his gun at them, despite Ram Bharari's admonitions.

A puff of smoke, a loud explosion.

Hundreds of birds took wing from the surrounding greenery and the nests in the trees. They drew wobbly grey and white lines through the dark heart of the sky, broken routes curving in the air. The air grew heavy with frightened birdcalls.

It was as if Raj Chandra had woken himself up with the gunshot. He broke out of his daze as if the sound had got the war-drums beating in his mind. He couldn't just wait here any longer. A cormorant floated in the lake, its head resting on a stretched-out wing. Raj Chandra left behind the most beautiful eyes in the world and galloped towards the den of the enemy—his own home.

Fifteen

Who was a friend, who an enemy? It was like Kurukshetra, where the opposing armies were all kin to each other. Like Gandhari, who had chosen to cover her eyes with cloth, Ma Shumitra could only see darkness all around. Rajendra would not allow any money to move out of the treasury, and her blessed son would not abandon his proposed lake. Fearful and anxious, she counted the hours late into the night.

Perhaps news of Inga's missive had reached her ears; her windows were open even on this winter's night, a tiny lamp flickering inside. Raj Chandra spotted the light from the entrance to the inner wing and moved away. He didn't make it to Phuleswari's chamber. Suddenly Jugindor appeared in front of him with sleep-dazed eyes. His servant was gradually turning into a night owl.

Whether Raj Chandra returned home or not, he kept guard all night around the outer wing. He was free during the day. Daytime was the time to eat and sleep dally with your wife, when no one bothered you.

Raj Chandra had never wondered before whether this had been arranged by Ma Shumitra or Rajendra Khura. Right now the way Jugindor emerged—whoosh!—out of the darkness, was just like a spy. This constant yawning was fake. The letter declaring war had arrived from Dewanganj, yet nothing in his half-shut eyes gave any clue to the situation. The fellow hung around the outer house as well. If he brought back no news, what business did he have there? Yet to shout at him now would muddy the waters prematurely. Raj Chandra dismissed Jugindor and went to bed, covering himself with a quilt.

As the night deepened, Raj Chandra felt more and more confused. Inga's message must have reached already—how could the whole household be asleep then? Or was it some other conspiracy that was gathering shape on this side? The trouble was, if the quarrel was inside one's house, it was hard to figure out who was taking which side. There was no use worrying. Raj Chandra locked away those emerald eyes in the little box of his heart and turned on his side. Let the lake dig itself—now he needed to sleep.

Raj Chandra dreamt of neither Gulbadan's eyes, nor Rongomala's face—he dreamt of the little cormorant with its swivelling neck. The bird twisted its body and took off from the water. He followed it for a while. He even thought of shooting it again. But when he looked downwards, he shivered in fear. He had flown so high; how was he to get down! The gun slipped from his fingers. As he flew this way and that like a fallen leaf, Raj Chandra scrambled awake in his bed.

A messenger had arrived from Lamchor. Kali Charan Guha had passed away. The moneyed man had been suffering for days before he passed, yet not a single person from the royal household had gone to visit him. His daughter was here but gone—as if she had already settled all her accounts with this world. She had been weeping since daybreak for the blood shed by a bird that had been shot in her dreams. She wasn't paying attention to her father's death. Not dead, yet, still suffering—it was hard to tell whether the young girl spoke of her father or the bird. But since she had also mentioned a yellow beak, white neck and pitch black colour, it was most likely a bird, not a human she was grieving. Probably a cormorant.

Ma Shumitra left Phuleswari's room fuming. She was the one burdened with all this trouble! The palanquin from Lamchor stood waiting at the gates. If the daughter-in-law did not go to her father's household on such an occasion, Ma Shumitra would have to take her share of the blame. No one cared about what crazies and fools she had to deal with day in and day out. That Heera was pulling the strings from behind the scenes. That whore was worse than the devil. She was going around spreading the word that once the royal family managed to smuggle the barren daughter-in-law back into her father's household, they would never take her back. Everything she said reached Ma Shumitra's ears. But how could she respond? Her own son Raj Chandra was the one who had destroyed Phuleswari. He had returned from that pilgrimage and was now embroiled in this lake business. Oh, you fool, the moneybags man had just died. You could skin your mother alive and still not reach the bottom of that lake. Ma Shumitra wailed at her son's door. Raj Chandra was stunned. His father-in-law's death had not made him newly anxious about money. That was an old story. So far he had managed to get all he wanted by either breaking into the royal treasury or his wife's coffers, procuring loans, by cheating people, or by sleight of hand. The only new thing was going to war with his uncle. Certainly, it was to be regretted that his father-in-law had passed away at this most inopportune time. If he had been alive, he could have been persuaded to side with Raj Chandra. Still, he could not produce fake tears like his mother did. It was also impossible to visit Lamchor now. The message from Dewanganj had arrived just yesterday. Now he needed to stick close to Rajendra Narayan and try to figure out his moods and moves.

Raj Chandra found the courthouse transformed as if by magic. As if a pack of tigers had suddenly turned into cats. Rajendra Narayan sat with bags full of money ranged in front of him. Beside him stood his treasurer, as well as Chanda Bir, and others who basked in his favour. Everyone behaved humbly, their faces beaming with generous smiles. Kali Charan Guha's death had not cast a pall anywhere. Chanda Bir's blood boiled in joy at the slightest sign of war. It wasn't unlikely that these events would make him smile. But what about his uncle, who pissed his dhoti at the sound of a gunshot, who couldn't move a step without an armed guard? What had happened to him today? Raj Chandra felt bewildered. His groom had been instructed to keep the horse saddled. Ram Bharari was waiting, hidden somewhere in the bushes by the lake. If a commotion arose in the outer house, Ram would emerge from the undergrowth, and Raj Chandra would show up by the lake. The two of them would gallop straight to Dewanganj. There, he might even run into Gulbadan. Therefore, Raj Chandra had dressed like a prince. The prince would be brandishing a posy of wild mustard flowers, stem and all, plucked from the roadside. And now all these plans had come to naught.

Raj Chandra had just set foot outside with the bags of money when Rajendra spoke in a honeyed voice from behind him. 'Raj Chandra, my son, I'm in a bit of a quandary. Why don't you and our daughter-in-law represent the family at the last rites for your father-in-law? The palanquin awaits.'

He didn't need to be told that his uncle was in a bit of a quandary. Who would not be in 'a bit of a quandary' after receiving such a missive! Still, this blatant attempt to remove Raj Chandra from the scene by packing him off to the last rites of his father-in-law was not going to work. Let the palanquin wait.

Raj Chandra trundled off like a camel, weighed down by the bags of money. If he went to Dewanganj now, Inga would snatch the coinage like a hawk, as was his nature, and dismiss Raj Chandra right from the door. He would never reach that long room in the inner quarters. He would neither have his cake nor eat it. The fellow had called for war on his own; let him figure it out himself. Raj Chandra was done with all that. The expenses for the lake, the issue that had given rise to all this conflict, well, that was now taken care of. Now he just needed to begin the work.

Ram Bharari scratched the back of his neck and agreed. He had been sitting hunched under a bush for so long that his foot had fallen asleep; and here was the master, hurrying and rushing at everything. If you were slow to keep pace with him, you were in trouble. The horses were haltered nearby, ready to go. At Raj Chandra's scolding, Ram moved ahead, whip in hand, shaking his foot. Their horses galloped the miles towards the Mog neighbourhood where Ramya Mog, chief of a clan of diggers, lived.

Although it was near his mansion, Raj Chandra had never set foot inside the Mog settlement. He had heard that once upon a time this whole area used to be a jungle. Tigers roared even in daylight. When he was young, Ramya Mog had journeyed with his people from Rosang to here, a long trek via Diyang. The tigers fled from the hundreds of glinting machetes and wicker baskets they carried. The jungle was cleared and the land settled. The hard days of homelessness were over. The Mogs had a monopoly over all the digging for water that took place in the entire pargana. With his clan surrounding him, old Chief Ramya lived like a king.

When Raj Chandra entered the Mog settlement, Chief Ramya was lying naked on a woven mat in his yard. Just like trees, human bodies sometimes need to be fed sunlight. This body made of dust would indeed turn to dust one day. Still, when the lord above had granted the ability, why deprive the body of comfort and joy? One of his five concubines was massaging his arms, another his feet, and the youngest, who was ten years old, was jumping up and down on his back like a frog. Was he a man, or a giant, or a tree trunk! The exertion was making his wives pour with sweat even in the bitter cold of the month of Poush. His name sounded outside, three times—'Ramya! Ramya! Ramya!'. The chief's musings vanished from his mind like mist. Who was this fool, standing at the entrance to his house and calling him, an elder whose years had led him to death's door, by name? The boldest among his five wives peeked through the yard-fence with a pole in her hand. Then she dropped the pole. She bit on her tongue, and came running to him. The elephant had stepped foot in the poor man's hut. Chief Ramya could no longer remain flat on his back, naked.

After he was formally engaged to dig the lake, Chief Ramya began banging on his brass drum. The very earth trembled. It was almost noon. None of the diggers were home. They had all gone out to chop wood in the forest nearby. Each man had his own belly to fill, and five to seven hungry mouths to provide for. They required decent clothing to cover their asses. The chief's drum-call wasn't just music; it was like the last horn blowing on judgement day. Everyone dashed back. They left their work and gathered in a crowd. Ramya called them by name, one by one, and the men moved from the left side of the yard to the right. Soon the left was empty. They counted heads and made sure that there was not a person less, nor more than two hundred. Every man was present and accounted for.

Raj Chandra's horse was standing still, paying close attention to Chief Ramya's activities. When the whip landed on its back, it flew as if it had wings. Behind him sped the black horse with Ram Bharari in the saddle. The pair of horses galloped off, leaving a trail of dust, growing smaller and smaller until finally they disappeared. Two hundred workmen stood in a line and watched them go. Then, with their shovels and their baskets, they took the path by the pond, then by the bamboo thicket, towards the Nor house. Chief Ramya led the way, clomping ahead in his loincloth, carrying his basket and his machete. He had left his heart in the bamboo grove by his house, where his five wives stood to bid him farewell. They bit on their sari-ends, their eyes brimming with tears.

Heera wiped her tears away and walked to the pond to bathe. Her blue eyes were bloodshot; she had been crying since dawn. Her tears had dampened the patch of her sari covering her heart. Her tears were in mourning for Kali Charan Guha, but more so from the sting of Ma Shumitra's words. Who wanted to live in a house like this? Apparently, it was Heera the slave's fault that Phuleswari, the daughter-in-law, did not want to go to her father's house. It was also Heera's fault that the royal daughter-in-law was seeing the blood of birds in her dreams. What, did she sit by the heads of these queens and make them dream? Let a few more days pass. Heera would then see about Ma Shumitra's arrogance. God would take care of it—Heera quickly looked heavenwards. She touched her forehead. Of all the things that could have happened, now, there was hot bird shit on her forehead. A crow flew overhead, cawing. Where was the bird escaping to after shitting on her?

The empty fields, devoid of trees or underbrush, began at the bank of the pond. Now that the crops had been harvested, everything looked balder than before. The Mog diggers emerged like shoals of carp. They were on their way to the Nor house to start digging the lake. Their hair was tied at the back with colourful rags. So many men carrying so many baskets and shovels. The bald fields grew dark in the middle of the day. The father-in-law's funeral pyre was being put together, and here was the son-in-law arranging for this lake to be dug. The first shovel was breaking turf on such an inauspicious day; would the water rise at all? This was Kali Charan's misfortune; he had poured his wealth into this household like water, and yet not a leaf had fallen to mourn his death. If people could know things beforehand, they would never be needlessly cruel. If anyone in Babupur had shed tears at his death, it was Heera the slave, whose back still bore the clear scars of that metal falchion. There was a salty, bitter taste in her mouth. A salty, dank smell all over her skin. With everything she had endured, it was hard to separate the good from the bad. The sweet and the bitter were too intertwined. Heera sat by the pond and rubbed herself all over with Fuller's earth. She scrubbed herself harshly with a loofah. The scar on her back tingled now and then. If only someone would gently massage her back! It was quiet all around her. A kingfisher perched on a low-lying mango branch poised to dive. Heera sprinkled water around her with her hands and descended into the cold pond. She rinsed her mouth a few times and then closed her eyes before plunging underwater several times. Let all signs of the dead man wash away in the waves.

Heera had barely emerged from the water when someone carried the news to the pond's side—Phuleswari had begun wailing and grieving. The girl had been fine; she had fallen asleep, mourning the dead birds. That Shunonda and Mejo Thakurani, they never did anyone a good turn, but jumped at the chance to harm. Mother and daughter had slipped into Phuleswari's chamber when no one was around. Her father was dead; and here lay the daughter, fast asleep—what on earth was going on? If one didn't wail and rend one's hair, would grief ever let loose one's heart? Now it was done, and the aftermath had to be dealt with.

Phuleswari was now adamant that she wanted to go to her father's house. Where were they supposed to find palanquin bearers or guards to accompany her at this hour? The Lamchor palanquin had been dismissed early in the morning. The winter's day was gone in the blink of an eye. So it was just the question of one more night. It would make no difference to start for Lamchor tomorrow morning. God had not written in Phuleswari's fate to let her see her father's face one last time—what could be done! Phuleswari was not listening to any of these explanations from her mother-in-law. She was bashing her head against her bed; her skin had split open and was bleeding. Unable to deal with any of it, Ma Shumitra herself had sat down with her legs apart and begun weeping.

Heera ran in, still in her sopping wet clothes, and stopped at the door. There wasn't an inch of space in Phuleswari's chamber. The old and the young, the slaves and the servants—all the women in the royal palace were jostling for space in the room. The news of the death had arrived that morning—and now in the evening, here came the tears. What fakery! Ma Shumitra's eyes were glinting with crocodile tears. Such a close relative had died, and nothing in her every day routine had changed, nor had her son stopped his lake-digging. Heera gazed at her clean, bathed body. The musty smell of salt hit her; a salty, bitter taste settled on her tongue. As if the scar on her back was a fresh scab, it burned. Heera had goosebumps all over. It was probably just the cold.

While the inner quarters were in such disarray, a new drama unfolded in the courthouse. There, a return letter was being drafted, in response to Inga's missive. A letter that proposed alliance instead of war. Chanda Bir had to spend many an hour explaining the pros and cons. Inga Chowdhury did not lift a finger without it profiting him in some manner. He was using Raj Chandra as a cover and was really waging a takeover of the kingdom. If the man thought the roars and big talk of the nawabi era was all that he needed to pull it off, he was in for a surprise. The reign of the jabans, the Muslims, was over. Chanda Bir was no mouse hiding in a hole. But everything in good time. Right now, an invitation to alliance would salt this leech. Also, it would give Chanda the chance to reconnoiter the lay of the land in person.

Chanda Bir himself was illiterate. Rajenda Narayan was formulating his words into proper language for a formal letter. Chanda had also advised him to keep the clerk in the dark about all this. The zamindar Rajendra had grown old. Chanda Bir had to keep his eyes and ears alert. His arms were strong, his wits sharp. The rest was in the hands of the gods.

Sixteen

Anything could happen if God willed it. Instead of war, a message of alliance had just arrived from Babupur. Inga Chowdhury bellowed with laughter as he broke the seal and read the contents of the letter. Frightened, the pigeons pecking in the yard flew off in a flurry of wings. Bhelu Chowdhury's heart raced. He couldn't not be in awe of his Bhai shaheb's courage. However, his slight lack of acumen was wreaking all kinds of havoc. Indoors, he was playing with a live fire like the younger bhabi saab. Outdoors, he was creating new enemies on a whim. Bhelu didn't approve of such caprice. How quickly their kin had lost their throne! Destruction was descending upon the line of the Dewans as well. These infidel, *firingi,* foreign rulers were ready to exploit them, if not directly attack them. Faithful Muslims should act in *tark-e mawalat*—there was no protest better than non-cooperation. The fakirs and darbesh, the holy men in Mymensingh district, not far from their own land, had begun their jihad. Sharpened blades glinted in their hands. Regrettably, Bhelu himself was a coward. He would not be able to take part in the actual battle. But at least he could plead to Allah on behalf of the mujahedin who were risking their lives.

He moved into the room without his brother noticing, and latched the door. Spreading his prayer rug on the floor, he prayed two *rakats* of *nafal* namaaz. He picked up his tasbih from his lap. His fingers counted the beads at a quick but gentle pace. His surma-lined eyes were half shut. He had put the jihadi warriors completely out of his mind. His heart pined and struggled—when would he be free of this life's prison? An older brother ranked just after the father; Bhelu could never be disobedient to Inga bhai shaheb. Otherwise Bhelu would have left for the holy city of Mecca long ago, on the pretext of completing his hajj. Mecca was the palace of his soul's freedom. It pulled at his heart. When he closed his eyes, he grew wings and flew there. He could see ripe dates clustered between palm fronds, and caravans with camels and Bedouins. Sand gusted against his skin; he could feel it hot beneath his feet. He joined a caravan and began an endless journey. Many moons grew full and wasted away to nothingness. Desert sands slipped away, loose, under his feet. The dry simoom winds blew. The ordeal of the road seemed like nothing. He, the traveller, sought signs of his desired destination. His eyes were sleepless deserts—they glinted and burned; whose dark shadow befell there today? The prayer beads stilled between his fingers. Ya Khuda! Chanda Bir had begun showing up even in his prayers and meditations! Like Azrael, the angel of death, he had begun to enter through locked doors. Bhelu would have no refuge from that ruffian in this lifetime.

About a month later, when he spotted Chanda Bir at the vestibule of their mansion, Bhelu shivered as he recalled that evening. Rajendra Narayan had arrived here in the spirit of friendship, seeking alliance; why bring this thug with him? They were guests, so they couldn't be treated with discourtesy. Rajendra Narayan Chowdhury descended from the palanquin, leaning heavily on his cane. The guards and soldiers accompanying him rushed over. Chanda Bir remained astride his horse, peering this way and that, as if he was a grandee. It looked like he had an Arabian steed. The horse matched the rider.

Bhelu was so angry and dejected, he was speechless. But he tried to convey to his brother, through meaningful glances and gestures, that this giant was Chanda Bir. If you wanted war, then this was the time to take his measure. Later would be too late. Inga

Chowdhury was usually focused on himself. He would miss an elephant if it walked past him. Laughing, he emerged to welcome Rajendra Narayan with an embrace. Once they had embraced, the two walked to Inga's personal chamber, grasping each other by the hand. A guard was posted at the door. What else could Bhelu do except stand in the courtyard and watch Chanda Bir put on airs?

Nothing lacked in their hospitality. They had been preparing for this visit for a month. The food was fabulous: every guest had dipped their hands up to their wrists. Where was Chanda Bir? If a Dewanganj guest returned unfed, his bhai shaheb would torch the cookhouse. Bhelu searched near the main entrance. No sign of Chanda. Nasir Mohammed, his esteemed brother's only son, the only flame granted by Allah to keep alive the Dewanganj line, stood near his horse. The deeds of this small child were astonishing. Not a smidgen of fear darkened his heart. He barely came up to the horse's tail, but here he was, jumping up and down, trying to mount it. He held a cane, as if he were wielding a whip. Every time Bhelu looked at his beloved nephew, his eyes teared up.

Bhelu Chowdhury wiped his eyes with the end of his scarf and walked away. Who knew where Chanda Bir was lying in wait? He could see the moat surrounding the three sides of their fort from the roof of the second floor. Their ancestors had built it thus to keep them secure. Now, lacking maintenance, the water was black and malodorous, especially during the dry season. Was Chanda Bir diving in and out of it seeking sunken treasure, or was he merely trying to estimate how deep it ran? Fear bit into Bhelu's guts. This had to be a trick; a proposal of friendship hiding the will to war. He should tell bhai shaheb about his discovery as soon as possible. To make things worse, suddenly the secret entrance behind the moat slid open. The sound of undammed laughter floated out. His younger bhabi sab, Gulbadan, stood hugging the vine-covered, hidden entrance, giggling madly. Her gaze flitted across the moat like a butterfly.

Bhelu Chowdhury's heart was ripped asunder. Bhai shaheb was wrapped around the little finger of his new bride. He would pay no attention even if Bhelu brought a complaint against her. Instead, poor Bhelu would be burdened with the allegation of eyeing his brother's wife. But who could thwart Chanda Bir? He would enter like a needle through the secret entrance and emerge like a battering ram. Allah forbid that Bhai shaheb had to pay for his naiveté with his life! Bhelu Chowdhury held his temples and slumped on the ground.

On the other side of the moat stood Chanda Bir, towelling himself dry with a gamchha. He couldn't make up his mind about what to watch: the secret entrance or the beauty who stood there. If the gods had not chosen him to be their favoured one, would the goddess of luck have delivered herself to his hands before he had even asked!

Chanda Bir was riding right alongside the palanquin of his master, Rajendra Narayan. He was ready to swallow a stone and wait to digest it, but the old man was impatient. Like a turtle, he stuck his neck out of the palanquin and jabbered the whole way. The master was enamoured of his own prowess at statecraft. If Inga was a maestro, he was no less. Inga Chowdhury had completely omitted any demands of the quarter of the zamindari. Rajendra Narayan had volunteered to hand it over to the rightful heir, his nephew Raj Chandra. Asking for a month's time to do this was merely a delaying tactic, deceit. It was a meeting of mountebanks. That was all.

What Chanda Bir had witnessed or done at Inga's residence were not things he would shout out in public. And what was the point in making declarations anyway? There had already been too many words. What his master needed now was deeds; not words. It didn't seem likely that they would be impeded. Inga Chowdhury lacked the strength and support required for war. His reign was over. His own son was still a child. His younger brother was worse than a woman; high as a kite all the time, without even the aid of drugs. He sleepwalked the entire fort through the nights. 'But,' Chanda Bir lowered his face and said to Rajendra Narayan, 'as long as Inga is alive and above ground, you will have no peace. He will hide like a poisonous ant, and, in secret, prepare to bite you again and again.'

Chanda Bir didn't wait to see his master's expression change. He reared up his horse and galloped ahead of the palanquin. His thoughts were at the bottom of the moat. The water had seemed infinite; he couldn't guess how far down it went. If they could somehow cross it with all the equipment they brought with them, they would win. The goddess of luck herself had emerged to show him the concealed way.

May he never again have to gaze upon the wrathful visage of the goddess in this lifetime. Even the heart of a warrior like Chanda Bir trembled in terror when he recalled that vision. He had broken into Inga Chowdhury's mansion through the secret entryway. The place was like a maze. He couldn't figure out which chamber belonged to whom. Every few yards there was one hallway after another, buildings, a Turkish bath, twisting staircases, vertical walls laid out. Chanda Bir entered and exited various structures. His *kirich* was tucked into his waistband. Behind him trailed ten loyal guards, brandishing pikes. They were dousing the cressets flaming on the walls as they moved forward. But they were finding it difficult to proceed quietly remaining hidden in the darkness. Bright moonlight jumped on the assassins, illuminating them.

The dark nights of the new moon had passed while they crafted a ladder of sixty arms' length. Although Banchharam Barui had built the ladder all by himself, and only at night, Chanda Bir had stood guard while it was being constructed. Inga Chowdhury's palatial fort wasn't too far from Barui's hut. The very wind could carry rumours. They wasted a few more days while they cobbled together the other tools they would need. It would have been a good idea to have procured some more information about the inner workings of Inga's household from the bangle-seller Maymuna. It wasn't as if she hadn't gathered any intelligence. Maymuna travelled to Dewanganj every single day, with her two hijras carrying wicker baskets full of bangles on their heads. Although they were covered in gold and jewels, the women of Inga's household fancied covering their arms in the latest bangles of belwari glass. They held out their wrists to Maymuna and, as she slipped the bangles on, chattered endlessly about their joys and their sorrows. 'For shame, *tauba tauba*,' Maymuna lightly slapped her own cheeks in contrition and said to Chanda Bir, 'Babu, please don't ask me more. It shames me to have to tell you all these awful things.'

Although Maymuna was Rajendra Narayan's tenant, she was a Muslim, like Inga. Forcing her to tell more than she was already volunteering was risky. It might make her suspicious. Chanda Bir backed off that day without uncovering any information about Inga Chowdhury's bedchamber.

Would his boat sink just as he was about to hit shore? There could be no face-to-face battle with war drums beating when all he had for support were ten pikemen and guards. If they tried that they would be flattened like dough by Inga's men. He had left home that day swearing an oath: like thieves in the night, they would infiltrate through the secret entrance; they would carry out the assassination and leave the same way just as quietly. Although their mission had not been carried out successfully yet, the path to retreat was still open. The ladder lay there, spanning the moat.

Chanda Bir retreated step by step with his men and stopped by the ladder. They had neither tobacco nor opium with them. For over an hour they had been fumbling around, as if playing blind man's buff. Earlier, they had had to travel miles carrying this ladder that was sixty arms' length. His men were extremely discontented. Chanda Bir was beginning to worry that instead of Inga, they were going to go ahead and stab him with their pikes. If he tried to strategise with them over this mission now, the night would be over. These jaban Muslims had the bad habit of rising while it was still dark to say their dawn prayers. He would have to do what was needed right now. And Chanda Bir would get it done himself. But he would have support—that was essential. Chanda Bir left orders that they were to emerge like lightning as soon as he gave the signal. He entered the living quarters of the mansion by himself. By then, the moon had moved enough to be hidden by the dome of the mosque in the western wing. Darkness and shadow surrounded him.

The hours of the winter's night were almost over. Everyone lay comfortably asleep. Not even a leaf stirred. Suddenly he heard a dog whining. But Muslims were forbidden by their faith to keep dogs. What was it then? Chanda Bir hid in the shadow of the slanted stonework and waited. A woman ran out in front of him. She was dressed in a long skirt, her torso naked, her hair dishevelled. The hem of her skirt swept the yard as she crossed. The figure clomping heavily after her was Inga Chowdhury; Chanda Bir had no trouble recognising him even in the dark. So his prey was coming to him! Chanda Bir hacked at him twice with his kirich. The first time it slid off the fabric of Inga's achqan. His next lunge didn't miss its mark. The single-edged blade lodged exactly where he meant it to.

Inga Chowdhury twirled like a bumblebee and fell on top of his killer. On one side, a wounded tiger; on the other, a bear wielding a kirich. The two tussled in the alcove under the slanted wall. Bhelu Chowdhury, the sleepwalker, watched the fight from the balcony upstairs.

Actually, Bhelu saw nothing. He had left his bed and exited his chamber, but his dreams still spread their wings across his eyes.

He could see himself, solitary, roaming the battlefield of Karbala. The sky and the land were joyless. The wind wailed a lament as it blew dust everywhere. The weeping of women and children from days of yore floated from afar. His chest was about to explode with thirst, but there was no way to raise a handful of water to his lips. The enemy had besieged the river Euphrates. Lamentations rose from all sides. He felt cold even within the burning of the desert. Step by step, he walked towards the Euphrates, where he would have to push back the enemy and reclaim the right to water. Or else the Prophet's line would not survive. Bhelu held his sword high and leapt down the stairs. He crossed the courtyard and darted between the slanted walls. Beyond the last building lay the moat, where both water and enemy waited. By the time Bhelu reached the walls, Inga Chowdhury had already been decapitated. Although he slipped on the hot blood and fell, Bhelu put his weight on his sword and pulled himself upright. He began walking. His destination: the banks of the Euphrates.

Again, Chanda Bir struck from behind with his kirich. Although he had a sword, Bhelu Chowdhury did not resist like his brother. He pulled himself along the ground for a few yards, to reclaim his right to the river. Then he fell back. A shadow stepped carefully around his head and slipped quietly away. As Bhelu gazed upwards, the night sky lowered to his face like a black shroud. Countless stars glinted, wan and mournful. He fought hard to keep his surma-rimmed eyes open. The stars began blinking out one by one, and then all of them together—they were gone. The spiralling wind wailed in mourning.

What was this noise that assaulted his ears? Chanda Bir was blood-crazed. He had finished off the father and uncle of that little boy, Nasir Mohammed, and was now searching for the child in every nook and cranny. Never let enemy seeds or saplings survive to sprout. That was how generational vendettas began. When he heard the wailing in the wind, he raised his kirich and turned around. About ten feet away stood the woman with dishevelled hair in her long ghagra. Her eyes burned. She looked exactly like Goddess Kali.

What had he done to turn the goddess against him? Secret assassinations were wrongful, but what else could he have done? The bloodied kirich fell from Chanda Bir's hands. Joining his palms in supplication, he begged the goddess's forgiveness. It was not granted. She would have sliced his head in two with her sword, if one of his men hadn't run his pike straight through her back.

How did it happen? God knew, Chanda Bir had not yet let the signal pass his lips; the pikeman had done this on his own. The earth shuddered beneath Chanda Bir's feet. The pike had entered through the goddess's back and exited through her head. Great gouts of blood spurted out. Yet she still held her blade overhead and laughed. The skies and the wind seethed. The doors and windows of the Dewanganj mansion were slamming open. Somebody blew on a horn. A great clamour burst forth. Chanda Bir came to his senses when his companion shoved him. He could no longer tarry here, looking for Nasir Mohammed; he would have to take care of that later. Right now, they needed to save themselves. He who fled survived. The assassins discarded their weapons in the courtyard and melted away into the darkness.

Since that day, the goddess had been ritually established in Chanda Bir's house. He worshipped her every evening with ringing bells and incense. Mounds of blood-red hibiscus were piled high near her feet. The goddess's idol, crafted on special instruction in the likeness of Goddess Kali, had her long tongue sticking out as was the custom and held high a kirich; through a hole in her chest gushed a constant stream of blood. Even the garland of human skulls encircling her neck could not hide the blood. It drew the visitors' gaze right away. The goddess wore a large stud on her nose and was dressed in a ghagra so long it swept the ground. All three of her eyes were emerald-green and edged with surma. They burned.

At first, Chanda Bir couldn't bear to raise his eyes to her. Terror raised goosebumps on his skin. Gradually he grew used to it. His heart grew stronger. What did he have to worry about? It was the goddess's goodwill that had allowed him to decimate Inga and his line. The goddess's kindness was hidden deep: under her hard earth flowed the streams of her kindness. She would not turn away from her son. Chanda Bir would soon have to rid himself of another thorn in his side, just like Inga Chowdhury—the one at the Nor house. If only the Mother, the Goddess, bestowed her blessings.

Seventeen

The digging of the Nor lake was almost complete. The *chand kuwa*, the little borehole to allow groundwater to trickle through, was being constructed. This required some rites and rituals. Two hundred diggers had slaved bone-breaking hard day and night for four months; they would fill their bellies with yoghurt and flattened rice on the day of the rites. Rongomala had barely made this proposition before Raj Chandra jumped up in excitement. Raj Chandra Chowdhury could never think of doing anything in proportion. Truly a man of zamindari lineage. It was in his blood—if looting, let it be a king's ransom; if hunting, let it be a rhinoceros. The more ostentatious the arrangements, the more money he needed. His sack of money was already depleted just paying the half-wages for the diggers and their daily ration of food. The greedy bastards ate indiscriminately. They only moved away from their plates when their bellies were swollen like tightly strung drums. But they had dug quite a lake. Once the water began rising, it would look like a sea, not a mere lake.

The first few days after the work began, Raj Chandra had peeked through the blinds from the stilted cottage and watched the digging from afar. Later he went over, a parasol shielding his head, and supervised in person. The Nor girl's lust for this lake had now possessed him. During the reigns of Raj Chandra's father and grandfather, such lakes were a dime a dozen—not even the flies hovering in the palace could tell when eight or ten such lakes were dug out and formally established. There were people to take care of things like that. But Raj Chandra had recently learned something new from Rongomala—there existed a different kind of satisfaction in partaking in physical labour. Their boiling love had finally quieted itself and simmered into cream. Today Rongi was not merely another beauty; she was Raj Chandra's soulmate. Such intimacy could only be born after living together, after knowing each other so well for so long.

No longer could one lovebird fly high while the other remained destined for dirt. For the last few days, Raj Chandra had been considering performing the water rites to elevate the caste status of Rongomala, the daughter of the Nors. Many kings and emperors had raised the caste of Hindus so lowborn they were not allowed to practise or participate in any religious rites at all—raised them to be at least shudra. No one had uttered a single word of objection. These days one could get away with anything if one had power and wealth. Now he had a chance. He could slip this in under the cover of all the clamour over the formal establishment of the lake. Raj Chandra ordered Durga to bring pen and paper. His first missive would be sent to the Goshai house in Maizdi. Those who sold themselves for a handful of cowries would drool if they smelled gold. Their nostrils were rotting from having to sniff the faux snuff made from snail shells. If you paid enough you could even obtain tiger's milk. A hookah dressed with aromatic tobacco—ah! Who didn't want good food and nice clothes? If he could lop off the top of the palm tree, the vines would collapse by themselves.

Raj Chandra dipped his nib in the inkwell and made a mark on the paper. His own calligraphy looked awkward. The letters seemed to be jumping on each other. Rongi had a good hand for letters. Her characters were sharp but rounded like pearls. As soon as she sat down, poem after poem emerged from her pen. She didn't need to work by the sweat of her brow. However, there was no call to write poems to these old Brahmins. A few lines of soft and hard prose would do quite well.

When Raj Chandra offered her the ink and inkwell, at first Rongomala ran off. She giggled as she fled. She was stumped when she heard the proposed contents of the letter. She plopped on the floor with her head in her hand. Her heart was thumping. Raj Chandra's whims were endless. What if she lost her life trying to raise her caste status? Well, if she died, so be it. She had it all now; why should she still sit on the bottom rung of the ladder? Good or bad, she needed to see this through to the end. She tucked her sari-end into her waistband and picked up the pen.

Beautiful Rongomala sat hunched, writing the message, surrounded by numerous discarded drafts. She was writing, scratching it out, crumpling up the paper, throwing it away. In between, she pulled on the hookah. She had never, in her lifetime, had such an important job. Her fingers were aching from just penning the high-status invitations—when would she finish the low-status ones? Still, it felt like no hardship. Durga was going back and forth in the burning noon sun between the stilted cottage and the inner quarters of her house, carrying paan, chewing tobacco and drinks. She didn't have a moment to spare. Raj Chandra sat on the thick mattress, leaning against a bolster, watching the fun. His upper body was naked. Even the breeze of the *punkah* was insufficient to cool the burn of the summer months. However, he was quite amused by the song and dance he had created by raising the mere possibility of elevating the Nors' caste status. Even that Golap Raiya, whose face was perpetually dark like rainclouds, now smiled as if the moon was breaking out from behind clouds. Whatever Rongi needed at the moment—pen, inkwell, paan, tobacco—he sat there supplying with a smile.

Golap Raiya's days were not going too well. His whore in Rajganj was being wooed desperately by a rising trader with fresh money. The scales were weighted in the trader's favour. Golap Raiya had returned because he couldn't stand his lover snapping at him or hitting him with the broom every other minute. Now he was at the beck and call of his little sister. He stood beside the lake, patiently holding a parasol above Raj Chandra in heat that could crack wood. Raj Chandra rather liked Golap Raiya. He looked like a tart, and he dimpled when he smiled. He seemed transformed when Raj Chandra asked him to wax and seal the letters; he left Rongomala's side and sidled closer to Raj Chandra.

Ram Bharari was also aiding the effort. Ram was responsible for counting and bundling the money. Each high-status invitation was being sent with some gold and ten silver coins. And the low-status invitations were five silver coins per person. Although the amount of gift money varied, no one, whether Brahmin or not, whether family or not, was being left out. However, even if some folks might not agree to sit down and eat at the Nors' due to their low caste status, the Goshais would not be allowed a chance to refuse. Raj Chandra issued orders to hold hostage the holy books belonging to the Goshais, and went off to the pond to bathe.

Ram Bharari returned while it was still daylight. With him was Chullu Singh. The horse was loaded down with all the books and treatises captured from the Goshai households; torn pages trailed them like discarded rags. The black horse was digesting a few of the pages at the moment. That fool would eat anything; most of the time he had no idea what he was even chewing on—Ram Bharari lovingly slapped his horse's jaw several times. As if conceding to the allegations, the black horse lowered its head and swished its tail. Ram Bharari bared his teeth in a smile. They had faced no trouble at all in getting hold of all these books. The deed had taken no more than a couple of hours. What had taken up much more time was the distribution of the invitations and the money. The Goshai household had emptied out as soon as Chullu Singh planted himself in the yard. By the time they had begun pulling people out from the pond one by one, and from where they were hiding along the banks, to tuck the letters of invitation in their hands and to count out the money allotted to them, the books had all been loaded on the horse. In a wall-niche, Ram Bharari had found a volume composed on palm fronds and tucked it under his arm. The Goshai Thakurs had got no chance to protest. But on the way back, Ram Bharari had already heard that the Goshais had ganged up and were heading towards Rajendra Narayan's court to lodge complaints, the tiki on the backs of their heads swinging. The trouble was about to start.

The next day, similar reports began arriving from all over. Although the big zamindaris and other landholding houses had not been looted like the Goshais', receiving letters of invitation from the Nor house had triggered their outrage. They were probably already on their way to the Shindurkait palace. All these high-caste leaders feeling disrespected by the Nor house were really Rajendra Narayan's puppets. The remainder, who stood with their feet planted in two separate boats, were minor in number; they were small fry. They were terrified just thinking about what might happen—or not happen—if Raj Chandra became zamindar. The whole issue of caste was just a red herring; all camps were invested in whatever served their own interests.

Raj Chandra cared nothing for any of this. People were going to Rajendra Narayan seeking justice as if he was a grand qazi or a hekim! Rajendra Narayan was a swindler beyond compare. He was ruling by defrauding his own nephew out of his inheritance. This was a matter that should be settled post haste. Raj Chandra prepared himself to go to war with all the small fry on his side.

The auspicious hour for the establishment of the lake was the day after tomorrow. Unfortunately, although those bastards had rejected the invitations, they had not rejected any of the cash gifts. All that money had just gone down the drain. Orders had already been placed with dairy suppliers, the sweetmakers and confectioners. Clay pots full of sweet yoghurt, mithai and palm sugar would begin to arrive on the eve of the celebration. Then there were all the ritual benefactions for the Brahmins; the donations, the charity payments, the payments for the labourers. All in all, he needed a huge amount of cash. It would take several days to even secure a mortgage deed and obtain a loan from a moneylender.

When even Ram Bharari had failed to think of a solution, a missive arrived from Rajendra Narayan's court. Raj Chandra's preparation for war floated away. His anxiety over money also disappeared. Although the penmanship was his uncle's, the language seemed to belong to someone else. Rajendra Narayan was volunteering a payout to his nephew—such an occurrence was a rarity in their history. Not only was he offering money, he was actually offering to pay to have the lake formally established.

This had to be a booby trap, laid by Chanda Bir. As soon as Rongomala said the words aloud, Raj Chandra hesitated. The next moment, he felt insulted—so he didn't know his own uncle's heart, but this lowborn Nor girl did? If you let them, women climb right on your head! They try to sermonise you at every turn. If Rajendra Narayan was willingly giving him a sackful of money for the digging, why would he skimp on paying some more for the formal inauguration of the lake? It was quite clear from the letter that the complainants had all been dismissed. However, Raj Chandra had no interest in whether the complaints made by those bastards had been dismissed or granted any credence. He would see about payback when he got the chance. The issue with the Goshais was different though. If they held their holy books dear, they had no choice but to present themselves at the Nor house. Raj Chandra couldn't care less about them once they departed from the Nor house—whether they cleansed their faces like cats, or whether they consumed cow dung to purify themselves. The idea was to allow the Nor people to participate in the water rites. Those who were amenable to the idea had already been instructed to prepare and appear the next day at daybreak.

Raj Chandra made Ram Bharari responsible for everything at the Nor house and started back home. Rongomala stood by the pond, leaning against the mango tree, her sari-end held to her eyes. The branches lowered themselves over her head, weighed down by green mangoes. Springtime cuckoos warbled nearby. The vast emptiness of Rupsingh's Plains spread out ahead of him. His horse kicked up dust. Every single time this man departed, he left her bereft. When he returned, her heart was full again. How could she live without him? He wasn't her husband—they were not married—she couldn't tie him to her sari-end till death parted them. He would remain with her as long as he was dazed by his desire. When his eyes opened again, he would fly off. That was how it was. Rongomala's heart couldn't accept it. She wanted to wail and scream, or run after him, following the path Raj Chandra had taken to leave her behind.

Chanda Bir's house fell on Raj Chandra Chowdhury's way home. He had heard some gossip about Chanda Bir installing a new Kali idol in his temple. An unending stream of blood flowed from the goddess's breast. Word of her beauty was spreading far and wide. Before this, no one had ever seen or heard of Kali, the Mother, the Goddess, appearing in Muslim garb. That too was news worth discussing.

Although Chanda Bir wasn't home, there was no lack of hospitality extended to Raj Chandra. A seat was laid out for him in the open yard, under the shade of a tree. One by one water from a green coconut, paan, chewing tobacco and a hookah arrived. Chanda Bir's old father sat nearby on the porch, inhaling snuff and sneezing like a cat. Chanda Bir's son Tara rushed about, taking care of Raj Chandra's needs. However, the young fellow seemed to be suffering from a distinct forgetfulness about taking Raj Chandra to view the goddess. He stammered. He hemmed and hawed about having to ask his mother or maybe his grandmother, or it had to be an auspicious hour or some such. Raj Chandra got hot. 'Go on, go tell your mother, your grandmother and all your fourteen generations that it's your real father who has just arrived here.'

What was this vision the goddess had granted? But this was Gulbadan! The emerald-eyed, mixed-breed woman from the western lands—two months ago, the enemy had seized her soul alongside her husband's and her brother-in-law's.

Although late, Raj Chandra had hastened to Dewanganj. Inga Chowdhury had done him a great favour in his last days. If he had not written that letter, it was doubtful whether Rajendra Narayan would have given Raj Chandra the money for the lake. However, by the time Raj Chandra reached Dewanganj, they had all been buried. Fenced by bamboo, three graves lay side by side, adjacent to the domed mosque on the west side of the mansion. Fresh chaff had been spread over the moist earth. Nasir Mohammed was sowing cloves of garlic in that earth with his tiny hands. Raj Chandra's heart was breaking, but he was Hindu, and wasn't permitted near the graves. He watched from afar. The tiny grave on the left was Gulbadan's. The freshly laid earth looked crimson, as if someone had just sprinkled abeer powder all over it.

Manohar Gazi sat in a chair in front of the mosque, stunned with grief. He paused many times while speaking to Raj Chandra. How had he not known that Inga had enemies who could take his life? It was all fate. If kinfolk separated and kept their distance from each other, of course enemies would spawn to seize a chance! Although Manohar Gazi's words were about Inga, Raj Chandra shivered as if they had been thrown at him. The courtyard was packed with people. Inga's brother-in-law Aman Khan, Gulbadan's brother, was there as well. The lad knew about Inga Chowdhury's missive to Babupur declaring war. It had all happened right in front of him. He might have discussed it—the feud between the

Shindurkait Chowdhurys and Inga's involvement—with Manohar Gazi before Raj Chandra had shown up; in fact, it was natural if he had. It wasn't as if the three corpses had materialised out of thin air. Fortunately, Manohar Gazi spotted Nasir Mohammed approaching and changed the direction of his conversation. As soon as he called to his nephew, the boy flew over and fell onto his chest as if he were a baby bird. From now on, that is where he would stay, close to his uncle's heart. Manohar Gazi was taking him back to Meherkul with him once the milaad and the full recital of the Holy Quran for the dead had been completed. The foe that had suffered no qualms in assassinating a woman would surely not value a child's life. The only good piece of news amid all this was that a kirich and a pike had been recovered as clues from the scene. These weapons would lead to the identity of the enemy.

Raj Chandra became eager to let Manohar Gazi know right away that he had already identified the enemy without the benefit of any weapons collected. The clue was the emerald-hued eyes—the pigment that graced the three eyes of Chanda Bir's Goddess Kali. Then there was the nose-stud the goddess was wearing, and her clothes. In fact, even the deep wound in her chest, from which gobbets of endless blood flowed, was exactly the same. If Manohar Gazi had seen the dead body, he would be astonished to see the goddess. There was no harm if he didn't see her, though. Everyone was talking of Gulbadan's blood-drenched shroud. They said that even after she had been laid in the grave, the blood kept oozing out of her chest. But it was useless to hear others talk about the tint of her eyes and the shine of her jewels. Whoever had lost the chance to lay eyes on her in life had wasted their own. Even if that person happened to be Manohar Gazi. Gulbadan had been his younger sister's co-wife and Manohar Gazi had not approved of Inga's second marriage. He had not visited Dewanganj a single time since the day of that wedding. He had finally come: to take part in Inga's funeral prayer. What use was it to take this jaban to see the Kali at Chanda Bir's house? Rather than gaze at her with his eyes, he would more likely itch in his fists to demolish her.

Two months had passed by, and still there was no news of Manohar Gazi identifying the foe through those recovered weapons. Neither was there any sign of any other activity. As if the man had forgotten all about war and conflict now that he had his nephew close to his heart. How did the blood of Shamser Gazi's heir run cold like a snake's?

The subtle justice of the qazi-system had vanished from this land. It was jointly ruled now by the British and the zamindars in name only. Who was ruling? How were they ruling? No matter whether people lived or died, these British rulers seemed to do nothing other than collect double revenues, and seize kingdoms by hook or by crook. These vampires were sucking the entire land dry. Murders and other crimes were rampant; where were people to ask for justice? He who had power, ruled. Raj Chandra himself had knocked on many doors over the last few years and still not been able to wrest back his own inheritance, a claim that didn't even need witnesses or proof. Pratap Narayan's conditions identifying an heir were as clear as daylight—and yet …

The closer Raj Chandra got to the palace, the angrier he grew. Gulbadan's face floated in front of him; her emerald eyes, the gem on her nose. The tinkling of her bangles and her laughter had vanished into air. Now her eyes burned. Manohar Gazi should come here, even if just once. He would lose nothing by casting his eyes on the goddess. The jaban Kali at Chanda's house had at least this going for her: a single viewing was enough to make the blood boil.

Eighteen

When he heard of Raj Chandra's arrival, Rajendra Narayan dismissed his court early and got up. He was hurrying off to the inner quarters of his household, as if Mejo Thakurani herself was waiting around to serve him his afternoon tea. Chanda Bir winked and followed his master. Some of the courtiers understood what was going on, some didn't. It was serious. Everyone was talking about the water rites being performed to raise the Nor girl's caste status. What horror! The only way now to safeguard the sanctity of their faith was to go into exile. Although Rajendra Narayan had formally accepted the allegations of the complainants, many had not left his palace yet. They were milling by the lakeshore, or in the main courtyard, chatting in groups. Some were busy hiding behind the shrubbery and smoking opium. Everyone seemed to be going through a bad patch. At least Raj Chandra's letters had given everyone something to do after a long while. Something to do, as in gorging themselves on Rajendra Narayan's dime and smoking it up while raising a racket. It was as if there was some festival going on at the palace. At the main entrance lay huge piles of used banana-leaf plates, broken clay cups, yoghurt pots, melon peel and green coconut husks. Crows and dogs fought over these remnants.

Although the air seemed heated all around him, Raj Chandra did not have the time to glance left or right. The day was moving towards its close. He jumped off his horse and made a beeline for the courthouse. The court chamber was empty. A few low-tier courtiers were standing flush against the wall fearfully. They appeared to be rendered speechless as soon as they saw him—as if Raj Chandra was Yama himself. He had to shout at them several times to evoke a response. Raj Chandra strode off towards the inner quarters of Rajendra Narayan's wing.

Phuleswari Rai was in the inner courtyard, wrapping a bandage around the broken leg of a heron. Prafulla Kumar sat hunched near her, his hands on his knees. His eyes never left the wounded bird. How pretty were its long, golden legs! And the doings of his addlebrained aunt were also worth watching. She had recited an invocation to Lord Indra, and spread a paste of slaked lime and fresh turmeric on the heron's leg, and it was all better. But Prafulla Kumar was against releasing the bird. It had been six months since his own leg had broken. He walked with a limp now. Nevertheless, he had spent the whole afternoon running around, and slipping and falling, before managing to capture the heron. His mother didn't approve; she didn't have an aviary like his crazy aunt either. He had discovered a broken, old cage a few days ago, during his wanderings. Today he had cleaned it up and lined it with straw so the heron could rest comfortably. He had hung a couple of swamp barb fish from the top of the cage with twine so the bird wouldn't cry when it was hungry. But it was only after he was done with all his arrangements that his crazy aunt said, 'This cage is too small for this heron. It'll die. Let it go, love.'

Prafulla Kumar wanted to cry. He felt angry at his aunt too. Did he have to listen to her just because she had healed the heron's leg? Why, he didn't even pay attention to many of the good things his mother and grandmother asked him to do. When aunt and nephew were about to quarrel, Raj Chandra arrived. As soon as she spotted her husband, Phuleswari covered her head and face with the length of her sari-end and left the inner courtyard. Prafulla Kumar jumped up in joy. 'Chandra Mama! Chandra Mama, look! I caught a heron!'

Raj Chandra severely disliked the clingy nature of this child. A cobra's grandson was a cobra himself. And what business did Phuleswari have in his uncle's wing anyway? Just because he was away, everyone seemed to have sprouted wings, and was doing as they pleased. Let today and tomorrow pass, he would take the measure of every single person here—Phuleswari, his mother Shumitra, Rajendra Khura …

'Chandra, my son, have you arrived? Come, come …' Rajendra Narayan stood up from his bed and came forward when he spotted his nephew on the threshold. Chanda Bir bared his teeth in a smile. It was the same smile he had sported on his face the day the bag full of coins had been proffered to Raj Chandra after Inga Chowdhury's challenge had arrived. Raj Chandra stood stiffly in the doorway. He was feeling dizzy from the heat. Mejo Thakurani, his aunt, began bustling about. Where should she invite him to sit, what should she bring him to eat! How long it had been since Raj Chandra had appeared in her home like the moon! The little boy he once was, who would come to her, his new aunt, to sit on her lap and be fed by her, to be bathed by her, and Ma Shumitra would return empty-handed, weeping, with her sari held to her eyes, because the child refused to leave his aunt until he fell asleep; now that he had grown up, had he completely forgotten his aunt?

Raj Chandra did not have the time to listen to this whining. He was stunned and speechless at the intimacy he was observing between Chanda Bir and Shunonda. His uncle and aunt were pretending not to notice. When Chanda Bir left the room, Shunonda followed in his footsteps. Let everything go to hell; Raj Chandra needed money at this moment. But why was Rajendra Khura delaying him by promising to give him the money? What trick did he have hidden up his sleeve? He was saying that the money rested safely in the money chest in the outer house—let their beloved Raj Chandra first calm his belly with the food that his loving aunt was serving him. He was taking money that was rightfully his; who could dare say a word against that? Raj Chandra could take the heat; what he couldn't take was this smarminess. He sat there squirming.

Shunonda returned. Alone. Not a word passed her lips. She laid out his seat herself, and arranged the servings of food in a semicircle. Which way had the sun risen this morning? The same Shunonda who had once refused to move a muscle was serving him herself, despite having scores of maids and slaves at her command! She had not spoken to him since she had returned a widow, bringing her son with her. Anyway, forget about the food; it looked like the crystal goblet contained a cool whey drink—Raj Chandra's thirst seemed to grow. He should wet his throat if only to better interrogate his uncle. Also, he could not completely ignore his aunt's repeated wheedling. Since he had to accept something from what they were offering, he might as well accept the drink.

Although Phuleswari had covered her face and disappeared when Raj Chandra showed up, she gradually made her way back to Rajendra Narayan's wing. Sleep and tears; she had used up all she had of both. Her days of singing like her birds were over. Ma Shumitra's quarters, her own chamber—she felt like a stranger everywhere. Her aviary looked dilapidated, uncared for. Putting out birdfeed twice a day, changing their water, cleaning the cages regularly, covering them up during the nights of winter and the rains—Heera still did it all, but the bustle and care of the past were no more. Neither were there any new birds. This time Phuleswari had returned from Lamchor empty-handed. Her brothers had completed their father's *shraddho* in a slipshod manner, before sending her back in her palanquin. Let alone her husband, they couldn't be bothered to wait for anyone from her in-laws' household to arrive.

Apparently, this was a slap in the face for her mother-in-law. She had stopped speaking to Phuleswari. Their rooms faced each other across the yard—and they weren't on speaking terms!

Phuleswari couldn't deal with her mother-in-law's neglect. She tried to shrug it off and began going off to Mejo Thakurani's wing of the palace. Although Shunonda was older, she would place her hand on Phuleswari's shoulder and sit her down to play pasha. She didn't cheat when they played, either. She joked with Phuleswari, 'Oh, *bou-rani*, Prafulla is your child. What do I have left in my life? I live in my father's house now; what power do I have to provide him with anything? You should take care of him, love him and nurture him. Kumar admires you so much!' One day, Mejo Thakurani explained the state of affairs to her clearly. This feud between uncle and nephew would be easily resolved if only Phuleswari adopted Prafulla Kumar. Prafulla was of the same lineage; he was of the Chowdhurys, if not on his father's side, then at least on his mother's. When he was older, he would ascend to the throne. Let Raj Chandra live the way he wanted to. None of his desires would be unmet. He would get twice his allowance every month.

Phuleswari didn't understand all these twists and turns. She liked Prafulla Kumar. She could give him everything she had—except her aviary. The little boy wouldn't leave the birds alone. He wanted to hold them tight in his fist, even if they choked and died. He had pushed and shoved until he had that heron inside his cage. How was the heron supposed to swallow fish in a cage where it didn't even have space to stretch out its neck? Phuleswari didn't stop Prafulla from doing what he wanted. But she didn't cede the courtyard to him either.

She glanced from the corner of her eye at Rajendra Narayan's chamber. Her feet had grown numb from standing in the same place. No matter how long it took for the man to emerge, this time she would not hide her face and flee. She would stand right in front of him, right in his way. How many days had it been since she had even glimpsed him! She wanted to see whether Raj Chandra had anything to say to her as he left, whether good or bad.

Raj Chandra stood on the threshold. He descended the steps, wobbling like a toddler who had just learnt to walk. He didn't notice Phuleswari; he wouldn't have noticed an elephant if it had passed right in front of him. Everything looked blurry. The world twisted and turned around him, as if he were riding on a Ferris wheel. When Jugindor, his servant, ran over and stood in front of him, Raj Chandra lunged at him and placed his head on his shoulder. Chanda Bir rushed over from another direction. The two of them pushed and pulled him to the outer chamber.

The man had marched into his uncle's chamber. Why was he now emerging tottering, barely able to walk? Phuleswari ran straight to her mother-in-law to tell her what was going on. Each Tuesday, Ma Shumitra held a puja for Goddess Lakshmi. She had just placed the offerings for the goddess on the stove. She was busy with the placement of the holy *ghot*. Phuleswari felt like she was a bug as she stood in the doorway, calling out, 'Ma, Ma!' She called so many times, and Shumitra didn't even turn to look at her once. So, her gods were more important to her than the life and death of her son? Who knew whether the uncle and his wife had conspired to lay a curse on him? But if they had, what was it to Phuleswari? She was the daughter from a different household, and a barren one at that; one whose husband existed but was absent. Even Heera repeated this to her. But Heera at least, at Phuleswari's pleading, agreed to sneak a peek at the outer chamber. She came back to tell her, 'Didimoni, Raj Chandra Chowdhury has drunk all that bhang and is just lying there, asleep. Don't worry about him.' Other residents of the palace weren't worried about him either. The longer that madman stayed asleep, the better.

Chanda Bir was relieved the most. He was quite sure that Raj Chandra would not awaken from this black sleep before dawn. Chanda Bir had much to do before then. His slightest mistake today could cost them dearly. The Nor house did not have many men, and they were unarmed. Apart from the blades and spatulas used in the kitchen, there were no weapons in that house. The problem was the two hundred diggers loyal to Chief Ramya, who were camped in tents nearby. The number of baskets, shields, machetes and shovels they had with them were beyond count. They were stronger than most. If the chief disagreed with him, the two hundred diggers would readily go to war; give up their lives if need be. Chanda Bir prepared himself for these eventualities and quickly entered his temple.

Why were there tears in the goddess's eyes? Who was she desperately weeping for, her stole held against her mouth? Chanda Bir couldn't see clearly because of the incense smoke. The goddess seemed to be sobbing when he held the lamp closer. The Mother was against it. She had objections to him, her son, going to war. Why, oh Mother, why? Did it mean that Chanda Bir would go to war but not return? What did your divine sight show you? Please, speak, oh Mother!

Chanda Bir began to sob loudly, and prostrated himself at the feet of his goddess. He didn't know for how long he lay there. He sat up when jackals began to howl from the forest nearby. A pile of ashes sat in the censer. The goddess's eyes were dry as bones. Once the smoke dissipated, her eyes glowed again in the dim light. Chanda Bir pulled out his kirich from his waistband and touched it to the goddess's feet. If there was danger, let it come; without war Chanda Bir's life meant nothing. It didn't matter whether that war was to place Shunonda's son on the throne, or to uphold the sanctity of faith.

It was war only in name though. In truth, it was no more than a fight between two neighbourhoods. The weapons were merely sticks, pikes and falchions. Only a few men with swords and shields had to be taken along to give the whole thing a more war-like appearance. The side with more men would win. Chanda Bir had no difficulty in procuring enough men to encircle the Nor house completely. Who did not want to destroy an attack on the faith? Chanda Bir started off for the Nor house with double the number of Chief Ramya's diggers. On the way, they heard jackals yowling and owls hooting while bats glided overhead. The land and sky around them were permeated with harbingers of ill fate. Chanda Bir's heart thumped steadily as he walked.

Chanda Bir had never gone to war with such a large command. It would have been one thing if these were regular soldiers. The lion's share of these men was wielding weapons for the first time in their lives. But they lacked nothing in bombast and talk. Their tongues flapped faster than their blood boiled as they marched to save their faith. Every single one of them was busy jabbering about himself. Forget about paying heed to orders, they barely listened to each other. These cowardly windbags could at most be guided to the lakeshore. Even if they weren't capable of doing actual damage, their mere presence in such large numbers would count for something. If the diggers saw half a kingdom's worth of men advancing and just decided to flee, that would be a blessing. Then he wouldn't need to bloody his hands for no good reason. Although the battle was one-sided, hopefully these pretend fighters would understand that the real fight was at the Nor house itself. Otherwise, lusting after some renown, they might go after the small fry. The men were growing more and more out of control as they got closer to the Nor house.

Next to the Nor house stood a raised shore, built with the freshly dug earth born of the lake's womb. The tents set up by the diggers lined the elevated lakeshore. The last one belonged to Chief Ramya. Usually they were awake around this time. After their night's supper, all the men who had musical skills gathered in the clearing with their drums and other instruments.

Come, oh, Mother Mogini, come
My lifetime passes, Mother, in singing of yours.

In tent after tent, the men sat gambling. Winning and losing—even gambling novices lost sleep in excitement. Some sat solitary, counting the days till they could go home, planning and dreaming of the things they would purchase from the Rajganj marketplace once they had been paid in full. Five among them suffered a terrible habit. They rubbed salt on the dead skin of almost-healed scabs and found pleasure in the lingering itchiness. Today, the doings of the two hundred Mog men had been suspended by a single order from Chief Ramya. They had barely settled down with their paan and tobacco after their nightly meal of rice, when the chief came to hurry them into their tents. The special water-drawing ritual was to be performed tomorrow morning. The chief himself entered his tent, doused his lamp and went to sleep.

Chief Ramya wasn't feeling very well this evening. He shivered as fever took hold of him. Two lackeys sat near his feet. They tailed him throughout the day and even slept in his tent at night. If he asked them to give him a massage, they would set to it with enthusiasm; that wasn't the problem. It was Ramya himself—he was ticklish. Tomorrow they would set off for home. Ramya smiled and wept in the darkness as he thought of his five concubines. Apart from his middle concubine, the other four were always flitting around, doing housework. They had no patience with sitting idle. Since there was no saying when he, the master of the household, would return, they would surely make themselves up with oil and kohl, tuck some paan in their cheeks and go off to reconnoiter the neighbourhood. Generally, they were ready to offer up their lives for him. But out of sight, out of mind. Perhaps they had found a newer master in some other village, and by now they had all disappeared. His middle concubine, the one with the leisurely air, lolled in the yard; hopefully the others had left her there. At least there would be someone in the house. This was how each time Chief Ramya was contracted for a lake, his household of five concubines was shattered. When he finally returned home and called out their names, his voice echoed and bounced right back at him … Ramya's eyes flooded with tears.

Ramya's youth was ebbing; he was turning soft. Who knew what whim had led him to leave his house built on stilts to see the end of the mountains! That time had been the glory days for Rosang, his birthplace. There was no dearth of food or crops. Rosang had recently been taken over by the Burmese king Bodawpaya. The refugees were lining right up to the mountains of Diyang. Retaliations against the usurper were being launched from the border mountains, the valleys and the dense forests through which even ants couldn't pass. If Ramya Mog had the strength he once had, he too would take up arms. Age diminished a person. There were certain animals though that returned to their place of origin just before they died. Why shouldn't he do the same? His muscular body shivered and quaked more from emotion than the fever. In a little while, he lost all sense of who he was or where he was.

Rongomala had just dozed off after waiting for Raj Chandra when she began dreaming—a palanquin had stopped at her gate. She was to be taken to the royal palace, bedecked in flowers and sandalwood paste. A celebration was taking place. Rongi was naked. She couldn't find her clothes anywhere. There was nothing she could use to cover herself and her shame. How could she go out in such an exposed state? A furore erupted outside at her delay. The palanquin bearers were refusing to leave without her. And she was refusing to go outside naked. When the fight reached its peak, Rongomala woke up. By then, Chanda Bir's army had launched their attack on the diggers.

As the assault began, the diggers were like a herd of sheep being attacked by a tiger. Still dazed by sleep which hadn't even deepened, they began to flee whether they understood what was going on or not. There was no lack of forest or undergrowth around them. They could have just hidden there in the dark. But

Chanda Bir's army impeded them. They entered each tent and attacked the poor labourers who had not been able to escape. Chief Ramya came out of his stupor. When he saw that both the men in his tent had been overpowered, he began banging on his brass nagra-drum: Boom! Boom! Boom! The earth trembled. Even the men who had hidden themselves in the jungle could not evade that call. They returned to arm themselves. The damage was extensive on both sides. The borehole in the lower part of the lake brimmed over with blood.

As soon as Chanda Bir felled Chief Ramya, he took off for the Nor house, wielding the shield and machete he had taken from the chief. The chief's head had been cut off; now the diggers would run. The fickle, pretend warriors had disappeared as soon as the shovels had descended on them. By now they were probably back home, waking up their wives and daughters to recount tales of their epic heroism. Over here, if the bird escaped its cage, it would be very difficult to capture her again. It wouldn't take long for that siren to seduce and make fools out of the few men who had the Nor house surrounded.

It's possible that if Rongomala had tried some seduction like that, she might have succeeded. As soon as she heard the commotion from the lakeshore, she knew the diggers were no more than thorns in the side; the foe had attacked in the dead of night to finish her off—to besmirch *her* name, to end *her* life. She jumped up and secured her door. No matter how preoccupied he was, Raj Chandra was sure to show up at the last minute, galloping in on his horse, before this barricade of *shaal* wood fell. Ram Bharari was probably on his way home right now. He was supposed to return early with Raj Chandra. There was a lot to do before the water rites.

Inside, the servants and slaves were floundering about, weeping and wailing. Chullu Singh left his post at the main entrance and ran indoors. Rongi did not unbar her door. Whatever danger drew near was coming to get her. The others were just extra. She lifted her blinds and ordered Chullu Singh to strengthen security all around. She called Durga and told her to make sure Golap Raiya was all right. Her brother loved sleeping. And when he'd had a few drops to drink, there wasn't much difference between his being awake and being asleep. The whole world could be laid to waste; he would be immersed in his dreams. Durga might or might not have heard the instructions Rongomala had shouted out. She was busy in her room, filling up a bell-metal vessel with all her silver. When she emerged, she was skewed to one side, weighted down by the pot. Lopsided, she ran across the yard and entered Golap Raiya's room. Then she ran into the yard again, and shouted, 'Oh, sister, Golap has fled; his bed is empty.' The words had barely left her lips when a terrific blow landed on her, separating her from her pot full of silver. The sounds of metal echoed in the yard. Rongomala lowered her blinds. Her brother had been smart enough to escape. Oh Lord, let him live!

Who could ever save themselves from such a great foe by simply bolting their door! Rongomala had perhaps a few more moments to live. While Chanda Bir's men were using the rice husker as a battering ram on her door, Rongi stood in front of her mirror, which spanned a whole wall. It was like a reprise of that night when Raj Chandra Chowdhury had first blown into this house. Her father Atmaram, unmoving like a rock, amid the wailing of her mother and brother. With pursed lips, he had silently recited slokas from the Gita: *Lead us from dishonesty to honesty; from darkness to light; from death to immortality.* That evening, Rongi had held a mirror to her face, and dabbed her little finger in the kohl vessel before lining her eyes with kohl. On her forehead, she had placed a crystal dot. She had reddened her lips with paan.

Today, she had no lack of fragrant oils, kohl, alta dye. Raj Chandra Chowdhury had given her everything—in exchange for her life. Today, finally, her summons from the palace had arrived.

Her palanquin, to be carried by eight bearers, stood ready at the main gate. Rongomala delayed no longer: she pulled out her jewellery, her ornate saris and bodices, and began dressing herself with great ostentation.

When Chanda Bir entered Rongomala's room, he was dumbfounded. This woman for whom they had just constructed a chopping block in the yard—how was she preparing herself! As if she was a bride; as if they were here to carry her to the wedding canopy. He couldn't even touch her. She walked out like a queen, her head held high. Chullu Singh, Durga Dashi—she called them by name, one by one. There was no response. In the flickering torchlight in her yard stood strange men with a baffled air about them. The wind of these last hours before dawn rustled in the trees surrounding the Nor house. Spring leaves fluttered. Where were all the familiar faces? She would not get the chance to bid farewell to any of them.

At that very moment, Rongi's eyes alighted on Golap Raiya: his neck was stretched out on the butcher's block, his hair mussed, tears coursing down his cheeks. Oh Lord, even her brother hadn't escaped! Rongi's trance broke. Her straight spine twisted. A hawk-like scream arose from deep within her; a scream that sundered eardrums. She had barely taken two steps towards her brother before she too was trussed up and spread out on the chopping block. In life, brother and sister hadn't been able to live in the same house for too long, and here they were, about to die together. Their sorrow made the leaves fall, made the birds of the forest forget their song, made the wind choke and turn silent.

The machete in Chanda Bir's hand glinted in the dim light of dawn.

Chanda Bir raced across Rupsingh's Plains. Behind him trailed a pretty, twisting line of red blood. How much blood could a severed head release! Even winding it in seven layers of a thick shawl had not staunched it. The blood seeped out like tears from a broken heart. Only God knew whose fault it was—the poor thing was weeping for herself today. The Nor house was now desolate like a cremation ground. All the slaves and servants had fled through the backdoor at the first sign of danger. Chullu Singh's massive corpse slumped at the front entrance. Anyone wanting to enter that house would have to step over his body. He had guarded his *mai-ji's* door with his life. Rongomala's brother was dead as soon as he had been caught. The young man was bound for heaven, chopped in two on the block. Even if Durga could manage to recover from the great blow from the *ray-bansh* bamboo that had landed on her head, she would never walk again. Her pot full of silver had been looted.

Chanda Bir had a clear conscience. He was returning with Rongomala's decapitated head precisely as he had been ordered to by his master. He had not touched even a straw belonging to the Nor house. But why would the others abide by that? They had fought through the night, and at dawn, with deafening war cries, they had commenced looting. Whatever they managed to get their hands on was their gain. The fixed wages that Rajendra Narayan paid them didn't fill even a corner of their bellies. Only Chanda Bir had no worries like that. The great munificence of Ma Chandi meant that the odour of blood was enough to fill his belly. This bleeding, severed head was the symbol of his victory—a treasure richer than a thousand gold coins. He placed it gently on the grass before transferring it from one hand to the other. This night was passing very slowly. The light of dawn was almost here, but not quite. He had returned after triumphing in a great battle. There should be cheering in the streets; instead, the streets were barren, with not a soul to be seen. Except on the other side of the road, there were people headed for the Nor house, carrying pots full of yoghurt. There were also bullock carts transporting sacks full of flattened rice, and earthen vessels full of palm sugar. The offerings for the water ritual would do for the funeral feast for the Nors. Chanda Bir walked faster. The great treasure he carried had to be delivered at his master's court before Raj Chandra awoke from his slumber. Flocks of crows wheeled overhead. They were carrying the news of Rongomala's killing to the palace.

Nineteen

Oh, faithful one! Allah, the Exalted, has crafted you from clay.

Be as humble as earth … Do not be angry like fire.

Ram Bharari spotted the crows flocking above the palace and reined in his horse. It looked like a midden. What had happened—had Rajendra Narayan died? No matter how powerful one was, death was beyond all calculations; it struck like lightning from the sky. Ram Bharari had slept through the night like a corpse. If his wife hadn't jerked him awake this morning, he doubted he would ever have woken up again. All this labour for the water rites had left life barely pulsing within his body; he did not have a smidgen of energy left. He had returned from the Nor house quite late last night. Raj Chandra Chowdhury still hadn't come back with the money by then. Ram Bharari should show up early. If the master woke up and he wasn't close at hand, there would be hell to pay.

Ram Bharari turned his horse away from the palace. A few yards farther, he saw Chanda Bir walking towards him. The servant, dressed up like a warrior, on his way to the palace this early? Chanda Bir was skewed to one side, pulled by the weight of the bundle he was carrying. He was probably just returning from some burglary. Ram Bharari would have just ridden past him, but he stopped when he spotted the blood spatters on Chanda Bir and the blood oozing out of the bundle. Who had this brute destroyed before the day had barely begun? He wasn't even looking around. Even when he saw Ram Bharari waiting, he strode off without stopping, still off-kilter, as if he was walking in his sleep.

Ram Bharari sat thunderstruck on his horse. The sky above the palace was black with crows. The path was flowing with blood. Which way should he go now? East or west? The palace or the Nor house? His duty was to go wherever Raj Chandra Chowdhury was.

As he cantered towards the Nor house, it seemed to Ram Bharari that he was following a trail of blood. Whether he galloped through a field, or steered his horse onto the road, there was no avoiding the blood. It followed him quietly, like a shadow. He felt goosebumps all over. It was beyond him to travel across this frightening lakeshore; if only someone would take pity and come with him. Ram Bharari raised his eyes from the ground. There was no one to be seen in any direction; ahead of him, everything was ablaze. The western horizon was dark with smoke. The smoke and fire in the direction of the Nor house determined Ram Bharari's destination. He whipped his horse and galloped towards the palace.

There were no guards at the main entrance. The broad doors to the outer house also stood wide open. He clambered down from his horse and peeked inside. The chamber was empty. On the floor lay a bell-metal platter displaying a severed, bloody head with long hair. As he flipped the head over with his cane, Rongi gazed up at him, clear-eyed, like a woman alive. The beautiful face was covered in blood. Ram Bharari grabbed his temples and fell to the floor. It was all over. Wherever Raj Chandra was, whether on land or in the sky, he had to find him right this moment.

By the time Ram Bharari had awakened Raj Chandra and galloped his horse to the Nor house, the stilted cottage had been burnt to ashes. The roof of the upper storey of the main house was still on fire. Although the attackers had disappeared, no one was approaching the place. Everyone stood at a distance, watching the fun. Was Ram Bharari supposed to try and douse the fire, or take care of Raj Chandra Chowdhury? The master didn't know of Rongomala's fate yet; as soon as he had seen the Nor house ablaze, he had gone crazy. He kept running towards the inner quarters of the house from the bank of the pond. Chullu Singh, Rongomala, Golap Raiya—he called out the names again and again, and when he got no response, he grew angrier. The tents that had been set up along the lakeshore were in disarray. Every single one of them were cowards. They had all disappeared as soon as they sniffed danger.

It wasn't long before Raj Chandra's confusion disappeared. When Ram Bharari was calling out to people and organising them to put out the fire, Raj Chandra noticed Chullu Singh's corpse sprawling at the main entrance. He leapt over Chullu's thick body into the inner quarters. A great roar erupted from the yard. His wails rose above the clamour of the raging fire. Ram Bharari reached the spot to find Raj Chandra rolling on the ground beside the chopping block with Rongomala's decapitated body in a close embrace. Nearby lay Golap Raiya's body, hacked in two.

What difference did it make now whether the Nor house burned or was saved? He would take his revenge on his uncle. His heart would not be soothed until he placed Chanda Bir's neck on this same chopping block. Raj Chandra mounted his horse and galloped off to the palace. Ram Bharari entrusted the three corpses and the unconscious body of Durga to the care of neighbours and followed his master.

The palace was silent like an abandoned house. As if night had descended in the middle of the day. Rajendra Narayan and Chanda Bir had both gone into hiding very early that morning. In the later hours, in several installments, Mejo Thakurani had fled with Shunonda and Prafulla Kumar and all her slaves and servants. Everyone Raj Chandra wanted within his grasp had disappeared. When he tried to set fire to his uncle's wing of the palace, despite Ram Bharari imploring him not to, Mangal Singh materialised as if he had just emerged from the earth. His men were with him: their sticks thumped the ground, their swords clanged. Matching Mangal Singh's strength was no easy feat. He wasn't human; he was more a blind ogre. A naked sword in one hand, a stick twirling overhead in his other—there was no way to predict which direction his attack would come from. Raj Chandra departed from his own home, driven out by servants and slaves. He had been made a pauper while he slept. He had had no clue! What he had planned for today; and what had actually happened! She who was supposed to be raised from her caste status now lay dead—her head was displayed in the palace while her body sprawled in her own yard.

Raj Chandra couldn't think. It felt as if both his mind and body were controlled by someone else. It took all day, well into night, to get Rongi's head and body in the same place. Like a machine he assembled the funeral pyre, and set the flame to her face. When Rongi's pyre blazed in the mild spring breeze, he was still befuddled. As if through someone else's eyes, he watched the beloved body turn into ashes. His heart and soul burned to ashes, right beside Rongi's deadbody.

When Raj Chandra awoke again, he was already far from Babupur. He had galloped his steed to Meherkul, Manohar Gazi's abode, two days away. Gazi had given him shelter with due honour. He encountered no lack of hospitality or care. The guest quarters, the *mezbankhana*, were set along a lakeshore, facing southwards. In front spread out a long veranda. Behind, a separate cookhouse. Whatever he wanted was stocked right at his fingertips. Servants waited around to carry out his every desire. If he called for one, ten showed up. And all of this Gazi had arranged from behind a veil of quietness, without any bombast or talk.

About a week later, when it seemed like Raj Chandra had regained his strength, Manohar Gazi showed up with much pomp and circumstance. Gazi's favourite elephant, Sher Ali, stood at the main entrance, accoutred in a red covering with golden tassels. It had rained during the night. The day's light had not come out in full force yet. The courtyard was awash in silken light, as pale as curdled milk. Raj Chandra splashed water on his face and climbed onto the howdah on the elephant's back. Gazi was taking him on a bird hunting expedition to the Lalmai Mountains. The elephant climbed higher and higher along the red dirt slopes, decimating the rain-washed trees and undergrowth. It had a regal air about it. Even down on its knees, the animal exuded arrogance. Raj Chandra set foot on the newly sprouted grass and stretched his limbs. Ram Bharari held out his gun and ammunition with alacrity.

The forest ahead of them didn't look wild, it looked like a laid-out orchard of *shaal* trees. The narrow track through the trees was clear of any thorny obstructions. In the soft light of dawn, chandanas, parrots, parakeets and mynahs warbled and chirped joyfully in the trees. Had Gazi brought him to this sanctuary to test his shooting skills? It was possible. Outside the Bhulua region, who would know about the prowess of Pratap Narayan's heir? Here, even Bishwambhar Sur was a nobody. Raj Chandra felt disheartened. He trailed Gazi with a distracted air. They walked a little further and just when he, at Manohar Gazi's signal, took aim and was about to shoot, from afar came the birdcall—*Rat Chandra! Rat Chandra!*—Black Moon, the mynah's shrill lament. Raj Chandra's hand shook.

When Raj Chandra missed his shot, Manohar Gazi smiled to himself behind his beard. His assessment had been correct. This fellow with the long sideburns was useless. He had immersed himself in pleasure-seeking day and night. He had become an ace at playing the flute for women, but had not practised any useful skills. A man who couldn't even shoot down a bird wanted to go to war! He should just give up this jihad of his and return to fall at his uncle's feet. His uncle was his father's brother—they were of the same blood. Even if he did not manage to wrest his inheritance from his uncle, he would at least be granted forgiveness for his insolence. And if he returned riding an elephant, well, that would be quite a feat. Who knows, if the uncle saw the nephew slide down an elephant's trunk right at the palace entrance, he might even bow down.

Manohar Gazi knew the measure of Uday Narayan's line quite well. They were greedy for ostentation and were proficient at showing off their extravagance at the expense of others. The only regret was that Inga Chowdhury had lost his life in an untimely manner simply by sticking his nose into the quarrelsome affairs of this vulgar bloodline.

Raj Chandra Chowdhury had folded at the very first ace Gazi had played. Ram Bharari stood behind them and bit his tongue. As if not Raj Chandra's, but his own honour had been sullied. What had happened to the man? What was gone was gone. Was the man thinking of giving up on his life for that Nor woman?

Several Tipra women filled their water pots from the waterfall and, the pots balanced on their heads with ease, climbed up the steep incline. Their bodies were barely covered in the two strips of fabric they wore. Ram Bharari had never seen such shameless hussies in his entire life. Their airs, their complexion, the wave in their hair! But Raj Chandra barely glanced at them. On the way back from the hunt, Ram Bharari mocked,

I used to be a greedy kitty
Now I'm such a saint
I pray and pause and supplicate
I've taught me such restraint!

Although a servant, Ram Bharari had been his companion since childhood. He had never deserted Raj Chandra's side. It wasn't as if Chowdhury didn't understand what he was implying. But he paid no mind. Since they had arrived in this foreign land, Ram Bharari seemed to have grown bolder. He started to drool anytime he spotted a hussy.

At night, in bed, Raj Chandra thrashed around like a wounded bird. Rongi's alta-painted feet on the funeral pyre floated in the darkness. For whom had she dressed herself so beautifully before her death? Each hour of the night rolled into the next. Someone had stolen all the sleep from his eyes. From a distant shore drifted the broken words from a song:

> *My heart burns, my heart burns*
> *I wanted to build my house in the shade of a tree*
> *My heart burns.*

Raj Chandra could not remember the last time he had wept. The soft pillow under his head grew heavy with his tears.

After that day, Chowdhury was called into Manohar Gazi's personal quarters frequently on this pretext or that. Sometimes there were *mushairas* or musical soirees that lasted the night. As long as he was immersed in the warmth of song and liquor, his wings were clipped. Who would care to know that Raj Chandra's weeping heart flew here and there and everywhere?

Thus the days passed. The months flew by. When Raj Chandra demanded to visit the high earthen borders built beside the Gomti river, Manohar Gazi sent a pair of men with canes with him. It was a beautiful place. The Gomti's waves sounded its music below. Ahead of him lay the enigmatic green mountains of Tripura. Restful, gorgeous, and with endless wealth. The mountains played hide-and-seek with the clouds and beckoned him from afar. Raj Chandra wanted to run there. Or perhaps to stand here and call, to get the Agartala palace to respond to him promptly. How long could he hide away in this Muslim's shelter with his tail tucked between his legs? Even if the Tripura king no longer had the power he once had, a dead elephant was still worth a fortune. The king of Tripura could still crook his little finger, and that would be enough to dethrone Rajendra Khura. One day, in a wine-induced stupor, Raj Chandra mentioned this to Manohar Gazi. Gazi's radiant mien darkened. He twisted his hennaed beard in his fist. When he looked up again, in the light of the candelabra, his eyes glowed red like twin setting suns. Raj Chandra lost his bliss. A life-size portrait of Shamsher Gazi astride his horse hung on the wall in front of them. The white stallion, almost sage-like in appearance, stood with its rider, its head cocked to one side. It was star-marked, black on white. The rider held the reins in one hand, in the other was a naked sword. The long tail of his turban streamed in the wind like a cloud.

From that day onwards, Manohar Gazi's tongue was unlocked; words flowed from him. But the conversation, accompanied by wine, was always the same, and the hero of the stories always the same as well—Shamser Gazi. From Gazi's wars to his wrestling prowess to his charity work. Back then the borgis, the Marathi invaders, were frequently attacking the western region. As a result, the prices of goods skyrocketed even in the marketplaces of Tripura. Daily necessities were dear. Shamser Gazi fixed the prices for basic foodstuffs such as rice, lentils, oil and ghee. Long schedules detailing the prices were nailed up in every marketplace. All shops had to abide by the set prices, otherwise traders faced harsh penalties. Under Shamser Gazi's rule, even the poor farmers of Lower Tripura were able to live on milk and rice.

Shamser Gazi had tried to light the lamp of knowledge in all homes. Once he took over the throne of Tripura, he established a maktab spanning half the Udaypur palace compound. He brought a blind Hafez, a scholar who could recite the entire Quran from memory, from Sandwip to teach at the *maktab*. From Lucknow came a Maulvi to teach Arabic. From Jahangirnagar came a Hindu Munshi to teach Persian. A well-known Pundit was pulled in from Jugidiya to teach Bengali. Shamser Gazi's expansive vision missed nothing. Nothing was too small. Gazi had begun his reign with his imagination stretched over a thousand years. He was a rare one—a ruler so learned, skilful, wise and illustrious was hard to find even among kings and emperors. He held aloft the banner of liberty for the poor and oppressed. He cleared the way by pulling out all the weeds. It was fate that stopped his dreams from reaching fruition.

Manohar Gazi remained silent on how the nawab, Mir Qashim, summoned Shamser Gazi to Murshidabad and blew him up with cannons. If Raj Chandra pushed him, Gazi retracted like a snail in its shell. Whose heart did not break to speak of such sorrow? Still, after a while, he began again, saying, 'Chowdhury, patience! Patience! Today I shall tell you the whole story.' What was there to say about Alizeh Mir Qashim, Nawab of Bengal, Bihar and Orissa? He was a man who was both good and evil. He had bribed his way to the throne, but he couldn't tolerate being at the beck and call of the infidel British rulers. He had paid for his sins while still in this world. 'You sow what you reap,' Manohar quoted from the *Bostaan* and returned to his saga. Shamser Gazi had not been born in a royal family. He was of peasant stock: a dwarf reaching for the moon. He had made it, though. But the rights of those who ruled through generation after generation came first, even if they were wicked and unjust. To Mir Qashim, Krishna Manikya, the deposed king of Tripura, seemed kindred. He acceded to the plea for help from the Hindu king.

Manohar could not finish his tale. His mournful tears dripped into the empty goblet in front of him. When he looked up with his swollen eyes half-shut, his gaze moved beyond everything to where the illustrious Shamser blazed like a spark before dying out. How could Manohar Gazi rise beyond this sorrow?

It was hard to take the measure of a man whose heart seemed so softened with tenderness. Compared to Gazi, Inga's heart had been like a crystal goblet; the insides were clearly in view. People were both good and bad. While Inga had lived, Chowdhury had not appreciated the weight of this quality. Now, day and night, it was Inga he sought in Manohar Gazi. Inga—who did not calculate pros and cons, who slammed his silver cane on the ground, who spat red into the spittoon and roared for war.

Who was Manohar Gazi afraid of? Although Meherkul was just a breath away from the Tripura king's domain, these days it was governed under the Roshnabad district. A *gorah* British man was the master of this realm, a man who had no thoughts other than taxes and revenues. Anyway, the war wasn't going to take place here. Neither was it being waged on false pretenses. Chanda Bir had destroyed the bloodline of the son-in-law of the Meherkul zamindars. Plunging his hands in the blood of such a foe would only prove Manohar Gazi's title of gazi or warrior.

One day, to rile Manohar Gazi, Raj Chandra recounted the tale of Chanda Bir's jaban Kali, his goddess icon in Muslim garb. Gazi was a man of gravitas and did not laugh very often. But when he heard the story, he chuckled. The next moment, his moon-like face darkened as if spattered with ink. Gazi despised that crazed woman. He had no desire to listen to whether, after her murder, Gulbadan had become Kali or Durga in the assassin's hands. His only concern was his little sister, the recently widowed Mehrab. His sister had been wilful since the day she was born. Now she was being stubborn about returning to her own home. Why would a duck fear a storm—this was her constant mantra. She had stopped eating and drinking. She thumped her head against any solid thing. Witnessing her pain, as hard as death's torment, was difficult to bear. Yet Gazi could not send her back to Dewanganj. Neither mother nor son would be safe as long as the assassins were alive.

Raj Chandra looked up. But Gazi didn't say another word, as if he had clad himself in iron armour. His expression was sombre.

The boat had sunk so near the shore! Raj Chandra replaced his wine goblet and left. No matter what people said, there was very little hope of getting milk from such a cow.

There was only one person in Meherkul, Nasir Mohammed, whose mere shadow was enough to make Raj Chandra's heart spread wings like a joyful peacock. Tiny and frolicsome like a little pony, his feet rarely touched the ground. Every morning, he showed up at the Miah Shaheb's doorstep for his lessons, wearing his little skullcap. The rest of the day he was either in the stables or the elephant enclosure. He was usually dressed in loose pants dirtied by sweat-salt, and a white or sky blue shirt dotted with mould. He was friends with all the grooms and mahouts. He rarely came near Raj Chandra. If he beckoned the boy to come close, Nasir Mohammed ran off. Sometimes he made faces at Raj Chandra from atop an elephant calf. The fatherless boy was growing up. He roamed far and wide, the pouch in his shirt heavy with slingshot pellets.

One day, he took out the left eye of Ram Bharari's black horse with his slingshot. Ram Bharari was about to get rid of the old nag for a pittance anyway, since it was suffering from arthritis. But now, at this chance, Ram slapped his chest in grief and wept and wailed loudly, as if he were mourning for the Karbala. Gazi was enormously embarrassed. Right away he ordered for a black horse from his own stables to be brought forth as replacement for Ram Bharari's horse. His nephew couldn't care less though. He still behaved the same—arrogant, reckless. But he didn't play the fool like his father. He was stubborn. He had perfect aim. Already he was setting aside his slingshot and taking up a bow and arrow. His trainer was a Tipra archer. Raj Chandra recalled his own childhood. If only he could somehow travel back to Nasir Mohammed's age by magic!

At the height of the rainy season, Karim Sheikh arrived in Meherkul, carrying a message that began Raj Chandra's life anew.

It was a long letter. Line after line of shaky, uncertainly copied words, ending with Ma Shumitra's thumbprint, cried in agony over missing her son. Alongside all that grief was urgent news. Rajendra was paying for all the evil he had wrought: his old haemorrhoids were acting up again, leaving him in intense pain. He couldn't shut his eyes even for a moment. The man spent all his nights sitting up in his bed. Once, at midnight, there was a knock on her door. Rajendra's hair was a bird's nest, his eyes bloodshot, a sheaf of documents in his hands. There were all kinds of nonsense in those pages about the revenues and tolls and whatnot from the previous year. The zamindari was paying out more than the revenue that was being collected. It took the whole night for the two of them to look through all the documents. But in Ma Shumitra's opinion, if God had written it in your fate, your belly would be full. It was an old excuse—this claim of a bad year. Dividing up the zamindari and all other assets would benefit both sides. Rajendra did not disagree. It wasn't right that her dear son Raj Chandra was exiled and taking shelter at a Muslim abode, especially at such a time. The remainder she would explain in person.

As if it were a summons releasing him from fetters, his mother's letter left Raj Chandra dancing with joy. If he could have, he would have flown home right there and then. Ram Bharari was the one who impeded him. 'Babu! You should take your leave of the Gazi first. Or else, later he'll go around saying Raj Chandra Chowdhury sneaked off like a thief.' Raj Chandra came to his senses. Ram Bharari was right. Not bidding farewell to the one who had sheltered him in his time of trouble would hurt his feelings. It wouldn't look good. Raj Chandra galloped towards the raised earthen borders of the Gomti river. Manohar Gazi had set up camp with his men to guard the borders before daylight.

The mountain rivers had cracked open several deep fissures in the earth along the embankments. Excavating earth, carrying in loads of rocks—there was a lot of work involved in trying to keep the dam shored up. Hundreds of men were labouring. The zamindar himself was there, overseeing the work, despite the pounding rain. If this rain and the ensuing floods could not be contained, the entire district would go under. Gazi was in dire danger.

When Raj Chandra showed up to bid him farewell, Manohar Gazi dismounted from his horse. His achqan was soaking wet. He was carrying his turban under his arm. Water dripped from his long, curly hair and beard. When they embraced each other in farewell, hot tears fell on Raj Chandra's forehead. This world held such people whose only iron was in their invisible armour! When he remounted his horse after promising they would meet again in better days, Raj Chandra stood stock-still for a while. He didn't understand—once the rainy seasons were over, who would travel to meet whom? He wanted to shout and ask Gazi. By then, the heavy rain had placed a fine, silken veil between the two of them. Everything around him looked hazy. Like a watermark, Manohar Gazi appeared in the distance, then disappeared where the embankment restraining the Gomti river curved away.

Twenty

When Raj Chandra's boat docked near the palace, it was past midnight. Silence reigned. Not a soul was near the lakeshore other than the people on the boat. A jamkuli bird sat in the cotton tree by the lake, calling in an ill-omened voice. The surroundings felt eerie enough to raise goosebumps. Ram Bharari got properly scolded by Karim Sheikh for fumbling in the dark trying to light a lamp. He dropped the flint into the water. On their return journey, the chief boatman, Karim Sheikh, had been the one in charge. The passengers as well as the crew had all danced to his tune from beginning to end. The cooking boat and the boat carrying their horses had yet to reach. Still, they couldn't sit here waiting in the dark while danger loomed. Leaving Ram Bharari waiting by the lake, Karim Sheikh escorted Raj Chandra to the main entrance flanked by stone lions, exactly in accordance with Ma Shumitra's instructions. She herself had been waiting there since midnight.

Raj Chandra stood at the main entrance for a while. He felt hesitant to just walk in. He was returning as he had left. Nothing seemed to have changed in the few months that he had been away. He was reentering his home quietly, like a thief.

Ma Shumitra was waiting. When he spotted her thin silhouette moving in the liquid darkness, Raj Chandra walked towards her. They inched together towards the inner quarters. They crept through the inner yard, then along the passageway, straight into Ma Shumitra's bedchamber. She had arranged for everything required for her son to wash up, change his clothes and eat to be set out in her own room. She had personally supervised everything. Even when he sat down to eat, she did not send for Phuleswari. Instead, Ma Shumitra dismissed all the slaves and servants and emptied out her chamber.

How could she have been completely transparent, especially in a letter that was drafted by the palace estate manager? Who knew in whose hands such a letter might fall! The truth of the matter was that Rajendra Narayan was a charlatan of the highest order; he was not a man of his word. Fortunately, she had been able to persuade the Nayeb-e-Reasat, the chief revenue collector, to take their side. He had been in a disagreement with Chanda Bir, so these days he was thoroughly against Rajendra Narayan. The nayeb's advice would be very valuable before they commenced negotiations over the division of the zamindari. This was a country where the rivers gobbled up the land. They would have to make sure to learn the precise and detailed situation with each estate and territory, with land broken by the river, and alluvial land.

In the old days, Raj Chandra would glory at such skullduggery. He would have run off immediately to the nayeb's residence to conspire. But his world had been turned inside out. He, heir of Pratap Narayan, had become a vagrant, and not by choice! Was his mother forgetting that if Manohar Gazi had not offered him refuge, her heart's treasure would have lain discarded in the dirt? Raj Chandra dumped water on his plate which was still full of food, and got up. Ma Shumitra grew agitated. After all that had happened, she couldn't possibly send her son to stay in the outer chamber with only Jugindor to care for him. The times had taken a turn for the worse. If their enemies found a chance now, they would feed him dhatura seeds straightaway instead of merely bhang. For the time being, her son should stay in Phuleswari's bedchamber. However, a wife existed to give birth to a son—she, as mother-in-law, had nothing more to say about this barren daughter-in-law. When the time came, her son would understand everything.

Ma Shumitra was ready to bring order to her son's life: outdoors there would be the zamindari, indoors a new bride clasping the new heir to their bloodline. Rongi didn't exist anywhere—neither in the lines of his mother's letter nor of her face. Even in death, the Nor girl remained an untouchable in the palace. Raj Chandra lowered his head and exited his mother's room.

Phuleswari's chamber was nearby. A lamp flickered faintly inside. The weak light seeped through the blinds and fell on the veranda. Midway, Raj Chandra's heart began keening in grief. Someone was singing a plaintive melody,

At Rongomala's sorrow even the leaves do fade
What dark evil Chanda Bir has made.

As Raj Chandra stood stock-still, the voice melted away like a sudden gust of wind. The low hanging branches of the trees in the orchard swayed gently in the breeze. The thin air bore a strange lament in human voices.

Phuleswari moved away from her window when she saw Raj Chandra. She was awake so late because she could no longer sleep at night. In the evening, at Heera's coaxing, she had washed and even dressed up a little. Then she had held the mirror up to her face and searched and searched—yet the mirror did not reflect Rongi's face. Within moments the image in the mirror grew blurry. No matter how many times you called on them, the dead did not return. If the man came back, he would return alone. Which is what had happened. Like a snake that had lost its gemstone, he lacked shine, he looked sad.

Phuleswari Rai's jewels weighed heavy on her body today. She took off the swan-shaped earrings and had just slipped her fingers into the clasp for her bracelet when Raj Chandra grabbed her hand. His touch was cold like a corpse's. The light in his eyes had gone out. This was no person; this was a shadow. When Raj Chandra crawled close to her in bed, Phuleswari felt numb. The woman whose guise she had taken on to meld her own body with the king's had dispersed into the five elements. Phuleswari moved away and pressed her lips against the cold wall:

Wall, become a tree, I shall climb to the top and stay.

The man did not force her as he used to once. When she turned on her side and sighed, a rash of ashes flew at her from somewhere, replete with the raw smell of burning bodies.

In the morning, Raj Chandra awoke to the same sad song. Who was singing? Phuleswari still lay asleep on the other side of the bed, happily snuggled against the wall. She was sucking her thumb. The song seemed to be drifting over from Phuleswari's aviary. Raj Chandra exited the room and ran into his mother. Ma Shumitra was pacing outside Phuleswari's door instead of being in her prayer room. Clearly, she had not slept all night.

She had felt agitated every few minutes recalling some brazenness that Rajendra Narayan had inflicted on her. Once she thought that someone had climbed down from the slip-covered chandelier and was trying to strangle her. Nearby stood Chanda Bir, wielding a trident like Lord Shiva. Ma Shumitra's life force trembled at her fingertips. She couldn't bring herself to shut her eyes. She left her bed and paced. By the time dawn's light had broken through clearly, she had already made several rounds of the inner courtyard and the gardens. Even if he was asleep, it had comforted her to know that the son she had carried in her womb was nearby.

Ma Shumitra now walked along the garden paths with Raj Chandra. When Pratap Narayan had been alive, these had been the pleasure gardens for husband and wife. In those days, there had been more flowerbeds than fruit trees. Different flowers graced the soil in different seasons. Their fragrance spread beyond the palace, especially during the rainy days. Lotuses bloomed in a small pond in the middle of the gardens; beside the pond was a small, trellised grove where flowering vines twined. The grove was surrounded by rosebushes and many kinds of night blossoms, spreading their perfume. Husband and wife had spent many moonlit nights here, in laughter and play.

She had not walked this way since her husband's death. This part of the garden was now overrun with weeds and unchecked shrubbery. When Phuleswari had arrived, a segment of the garden had been cleared to make space for her aviary. The gardener Haradhan Mali had been sent from Lamchor to take care of the gardens, which had grown lush again with flowers, fruits and birds. But now that the money had dried up, the gardener had disappeared.

Phuleswari had lost her wits alongside the child in her womb. She had no control over herself; how could she pay any attention to the gardens? In any case, that motherless girl, brought up all her life by slaves and servants, had been half a savage to begin with. Her behaviour was more like a bird's than a human's. What could she, the mother-in-law, do? She had tried. Now Phuleswari had composed this song, *At Rongomala's sorrow* … It was not nice to speak ill of the dead. The poor creature had been dealt with unjustly. Still, it was sinful to bring up her name. And that Heera! Instead of curbing Phuleswari, no, she was sticking by her day and night and encouraging all this bad behaviour. That hussy's nature wasn't to do good for anyone; she could only wreak evil. This garden was now the place where the royal daughter-in-law and her maidservant hatched their plans. They spent hour after hour here, day after day, and yet neither ever noticed that the walkway was overrun with weeds.

As she walked barefoot through the untamed undergrowth, Ma Shumitra tripped again and again. Added to that annoyance was that every time a bird warbled or a leaf trembled, Raj Chandra would stop short and prick up his ears listening to who knew what, his expression sad. She stood beside him, surprised. She listened to the wind. She could hear nothing but the murmuring of the trees. Had her son gone mad? Who was she walking with? However, she couldn't stop now.

Ahead of them stood the outer boundary wall of the palace; behind them, Phuleswari's quarters. Ma Shumitra's rooms were hidden by trees. From there to this wall—that was the extent of Raj Chandra's inherited share of their home. If a fair division was made, there was no doubt that he would get this much. Then Ma Shumitra would revive this garden with her own gardener. Then there would be more flowerbeds than fruit trees as there used to be. Flowers of many different colours would flourish. She would sit on a swing in the grove, with her grandson in her lap, and enjoy the breeze. There was no point in telling Raj Chandra any of this at the moment. He seemed quite distracted. Let a few more days pass. Let Raj Chandra settle back into his home. Ma Shumitra forgot the nightmare from earlier and, with each step, began weaving her new dream.

A narrow canal ran beside the boundary wall. A makeshift bamboo bridge was enough in the rainy season. The rest of the year, people just walked across. This season, they had engaged labourers to widen the canal. The bamboo bridge was missing. The work had progressed very quietly. Were they building a moat—were they scared of an attack? Mother Shumitra's brow creased. The song of sorrow vanished from Raj Chandra's mind. His jaw clenched. This time, both mother and son had set foot in the same old trap. That eternal shyster Rajendra Narayan had said one thing, but he was doing another: secretly, he was still preparing for war.

The nayeb or chief tax collector, Harendra Ghosh, said the same thing when he sat down to lunch with them. He had pretended to go home from the courthouse and then, pivoting abruptly, had scuttled over to Ma Shumitra's wing. The elder mistress of the palace had summoned him—she needed a secret meeting right away. There was no way to avoid the summons, especially since the chief tax collector's own interests were involved. The court would reconvene once the sun moved westwards. It would be midnight by the time they would wrap up the day's business. Although she was elderly, it was unseemly for a man to visit the independent widow's chambers at that hour. The rumours would ride the wind; even if she was a woman with an adult son around. They might as well take care of their discussions right now.

But such discussions could not be resolved at one sitting. Neither were they ever over and done with. The tax collector's eyes bugged out in surprise when he discovered that Ma Shumitra had no knowledge of the moat being dug around the palace. So, Rajendra Narayan hadn't informed her. But if she couldn't keep tabs on what was going on right under her nose, how would she keep up with what was taking place behind the scenes? The sum of it was that they would need loyal men at every turn. They should know right away if even a single leaf trembled in a tree. The excavations for the moat had begun when the rumours that Raj Chandra had taken shelter at Manohar Gazi's abode were substantiated. The digging was halted midway when new information arrived: Raj Chandra was now a rat in a trap. Uncle and nephew, Manohar Gazi and Nasir Mohammed, were en route to the holy city of Mecca to perform the Umrah Hajj.

Raj Chandra was startled. The information was accurate. The date for Manohar Gazi and Nasir Mohammed's departure for the Umrah Hajj had been fixed. It was Bibi Mehrab who had hindered their plans. Her older brother Manohar Gazi had become long in the tooth, so it was natural that at his age, he would want to gain Allah's favour by kissing the sacred black stone—Alhamdulillah. But why drag his sister's little treasure along on this journey? Did Bibi Mehrab have anyone left in this world other than her son? Gazi's face had paled at this question. He had forfeited the hefty advance he had paid for their ship. But how did the Babupura people know the ins and outs of all this Meherkul gossip?

Such was Chanda Bir's prowess. He had agents everywhere. If he threw out a net and pulled it in, there would be hundreds caught like small fry.

What was he saying, this tax collector whose days and nights were spent with his nose stuck in documents and books? So he knew the ins and outs of Chanda Bir quite well. What bushel had he been hiding his light under all this time? Ma Shumitra had displayed quite astute judgement in persuading him to take their side. Raj Chandra's wounded heart revived.

But Ma Shumitra deflated like a pricked balloon. She was bewildered: who was right? Harendra Ghosh or their old estate manager? A few days ago, the old man was on his way back from the marketplace when Rajendra Narayan had grabbed him. 'Please, give me some advice. This estate that was handed down by our fathers and grandfathers—who am I supposed to hand it over to? Who knows in what land our son Raj Chandra has hidden himself!'

'That is a complete lie,' said Harendra hotly, as he picked the bones from his fish. 'The master's bluster grows by the day. He goes around telling lies all the time to keep in the good graces of others.'

The servants and slaves had all been dismissed as soon as the food had been served and the door had been latched shut. The mistress herself, Ma Shumitra, would serve whatever they needed. The tax collector was licking his fingers, scraping his plate and licking them again, yet Ma Shumitra had completely forgotten to spoon some amshatta chutney onto his plate. Then, while chewing on paan, Harendra Ghosh made a statement which landed on her head like a thunderbolt. A pair of hand cannons abandoned by Portuguese pirates had been languishing in the armoury since the days of Mahesh Narayan. On Chanda Bir's advice, Rajendra Narayan had recently had them brought out to be repaired. Chief Tax Collector Harendra Ghosh had been summoned to the courthouse's inner chamber at an odd hour for this purpose. It wasn't possible for him to comment, right to the master's face, on the wisdom of wasting money at a time of scarcity. He was merely a servant bound by orders. Chanda Bir had trudged off, clutching bundles of cash. The airs he put on! As if he was the chief quartermaster of the imperial army of Delhi. Even the tax collector himself was feeling harassed. If there was any fuss over the revenues and tolls being collected, he had to apply to that ignorant fellow Chanda Bir for the use of even a couple of men. All the guards, the pikemen and the like, were under his command. Because the Nor house raid had earned the ogre a promotion. The sum of it was, if there was war, Raj Chandra couldn't count on the army of his ancestral estate. He would have to seek support elsewhere.

Chief Tax Collector Harendra Ghosh was about to say a few more things. But in the middle of his speech, Mother Shumitra opened her door wide, saying, 'It's time you left, I have too many things to do,' and effectively broke up their meeting. Even if it irked her son, what else could she do? The moment war had been mentioned, her head had begun to spin. Then, Harendra Ghosh, by explicating the whole situation, had just made it worse. Nayeb-e-Reasat—a mouthful of a title. But, in action, he was a lame duck. What use was it to listen to the excuses and prattle of someone who had greyed his hair counting other people's money? Rajendra Narayan's nature was to break his word. He was probably just using his promises of dividing the zamindari as a delaying tactic. If war was inevitable, Mother Shumitra needed a second Chanda Bir, a warrior, whose word would be command to her army. Her son, despite all his training from childhood, had not turned out to be a warrior. He had wasted his life hunting birds and playing the flute.

Although he had no flute in hand, Raj Chandra left the palace soon after the tax collector. He was already tired of the swift changes in his mother's moods—this moment sunlight, and the next, a storm. How did women live confined to these inner quarters? It was like a prison sentence, a lifelong one. On the way out, Raj Chandra picked up Ram Bharari, disrupting his daydreaming. Ram had grown a layer of fat from lolling in the servant quarters in Manohar Gazi's abode. Even when he slid his foot into the stirrup, he couldn't manage to mount his steed. Two men had to be called over to push and shove his ass onto the horse. He was panting as he held his whip, his chest heaving like bellows, as if he had expended the full sum of his energy just mounting his ride. If the man had stayed any longer at Meherkul, he would probably have volunteered to convert and be circumcised. Such was the power of nawabi luxury.

Raj Chandra and Ram Bharari sat astride their white and black horses. The two of them galloped through dusty roads like they used to in the old days. Leaving behind the royal turnpikes, they took the earthen borders by the crop fields; they jumped over canals and ditches. They led the horses through water that reached up to their hocks. Flute melodies coursed through their veins as they used to in the old days. Suddenly, from far away, the sound of weeping drifted towards them. The horses came to a standstill at the newly raised bank of Rongomala's lake near the Nor house.

The lake had almost turned into a sea as the water overflowed the banks in this rainy season. Just as they had once imagined. The water roiled in the brisk breeze. The clear water was like a mirror. However, people rarely visited the lake, let alone wash or bathe or fill their water pots there. Fear and respect had joined hands to bring forth these lines from their tongues:

Chanda Bir was such a brave soul, oh brother, such a brave soul
he is

Nine hundred Mogs had their heads chopped off by a single stroke of his.

Chief Ramya had brought no more than two hundred men with him. People cared nothing for accuracy. Even Raj Chandra didn't know how many diggers had survived the attack and managed to make their way home. Their blood swirled in the depths of the lake. Who knew how many rains it would take to wash that away?

The only one who didn't worry about such things was Ayna's husband Adam Ali, the man driven mad by love. Every single day, he journeyed to the lakeside from Shudharam, completed his ablutions in the waters of Rongomala's lake and stood on the bank to say his prayers. It was a long path he walked. If he couldn't make it before the early afternoon hour for the Zohr prayers, he stayed long enough to say his late afternoon Asr prayers. But he never missed his namaaz hours. Today, Adam Ali arrived while Raj Chandra was still there.

Raj Chandra loosened his horse's reins and squinted into the distance. The water in the lake glinted in the sunshine like the liquid, tearful eyes of Rongomala. The wind swept the water into high waves. Ram sat astride his horse in the same pose, keeping close to Raj Chandra. He couldn't decide whether to dismount or not. At that moment he noticed a passerby crossing the ditch with his shoes tucked under his arm. The man was wearing a red lungi, raised about a hand's breadth above his ankles. His torso was bare, and on his head, he wore a tiny gold-embroidered skullcap, like a child's. As if the two horsemen right in front of him were invisible, this odd man placed his shoes on the bank and scampered into the water until it reached his knees. He spread the water with his hands, creating ripples. He rinsed out his mouth and completed his prayer ablutions. He ran his fingers through his sopping beard and then clambered up the bank. He stood in prayer as if the grass itself was his prayer mat. He prayed for a long time.

By then, the other side of the lakeshore had disgorged four boys clad in loincloths. They grasped clods of earth in their hands. They came here about the same time every day, when Adam Ali showed up to pray. Today, when they spotted Raj Chandra, they tried to flee. Ram Bharari galloped towards them. They were just young boys, quaking with fear. One had even pissed his loincloth. Ram Bharari jumped off his horse. 'Hey, you monkeys! Why did you bring those clods of earth with you?' The one who had pissed himself pointed towards Adam Ali. 'That madman. We brought the clods to pelt him with.'

By then, Adam Ali was sitting facing westwards, his palms spread in front of him in prayer. His eyes were closed. The madman reeled side to side while he chanted his prayers. His voice, low, dripped sorrow and woe. For whom was he weeping at Allah's court? Was the lover he mourned the Burmese lass or Rongomala? A true lover's heart made no distinctions. His yearning soul had taken wing towards the place where Rongomala had journeyed six months ago. The yearning lover's weeping made the whole world heavy with sorrow.

As if someone had thrown powdered chilli in his eyes, Raj Chandra's eyes burned. His horse crept forward in a crouch and, his rider still astride, gradually made its way down the steep incline of the lakeshore. The sun had moved farther down the horizon and the crops shimmied in the light breeze. The wind carried the hum of the same sad tune that had floated towards him that morning from Phuleswari's aviary.

Twenty-one

Ma Shumitra had disbanded Phuleswari's bird school. At her sudden onslaught, some of the birds took shelter in the cages, some in treetops. Phuleswari had retreated to her own chamber. Still, Ma Shumitra's rage continued unabated. Cane in hand, she rampaged through the orchards and the gardens. 'Some have fun while another's house burns. This daughter-in-law might have been born in a human household, but she's no human being. What is this creature that Lamchor's Kali Charan palmed off on me with all his money? I can't keep this thing, this creature, nor can I throw it out.'

When she spied Ma Shumitra's angry figure, Heera disappeared from the aviary as fast as she could. But this whole palace was nothing but a large cage. She ran up against Ma Shumitra coming and going. There was barely any room to breathe. A wall had been erected between Ma Shumitra's wing and Mejo Thakurani's wing. The separation between the two descendant households was complete. Pots and pans, plates, glasses and bowls—each wing had their own now. Even the slaves and servants had been divided up; they continued their quarrels through the chinks in the walls and the fences. The courthouse, the storehouse, in fact almost all of Babupur district was in Rajendra Narayan's control.

Ma Shumitra guarded the little pond beside the inner quarters. She couldn't survive unless she handled water day and night. Since she herself had put up a fence of thorny branches, Mejo Thakurani had no way to get to the pond anymore. They were using water hauled in from the lake for all the cooking, cleaning, bathing and washing in that wing.

Heera reached the pond through the back entrance. The afternoon sun shed gold onto the water. The fragrance of coral jasmine and orange jessamine blossoms arrived in gusts with the breeze. The birds trilled in many voices in the trees. Heera's heart danced as soon as she set foot outside. Ahead of her lay the newly dug moat. She looked this way and that and climbed down the bank. The water came up to her waist. She raised her clothing as she crossed. Her sari-end streamed in the wind as she walked along the raised earthen ridges of the field and sang.

Suddenly, Durga Dashi whooshed out from the reeds. Heera's singing stopped. Oh, it was that crazed woman, the one who roamed the streets ever since the Nor house had been ransacked. Instead of being grateful for the rice or the cowrie-coins people offered her, she kept begging for silver. Durga held out her begging hand to Heera as well. She pointed to Heera's anklets and said in a sad voice, 'Won't you give me one of your kharus? Please? If I wear them they will tinkle when I walk.' Well! What fancy! But then, a madwoman was something to fear. Heera stopped herself from responding to the madwoman and bolted. She ran straight to Karim Sheikh's home.

Her heart was racing. Her throat was parched. Heera sat down and accepted water from Somiron Bibi and drank all of it at one go. At least her silver anklets still hugged her ankles; she hadn't had to sacrifice them. But that slut who used to queen it over the stilted cottage, what an end she had come to! She was dressed in rags. Her hair was ropey. Her skin, as dark as the sky, was smeared with dirt and clay. Her skeletal body exuded a smell like that of a duck pen or a chicken coop. Who knew how long since she had last eaten or bathed! Perhaps she should have called the madwoman in and fed her a fistful of rice.

Karim Sheikh sat facing her on the stoop, swaddled in a quilt. It was unclear whether he had heard her talk about Durga becoming a beggar. Heera and Somiron Bibi were speaking in low voices. In the last few months, Karim Sheikh's hair and beard had turned completely grey. Chanda Bir showed up at his doorstep every single day to issue some new threat. If he didn't swear fealty to the master, Rajendra Narayan, he would be imprisoned. His house would be ravaged. He, along with his wife and his offspring, would be sent into exile. However, this didn't seem to be worrying his wife. She had different concerns.

Her husband sat on the stoop day and night, bundled in that quilt, and snapped at her whenever she tried to talk to him. He was constantly hitting their mute daughter. 'Torture, the torture of the grave, has descended on us right here on this earth.' Somiron Bibi took the *kaun* porridge off the heat. She pulled Heera behind the house. She lowered her voice as she changed the subject. Her world was darker without Ayna. Her daughter was so afraid of her father that she hadn't dared to visit once since she had left. Ayna was sending message after message—she was in great distress and she was starving. Her husband wasn't working. Her dear father had been right. The man had completely lost his wits after eating the vulture meat that those witches had cooked for him.

Adam Ali had been raving a few days ago, and they had to call in an exorcist to get rid of the djinn possessing him. But that had led to newer complications. The mustard oil in the eyes, the burning red chilli in the nose—none of it seemed to be working. In the darkness, the exorcist had been hitting his ass with the plank used to bar the door. Ayna and her mother-in-law wept and flailed in the yard, tormented by the situation. But once Adam Ali's skin split open and oozed blood, a strange thing happened—the djinn possessing the man confessed that it was actually Rongi's ghost: Rongomala, a woman whose shadow Adam Ali had never seen. But he had heard of her. Who hadn't? Even though she had been a whore, her murder by Chanda Bir had made people mourn her. Even the birds had grieved. The trees had shed leaves like tears. Babes had refused to suckle. The loss of the most exquisite one had blinded the entire kingdom. This wound could not be healed. However, the living had to work and eat.

Everyone eventually returned to their work and their lives, except that fool Adam Ali. Seizing the chance, the ghost of the dead beauty took possession of his body. Rongomala's spirit was so iron-willed that she refused to leave even after the beating, even after being forced to sniff the bones of dead cows. After abject pleading, the ghost stated in a nasal tone: if Adam Ali visited Rongi's lake every day and performed at least one *wakt* of his namaaz there, she would release him.

The spirit had shown Adam Ali a way out; but what about Phuleswari Rai? Rongomala was granting release to one but taking possession of another. Her ghost cared nothing about whether the one she possessed was a man or a woman. When Rongi had still been alive, Phuleswari used to try to dress up like her. That was different, though—many women wanted to compete with the whores that their husbands kept. But why all this drama over her now that she was dead? No one paid any heed to Heera's words. Rongomala's song would begin even before dawn could break through. It was as if even the birds in the aviary had forgotten all else and sang that same tune. Dispersing Phuleswari's bird school today was the only good thing Ma Shumitra had ever done. If this only put a stop to that ghostly singing in the palace!

As soon as she returned, Heera was summoned to Phuleswari's bedchamber. She wouldn't let Heera out of her sight for more than a moment! When Black Moon spotted Heera hurrying toward the room, instead of squawking *Baandi, Baandi* from his perch, he began singing Rongomala's song. The other birds joined in with Black Moon. They had already learned the lesson by heart; it made no difference whether the bird school was disbanded or not.

Phuleswari sat on her bed swinging her legs and giggled. Heera felt as if she had lived in darkness all these days, and today, finally, her visit to Karim Sheikh's house had opened her eyes: she saw Phuleswari and Rongomala as one, like twin sisters in the womb.

Heera's belief that Rongi had left Adam Ali and was now possessing Phuleswari grew firmer when Phuleswari asked to exchange beds with her. Heera stepped back in anger and disgust. This grass widow finally had her husband all to herself! And now she was asking to exchange beds. She was trying to send her servant to her husband's bed while keeping herself aloof. This had to be the machination of Rongi's spirit. Alive, she had kept Raj Chandra Chowdhury in complete control. Now, dead, she had lost her body; what else did the poor creature have, to retain control of her man? With no recourse, she had possessed Phuleswari. She wouldn't allow Phuleswari to be a proper wife to Raj Chandra.

Phuleswari had been restless ever since her husband had returned. As soon as night descended, she began twisting and squirming. And now, she was trying to deter him from sharing her bed. Jealousy, that's all it was. That Nor girl's belly was full of jealousy. Who could exorcise such a jealous spirit? Heera could attempt to summon the same exorcist from Shudharam who had treated Adam Ali. However, the exorcist was Muslim—what if the spirit demanded that Phuleswari perform a wakt of namaaz every day? That might be a problem. Phuleswari was the daughter of a Hindu household; she had never learned *duas* or such.

In the end, Raj Chandra saved Heera from her dilemma. He spotted an empty room at the other end of the inner quarters and volunteered to stay there. Two mercenaries with guns guarded his door. The boundaries between the inner and outer quarters disappeared. Late at night, unknown men from far-off lands came through the back entrance into their wing. The employees guarding the main entrance were all loyal to Rajendra Narayan. Those who had recently shifted allegiance to Raj Chandra were all keeping their feet planted in both boats. They worked for Rajendra during the day, and at night, tiptoed their way to Ma Shumitra's wing, to plan their conspiracy. The others were merely bees lusting after honey. Raj Chandra was fumbling his way forward in the darkness by throwing clods of earth ahead, to scope out the lay of the land. This was no time to play hide-and-seek with his wife. And anyway, force could only be exerted on someone whose heart ebbed and flowed with love. But this woman's flower had withered while still in the bud. She had been over the moon when her husband had absconded. Now that he was back, she was in a fix. She couldn't figure out where to hide herself. Phuleswari's birds were also insufferable. Every day they sang songs of sorrow. What use was it to listen to any of this? A man's job was to go to war.

Raj Chandra woke from his siesta alone in his chamber. His heart raced as if a herd of horses was galloping across his chest. A bitter taste overlaid his tongue. Manohar Gazi had shown up in his dreams, in the middle of the day. He appeared as a sage dressed in white, sitting in a howdah atop his favourite elephant Sher Ali, waving his hands as he slowly disappeared in the murk. Sher Ali swayed as he walked at a leisurely pace like a king. He could still hear the trumpeting of the creature. Gazi had promised him they would see each other again—when would that auspicious day arrive? It had been almost a year. Clouds grumbled in the sky; another rainy season was about to descend.

Prominent people from his own faith had taken a stand against Raj Chandra. That letter of invitation for the water ritual had turned out to be a disaster. Since then he had not left out any jaban-Muslims or any *Nassara*-Christians in his pleas for help. Everyone was just playing him. Last Sunday, on church day, Raj Chandra had visited the indigo kuthi, the textile bungalow. He had been hoping that, if necessary, perhaps he could procure a few red-coated soldiers from the *kuthiyal* Englishman. The sahib was busy clicking his tongue, as if he couldn't hear Raj Chandra at all, expressing sorrow that instead of bullets, Rongi had been murdered by *dhama*-machetes. Then—*gurum, gurum*—he pulled on his hookah again.

It had been eight or nine years since they had last seen each other. The sahib had discarded his British raiment and turned into a native landlord. His face was graced by moustachios with waxed ends. He was wearing a mulmul shirt and a pair of flowing pants loosely tied around his waist. He no longer wore his hair in a ponytail; instead, his blond hair was wrapped in a bright red turban. Beside him burned a silver narghile with glowing coals. Everything was native. In fact, inside his bungalow, where the sahib had set out at least ten rooms as the zenana mahal, the women's wing, blonde, white women were curiously absent. Rumour had it that his domain was ruled by five native women. As he approached the entrance to the bungalow, Raj Chandra spotted a group of half-breed children running and playing in a field nearby.

It was a meeting in name only. Evening melted into night, and the sahib remained ensconced in another world. Although his bad habit of using his telescope to lust after women had lessened with age, his lewd nature hadn't changed much. He wanted all the details about Rongomala. And the whole time, he was sneaking sideway glances at Rongomala's lover, Raj Chandra.

Tales of Rongomala's beauty had travelled from tongue to tongue and reached the sahib. He had not had time to cast his bait her way. And then, that beauty had been killed. The murder had been quite a nine days' wonder. The discerning had even composed songs about her. Once a young potter, here to plead for a loan, had sat under a tree, humming,

Rongomala's beauty was such, they said,
Raj Chandra for her did lose his head.

This was what all his efforts had yielded! Was this man a human being or a jackal of a merchant? This sahib's palm was never held out to give, but always stretched out to grab. He would promise one thing now, and then later ask for payment per soldier. Raj Chandra felt he couldn't bear to even look at the shine of the sahib's hazel eyes. *Oh, mistress, I don't want your alms, just get your dog off me.* Pratap Narayan's son, Raj Chandra Chowdhury, had no need for these soldiers uniformed in red or blue coats. He stood up suddenly and marched out of the room. The sahib was by then banging on the table singing Rongomala's song in a hoarse voice. His accompanists, waiting nearby in the forest, began hooting and howling. The man was whimsical like a king. But merely a jackal king.

Raj Chandra washed his hands of the whole business and swore that very day that he would never, ever in this lifetime ask that jackal for help again. Whether he lived or died, he would achieve what he could on his own. But why had Gazi shown up in his midday dreamscape? What did it mean? Raj Chandra sat fretfully on his bed till late afternoon. As soon as the night grew late, the night owls would begin their comings and goings. Nothing was actually happening; it was all just useless talk. All of them could go to hell. Raj Chandra latched his door and settled down to smoke some hashish.

As soon as night descended, Raj Chandra got rid of his own hired guns and left the palace. In a stupor, from the drug, he galloped his horse down unfamiliar paths. His body floated in the wind like a feather. Who cared if this would make Ma Shumitra angry? What use was all this conflict and war in this lifetime anyway? Thanks be, at this hour there was no one to his right or his left to guard him; he was completely alone.

It wasn't too late in the night yet. Although the rooms in Chanda Bir's house were illuminated by lamps, there was no sound of the people within. Perhaps everyone was busy eating supper.

Raj Chandra tethered his horse to a tree and walked forward on uncertain feet. The entrance to the home-temple stood open. The scent of burning incense and sandalwood permeated the air. The oil in the lamp was almost gone; the flame had grown low. Raj Chandra stood at the entrance and made eye contact with the goddess. The goddess seemed to move. Her emerald eyes glinted in joy. Her nose ring quivered. When Raj Chandra brought his palms together to pay his respects, the goddess seemed to find his gesture vastly amusing. She giggled loudly like in the old days. The thrum of her laughter resounded across the world. People left their food on their plates and ran to her.

Raj Chandra fled with his tail between his legs. Behind him pursued the discarnate, goosebumps-raising noise of the imprisoned Gulbadan laughing and weeping at the same time. The din followed him to the main entrance of the palace. Then, in smouldering pain, it turned back. Raj Chandra knew the goddess was hungry. She wanted blood: the blood of Chanda Bir.

Twenty-two

Nothing in this world happened without intercession. Some money needed to be spread out here and there. Ma Shumitra agreed. The tax collector was not talking nonsense. When Rajendra Narayan did not respond even after being summoned several times, Ma Shumitra played her ace. From her iron chests and from beneath the ground emerged bundles of money. If, in these dire days, they didn't use all that wealth that their Lamchor in-laws had sent over, it would all go to waste. She handed the money over to her son. Raj Chandra, with Ram Bharari by his side, sped off in a different direction each day. Money flew every which way. In the dark of night, they were stockpiling ammunition and other gear in Ram Bharari's barn. The other estate owners, landholders and traders lined up behind Raj Chandra, contingent upon the cash advances he made them. Even the madmen, the unemployed and the drunkards were not left out. In fact, they seemed to constitute the lion's share. Now all they needed to do was set a date.

On the day Raj Chandra was supposed to raise the banner of war at the Chandraganj marketplace, he woke at dawn and dressed himself like a warrior. Then he went to bid farewell to his mother. When he left, Ma Shumitra entered her prayer room and shut the door. Her son was being forced to take up arms to gain possession of what was rightfully his by birth! Only God knew who was responsible for this. Today would go either to Rajendra or to Raj Chandra. Mother Shumitra would not open her door until there was news, good or bad.

The war drums sounded in the afternoon. Both sides had swords and shields and cannons and guns. Battle commenced. Ear-shattering booms rang out. The women of the palace—the daughters-in-law, the daughters, the servants, the slaves—had gathered by the pond in the women's wing to watch the fun. Each person was shouting justification for whichever side they supported. It was as if another war would begin, right there. In the middle of all this, when a cannonball hit a kewra tree not far from them, Heera pulled Phuleswari away from the pond. Phuleswari was thrashing about. She didn't want to go back indoors. Heera pushed her into her bedchamber and locked it from outside.

The birds were screeching in the aviary. Why should they stay caged, only to burn to death, especially since they had wings? It was the two-legged, wingless humans who were in trouble—what should they do, where could they go? If they lived in a walled-in palace like the royals, that would have been one thing. But most of their houses were flammable. Their lives were easier to turn into ashes. All the folks who lived in the vicinity of Chandraganj marketplace began evacuating their neighbourhoods, fleeing like insects.

From the other side, Adam Ali alone waded in against the tide. He carried his sandals in his hand, while on his head rested a turban embroidered with gold thread. These familiar paths and streets seemed strange to him today. Even the air smelled different. The news of war between uncle and nephew had spread everywhere. No one was sitting at home today. People assembled in street corners, crowding every nook and cranny. Even those fleeing with bundles stopped a moment to look at Adam Ali. They waved their hands at him and told him not to go any farther. Now and then, gibberish fragments reached his ears: 'Why is that madman headed that way?' 'Oh, you fool, don't go that way, go this way!' 'Death has summoned this madman. That's why he's rushing that way.' 'Is he an idiot? Can't he hear the cannons roar? Utterly mad.'

Although Adam Ali had become accustomed to being harassed as a madman, occasionally it gave him pause. Why did people call him crazy? Did he dance in the streets wielding a branch? Did he chase children? They were just ignorant. In this lifetime, he had neither heard gentle words nor had he been fated to receive a speck of kindness. Whenever they had the chance, they clobbered him with clods of earth, or spat on him. Anyway, Adam Ali did not have the time to listen to the claptrap of all these people. With every step, he chanted Allah's name from the depth of his guts, as if he was about to embark upon a jihad. His chest rose and fell with the rhythm of his stride.

Once upon a time, this area had been terrorised by frequent attacks from Mughals, Mogs and Portuguese pirates. The alluvial soil of this region had been reddened by the blood of many different races. Once upon a time, the night winds had quaked to the drumming hoofbeats of the countless horses of the imperial army. But that had been a long time ago. All those memories had been erased in just a few generations.

Adam Ali did not comprehend what the blasting whistles or the pounding *nakara*-drums meant. He was close to the Chandraganj marketplace. Rongomala's lake was still about half a mile away. The hour for the Zohr prayers had passed; it was almost time for Asr. It was a longtime habit—he was feeling uneasy about missing his prayers. But before he had passed the marketplace and reached the road, he spotted Raj Chandra in iron armour, astride his white steed. He stopped walking.

Raj Chandra was galloping from one end of the battlefield to the other. Many of his soldiers had drunk bhang before coming to battle. The hired gunners seemed to be targetting swamp demons rather than battling foes—every cannonball was landing either in an empty field or on the kewra and tamarind trees. This was bringing much joy to the infantry, who were already high on bhang; they could barely breathe, they were laughing so hard. How many things could Raj Chandra take care of singlehandedly? One drop of piss was enough to spoil a barrel of milk. Raj Chandra's whip whistled in the air. He was dripping sweat and still he couldn't get these bastards to line up. So much money just gone to waste, and now his life was about to, as well. His face was burning with anger.

Raj Chandra's bright red face aroused some tenderness in Adam Ali's heart. His eyes shone. What a commanding young man! And why wouldn't he be? He was Rongomala's lover Raj Chandra Chowdhury. Since the Nor girl had been murdered, a beautiful young woman, armless and legless, was showing up in Adam Ali's dreams. Endless tears trickled from her beetle-black eyes. She wanted her body back. It was very strange. Adam Ali was in a quandary. Even when he tried to explain, the beautiful woman wouldn't listen. She tugged at his skullcap with her invisible hands. Her words were cutting; but her voice was honey. She laughed while pretending to weep. And her coquetry! It didn't matter what people said; he couldn't just dismiss the capricious requests of such a woman. But other than raising his hands to Allah in prayer, what could a penniless, destitute man like Adam Ali do?

Suddenly Adam Ali awoke from his stupor. A tumult had broken out behind him. Chanda Bir and his army had arrived, hollering war cries. Raj Chandra's forces had dispersed like bees fleeing a broken hive. Adam Ali's prayers for the day were done for. He pushed through the throng and stood under the pakur tree in the middle of the marketplace. He placed his slippers at the base of the tree and pulled his lungi up between his legs, tucking it in tightly at the back.

Chanda Bir's men held their swords high as they attacked. The ground trembled as the horses stamped. Naked blades glinted through the air. Adam Ali's eyes dazzled. With his hand on his forehead to shade his eyes, he sought Chanda Bir. He would provoke a reckoning with that murdering brute. But what could he accomplish with empty hands? At least if he had a sword or a machete, he could grab hold of the handle and swing it this way and that. Allah was ever merciful; he granted the prayers of his truly faithful. Suddenly a giant of a man fell right in front of him, an unsheathed sword in his hand, a kirich tied to his waistband. He was engaged in hand-to-hand combat. It was hard to tell who was on which side. Adam Ali shouted *Allahu Akbar* and leapt into the fray, gripping the man's waistband. His aim: to seize his kirich.

God only knew what was written in their fates today. As the day waned, the silence of the grave descended all around them. Even the wind was quiet. Not a sound came from anywhere. Step by step, Heera edged away from the pond.

In the early evening, the sounds of ululation arose from Mejo Thakurani's wing. The clanging of bells and cymbals deafened everyone around. Raj Chandra Chowdhury had been defeated by Chanda Bir's army. They had fled the battlefield. In the second hour of the night, after chasing Raj Chandra to the end of the kingdom, Chanda Bir returned with his men pounding the war drums. Rajendra Narayan had spent the whole day guarding the courthouse. When he heard the victory drums, he heightened the security measures for Mother Shumitra's wing. Whatever celebrations were in order would take place in the outer courtyard. Rajendra Narayan had issued strict orders—if anyone took even a step towards the inner quarters, his head would be chopped off. Even though circumstances had made them enemies, Ma Shumitra and Phuleswari were still the mother and daughter-in-law of his household. Any assault on their honour would be an insult to the Chowdhury dynasty.

Ma Shumitra spent that night in her prayer room. When she emerged the next day, the bristle of new hair on her head had turned grey. She looked half the height she had been the day before. She stood in the yard with her suddenly smaller body. She glanced at everyone shyly, as if she was a new bride meeting her in-laws for the first time. Then she started towards the pond with her bell-metal pot in hand, like she did every day.

Heera trailed behind her; all the other slaves and servants, including Kalitara, stood frozen, watching her. No one had the courage to come forward. The pond and the jetty had been seized overnight. Because the son had lost the war, the mother had lost her right to bathe in the pond. Ma Shumitra returned from the thorny fence that had gone up overnight. She embraced the tulsi tree that stood on a plinth and slithered down to its base. Everyone thought she was about to strike her forehead and begin a lament. But her eyes were dry and her gaze vacant. No one looked away from Ma Shumitra, as if she were some exotic caged beast right in front of their eyes.

She started towards the garden walkway, still carrying her bell-metal pot. The cool dawn breeze blew through the trees. The birds sang Rongomala's song. Ma Shumitra stopped walking and cocked her ears. A sad smile blossomed on her wrinkled face. Gradually, the maids and slaves made their way towards her. By then, the mistress of the royal household had climbed into the tiny pool in the middle of the garden. The water, viscous and covered in rotten leaves and moss, came up to her knees. Still, she submerged herself in it, standing up and going down again and again. As if she was a drunken elephant in a puddle. When she was pulled out of the rotten pool, she was shivering like someone possessed, and her eyes were bloodshot. That night, her body burned with a high fever and she began talking in delirium. The next day, the royal physician was summoned. His remedy yielded no improvement. The fever rose, and with it, her delirious speech. The physician gave up and left. On day three, Rajendra Narayan appeared and, sobbing woefully, prostrated himself at his sister-in-law's feet. After all was said and done, she was still his playmate from childhood—they had been so close in age.

Back then, he had not yet learned to swim. Shumitra Devi had just been wed to his brother. He remembered watching her the first time she returned from her naiyor visit at her father's household. She descended from her palanquin with her jewellery tinkling against her body. She had been wrapped in a *nayansukhi* sari from Dhaka, the fabric as fine as cobwebs. The child-bride had shown up by the pond all dressed up, carrying an armful of dolls and other toys, and found her brother-in-law sinking and bobbing in the water, about to drown. Ma Shumitra had always been a woman to take risks. She had jumped straight into the water and pulled Rajendra out all by herself. He couldn't let her die like this—she who had once saved his life. Rajendra Narayan banged his head against her bed and swore an oath to relinquish his claim on the pond. This promise worked better than any medicine. Having reestablished her rights to the pond, Ma Shumitra gradually recovered.

After such a war, there was no way to sit indoors and know who had died and who had survived. This wing was now worse than a dungeon. The main entrance was carefully guarded. Anyone coming or going through the back entrance was subject to searches by Chanda Bir's men. The old estate manager sent the fresh produce for each day with one of the guards. Even a man so old he was close to death didn't have permission to enter, as if they were fully veiled Muslim women. Heera felt stifled. She looked for her chance—the moment Chanda Bir's men relaxed their guard around the back pond, she was going for a quick visit to Karim Sheikh's house.

Ma Shumitra, now that she had permission to go to the pond, spent her days there. After losing the war, her son had again become a fugitive. The wealth she had saved, painstaking coin by painstaking coin—all of it had gone to waste. What else did she have left other than the pondside and her prayer room? One day, as she was walking back from the pond, birdsong caught her ear. That wicked girl had again set up her bird school. She was snapping her fingers and trying to teach the birds songs. What could be done with her? What pleasure did she find in teaching the birds Rongomala's song? And anyway, where did the royal daughter-in-law learn words that belonged to the lowborn? Ma Shumitra's skin crawled in fear and repulsion when she heard it. She changed out of her wet clothing and walked to her prayer room, making a right turn at the garden. The sound she made latching her door shut was quite loud.

Phuleswari stopped her singing and rose quickly. Step by step, she moved towards the boundary wall. When her mother-in-law entered her prayer room, Phuleswari hid behind the trees and kept tabs on the diggers on the other side of the wall—when they arrived, when they left, when they settled themselves to laze and smoke, when they chatted with each other. She was very efficient about it; as if, lacking someone responsible, Rajendra Narayan had delegated the supervision of the moat to his enemy's wife. She plucked a line from her eavesdropping:

War is here, for Rongomala
Raj Chandra abandons his throne
Oh, war is here.

The birds in the aviary had abandoned the song about Rongomala's sorrow, and were singing this one now.

Twenty-three

Before the year ran its course, another war approached, as if Phuleswari's birds had just sang it into being. This time, there were no booms from firing cannons. The eastern sky raged with fire. Bamboo joints exploded in the blaze like gunshots. The winter wind carried with it the wails of people, and at times, the barking of dogs. Flocks of birds, suddenly evicted from their nests, wheeled overhead. They screeched and chirped, lamenting the loss of home. On this evening, Raj Chandra Chowdhury had looted and set fire to the Rajganj court. The entire marketplace burned to the ground. By the time people managed to draw water from the ponds and canals, the bamboo grove and the brothel next to the marketplace were ablaze.

Ma Shumitra fell at the threshold of her prayer room. Her son had turned into a dacoit! With his own hands, he was burning down the zamindari, the property of his forefathers. The boy's wildness was not unreasonable. With an uncle like that, what else could he do? Rajendra Narayan wasn't human—he was a monster. Unable to beat him in strength, the poor child had resorted to other means. But would this lead him back to the palace? As long as the monster was above ground, her son would keep languishing in the jungle.

Ma Shumitra looked around her with vacant eyes. Everything was gone. The chief tax collector Harendra Ghosh wouldn't come even if summoned. He had placed his hand on the sacred copper and tulsi, and sworn his fealty to Rajendra Narayan. Karim Sheikh had been thrown into the dungeon. The dungeon was worse than a cave; not a single crack or hole existed through which light could enter. Once locked up there, even if a prisoner managed to survive, they emerged blind. For what crime had Rajendra Narayan imprisoned him! If that Muslim boatman had been free, she could have sent him off to search for Raj Chandra. That man had been an ace at quietly getting things done. He was also peerless in his loyalty.

As if she had lost all her fingers, Ma Shumitra couldn't even raise her pointer to emphasize an order. Everything in her life, her fancies, her dreams were crumbling to dust in her loosened fist and slipping through her fingers. Rajendra Narayan was the one grabbing it all. Although he had not killed her, his sister-in-law, he had maimed her for life. She, the wife of Pratap Narayan, had to hold out her palms to him, pleading for her monthly allowance. And still, he played her as if she had a ring through her nose—he delayed, saying he would pay her today, maybe tomorrow, why not come back the day after. She couldn't bear this humiliation.

To save on expenses, Ma Shumitra had freed all her slaves and servants, bestowing upon each two seers of rice, twenty cowries and a plate. They were gone. The only ones who remained at their jobs were the Brahmin cook and the old maidservant Kalitara. Even their expenses she could barely manage. Most of her allowance was spent in maintaining Phuleswari's birds. What a nuisance she had been saddled with. If she tried to unlock the aviary and let them loose, it would be another major to-do. Phuleswari and her maidservant Heera would probably tuck their saris in the waistbands and jump on her. She would have to do it after she managed to palm off Phuleswari on her father's household. No matter how much Heera stomped around, she was merely a shadow. She would have to follow Phuleswari. They were travellers on the same path—bound together like an ox and its yoke.

But what else could she do to send Phuleswari to her father's house? It wasn't as if she hadn't already planned and tried out various methods of accomplishing this. During the conflict and the war, she had sent letter after letter to Lamchor. Not a single response came from that side. Finally, a month after the war at Chandraganj, an old and deaf messenger showed up at their main entrance. The sons of Kali Charan Guha had taken great care to send someone who would recite their message like a mynah, and wouldn't pay the slightest attention to or even be able to hear what the other side said. After a little bit of chitchat, the deaf old man said to Ma Shumitra, 'Don't send your daughter-in-law to her father's house. She will return a corpse.'

Oh, no! What an inauspicious thing to say! With such strapping young brothers, why would the girl become a corpse? Who would dare to do such a thing? The old man, who allegedly could not hear a thing, immediately picked up on Ma Shumitra's words and, as if he had a hundred tongues, began badmouthing Kali Charan Guha's sons. Those villains were horribly angry at Phuleswari. Their father had sent so much wealth in several shipments—bullock carts full of gold—to their sister, emptying out his treasury. When he was alive, they had been unable to stop him. Now they wanted to take out their anger on Phuleswari. Had the two stepmothers been around, they would have spoken up for the daughter of the house; but both the virtuous women had performed sati by burning themselves to death on their husband's funeral pyre. There was no one to impede the brothers now. Their way was clear.

Ma Shumitra was not one to just let it go. Kali Charan Guha's sons were still wet behind the ears. If they thought they could trick Pratap Narayan's wife by merely sending a pretend-deaf messenger, they had another thing coming. Let the night pass; in the morning, she herself would prepare the palanquin and accompany her daughter-in-law to Lamchor. The old man was here; he could serve as a guide. He would hold his umbrella overhead and lead the way. Ma Shumitra needed to witness this with her own eyes—how brothers could murder their sister.

The man who had been unable to hear anything so far suddenly suffered a bout of excessive flatulence as soon as Ma Shumitra spoke of her plans. As soon as it was dark, he went out carrying the water pot, and was never seen again; not even the servants searching throughout the night with blazing torches could find him. Such was the behaviour of that loutish, thieving family from Lamchor. *Don't smoke tobacco when the coals burn slow/Don't become kin with families born low*—the saying was absolutely true.

Ma Shumitra couldn't concentrate on her evening prayers. The *gulgula* smouldered in the incense burner. Its choking aroma perfumed the air in the closed room. Ma Shumitra sat with her palms together in front of the idol. Her head was full of thoughts that she was releasing upwards and which were vanishing like incense smoke. Even the Lord God was unable to resolve any of this. In the middle of her prayers and rituals, she tidied away all her puja paraphernalia and got up to leave.

Outside, the wind was frigid. The inner wing was pitch black. But it wasn't the bone-rattling wind that pricked her skin like thorns; it was the bright lights from Rajendra Narayan's wing. What conspiracy was being hatched so late in the night?

Although the actual words did not travel through the walls to this wing, the very walls and courtyard on this side were shaking from Chanda Bir's thundering and stamping. Today, the brute's heart had suffered a blow. Raj Chandra Chowdhury had looted the tax division and set fire to the Rajganj marketplace, including the courthouse there, right under the noses of at least ten soldiers and officials. This needed to be fixed, quick. Otherwise, one day the master himself would be murdered in his sleep. There was still time: that rebellious Raj Chandra had probably not yet crossed the borders of Babupur. If the master commanded, Chanda Bir would gallop his horse there and capture Raj Chandra alive. And if he begged or pleaded while he was being shackled—well, then his severed head would have to do.

Rajendra Narayan stared unblinking at Chanda Bir like a snake—as if in front of him stood not a person, but Yama himself. Had this butcher grown addicted to murder? If today he wanted to murder the nephew, tomorrow he would probably want to chop off the uncle's head. Every time Rajendra Narayan closed his eyes, he saw the severed head of the Nor girl staring at him from a bell-metal platter. The dynasty of Bishwambhar Sur had bloodied their hands with the murder of a woman now. What had this world come to? Even on this cold winter night, the sweat poured off Rajendra Narayan. He would be sweating buckets until this murderer left his sight. Rajendra forced his voice to rise several decibels and shouted, 'Why don't you just go now? It's very late; go home and sleep. Let me think about this ...'

Why was the old master being so pusillanimous? It was Chanda Bir who was actually ruling this kingdom through him. He was chief of guards in name only. In reality, he was the head of Babupur. Since it seemed like the master was losing interest in murder and mayhem, it was upto him to come up with some new plan. Something that would revive his appetite.

Recently, the East India Company had taken over the administrative court in Jahangirnagar. If they could manage to lodge a murder and mayhem case against Raj Chandra at that court, it would be a done deal. Money would talk. Who knew, Raj Chandra might even be exiled or sentenced to hang. The British firangi had their own rules for their courts—whoever filed a complaint first, won. They didn't bother with whether the complainant was a murderer or a thief.

Rajendra Narayan blinked repeatedly at Chanda Bir's words. His gout was bothering him. What was this idiot blathering about? After flying the grandiose banners of murder, maiming, assault and war so high, this fool now wanted to go and lodge a complaint against someone who he himself had made destitute. The mills of the gods grind slowly, but they grind exceedingly small. And in this day and age, there was no lack of rumour-mongers. Chanda Bir would barely notice when the fetters would be slipped on his wrist. The fellow had no idea that Bhulua was not the world, and that big cities were a different animal. No matter how many coins you shelled out, even if the wrongdoer was a zamindar, the law granted him no leeway.

If he didn't have to take this nuisance into account, there was no impediment to his travelling to Jahangirnagar. Rajendra Narayan's father and grandfather both had been in the habit of visiting Agartala, Murshidabad and Jahangirnagar as and when needed—they had stayed in those cities for years when necessary. Their wealth, their honour and their opulence had only grown from those connections.

As a child, Rajendra Narayan had demanded to be taken to see the Kal-e-Jamjam cannon on display at Jahangirnagar. He pelted the roof of their house with stones. He rolled around on the ground. But his old grandmother was unconvinced. In time, he outgrew this fancy. Until one day he heard that the Kal-e-Jamjam had sunk into the Buriganga. He felt as if he himself had been shoved into the depths of the river. He was choking under there, releasing bubbles to float up to the surface. Many years had passed since then. Rajendra Narayan had remained in Bhulua his entire life. Whether needed or not, he had never left his home. For Raj Chandra's father Pratap Narayan, visiting Calcutta had turned out to be fatal. Why anyone would visit such a rotten swamp of a place was beyond Rajendra Narayan. His brother returned in six months with the illness that came from living and breathing salty air. No physician was able to treat the illness. His everyday wholesome diet consisted of unripe banana spathes, water spinach soup and endless glasses of buttermilk. They smeared his skin with freshly ground raw turmeric paste. Nothing worked. He deteriorated until one day he just died.

Chanda Bir had heard this story so many times, his ears were about to fall off. Yama on one side, on the other the British firangi rulers—the master was dead before death had even arrived. He wasn't interested in taking any action apart from digging that moat. If this went on any longer, Babupur would be all moats and nothing else. There wouldn't be a single path left for a horse to gallop along, even in the dry season. He was pretty much digging a hole for himself to fall in. What good would it do Chanda Bir to increase his strength and prowess by warring under the aegis of such a man? Throwing in the towel when they were just halfway done. Chanda Bir salaamed Rajendra Narayan and stomped out of the chamber.

Chanda Bir's whole world had been upended today. He who torched houses had been forced to draw water from canals and ponds to put out fires someone else had set. The winter's night was only halfway through. The pillars of Chanda Bir's house shook as his old father hacked and coughed. He grabbed about a *powa*-worth of white arsenic from a pot hanging from a beam in the byre, hid it under his wrap and tiptoed outside. This was related to the inner workings of the palace; he could not afford a witness, not even his own father.

Grand ideas arrived right after the thief had fled. The nephew had looted and left as if he was the king, and the uncle was just now deciding to secure the main entrance. Two soldiers armed with guns stood guard with their chests puffed out even in this biting cold. When they saw the chief of guards returning at midnight, they performed elaborate salutes and held the gates wide open. He was the apple of the ruler's eye—what did it matter what hour he visited the palace? They did not want to challenge his egress and lose their jobs.

Chanda Bir puffed out his chest and strode towards Rajendra Narayan's wing. He walked straight to the entrance to the inner quarters. But then, he hid in the shadows of the columns and bided his time. As soon as the guards moved out of his line of sight, he slipped into Ma Shumitra's wing.

The lamps were out in every room. Even the wall-sconces in the passages were unlit. Was the mother glorying in the courageous deeds of her son in this darkness, or was she prostrate with grief over her fugitive son? Chanda Bir hid in the shadows and crossed the passageway. He knew every nook and cranny of this palace like the back of his hand. He also knew when each inhabitant went to sleep, when they woke, and which of them composed songs about whom. Like a burglar, he lay his ear against the blinds of Phuleswari's bedchamber. Had the royal daughter-in-law's insomnia disappeared? She was snoring lightly, like a baby. Chanda Bir moved away from the window shuttered from inside and fumbled his way forward, clinging to the stonework. This part was pitch dark, packed tightly with trees. He couldn't tell whether he still had eyes or not. As his vision gradually grew accustomed to the dark, his foes lined up in front of him, suspended in space; he didn't even need weapons to finish them off. All of them were fast asleep in their slip-covered cages.

At this hour, he could easily place a little bit of poison in the birdfeeders and give them their just rewards for singing vicious songs about Chanda Bir's deeds. That he would certainly do. But before that, he should do some push-ups, just for the fun of it. It would help him warm up and loosen his muscles in this cold. A foe is a foe—not to be ignored even if it is a mere ant. Chanda Bir had barely steadied his weight on his palms, with his head touching the ground, when something rustled behind him. Black Moon was waking up. He was giving Chanda Bir the side-eye through the slip-cover from his perch positioned beside Phuleswari's closed door. In the still-dark dawn, the bird couldn't quite tell whether this was an upside down human or some strange beast. Chanda Bir abandoned his diversion and stood straight. Blast! Here was the main culprit. So Black Moon was a light sleeper. If he screeched out 'Chanda!' even once, all these birds would start off with that wretched song. They weren't people, just birds; they didn't even need accompanying instruments, their voices were enough.

The birds never got that chance. The call of 'Chanda!' stuck in Black Moon's throat. Chanda wrung the mynah's neck and moved towards the aviary, clutching his pot of poison.

Ma Shumitra was late waking up this morning. It seemed as if the whole household had died. Even the birds were silent. No matter how late she went to bed, Mother Shumitra was used to waking up at the crack of dawn to the chirping of birds. What was wrong today? She hurried out of her chamber. Phuleswari's door was still shut. Nearby lay Black Moon's corpse. Ma Shumitra trembled as she entered the bird enclosure. Who had wrought such destruction? Not a single bird had been left alive. They all lay dead in their cages. This causeless massacre of innocent creatures—would the gods countenance this? They could have just opened the cages; that would have been enough.

Ma Shumitra returned to her room with heavy steps, as if she herself was the bird assassin. Whoever had perpetrated this, the Lord God knew, she had not ordered it. But then, that Chanda Bir had chopped off the head of that Nor woman; that too had been without her order. Whatever she wanted, happened somehow or other—if not today, tomorrow, if not this way, then that; someone or the other took care of it. Although, really, that didn't help things. Her little boy was still a fugitive. She was the mother, and yet she had no way of knowing where her child was sleeping or whether he was eating properly. Such was her sad fate.

Ma Shumitra hadn't changed into fresh clothing yet. The regular hour for her bathing and ablutions passed by. Her hand shook when she tried to pick up her bell-metal water pot, as if she was guilty, even though she was blameless. If she walked to the pond via the gardens, she could avoid being spotted by Phuleswari or Heera. It was like crossing the *Boitoroni*, the river of death—the path seemed unending. Her feet tripped on each other. Even in this bone-shaking cold, her skin steamed.

She breathed deeply when she reached the pond. Thick fog surrounded her. Lower down the slope, the fog and the water embraced each other. She pulled apart the veil of fog and entered the water. Water was freedom; water was the solution. Everyone knew that winter or summer, Ma Shumitra awoke at dawn, and the first thing she did was come to bathe. Her little visit to the aviary this morning was a dream, no more. She had barely ducked herself into the water twice before the wailing began. Phuleswari was weeping as if for the dead. Heera dashi was cursing at the top of her voice. Once her stock of curses was exhausted, the slut would come looking for her to lodge their grievances.

Ma Shumitra stood still in chest-high water for a moment. Although the terrible cold of Magh bit into her flesh and bones, she did not leave the pond. She hugged the water with both arms and plunged herself in again and again. When Heera arrived at the pond, she saw Ma Shumitra ducking herself again and again, like a cormorant. She was completely naked. She was in a trance. Her white sari floated nearby, like froth on the water.

Twenty-four

Whoever had perpetrated the deed, Heera knew they had done Ma Shumitra a good turn. She no longer needed an excuse to evict her daughter-in-law from this household. No storm was needed—the girl would fall on her own now, like a shooting star. Other than those birds and that aviary, what else in this household had been Phuleswari's, to which she could have clung and spent her days? Her husband was a fugitive. The ground beneath her mother-in-law's feet was unstable. Even if fortune smiled again upon mother and son someday, as a barren wife Phuleswari's place in this household would always be one of pity and neglect. Which—let alone Phuleswari—even Phuleswari's chief maid would find intolerable. In the meanwhile, all those pouches full of jewellery had slipped out of their hands.

If only that girl had any notion of what was good for her. It was Heera who would have to do the needful on her behalf, and that too would have to be done fast. That girl would die from grief over her birds. Already she was half-dead from her sickness and her sorrow. When Kali Charan Guha had placed this motherless little girl in Heera's lap, her itty-bitty face had been bright red, her eyes barely open, her tiny hands curled into fists by her temples. Heera had taken care of that tiny baby straight from the birthing house. She still had to do everything for her—clipping her nails, dressing her hair. Whether in joy or in sorrow, in sickness or in health, she had never left Phuleswari. In the interim, her father had died; her stepbrothers had turned out to be worse than enemies.

Forget about offering her shelter; if Phuleswari lay dead in the streets, they wouldn't spare her a glance. It seemed that Heera, the baandi, the bought slave, was the one in charge of Phuleswari Rai's life and her fortunes—she was her guardian. Heera had a lot of responsibility ahead of her.

Heera entered Phuleswari's chamber and made a list of possessions. This bedstead could not be removed without breaking the doorway wide again. For the same reason, they would have to leave behind the sandalwood chest. What remained were a few small, light pieces of furniture, and the metal utensils sent in several installments from Lamchor. Phuleswari's beloved gem-studded canopy could be stuffed into a box, and the domed moonstone lampshade could be carried by hand. They shouldn't leave behind those bolsters or those satin covers either. Who knew what whore would arrive in her stead and use them to relax.

As she went through her list, Heera propped open the lid of the chest. It was so untidy, as if no one had touched it in decades. When she discovered the gold opium box that used to belong to Phuleswari Rai's grandmother, Heera felt as if she had discovered the moon. In the twinkling of an eye, she tucked it into her waist pouch. She crouched, intently hunting for anything else that had somehow escaped the paws of dear Raj Chandra. All the diamonds and pearls and gold had vanished long ago. In a corner lay a heap of silver platters, attar dispensers, paan platters, vases and hookahs. Such knickknacks had once lain in Jaggeswari's attic in careless heaps. In the final days, to feed her addictions, Panna the whore had pawned them off one by one at the goldsmith's; items that were never reclaimed because she ran out of money or time.

Nothing was lost forever—whether it was pawned off or stolen. It merely passed from one hand to another. Although these things were crafted in different shapes, their essence remained the same. Heera's hands paused as she tied everything into bundles. She grew distracted.

Somewhere far away, someone was blowing on a conch. The back door to Jaggeswari's mansion stood wide open. A narrow walkway wended through the enormous orchard. Wet, rotten leaves and dead branches curled around her feet. Beyond that waited a tiny yard, neatly daubed with cow dung, and in a corner grew a handful of marigolds, hibiscus and medicinal herbs. Beside them grew tulsi, holy basil, on a cement plinth. There, the light had already been lit in a lamp fuelled by mustard oil. Away from the evening lamp, the back of the stone-hued mansion could be glimpsed through the trees. A whore's house. The main entrance was on the street. Small girls were prohibited in that place until their chemises were pushed up by budding breasts.

Elderly Jaggeswari's new den was at the other end of the yard, with the building for the whores to the right, just where the gravel-strewn path towards the river began. A lit ghee-fuelled lamp hung in a wall niche. On a shelf reposed a gold idol of Lord Ganesha, a relic from the days of her merchant lover. A garland of red marigolds was strung around Ganesha's neck that reached down to the bellybutton jutting from his potbelly. Night was descending slowly. There was no sign of Jaggeswari. She was standing on the riverbank, clasping a low-slung branch of the freshwater mangrove that stooped towards the water, gazing at the other side. Her white hair streamed in the wild wind of the Meghna river.

An image from such a faraway past! Heera was seeing something that was already lost, or was perhaps still barely existing. Human ingenuity could create a path where none existed; an abandoned house, a house wounded and broken from the river's assault could one day laugh again. What use would it be to tell Phuleswari before it happened? She would just gaze at Heera, uncomprehending.

Heera made up her mind. She withdrew her life here, and, in her imagination, decked out her home in another. Gradually the day of departure arrived. When her small bundles gathered into a mountain in a corner of Phuleswari's chamber, it finally occurred to her to wonder how they would cross Babupur's borders with all this stuff. Even if she managed to leave the palace with all this, they might get robbed on the way. Chanda Bir's men were experts at looting and killing. They had grown even better, honing their skills through war. If she was spotted leaving Ma Shumitra's wing with so many boxes and bundles, they would be sure to follow. And then, there was the risk of foreign bandits. These things weren't baggage—they were nooses around their necks. She should sell them off as quick as possible and have the money crafted into a string of gold coins. She could just thread the coins in her *kaiton* and hang it around her waist. Then she would see who tried to loot it while Heera still had breath in her body.

She did exactly as she planned. There was no way that Heera could visit a goldsmith. The only man she could think to entrust with this errand was the old estate manager. The man was a jeweller as well. Everybody knew that. No one in the Rajganj marketplace was skilled enough to fool him with fakery. But it was risky to hand the items over in broad daylight. Who knew who was watching? Under cover of night, Heera handed over a pair of enamelled silver vases to the old man and dreamed of the gold coins they would get in return.

A day passed, then another night. Heera had had no idea what a tattletale that old fellow was. The next day, Mother Shumitra showed up at Phuleswari's bedchamber, carrying the pair of vases. She had not visited this chamber since the day of the bird massacre. In her absence, Heera had finished bundling up all their things as well as her dreams of bedecking Jaggeswari's house with them.

Mother Shumitra was astonished to discover the bundles and the piles in the room. This was not Phuleswari's doing—this had to be that servant woman, Heera. That whore was trying to pull the wool over her mistress's eyes to secure her own future. She was grabbing the chance to buy and sell all kinds of things from the house. Ma Shumitra forced Heera to open up all her bundles for inspection. These lowlifes always set their sights low. The daughter-in-law of the royal palace was about to embark upon her journey with these bundles full of junk—the thought made Ma Shumitra's heart stop. But forgiveness and understanding were the essence of this world; with such a grand thought, she removed her gaze from the heaps of rubbish.

Ma Shumitra felt sorry for that uncomprehending girl. Her grief for her birds had turned her to stone. Her body looked as fragile as a bird's. Barely twenty, and already she was wasting away. Her face looked pale and wan without any makeup or adornments. Her hair looked coarse. She clasped a window-bar with her thin hand, staring unblinking at the empty aviary. The poor thing—with what ceremony she had entered this royal palace, and now what was she leaving with? No one could control destiny. All was the will of the Lord God, his whim. She released a long sigh and returned to her own room.

Ma Shumitra spent her entire afternoon with her door closed as she sifted through her jewellery casket. This was all the wealth she had left. She couldn't bring herself to take a single piece from here to give to Phuleswari. To give something to one who was already a ruin would be a waste. No one remained a fugitive his whole life. One day her son would return home. He would remarry and start a new family, a new household. She should save the jewellery in this casket for Raj Chandra's new bride. The woman whose womb would be the vessel to carry and spread the seed of Pratap Narayan through his descendants—she was the one who deserved these. Still, Ma Shumitra slid a set of thin gold bangles under her pillow before putting the casket away. The whole night lay ahead of her. She would decide in the morning whether she should return these bangles to the casket or whether they should adorn Phuleswari's wrists.

In the morning, Ma Shumitra jumped out of the pond as if a crocodile was chasing her. She had forgotten to put away the bangles from under her pillow. Her door was open. She could not rely on Kalitara who wouldn't notice if an elephant walked past her. Ma Shumitra forgot all about her bathing and ablutions and ran back to her chamber in wet clothes. Her heart was hammering in her chest. Although she found her possessions exactly as she had left them, she was still short of breath. She clutched the bangles to her chest and, with her eyes shut, laughed out aloud.

Heera watched from the doorway. She knew neither prologue nor conclusion of this little drama. She was just astonished at Ma Shumitra's clothing and her conduct. The floor was flooded. Every curve of Ma Shumitra's body was showing through the wet, white sari draped around her. And there she stood, her eyes shut in bliss, clasping gold bangles—what did all this mean, this early in the day? Heera turned around and left from the door without saying what she had come for. Why should she care about any of this, or anyone here, when she might be gone tomorrow? Heera trudged towards the pond, her anklets jangling.

She ran into Ayna's son Najar Ali near Karim Sheikh's house. The boy, a gold embroidered skullcap on his head and his torso bare, was shepherding a calf home. The skullcap on his head was the only trace he bore of his dead father. His appearance, his bearing, everything about him echoed his mother. Suddenly, as if lightning had struck the house, Somiron Bibi began wailing from the byre as she spotted Heera. Startled, Najar Ali dropped his skullcap and disappeared. The calf scampered away with a raised tail. How misfortune came to people! Her daughter Ayna's beloved family had been decimated by this quarrel between nephew and uncle. May Allah curse them! May He destroy their dynasty for good! *The higher burns Sita's pyre/Ravana's palace burns even higher*—may the Chowdhurys be reminded of that proverb with every breath!

Somiron Bibi emptied the vessel full of cow feed into the trough and returned to her yard, still weeping loudly. She was carrying pieces of sacking covered in smut. She sat down on her haunches, covered her head and began swaying back and forth. How long could someone hide her sorrows under a stone? Like burning husk: even without air, the flame burned low day and night.

Adam Ali had been mad. He had made all his mistakes in this life without quite understanding any of it. It was Allah who should have decided whether he ought to be forgiven or not. Somiron Bibi was worried about Ayna. The grief-stricken girl had turned to stone. She had a new baby. If she didn't have these encumbrances, then at least they could have remarried her and sent her off to take care of a new husband's household. Now, a young widow, how was she supposed to spend the rest of her life?

For the past few months, Karim Sheikh had been a prisoner in the palace dungeon. Ma Shumitra had never bothered to even enquire whether the family of her favoured chief boatman, his wife and daughters, had lived or died. The friendship of the rich was a dam built of sand. Here one moment, gone the next. She had lured him with dreams of land, and now, in the time of danger, she had retreated to hide in her hole.

Karim Sheikh had spent his life serving the deceased Pratap Narayan and his interests. Now, at this hour, it was on Somiron Bibi's shoulders that these burdens had been laid. With all this fighting and war, how was she to keep a young woman of Ayna's age safe without a man? She had been forced to send Amena to her uncle's house under the cover of night, and now she was regretting that decision. Her mute little girl had never been away from her since birth. Even if she died of hunger, she could never say, give me some rice. Somiron Bibi sat with her plate in front of her at every mealtime and could only think of her child. The lamp burned out. Somiron Bibi's rice stuck in her craw. For whose sin was Allah raining such havoc on them?

Household after household had the same lament. The men had all either joined Chanda Bir's army or they had gone into hiding. Young women had gone into exile. The women with grey hair were left behind to tend to the households. Arable fields were covered in weeds. They were neither being ploughed nor planted. If things continued like this, the lives lost to war would be nothing compared to the number of people who would die on the streets with begging bowls in hand. Dogs whined through the nights. The hawks and the vultures honed their beaks and their claws.

Heera stood in a corner of the yard, clasping a pole. She couldn't say a single word. No one had consulted her before waging this war. Still, she was a slave belonging to that royal household; her visiting the Sheikh household was like rubbing salt in Somiron Bibi's wound. Ayna hadn't come out of the house even once. Whenever Heera had visited in the past, Ayna used to have so much to say about her joys and her sorrows; her embrace had been like a vine. Ayna no longer needed a friend from the royal palace. Not even a year had passed since her husband had died; that wound was still raw. Who knew where Heera would be when finally Ayna's grief would be eased? Ayna and Heera: they had been friends. They had been there for each other for many years. Today, Heera left Karim Sheikh's house without bidding them farewell, her head hung low.

Heera returned home to a great commotion. Everyone was bolting. Apparently Manohar Gazi was riding in from Meherkul on a crazed elephant. With him rode Raj Chandra on his trusty steed. No one was worrying about victory or defeat at the moment. There was nothing those Muslims wouldn't do once they set foot here. For instance, perhaps Gazi would destroy all their idols and toss all of them in the water to drown. Or maybe he would assault the honour of the royal wives and daughters.

Throughout the day, in several installments, palanquin after palanquin fled the palace. Mejo Thakurani's wing had emptied out. That night, Ma Shumitra met with Rajendra Narayan. Her own son had become her enemy. He had dug himself a ditch and invited in the crocodiles. This was her father-in-law's homestead. Her husband had lived and died here; this was where his last rites had been performed. How could she leave all this behind, and where would she go? Her daughter-in-law was already looking outwards. It wasn't right to keep a young woman during a time like this. Ma Shumitra would see Phuleswari off safely and, live or die, she herself would remain in her prayer room. No matter how much Rajendra Narayan might disavow his sister-in-law, her son's zamindari was not more important to her than the honour of the Chowdhury dynasty.

Ma Shumitra had said all the right things to cool down Rajendra Narayan. She lay awake all night, unable to shut her eyes in sheer excitement. A mother's heart: she had sensed in advance that the wind was changing; that her son had learned through experience and finally found his way. Pratap Narayan's blood was galloping his way home. On his head a crown; in his hand a sword. Men stood by the roadside watching him. This was the zamindar they desired.

A thief may have ten days to call his own, but the householder needed only one. Rajendra Narayan's swindling had not lasted very long. Now he would be out on the streets. Mejo Thakurani had fled the luxury of the palace. Where were Prafulla Kumar and the future queen mother Shunonda today? Their usually light-bejewelled wing was like a desolate cremation ground. Rajendra Narayan was guarding the trash heap of his household like a decrepit vulture.

The next day, the air was heavy with gossip and rumour. Someone had heard that Manohar Gazi's army was marching towards Chandpur via Shahrasti, after crossing the Lalmai Mountains. Their ships were anchored at Chandpur. The residence of Gazi's cousin Damon Haji was close by. They could rest there for a few days before embarking upon the journey to the holy city of Mecca to complete the hajj. But why was the Hindu king Raj Chandra riding with Gazi? Had he partaken of beef with them and become a Muslim himself? Or were all these unfounded rumours being spread to throw dust in Rajendra Narayan's eyes? But Chanda Bir was not dozing. He was preparing his own army.

While everything was in such an uproar, Phuleswari's palanquin waited at the main entrance of the palace. All her boxes and chests were piled on a bullock cart. None of the bundles that Heera had put together were left behind. The possibility of being attacked by foreign dacoits was a lesser fear now, since two guards brandishing sticks were accompanying them. Ma Shumitra was dashing about, making arrangements for her daughter-in-law's visit to her father's house.

Ma Shumitra was in a kindly mood. She was feeling open and generous. She had pulled out the set of bangles and slid them on Phuleswari's wrist. Phuleswari stared at her for a few moments; then she bent down and touched her feet in farewell. The girl was so desperate for love. Tears dripped from her eyes. The bangles were too big for her; they almost kept slipping off her wrist. Even Heera was not leaving empty-handed today. Mother Shumitra had knotted a pair of actual *ashrafi* to her sari-end; coins of solid gold. Day could become night if the mistress willed it! The norms and rules of the palace had grown lax with war after war. The hierarchy no longer mattered. Perhaps this was a lesser evil. Heera could use those coins to bribe the cart driver, the guards and the palanquin bearers on the way. Heera climbed into the palanquin with a glint in her blue eyes. Today was her day of freedom. With her departure from Babupur, she was sloughing off her slave skin. From this day on, she was no longer someone's bought slave; she was the granddaughter of Jaggeswari of the port town of Laxmipur; she was Panna the whore's daughter—that was all.

Phuleswari huddled like a new bride in a corner across from Heera, with a heavy expression. One shouldn't be so glum at the auspicious moment of beginning a journey. She should get Phuleswari to laugh, even if it meant tickling her. Heera lowered the palanquin drapes, and from her waist pouch extracted the gold opium case. She stuffed the two gold coins inside and banged it shut. Then she began singing with all the joy in her heart.

Despite Heera's objections, Phuleswari had the palanquin stop by the pond beside the Nor house. The bamboo grove still stood there, as if poised to jump in. Where was the cottage on stilts? And that chandelier? His royal highness leaning against a bolster and smoking his hookah. Rongi's beauty shining through the plumes of smoke. Her reflection in the waves, like the glint of moonlight. The servant Durga darting from one end of the cottage to the other, tinkling her ornaments of silver. In her hands a spittoon, or a carafe or perhaps a paan box. Phuleswari broke out of her daze when a cuckoo began trilling overhead.

Rongomala had been murdered during one black spring. The spring before that was when Phuleswari had first seen her. And now, in this spring, Phuleswari was about to leave Babupur. The dust from Rupsingh's Plains blew in the wind. The world's breath was so hot! Rongi was lucky—while alive she had not had to learn what it was like for a person to lose everything and become destitute. She had gone in the peak of her existence, leaving everyone behind to weep for her. Raj Chandra had gone to war for her. And now he had become a rebel fugitive. So many vibrant people of Babupur, like Ayna's husband, had died. And Manohar Gazi was riding in from Meherkul on his crazed elephant.

Phuleswari was leaving her husband's house. She was leaving behind her empty aviary, the pond at Nor house choking with unchecked undergrowth, the now unrecognisable cottage on stilts. A river of blood had washed away all signs of love. Tears flooded Phuleswari Rai's cheeks. With her tears, she paid homage to the one for whom her life had been ripped apart, and slowly climbed back into the palanquin.

Phuleswari's palanquin sped from east to west. She was returning the same way she had once arrived. Where were all the people swarming the streets today? And that long caravan of bullock carts? Her aviary! She was leaving, having lost her beloved birds, having lost everything. There was no one to even bid her farewell.

The years in between had slipped away while she had been in a trance. Phuleswari had grown from a child into a woman. Heera's hair had greyed. Today, due to circumstance, Heera was in charge of Kali Charan Guha's daughter. When the palanquin didn't make the turn to Lamchor and continued towards Laxmipur, Phuleswari lifted the blinds and looked outside. Babupur was no longer visible. Ahead of them spread the twilight sky painted in blood. They were neither the rulers nor the subjects of the ground on which their palanquin sped. Beside the road sat houses full of unfamiliar people, forests and underbrush, uninhabited sandy islands. A little while later began lines of tall trees providing shade to the road. They seemed endless. The trees seemed to be travelling with them, keeping pace in quick steps.

Night descended while they were still on the road. Heera told the frightened Phuleswari stories from her childhood—stories of Jaggeswari. Tonight, Phuleswari was distracted. She stretched her neck out like a turtle and gazed at the starlit sky. Behind them the bullock cart creaked. The *hummm-hummm* chanting of the palanquin bearers sounded like the zikr at the shrine of a pir. It rose like a strange lament, slicing through the night air, rising and rising.

The palanquin stopped at the back entrance to Jaggeswari's house. Ahead of them rose a huge shadow, like a gigantic hummock of dark earth. The bullock cart driver raised his lantern, illuminating a narrow alleyway overgrown with weeds. Heera clasped Phuleswari's hand and started along the path. They avoided thorny growth and poisonous vines and made their way forward. The lantern followed them, spreading light. No human had stepped foot here in a long while. Snakes, insects and other small creatures were awake and alert. Birds rustled in their nests. A fox sprang out of a bush and stood still for a moment, startled. Then it tucked its tail between its hind legs and disappeared into the adjacent forest. Beside the forest lay a raised span of earth. What was once a yard was now guarded by a dense thicket.

Heera left Phuleswari standing there and stomped heavily ahead. Loudly, she shoved open the broken door to a room that no longer had walls. Inside, rats and bats screeched. Frightened, flocks of *jalali* pigeons began flapping about up in the crossbeams. The air grew thick with the sound of beating wings. Heera climbed the wide steps and entered Jaggeswari's house. From now on, this house was hers. She had returned, a free woman.

Twenty-five

A rumour for sure. Week after week passed, and there was neither any sign of elephants, nor of Manohar Gazi. Chanda Bir's spies were frustrated despite their best efforts; they returned to their homes and went to sleep. Their last report was: Manohar Gazi had just climbed aboard a ship, his head was shaved and he was dressed in the *ihram* clothing for hajj. A sizeable retinue accompanied him. Raj Chandra had disappeared into thin air once he reached Chandpur. So had Ram Bharari. A thorough combing of the place had not revealed any news of them. Gazi's ship had sailed through the river Meghna and was now in open sea.

What better news could arrive! Rajendra Narayan donned his princely robes and re-ascended the throne. But it was like the bed of arrowheads that King Bhishma had rested on; there was no comfort to be found. Who knew when his nephew would carry out another attack? Mejo Thakurani had bundled up their daughter and grandson and taken off for her father's household in fear of Manohar Gazi. They would not suffer any neglect there, so let them stay a while longer. Once he felt the circumstances allowed it, he would send the palanquin to bring them back.

Chanda Bir waited another week or so, then he dismissed his army and went home himself. He needed a rest. But Chanda Bir was a man of action. He could barely stomach his rice when there was no war or feud going on. Apart from the battle at the Chandraganj marketplace with that incompetent Raj Chandra, all the operations he had carried out so far had been assassinations. What joy did that bring? Manohar Gazi was a mighty warrior king, known throughout the region of Samatata. He had unerring aim. If Chanda had a chance to face him in fierce combat, then the title conferred upon him, *Bir*, or brave, would finally be justified.

Victory or defeat was a matter to be settled later; the war had almost happened but hadn't quite. War had knocked at their door and returned from the threshold. Gazi had gone off to the holy cities of Mecca and Medina with his tail between his legs. Chanda Bir stayed home and moaned and whined for days like a weeping demon from the sorrow of Gazi's departure. Then he prostrated himself at the feet of his jaban Kali.

This was the moment Manohar Gazi had been waiting for. Setting out with elephants, horses and men, beating the war drums—all of it had been a trick to scare Rajendra Narayan into sending a messenger bearing the white flag of truce. The messenger would arrive to find Gazi on his elephant's howdah, platters of offerings all prepared. He had only one condition—Chanda Bir had to be delivered to him. Days passed. There was no sign of either the messenger or a white flag. Gazi was annoying himself with the dust he raised. Rajendra Narayan hadn't fallen for his trap.

What did a bird have if its wings were clipped? Without Chanda Bir, Rajendra Narayan would see only darkness on every side. He busied himself, preparing for war. With things taking this unexpected turn, Manohar Gazi had to change his strategy. One whose tongue had been burned by slaked lime was frightened even of yoghurt. The throne of *Alizeh*, the Shiite nawab, had been dust for over two decades. Where could Shamser Gazi's clansmen be assured of safety under the rule of the East India Company? Their torment in this world had doubled. A man with a long robe and a beard was branded a dacoit as soon as he picked up his sword, even if he was only trying to avenge the murder of his sister's husband. Justice had vanished forever. If word about open war got out, any imprisonment, fines or penalties would be on Gazi's head; those Hindus, Rajendra Narayan or Chanda Bir, wouldn't even get slaps on their wrists.

Manohar Gazi began dismissing his elephants, his horses and his men little by little while still on the road. By the time he reached Damon Haji's abode, there were only six of them left, including Raj Chandra and Nasir Mohammed. If Allah, the most generous, blessed their endeavour, then this would be enough for a guerilla ambush. The rest was their fate.

Damon Haji's latest journey to perform the hajj opened the door of possibility. Manohar and Damon were about the same age. They were like twins in appearance and mannerisms. Rajendra Narayan's spies were fooled when they spotted Damon boarding the ship draped in the white ihram, with his head shaved. Their way was now clear. Still, patience yielded results. Although Raj Chandra Chowdhury no longer wanted to be patient.

Raj Chandra was highly annoyed at having to move around. It had been almost two weeks that they had camped at Damon Haji's residence. Raj Chandra did not have permission to set foot outside. He felt like he was a prisoner in the house. And then, there was the nuisance of these hundreds of books. Gazi was evangelising so much, his ears were rotting away and were about to fall off. Manohar Gazi was adamant: he would persuade Raj Chandra that the sturdiness and value of a Chinese urn was because it took forty years to craft one.

Although Gazi was slow in action, his words were not to be dismissed. Raj Chandra had taken his own measure by now—first he was defeated in battle, and his second foray was merely a robbery. Gazi had not let him off lightly when discussing these ventures. Like the azaan sounding every few hours, Gazi drilled this tenet into Raj Chandra—one should only engage with a foe after testing out one's own strength.

Was Chanda Bir's fist mightier than Gazi's then? Otherwise, why were all their forces dismissed as soon as they had crossed the Lalmai Mountains into Shahrasti? Raj Chandra examined Manohar Gazi's thick fingers intently. Each time he turned a faded page of the book resting on the wooden bookstand, the gems on his finger rings glittered in the candlelight. Behind him was darkness. Only a little space ahead of him was illuminated. Music was not customary in this household. Liquor was considered sinful. Raj Chandra yawned loudly and left the gathering.

It was pitch black outside. Everyone was fast asleep. Raj Chandra tiptoed up the spiral staircase, as quiet as a cat. He climbed to the roof. The lively noises of the nearby riverside dock hummed throughout the night. In between, the music and dancing by the hijra went on. Pinpricks of light flickered like fireflies in the hundreds. The starlit sky seemed to be diving right into the heart of the river. Light danced on the crests of the waves. A few boats drifted farther and farther, pulled away by the current.

Ram Bharari sprang from the darkness like a wraith. He was wearing a short shirt over his lungi and a white skullcap. Raj Chandra placed his hand on the boat-shaped hat on his own head and glanced out of the corner of his eye at the long sherwani and the tight, ruched trousers he himself was wearing. They were all dressed up like clowns, wasting their time in Haji's house. When would this posturing end? Ram's face was dark too. The light from the dock reflected in his eyes. There was bad news from Babupur today. 'Bou-rani, the queen, has left the palace.'

Ram Bharari had tears in his eyes. It didn't occur to Raj Chandra that the bou-rani was Phuleswari. It was Rongomala's face that floated in front of him. No matter how far away, she had to be somewhere. That face could not have been lost forever. He could only submerge himself in conflict and war briefly to forget about her. He didn't know whether grief burned a person to purity like gold. Perhaps Gazi knew. But whether he was imprisoned or hanged, he wasn't letting Chanda Bir off the hook. Raj Chandra was going to kill him with his own hands.

Ram Bharari agreed. That heartless brute had massacred all the birds, forcing the bou-rani to leave the land altogether! The daughter of the moneybag merchant was now a mendicant on the streets. The orphaned girl hadn't even found shelter with her brothers. Who knew where she was? He had heard that Heera had taken her to some derelict old house in Laxmipur, abandoned because of the advancing river. If their boat stuck to the banks of the Meghna and headed that way, it would be about a day's journey. Whether she was mad or a fool, she was, after all, the wife Raj Chandra had wedded with the holy fire as witness. How could she be allowed to live in the house of a whore? What did that say about the honour of the royal palace?

Ram Bharari's pleading scattered in the river breeze. What kind of a man had Raj Chandra been, and what had he become? He had changed forever. He was a blank page, on which Manohar Gazi scribbled whatever he pleased. Fate had ordained that he who once issued orders only followed them now. He didn't anger easily anymore; neither did he react to things. He was like solid stone. These days, even his lust had ebbed. Even when he was pushed into the rooms of well-known whores, he entered through one door and exited by another. He was lucky that none of them had taken a broom to him yet. What the man needed was an aphrodisiac. Since that wouldn't happen anytime soon, Ram Bharari reached into his pocket and pulled out a lump of opium. In another pocket, he had a clay pipe and a flint. The atmosphere was oppressive. Even exhaling seemed tiring. Every other word drew tears from his eyes. Perhaps smoking up would rid him of sorrow for now.

Today king and subject stood side by side. They passed the pipe back and forth. It was bliss in name only—where was the joy? People began in one place and ended up in another. Raj Chandra exhaled smoke, gazing intently at the dock. Wave after wave crashed upon the very spot where barely two days ago the ship had been anchored. Hundreds of people travelled to perform the hajj year after year. Each person was swathed in pieces of white fabric, and carried many bundles. From the roof, they looked like an enormous flock of white geese. If someone dropped a silver plate on them from above, it would never hit the ground. It would simply move from head to head, borne along by the tide of people. Damon Haji was the leader of the pack. This was his third time travelling to Mecca to perform the hajj. He had experienced many things in his life. Who knew if he would return from this journey? Cut the knots behind and move forward everyone, farther ahead, westward, farther westward.

The ship had set sail through the river and reached open sea—yet Manohar Gazi showed no sign of making a move. When Raj Chandra prodded him, he began quoting from the *Bostaan*. Chanda Bir had become a great warrior without even learning his letters. Yet they lacked the strength to defeat him in war. What was sauce for the goose was sauce for the gander—the plan was to trick the great warrior into a room with no escape route and no weapons, and slay him.

Although in the beginning Raj Chandra had felt perturbed, now he had begun to understand the wisdom of this strategy. Many rivers had been muddied. Why fly into battle with all guns blazing anymore? If Chanda Bir was removed from the picture, Rajendra Narayan would fall flat on his face. The zamindari would fall into Raj Chandra's grasp almost on its own. The only regret was that this facile calculation, as easy as one-two-three, had to be made by Gazi; it hadn't occurred to Raj Chandra.

Manohar Gazi had chosen Raj Chandra and Nasir Mohammed to carry out this assassination. Let those who had lost loved ones secure their revenge: blood in exchange for blood. But there was no harm in being cautious. Gazi made sure that his favoured muzzleloader was tucked safely under his long robe. Nasir Mohammed carried a bow and arrow while Raj Chandra had a sword.

This season was witnessing an unseasonal epidemic of cholera all over the region. This too was a sign from Khuda ta'Allah to his loyal servant. 'If He so wills, then danger can transform into good.' The three of them would disguise themselves as shamans out to rid the region of the epidemic and take to the road, astride their ponies, with some remedies. They would hide their weapons in their clothing. They would be altruistic wanderers. No worries about food or shelter. Thus, they would travel the three nights and three days to the house of Chanda Bir. Once the morning star rose in the night sky, they would crawl into the forest behind Chanda Bir's home-temple, flitting from tree to tree like shadows. In the second half of the night, they would attack the temple.

Attack a temple! Raj Chandra's Hindu heart shivered. What was Manohar Gazi's true design? To slay two birds with one stone? Would the jaban Kali disappear from this earth alongside Chanda Bir? She wasn't merely the goddess animate, but the emerald-eyed, half-breed woman Gulbadan. How she had run after him that night! Her laughter had concealed such heartrending sorrow. There was no point in telling that story to this Muslim. He would have to take care of business his way when they were in the field.

But everything was over in a heartbeat. Raj Chandra padlocked all the doors of Chanda Bir's house from the outside and had just set foot in the yard when he heard a clink from the direction of the temple. A single slingshot pellet from Nasir Mohammed's hands had been enough to decapitate the goddess.

Chanda Bir was alone in the temple. His eyes were closed from the joint bliss of devotion and bhang when the attack came.

Should he save the goddess, or himself? He was charging from one end of the temple to the other, like Hanuman, when his tail was set on fire. His naked, fleshy body jiggled.

When he saw Raj Chandra appear in the doorway, sword in hand, he finally turned around, brandishing his falchion, and stood his ground. The bright red symbol drawn on his forehead with blood-sandalwood paste glowed. That was the spot Manohar Gazi aimed for from his hiding place. His gun roared. The five-flamed lamp trembled. The temple air grew dense with smoke. Had the bullet missed the target? As if he had merely slipped on a banana peel, Chanda Bir shook his head and heaved his heavy body off the ground. He cocked his head and examined his wounded right arm. Then, step by single step, he moved towards Raj Chandra. In his left hand, he held the falchion reddened with sindoor.

Why was Raj Chandra not using his sword? Had he forgotten the lines from the *Bostaan—He who does not kill, even when the foe is right in front of him, is murdering himself.* Manohar Gazi moved a few steps forward and took aim. His gun went off before Raj Chandra's sword reached Chanda Bir's neck. Chanda Bir was finally killed by the one thing that hadn't been part of all their practice sessions.

When Chanda Bir's writhing finally stopped, Manohar Gazi lowered his gun and moved away from the door. He couldn't stand to be near burning incense or sandalwood. The smell of these things was awful, impure. If he could, he would have spread some attar and rosewater around here right away. That would also suffice to pay respect to the soul of the just deceased. Regrettably, in his hurry, he had not brought any with him. Gazi stood in the yard and signalled. Nasir Mohammed ran out of the bushes and launched himself to clasp his uncle's neck. 'Bravo, my nephew! Is everything all right?'

The child was wordless, trembling like a baby bird. Aiming his slingshot and decapitating the goddess's idol had been just another game to him. But he had not heard the sound of a gunshot before. And then the smoke, the shouting, the clamour. As if that night when his father, uncle and stepmother had been murdered had come again. Nasir Mohammed's arms loosened from around his uncle's neck, and he dropped off like a ripened fruit.

Here was trouble. Had the child lost consciousness? Where was Rajendra Narayan's nephew? Manohar Gazi picked up Nasir Mohammed and turned around. Raj Chandra was still standing at the same spot with his sword held aloft. There was a tumult rising around them, the booming sounds of doors being broken open, and yet he was unresponsive. Raj Chandra was trying to see something inside the temple. When Manohar Gazi grabbed him, the sword fell out of his hands. Suddenly, a severed head knocked up against his feet. Raj Chandra couldn't tell that it was jaban Kali's head. He retrieved his sword from the ground and followed uncle and nephew out of Chanda Bir's house.

As soon as they crossed the borders of Babupur, three riders with flaming torches guided three muscular horses towards them. Ram Bharari was one of the riders. From this point on, they would each find their own way home. Raj Chandra and Ram Bharari would be headed one way. Manohar Gazi would take his men and lead them back to Meherkul. Raj Chandra would remain in hiding a few more days, and once he figured out which way the winds were blowing, he would present himself in his uncle's court. The thorn in his path had been removed. Now it was Raj Chandra's responsibility to win back his throne, whether by forcibly removing the old man whose wings they had just clipped or by bringing him into the fold. If he did not have the strength to achieve at least this much, how would Pratap Narayan's heir rule his kingdom?

Darkness was giving way to light. Manohar Gazi spread his prayer rug on the grass and stood to say the *tahajjot* prayers. It was Allah's endless munificence that Raj Chandra had returned alive. The way that the brute had rushed forward brandishing his falchion—Gazi shivered at the memory as he positioned his hands on his chest in *tahrimah*.

All joys contained some sorrow. After three years or maybe more, Mehrab was set to return to Dewanganj. His sister was unlucky; she had never known her husband's love. And then, along with her co-wife, she had lost her husband and her angelic brother-in-law. Bhelu Chowdhury had not been of this world; he had been a child of heaven. Like a firefly, although his light burned low, it illuminated. Allah had called him back before his time. Nasir Mohammed would come of age alone, at the cold graveyard of a palace at Dewanganj, with no guardian sheltering him. But what right did Gazi have to hold on to the heir of the Dewan dynasty? Manohar Gazi raised his open palms in prayer to Allah, as if hiding himself. Tears trickled through his beard and dampened his robe near his heart.

When Manohar Gazi's shadow disappeared far into the light of dawn, Raj Chandra focused on himself. His naked sword was tucked in his waistband. It was smeared with blood; and yet, Chanda Bir had been killed. He had failed to save the jaban Kali. In this attack, Pratap Narayan's son had been merely a proxy. Manohar Gazi was returning home a brave warrior, pulling the final curtains over a war that had lasted for three years. Although it had now changed hands, on the throne of the zamindari would now ascend no one other than the rightful heir of Bishwambhar Sur. Dawn was breaking through slowly. Today the sun would rise in the skies of a Babupur without Chanda Bir.

Twenty-six

While humans made plans, fate laughed. But one had to make one's peace with circumstance. What else could Ram Bharari have done? Raj Chandra had indeed become king, but Ram had lost his position as flunkey. These days, it was honeybees of a different sort that buzzed around Raj Chandra Chowdhury. The courthouse echoed with words of wisdom they dispensed hour upon hour. Ram Bharari was illiterate, and he had never managed to learn the art or grace of leaning against bolsters in a leisurely manner to indulge in banter. He had followed Raj Chandra Chowdhury around until his hair had turned grey, sticking like a leech to his ass. He had spent his nights under trees with only a twisted coil of straw for a pillow. He couldn't count the number of castes and clans of people at whose houses he had eaten rice. At what point had he been supposed to educate himself? No matter what shenanigans he got up to—in the end, a zamindar's son turned into a zamindar himself.

But it wasn't as if Ram Bharari had been thrown to the dogs. Ma Shumitra was fair. She had kept him on in a nominal position to fetch and carry for her. Who showed even that kindness to anyone these days! It was impossible to set foot in the palace without stumbling on a servant or a maid. Those bastard servants and slaves that Ma Shumitra had freed right before the war had all scurried right back. They didn't want freedom; they wanted food in their bellies. Why else had Ram Bharari accepted this menial job! The machinations of fate and Ma Shumitra had led him to this.

Ma Shumitra had granted him permission for a pony and even allowed him a maintenance allowance. Which meant that if there were any errands that required travel, it was Ram Bharari who was summoned these days instead of old Karim Sheikh. He was on call day and night. Even when his body wearied, he couldn't refuse. A servant was a servant after all. He was no longer a flunkey, who had the chance to rub elbows with the king and lounge beside him on fine rugs.

Ram Bharari showed up at the palace with his pony at daybreak. From Babupur to Laxmipur—the distance of a kingdom. Ma Shumitra handed over a wok of hammered iron, a pair of crimson *cheli* saris, a pair of slippers, a tame parrot, honey, sweets, coils of paan, gunnysacks full of ripe coconuts and areca nuts. Her feet barely touched the ground as she floated in sheer joy. Tomorrow was the eighth-day celebration for Raj Chandra's firstborn son. At such a moment, a grandmother should harbour no ill will. It could cast a shadow on the fortunes and future of the grandson.

They were preparing gifts and offerings to distribute to all their friends and neighbours; why should Phuleswari be left out? All the folks there knew was that the daughter of the wealthy merchant had gone off to live at her father's because she wouldn't deign to share space with a co-wife. Ram Bharari was an insider. No matter what hell her daughter-in-law resided in, he would surely find her and deliver the goods.

Be that as it may, Ram Bharari was stumped. If this lot was loaded on the pony, where would his ass fit? The pony was more like the donkey which carried the rice donations for a dargah at the end of the harvest season—the donkey which followed the dargah's *Khadem* with a goatee, from one house to the next. Ram dumped two sacks of coconuts and areca nuts by the royal lake and climbed back onto his pony. Now he could converse with the parrot and slowly continue his journey.

It was almost evening when Ram Bharari finally reached Jaggeswari's house. Phuleswari was in the yard, scattering grain. She was surrounded by thousands of grey pigeons. As she spotted Ram Bharari entering the compound, Phuleswari put the grain basket on the ground, pulled her sari-end to cover her face, and disappeared. After all, he was coming from her in-laws' house. Who knew what news he was bringing after five years? He might even be here with some ulterior agenda. She had never heard anything good about this man while she had lived in the palace. And Heera wasn't around at the moment. Heera had postponed all hunger and thirst and stationed herself at the orchard since dawn. Phuleswari entered the house and locked the front door. Then she exited through the back door and slowly made her way to the orchard.

Harvesting the fruit of three to four hundred areca nut trees in a single day was no joke. Two tree-climbers were balanced on cross-beams near the treetops as they chopped off clusters of areca nuts with *hashuas*. Underneath the tree, three maidservants stood with Heera, holding a spread-out net. Piles of areca nuts dotted the orchard. Fortune's wheel had turned again. Heera employed many people these days. The areca nuts from her orchard were shipped to Jahangirnagar, Murshidabad, Delhi, and even to the east, to Rosang and Burma. She had more customers in Laxmipur than the town had flies.

When Heera heard of Ram Bharari's arrival, she dropped the net and ran homewards. Phuleswari didn't follow her. She strolled around the orchard, as if playing a game of blind man's bluff, and then headed for the fields where the northern wind blew cold. The sun was moving westwards. Behind her, light sparkled on the tops and the tips of the areca nut trees.

Countless sparrows and mynahs hopped about, pecking at the recently harvested rice paddies. An enormous heron emerged from the clumps of *hogla*. The heron raised its head and looked at Phuleswari Rai as if it knew her. She began making her rounds along the ridges. This was her routine. The northern wind had picked up and was now blowing hard. A flock of colourful birds flew her way, barely grazing the golden tips of rice swaying in a nearby paddy. Their wings glittered with joy. Although most of the rice paddies hadn't been harvested yet, after a long walk, she found a little space that had been cleared up. Phuleswari spread her arms out like wings and ran. The stubs of the harvested rice jabbed at her feet. A bangle slid off her wrist and fell to the ground. Today Phuleswari folded her wings before the chanting of 'bird queen, bird queen' began. She couldn't make sense of anything today. The tune she was humming kept breaking up and getting lost.

A muddy trail ran alongside the river. Phuleswari walked towards the jetty near their house, each footstep stitching the trail to the jetty. A *titi* bird sat nearby with its tail fanned out, warming itself in the sun. It looked at Phuleswari and parted its beak to send her some love. A kingfisher peeked at her from a burrow near the water. Ferruginous ducks cocked their heads and stared at her as they floated in the river. Phuleswari knew that even these birds that were merely annual visitors were like family. But she still couldn't forget her aviary birds. She had walked so many roads, day after day, and yet she never heard those melodies anymore. She sighed deeply, walked to the dock near the house and stood there. If she washed her feet here in the river and walked up the steps, Jaggeswari's chamber was right there. And a gazebo.

The river had pulled the *hijal* tree, the back garden and the gravel-strewn path into its belly, and for many years now, the house had been resting right at the edge of its maw. Right below the house, during high tide, waves crashed, and the river rose till all the steps were submerged and the water was level with the foundation of the house.

The sun was dipping into the river by the time Phuleswari walked up the steps to the gazebo. The water had turned crimson. A wedding boat carrying the groom's party drifted by, playing music. The groom sat in the bow with his wedding *topor* on his head. Tomorrow, the bride would pass along the same way, weeping quietly. The last passenger boat had just left the nearby dock. People were returning home, swaying on top of the carmine waves. So many trader dinghies passed by carrying goods, blowing horns, very late at night. Phuleswari Rai had nowhere to go. She was the Bird Queen in name only. Not even Heera knew how her wounded heart flapped its wings, how her heart bled like a bird with broken wings.

Heera had grown addicted to money. Even in her sleep, she kept counting and recounting on her fingers—ten areca nuts made one *gaa*, twenty-two *gaas* made one *kuri*. Phuleswari's heart ached. After five years, had Ram Bharari come to take her back to the palace? But then, where was her palanquin? She tripped as she descended the steps. Ahead of her floated the empty aviary. Rongi's face, now lost, floated in the waves. Ashes blew from Raj Chandra's skin towards hers. Everything was destroyed. Who could Phuleswari go to, where could she return, once again traversing this river of blood?

Heera heard all the details from Ram Bharari about the thorns that had now been planted forever to prevent Phuleswari's return to the palace. She didn't seem to care. This had been inevitable. She sat on her porch, smoking tobacco, and chatted about inconsequential things. The fire burned low in a clay bowl. Ram Bharari sat near her, comfortably settled on an embroidered seat. In his hand, he held the hookah nozzle. A silver platter with paan lay in front of him. Today, the special serving dishes had been retrieved from storage in the loft. Good or bad, this was the first time someone had arrived from the palace with some news. With him he brought the offerings for Ma Shumitra's grandson.

Heera left the gifts in a heap and hooked the parrot's perch over the door. The bird's feed—bananas and chickpeas—had been placed in front of it. The hubbub for Ram Bharari's dinner continued in the cookhouse. Many fried foods and vegetable concoctions were being cooked to the accompaniment of banging wooden ladles. Since Jaggeswari's days, no fish was cooked in the evenings in this household. The wind carried over the appetising smell of ghee, five spices and other seasonings in sudden gusts.

Heera hated cooking. Even the thought of sitting by the stove, blowing into a bamboo hollow to stoke the fire, made her feel sick. She had told Ram Bharari to rest awhile, and gone off to the marketplace. Then she had handed the vegetables she had bought to her maidservant and gone to bathe. When she returned from the riverside, shivering in the cold, evening had already descended. She changed into a newly pressed sari, lit a lamp, and came to sit on the porch. By then, the mute maid Ambika had lit a fire in the clay bowl with dried bamboo slivers and other fuel. She didn't have to call Ram Bharari. He stood and stretched and then came to sit with her. There was only this one night. There was so much they had to say or wanted to hear. The two of them sat by the fire and warmed themselves with paan and tobacco.

Ram Bharari poked the fire with a stick. Heera examined the goods sent from the palace as she talked. Suddenly her smile disappeared. Ma Shumitra hadn't thought of sending even a single thread for Heera! What resentment did the mistress still hold against her? Rajendra Narayan had exiled himself to the holy city of Kashi out of sheer sorrow. Mejo Thakurani remained at her father's house with her daughter and grandson, subsisting on a fixed monthly allowance. Ma Shumitra had gained control of the palace and the whole kingdom, yet her pinchbeck soul remained the same. What did the Babupur folk think of Heera, that she was still a bought slave? Tomorrow morning, through Ram Bharari, *she* would send a gold necklace for the new baby, as well as twice the goods that the palace had sent them. The mistress's flat face would be flattened further.

The whole night was ahead of her, but Heera couldn't wait. She got up right then and grabbed a thick shawl to wrap around herself. She lit a torch and, with long steps, strode away from the porch. From the yard, she called out to Ram Bharari, 'How long will you just sit there warming yourself by the fire? Get up, come. Let me show you my kingdom.' She was impatient to show Ram everything tonight—the areca nut orchard, the rows of coconut trees lining the riverside, the stone-hued silo that served to store the areca nuts, the dock, the gazebo—everything.

The flaming torches, held high, revealed the shapes of trees beyond the darkness. Like in the kingdom of wraiths, everywhere there were whispers and murmurations. The rats in the silo rushed at them, irked. Ram Bharari slipped on the moss and fell into the river when Heera was trying to show him the jetty. He was forced to bathe again in this winter's night. What could he say to Heera, formerly the chief maid of the palace, currently the areca nut tradeswoman? All of this was the misfortune that he, the unfortunate, carried with him.

When Ram Bharari returned after viewing Heera's estate, the fire in the clay bowl had gone out completely. Phuleswari stood with a lantern, trying to get the parrot to talk. Ram Bharari prostrated himself in the yard and paid his respects to bou-rani, the royal daughter-in-law. The daughter of the salt merchant, currently the bird queen: this respect was merely her due. But Phuleswari's unadorned body pricked his eyes like thorns.

She looked neither like a married woman nor like a widow. She wore a red-bordered unbleached sari and a burnt orange shawl. Aside from the pair of thin bangles on her wrist, and her nose-stud, she had nothing. Who was bedecked in whose jewels today, who jingled as they walked? All that had been looted from the Nor house had been accounted for and hauled back once Raj Chandra had settled himself on his throne. Phuleswari's jewellery had finally come to rest in the possession of Raj Chandra Chowdhury's new bride, after the slight detour of being in Rongi's hands. This world was but a game indeed, a strange one. When humans planned, fate laughed. Whether he had understood the consequences or not, Ram Bharari had done many terrible things in his youth. Now he was older. Let the news of Raj Chandra's son's eighth-day celebration remain locked in his tongue. Let the offerings lie on the ground. To hand it over to bou-rani, whether today, or tomorrow—let Heera be responsible for that.

Aggravation seemed to be Heera's lot in life. If that Ram Bharari ever came here again, she would break his leg herself and hobble him forever before he even reached the house. So, Raj Chandra Chowdhury had remarried and popped out a child; why did Ram Bharari have to come here bearing that tale? A man could never understand the sorrow and burn of a woman's heart. He had shown up here using that news as an excuse, carrying these things which Heera would not deign to touch with her foot. She had instructed Phuleswari not to touch anything either. However, a bird was a bird. Before she had even heard the news from the palace, Phuleswari had taken the parrot into her room, perch and all. The bird surprised even Ram Bharari by calling out *Rongomala Rongomala* at dawn. Soon the man had swayed off into the distance on his pony laden with goods. Now how was Heera supposed to douse this slow-burning fire?

Every afternoon, the women of the other trader households came over to play the Tiger Hunt board game, or cards, or *Golkodom* with Phuleswari. Today, she had closed her door in their faces. These were daughters and wives of important families—they had dressed up to come and see her. 'Bird Queen! Bird Queen! Why are you locking us out? We're your friends, Bird Queen!' They stood outside, calling to her like birds themselves.

Heera felt her head would fall off from embarrassment. Kali Charan Guha's daughter had no sense of propriety; she stomped off indoors. They were lucky that Kali Charan Guha wasn't an unknown in this area. Because the Bird Queen was his daughter, young or old, everyone respected her. Otherwise, here she was, separated from her husband, living in the house of a dead whore. And the way she dressed! Months went by without oiling or combing her hair. If you shook her clothes, half a kingdom of dust would fall out.

Yet, once upon a time, this girl would take so much time and effort to make herself pretty. Rongi's death had put a stop to that. It was then that this singing had begun. Unless they were mad, who did this for their enemy? And a foe she hadn't even seen properly? It was all God's game. As if everything was known beforehand: that, in the end, neither of these two women would have Raj Chandra, that the man would set up house with a third woman.

Oh, this heart that doesn't understand!
You remember nothing of the past ...

Phuleswari turned away from the river. Some kindhearted boatman sang as he rowed past. Night jumped in headlong on these winter days. From inside the house came the parrot's voice, sounding out its newly learned word: *Rongomala! Rongomala!* The bird had spent its days in a palace that was loud and full of light; was it suddenly afraid in this quiet, dark house? Was that why it was calling? The bird's voice trembled. Swiftly, Phuleswari descended from the gazebo.

Heera was sitting on the porch, smoking by herself, looking preoccupied. She was fuming. She was immersed in her own smoke. As if she didn't see Phuleswari right before her eyes. The parrot perched overhead, its leg shackled. Like the night before, Phuleswari picked it up by the perch and carried it to her room, to settle it over her bed. Parrots were a breed that loved to cut through their chains; if it survived, it would learn how to talk and sing just like Black Moon.

The bird stopped and started, but called out at every hour. Phuleswari couldn't sleep either. When had Raj Chandra remarried? And now, eight days already since his son had been born. In the palace, they were celebrating the birth of Ma Shumitra's grandson. The man whose rampaging had mangled her placenta and rendered her barren—why, nothing bad remained in his life!

What judgement was this? The king was on his throne. Instead of Rongomala, a new bride lit up his palace. Phuleswari had always been second best. She had had no man other than Raj Chandra in this life. And she had joined her body with his, pretending inside herself to be Rongomala. And now, when Rongomala's body had been burned to ashes on the pyre ... Phuleswari sighed. This lifetime had been spent for others. If not for people—for birds. If in the next birth she had the right to ask for someone, she would ask for Rongi. Today, after such a long time, she could hear Rongi's undimmed laughter drift from far away. When it wafted closer, it sounded more like weeping. The sound floated away again. Then moved closer. In the end, there was no difference between laughter and weeping. Phuleswari blew her lamp out, and hugged herself tightly.

Their son was Balgopal. He was very dark. Phuleswari held the boy's arm firmly while Rongomala poured oil and flowers on his curly hair. Today was his *mukhey bhat*, his first day of eating solids. Rongi was wearing the same white muslin worked in gold. She was covered in jewels. Her bangles clinked as she bathed their son. Her nose ring moved, although her face couldn't be seen. A lithe arm, the hue of cowries, held an urn full of oil towards Phuleswari. But there was no oil in it; it was filled with blood.

Scared, Phuleswari dropped the urn onto the ground. Rongi had turned into the wind. Her laughter faded in the distance, farther and farther …

The unpleasant smell of burnt oil hung in the stuffy room. The parrot rustled overhead. Phuleswari fumbled her way in the dark and poured herself a glass of water before returning to her bed. What hour of the night was this? A trader dinghy passed by, blowing its horn. When the sound grew faint, the crows in the port began cawing in concert. Phuleswari pulled her sari-end and wiped her eyes. Some unknown sorrow shattered her heart.

A new storm ravaged this household as if Ram Bharari had carried some evil wind with him. Another calamity smashed them before the year ended. How many disasters could Heera deal with? From early afternoon, some young boys belonging to the *Kaibarta* caste were going around, beating on a *dandera*-drum, creating a racket. A musical performance was to be held tonight, under the banyan tree near the fishermen's neighbourhood. It was a ballad: *Chowdhury's Battle*. The whole neighbourhood seemed to be excited. Even Phuleswari fell for the sensation. Such a public place; who went there other than coolies and labourers? Certainly not well-born women. But did anyone pay any attention to what Heera said? Whether she lived or died, Phuleswari *had* to go there. It was the same stubbornness, like that time when she wanted to visit the Nor house. Heera neither had the strength she had back then, nor was she a bought slave bound to dance to Phuleswari Rai's tune night or day. She dressed her tobacco and sat on her porch, smoking. Her face was like a glowing coal, burning. 'If the daughter of the Guha's clan wants to go, why doesn't she? Who's stopping her? There are many servants and maidservants in this house. She can just take one of them with her.'

Phuleswari walked barefoot in the sands by the river. The full moon shone bright above her; beside her flowed the river Meghna. On the other side stood row upon row of tall trees with slender leaves. As if all these things were reflections from another life. Phuleswari's feet moved slowly in the crumbly sand; she could barely walk. The maidservant Ambika followed her like a shadow. Ambika wasn't just mute; she was also deaf. Heera had not only refused to come with Phuleswari; she had made sure that it was deaf Ambika who accompanied her to listen to the singing. Farther away sat the shacks of the fishermen, with lamps flickering like fireflies. The wind carried with it the smells of rotten and dried fish. Far in the bamboo grove, a kanakua bird called, announcing the hour.

When Phuleswari pulled herself up the slope by grabbing onto the aerial roots of a banyan, she saw the place was packed with fishermen and potters and other men and women, buzzing like a swarm of flies. The horde was lit up by hajack lamps. In the middle of the throng stood a jaban man with long hair and a beard. A gamchha was wound around his neck. He held a three-stringed *sharinda* in his hand. Behind him, his backup singers sat in a row, dressed in faded vests embroidered with gold thread. The balladeer had arrived with his troupe straight from Babupur itself. His purpose was to make *Chowdhury's Battle* popular in this region.

Of war between Raj Chandra and Rajendra I sing
Of why uncle and nephew commenced this fighting
Such a long tale will take night after day
Let me pay honours to you all, and pray
Oh, oh, oh,
Chowdhury prepares for battle ...
God without form is the first Lord I praise
The Prophet He crafted from the light of His ways.
Let me tell you a saga of love good and true
Rongomala's story I shall sing here for you.

Whose game was this life? Like a lamp that had burned its oil, her life had been snuffed out before it had barely begun. And yet it wasn't over. An unknown minstrel had arrived to perform the ballad he had written about Rongomala's misfortunes. People were flooding in from every direction. Phuleswari covered her head with her sari and wound her way through the crowd. She found a corner for herself and settled down comfortably on a mat. The song tonight would be Rongomala's, all night long.

Translator's Note

Translating Shaheen Akhtar's writing has always been both a challenge and a joyful experience for me. This is particularly true for *Beloved Rongomala*. I have sought to find a balance between meaning and ease: hewing close to the text while making it accessible to a non-Bengali readership. One of the biggest challenges in translating this novel has been the lines from poetry and songs drawn from many different strains of literary traditions extant in Bengal, formal or informal, oral or written. Although they lent a wonderfully evocative texture to the original prose, I chose, with great sadness, to omit these to some extent. I have, however, retained the lines the author and I thought were essential to the narrative. The limitations of my translation notwithstanding, I hope that the English language reader will find *Beloved Rongomala* as captivating as I did.

Shabnam Nadiya

Translator's Acknowledgements

My abiding gratitude:

to the author, Shaheen Akhtar, for her trust in my creative spirit and her friendship, both of which have sustained me through the years

to my partner in love and literature, Mahmud Rahman, for being my beta reader, and for his patience and candour

to my dearest friend, Ashley Davidson, for reading the second draft, and for always being a willing listener

and to my father, Dr Nurul Islam, whose knowledge of the language and culture of the Chandpur/Comilla region was a lifesaver for me again and again and who I miss every single day